In Pursuit . . .

Joanna FitzPatrick

LD
PUBLISHED BY LA DRÔME PRESS

In Pursuit . . . is a work of biographical fiction. Apart from the well-known people, events and locales that figure in the narrative, all names, characters, places, and incidents are the products of the author's imagination or are used fictitiously. Any resemblance to current events or locales, or to living persons, is entirely coincidental.

Grateful acknowledgment is made to The Society of Authors as the Literary Representative of the Estate of Katherine Mansfield and to The Society of Authors as the Literary Representative of the Estate of John Middleton Murry for giving permission to reprint previously published materials.

Library of Congress Control Number: 2010909966
FitzPatrick, Joanna
In Pursuit . . . / Joanna FitzPatrick
1. Mansfield, Katherine, 1888-1923—Fiction. 2. John Middleton Murry, 1889-1957—Fiction. 3. Women writers—Fiction. 4. New Zealand / British writers—Fiction. I. Title

ISBN-13: 978-0-6154-1237-5
ISBN-10: 0-6154-1237-8

PRINTED IN THE UNITED STATES OF AMERICA
10 9 8 7 6 5 4 3 2 1
Second Paperback Edition

Cover painting:
northampton clamp scape
Samuel Payne © 2008
acrylic on paper

ladrômepress.com

à mon chéri

James

"I live to write."

— Kass Beauchamp, age 9, 1897

"'. . . as you ought not to attempt to cure the eyes without the head, or the head without the body, so nei-ther ought you to attempt to cure the body without the soul'; and this said Zalmoxis is the reason why the cure of many diseases is unknown to the physicians of Hellas, because they are ignorant of the whole, which ought to be studied also; for the part can never be well unless the whole is well.

"And Zalmoxis added with emphasis, 'Let no one, however rich, or noble, or fair, persuade you to give him the cure, without the charm.' And therefore if you will allow me to apply the Thracian charm first to your soul, I will afterwards proceed to apply the cure to your head."

From the Dialogues of Socrates, 469-399 BC

I know not how it falls on me,
This summer evening, hushed and lone;
Yet the faint wind comes soothingly
With something of an olden tone.

Forgive me if I've shunned so long
Your gentle greeting, earth and air!
But sorrow withers e'en the strong,
And who can fight against despair.

Emily Brontë, 1818-1848

In Pursuit . . .

Introduction

I discovered Katherine Mansfield at les fleurs bleues, a used bookstore in a village in southern France. I was flying home to the States and looking for a small book to read. You know the one. Not too large or bulky but entertaining enough to get one through a dull flight.

On a dusty bookshelf of English titles, I pulled out a slim book frayed around the edges entitled *The Garden Party and Other Stories* by Katherine Mansfield.

Katherine Mansfield? Why did I know that name? Then I remembered a quote in Virginia Woolf's journal: "Katherine Mansfield created the only writing I was ever jealous of."

Perfect timing, I thought, I had a six hour flight to find out why.

And I did. Ms. Woolf's jealousy was understandable. Every time I stopped to take a breath between stories, I thought, who is this extraordinary writer? Upon my return to New York, I read several Mansfield biographies and her voluminous correspondence. The more I learned about her, the more determined I became to re-imagine Katherine Mansfield back to life so that others might find inspiration in her remarkable story.

Katherine Mansfield Beauchamp was born in Wellington, New Zealand on October 14, 1888. Her father, Harold Beauchamp, was the Chairman of the Bank of New Zealand and believed like all upstanding British "colonials," that his children should be educated in England. At age fourteen, Katherine and her two older sisters were sent to Queens College, in London, a renowned progressive school for young women, where they spent three years acquiring a liberal arts education. Katherine thrived on language, philosophy, literature, and music. She studied the cello, attended concerts, and frequented museums and galleries.

When her parents came to fetch her, she had no desire to return to provincial New Zealand, but they wouldn't allow her to stay in London without a chaperone.

She had a ripping good time on the voyage home after she met a charming cricket player and back in New Zealand she became known as a wild bohemian. She had brief affairs with both men and women, camped out with the Maoris, and published some scandalous stories under various noms de plume. Her explanation for her transgressions: *Why be given a body if you have to keep it shut up in a case like a rare fiddle?*

Finally she persuaded her father to pay for her return passage to London and give her a very small allowance to cover her room and board. A bastion of upper class conservatism, her father perhaps believed relative poverty would drive Katherine back home. He miscalculated the higher value she placed on becoming an artist. She was more than willing to make financial sacrifices to achieve her ambitious goals.

On July 6, 1908, at nineteen, Katherine embarked from Wellington on a ship back to London and never returned to her homeland.

Prelude

Wellington, New Zealand, 1908

Katherine Mansfield Beauchamp, age 19

I SHALL END BY KILLING MYSELF, she thought, staring out her third-floor bedroom window onto the harbor. I've been back home for eighteen months, fifteen days, and six hours and I can't tolerate another minute. Pa keeps promising to talk about it but he never does. Mother says, 'talk to your father.' Jeanne, Chaddie, and Vera turn away saying, 'Give it up. Pa will never let you return to London. He's too afraid of the trouble you'll get into.' And my dear sweet little brother Leslie just smiles and says, 'Pa will let you go, just be patient.'

Oh! if only Grandmother Dyer were still alive. Why did she have to die just when I needed her most? She would have stood by me as she always did and convince Pa that I must live in London. And then she'd be the one who would miss me the most. No one else would miss me, I know that. Well that's not entirely true. Leslie would miss our walks in the woods and my bedtime stories.

Now that grandmother has died, oh why did it have to be so sudden, and before I got to see her again. Only the Trowells understand my desire to be a famous writer like my cousin, Elizabeth. Pa must know I can never become famous if I stay here. You would think after all the trouble I've caused since I got home, he'd be convinced to let me go.

It certainly has convinced Mother, especially after I wrote that story about my childish affair with Edith. Did she really take me that seriously? Oh yes, I adored Edith. Who wouldn't? She's beautiful. Talented. And she adored me. But after that week alone with her at our island cottage I knew it would never work. And Maata! Exotic

Maata. A real Maori princess. I probably shouldn't have asked Pa's secretary to type that story but I did warn her that she might find it shocking. She didn't have to show it to Pa. If that didn't convince him to send me away to London, what will?

Ha! And you call yourself an independent woman. You'll never survive in London if you don't take a stand now, here in this house.

She looked around her plush room. The lace curtains. Doilies on the tables. Pink bedspread.

I'm so sick of this room. I'm so sick of this life.

At that moment she heard a horn blast from the harbor and rushed to the window to watch the travelers wave good-bye to their loved ones on the dock as a large ship pulled away.

Oh why aren't I on that ship? Pa promised me I could go and then he said no. What changed his mind? Or rather who changed his mind?

She walked over to the door prepared to turn the knob and go downstairs that instant to her father's study and plead with him to book her passage on the next ship to England. Her hand dropped and she went back to the window to stare at the passing ship.

Coward. You might act bravely but you're such a coward.

She looked down at the family photo taken five years ago aboard the cargo ship *Niwaru* that brought her and her sisters to Queens College in London, where their parents dropped them off.

It's their fault. They're the ones who shipped me to England to finish my education. Didn't they realize that if I spent three years there studying and feeling the rhythm of that wonderful city I would never be happy anywhere else in the world?

And what's wrong with Vera and Chaddie? Why don't they want to come with me? On the ship coming home they wanted to. Pa would never have said "no" to the three of us. Maybe I can convince him that Leslie should go to school in London and I'll be his chaperone. No, Mother would never let him go. He's too young. Though I was only fourteen when I went.

Going over to London I was daddy's girl, sitting with him on the deck in longue-chaises watching the stars. Then on the return, after my so-called "scandalous behavior" on board with that charming cricket player, I spent most of the time in my cabin. Pa didn't talk to me the rest of the trip.

But now we're getting along. Well sort of. Didn't he help me get those first stories published in the *Native Companion*? He was proud of me then. He said I had as much chance as cousin Elizabeth of becoming a famous author. That was when I reminded him she wasn't a success until she left the colonies.

Maybe I should write to Elizabeth and ask her to convince Pa. No, I wrote her before and she never answered. She has no time for her silly, colonial cousin stranded in Wellington.

I even took classes in typing and bookkeeping at that horrible technical school thinking Pa would let me leave if I could make a living in London. But no, he said I'd never make enough to live the way I was accustomed to.

He doesn't understand me. I don't care about all this frill. I'll go through my wardrobe closet right now and throw out all those silly evening gowns. It was Mother who insisted I never wear the same gown twice. That's what I'll do, throw them right out. That will get Pa's attention when they float down past his window.

She swung open her wardrobe closet.

But that silver chiffon I just wore at my nineteenth birthday dance is really too wonderful to throw out.

I must get out of this house before I suffocate. I'll go to visit Julia. No I can't do that. We don't have anything in common anymore after she heard what people were saying about the "wild girl" and the "sinful behavior." She's even afraid of me now. Walks on the other side of the street.

I could visit the Trowells if they hadn't already left for London. I can't even practice the cello anymore now that my teacher Mr. Trowell has gone. And his son Arnold, my Caesar. He never answered my last letter telling him I dream of his embraces.

Pa helped pay their passage to England, why won't he do the same for me? That's what I'll do. I'll give my own benefit dance and collect funds for my passage.

She laughed.

Mother would disown me if I did that. But why doesn't Arnold write? He thought I was irresistible. Oh, who cares? From now on I will love only myself.

She looked at herself sideways in the tall mirror.

Hmm. I'm eating too much. I don't get out enough. Look how pale I am.

Oh, I really will end by killing myself. That'll show them. Yes, that's what I should do. Jump right out. Wave to Pa before I crumble to the ground beneath his window. But first I need to write a letter blaming them for my death. "If only you'd let me go to London." No that will never do.

Stop this moaning and complaining. Go downstairs right now and talk to Pa.

She tapped lightly on his door.

"Pa? Can I come in?"

"Yes, Kass, but I have a meeting in an hour and I must finish this report. I don't have time to talk."

From his bay window, she could still see the departing ship. She approached his desk.

"Pa, have you been thinking about what I said last night?"

"You mean about your asking me for the hundredth time to book your passage to London?" he said, without looking up.

"Yes."

"I haven't had time to give it any thought."

"Oh, Pa."

She plopped down in front of his desk and stared at him.

Patience. Patience. Everyone tells me to be patient. All right here I am being patient. I'll just keep drumming my fingers on the desktop until he pays attention.

At last, he looked up. "Yes, Kass?"

"I know I've caused you and Mother a lot of trouble since I got back home. Don't think me ungrateful for all you've done for me but can't you see how miserable I am? My life is rushing by and, besides the few stories I've published, I'm completely unknown and will remain so until I reach London. Why did you say yes I could go, and then change your mind? Why?"

"Your recent behavior has indicated to your mother and I that you are not responsible enough to be on your own in London. I have some control over your behavior here but in London, who knows what trouble you will get yourself into?"

"I only get into *trouble* because I'm so completely bored!"

"How can you be bored? You're constantly going to balls and tea parties. I just saw the accounts of your charges at the dress shop by the way. And about those hats you had made to your design. They were very expensive."

"Those bills aren't mine alone. It's true I get many invitations to parties, but so do my sisters. Vera and Chaddie are far more conscious of fashion than I am and spend much more on their clothes than I do.

"Just think, Pa, if I were in London you wouldn't have any bills for me at all because as soon as I'm a published writer I'll be independent of you. I've been taking typing classes. Until my stories are published, I can work and live on a small allowance and I'll even pay that back to you someday when I am famous."

"Kass, I have no problem giving you money. Have I ever been anything but generous to you?"

She thought it better not to answer that question and turned her gaze upon the ship slipping out of view. How many ships must she watch disappear from the harbor before she was a passenger?

She turned back to him, her eyes teary, and pleaded her case. "But what other reason could you have for not letting me go? If it's only my behavior, I can promise to stay out of trouble. You'll hear no bad reports."

"Do you think you can manage to keep yourself off the scandal page?"

"Of course, Pa. The only talk of me in the papers will be reviews of my novels." The ship disappeared from the horizon.

She leapt up from her chair, ran over to him, and jumped in his lap.

"Pa. Please let me go. I promise to be good. I'll make you proud. I know I will. I'll write to you everyday. I'll even report weekly to Mr. Kay at your London bank and he can report back to you on how well I am doing."

"Calm down, Kass. Stand up. I want to get something from my files. I have written to your uncle Henry asking him about proper housing for a young woman in London. He has suggested a lodge that takes only young, unmarried women, mostly musicians, pursuing their artistic ambitions. It appears there is a room available for a well-behaved, serious young lady."

"Oh, Pa." She jumped in his lap again and hugged him.

"Stop it Kass. You're wrinkling my tie."

"I'll go write Ida and the Trowells and tell them I'm coming."

She hesitated at the door.

"Pa, when will I arrive in London?"

He'd returned to his paperwork and didn't answer.

SHE WANTED TO LEAVE immediately but Mrs. Beauchamp didn't want anyone to think they were sending their daughter off because she had gotten into trouble. There were tea parties and a formal dance given by the Prime Minister's daughter, where Katherine performed a few mimes and sang. The *Wellington Courier's* social column described what the young guests, including Miss Beauchamp, wore and ate.

Finally her father handed her a passage ticket dated for departure July 6, 1908, and said, "I've spoken to the ship's captain and asked him to keep an eye on you as you are a young lady traveling without a chaperone."

What could be better than being alone on a ship without a chaperone? I mustn't let him know how excited I am.

"Thank you, Pa. I've dreaded taking this trip on my own. Maybe Mother could come with me?"

Katherine expected her to say no. Anything to do with her at this point was an irritation and an interruption of her mother's social calendar.

At the embarkation dock, Mrs. Beauchamp embraced her daughter stiffly. "Please behave, Kass. I don't want to read anything in the papers that will embarrass our family and make me come and fetch you home."

Katherine waved to her parents until the ship made a sharp turn out of the harbor and they disappeared from her view. The sudden shift in the ocean current forced her to grip the railing and brace herself against the gale winds. She was finally at the helm of her ship plunging toward the open sea. She threw back her head and exuberantly shouted, "I'm free!"

1

December 1918

The Elephant House—London

Grant me the moment, the lovely moment
That I may lean forth to see
The other buds, the other blooms,
The other leaves on the tree . . .
A Little Girl's Prayer—KM

DAWN'S LIGHT, like Romeo, slipped through the window and slowly unfolded, quietly painting the walls white. He stretched over her to gently touch the blooming jonquil bouquet on the bedside table. The jonquils, elegantly dressed in watery crystal, awoke; their tiny yellow flowers flattered by his touch. But he brought no warmth to Katherine and slipped away as stealthily as he'd come. "Farewell, Romeo," Katherine whispered, pulling herself up on the pillows.

She shivered and reached for her yellow bed jacket, tying its white silk ribbons for protection against the wintry chill. Too hoarse to call out to LM for a glass of water, she pulled the eiderdown up around her parched throat and waited for the sun to follow the dawn and wake the household.

Across the room, LM breathed deeply and steadily, her oversized body crunched into a child's pose, too large for the loveseat.

Katherine cursed her for leaving the laudanum on the bureau, its tempting bottle too far away to reach without hobbling across the room. But as quickly, she forgave LM, remembering she'd asked her to put it out of reach, to protect herself from its seductive power.

LM was an abbreviation for Lesley Moore. Her childhood name had been Ida but Katherine had changed it to LM, when they met in school fifteen years ago and became good friends. Katherine called her "Ida" only in anger or in public.

Ida would have preferred adopting her mother's maiden name, Katherine Moore, but the fourteen-year-old Kathleen Beauchamp had already taken it for herself, along with her grandmother's maiden name, Mansfield. From her earliest stories, she'd penned her name *Katherine Mansfield.*

The household slept on. Occasionally Jack snored on the other side of the wall. He had moved to the spare bedroom saying he could no longer share the same bed until Katherine returned to good health. His work was very demanding and he couldn't have his essential sleep interrupted by her hacking cough.

To muffle the mantelpiece clock's monotonous count, she reached for Shakespeare's *The Winter's Tale.* A piercing back spasm jerked her hand and several books fell onto the floor. She smothered her cry into a pillow and slipped under the covers, drowning in a sea of terrifying darkness that up until now she'd managed to hold at bay through the night.

KATHERINE AWOKE to LM's canary voice. "Good morning, dearie, did you sleep well?" Her face was hidden behind a breakfast tray weighted down with a full tea set, a stack of buttered toast and marmalade. LM plopped it down on the bed and Charles, disturbed from slumber, stood up and stretched out her thick, black and white, furry body.

"Off!" shouted LM, shooing the cat off the bed, just before her pink tongue lopped off the cream.

"Don't shout at her. What do you expect when you put a pitcher of cream in front of her nose. I don't mind if she has a taste."

"She's fat enough already."

"Come here, Charles. Don't let her scare you away." The cat leapt back on the bed and took another lick from the pitcher, before settling back down at Katherine's feet.

"She might be pregnant, you know. Haven't you noticed her swelling teats?"

LM turned away without answering. An irritating habit among a list of others, thought Katherine, glaring at her back.

"What a lovely autumn day," said LM, absently looking out the window over London's rooftops, a view Katherine could barely see from the bed. "What a shame you can't take a walk on the Heath. It would do you much good but it's too cold, isn't it, my dear Katie?"

Katherine closed her eyes and argued with herself, She's only trying to help. You're the one who thought the three of you could live in harmony. You're the one who argued with Jack that no one but LM knew better what you needed, that there was no one more loyal and dedicated.

"Careful, dearie, you almost knocked over the tray," said LM, suddenly towering over her and blocking the sun's warmth. "You know you mustn't dally today. Did you forget you have an appointment with Dr. Sorapure this morning?"

"No, I haven't forgotten," she answered, miming LM's tiny, chirpy voice, and forgetting her promise to be nice.

"Here, dearie, drink your tea while it's still hot."

"Is Jack awake?"

"Awake? It's ten o'clock, Katie. You're the only one who sleeps late in this house. He's down in the basement working with Richard setting the type to your new story."

"How do you know he's not setting the type to his book of poetry?"

"No, no. He said this morning it's your story."

"But which story?"

"I think it's the one you wrote in Bandol. The one with the French title I can never pronounce correctly."

"Je ne parle pas français?"

"Oh yes," she giggled. "That's it, though I could never say it so nicely. Heavens no, not like you. Now what was I saying . . . oh yes, Richard has designed a wonderful cover for Jen-nee—"

"What? You saw it before I did?" She coughed into her hankie and in a raspy voice said, "Will you please let them know that I must approve the cover before it's printed!"

"Now Katie, calm down. You don't want to bring on a fever, do you? I haven't seen it. That's just what Jack said. He remembers very well your anger when the Woolfs published your other story without discussing the cover. I'm sure he'd never let that happen again. You know the one I mean."

"*Prelude,* Ida! *Prelude*," said Katherine. "For someone who constantly tells me how wonderful my stories are you might think to remember their titles."

"Oh yes, how can I forget?" LM giggled again. "Well you know how ridiculously empty my mind is. But how could you understand? You're made so differently. Why, I remember back in school how you collected details like a squirrel collects acorns. Oh dear! I almost forgot to tell you that Jack won't be up to see you before dinner."

"How nice of him to take the time to visit his invalid wife."

"Oh my, aren't we grumpy today? But here I am chattering away and keeping you from your breakfast. Drink your tea, dearie. And after, shall I brush your hair? That always calms you when you're edgy. And certainly you want to look presentable for Dr. Sorapure. What dress shall I put out for you to wear today?"

Katherine pushed the tray away and pulled up the eiderdown. Charles jumped off the bed and ran out the door.

"Why you're shivering." She brought the shawl hanging on the chair in front of the writing table and wrapped it over Katherine's shoulders. "There now, we don't want you to catch cold, do we?" She handed Katherine a half-empty teacup. "Finish your tea and then I'll help you get dressed. What did you say you wanted to wear?"

"I didn't say. Please stop fidgeting around me. I'm too tired to dress. I was up all night."

"Did you have another night terror? I didn't hear a peep out of you all night. Why didn't you wake me?"

"I wanted to give you a break from administering to me."

"Oh, Katie, the way you have with words. I don't *administer* to you, dearie, I take care of you. And may I say it gives me great pleasure every day to do so."

"Well I don't know how you bear it." She sipped from the teacup and immediately thrust it back to LM. "This tea is cold and weak. When will you make a proper cup?"

LM ignored her again and leaned down to pick up the pillows knocked on the floor during the night. "Oh, who is this down here? Why little Rib. Why are you hiding under the bed? Katie's not angry at you, too, is she?" She picked up the floppy Russian doll and tucked it under the covers, then lumbered off to the other side of the room to straighten the medicine and perfume bottles. She returned to the bedside to restack the books and dust them off with her apron.

Katherine felt badly shouting at her and softened her tone, using her affectionate nickname. "Jones, please forgive me for being so unpleasant. I don't want to be like this. I've just been ill too long. I've forgotten how to behave properly. Bring me the hairbrush. I'll do my own hair. You should go downstairs. Doctor Sorapure will be arriving soon."

Five minutes later Katherine put down the brush when she heard Dr. Sorapure's light footsteps, followed by LM's heavy plodding.

"Leave us, Ida," said Katherine, when she saw her still lurking after ushering the doctor into the bedroom.

Dr. Sorapure opened his satchel and carefully removed the tools of his trade. He laid them out on her bed table: a stethoscope, a percussion hammer, a thermometer, and a small black notebook; not to record words, snippets of conversations, memories or detailed images like she did in her notebook, but for medical notations he would refer to or add to during his consulation with her. How different from my trade, she thought. I only need a pen, ink, and paper. He hung the stethoscope around his neck.

"Is that new?" she asked.

"Yes. Brand new. Far better for auscultations than the last one. And see this," he held up a rubber disc. "This fits over the chest piece as an anti-chill device."

A few months ago, on her thirtieth birthday, a pulmonary specialist told her, "You won't reach old bones." Then came a procession of stethoscope auscultators. She lost her modesty and no longer felt shy about unbuttoning her blouse in front of a doctor so he could listen to her crackling, disease-inflamed lungs. But none of them knew how to put out the raging fire burning within. With stethoscopes draped over white-collared, double-chinned necks and grim looks like mourners in a funeral procession, they shook their heads and threatened her with only four years to live if she didn't enter a tuberculosis sanatorium.

It still amazed her that a slight infection in her lungs after a cold could be the harbinger of early death. She was too young. The newspapers spoke of tuberculosis killing a thousand people every week in England but it wouldn't kill her. No, that wasn't possible. She'd only just begun to write stories that satisfied her. And what about that novel waiting to be written?

Dr. Sorapure was the first doctor who understood her desperation. From the beginning, she trusted his scientific knowledge and research. Their intellectual conversations about the immensity and wonder of the universe and the incomprehensibility of space had calmed her growing fear of death. He also recognized the importance of her work, which she would be deprived of if she moved into a sanatorium. He suggested a home cure that would allow her to continue writing.

She now watched him as he carefully siphoned the seductive amber tincture of opium from its vial and added it drop by drop to the alcohol in the green Bohemian glass bottle—his gift to her. She'd worried

LM would clumsily knock it over and break it and she had instructed her to only touch it with permission.

Dr. Sorapure pulled his chair closer to her bed as if they were old friends and he had come to talk about literature. LM still stood behind him, looking over his shoulder.

"Ida, I said you could go. I'll call you if I need you."

"Shouldn't I stay?"

"Ida, go now."

She swung around, quickly hiding her hurt face but Katherine noticed and felt guilty.

"So Mrs. Murry how are we doing today?"

"Well, let's see. My back screams. My head moans. I have to crawl across the room to get to my writing table only to find my fountain pen's too heavy to lift. And oh yes, my right lung feels like someone is plunging a knife in it every time I breathe. Otherwise, Doctor, I'm just fine." She preferred to mock and exaggerate her symptoms. Otherwise they were thoroughly boring and even she was tired of hearing them.

"Let's have a listen, shall we?"

He was right. The new rubber disc didn't make her jump out of her skin when he pressed it against her chest. "Breathe deeply," he said.

He had her turn over and tapped her back several times with his hammer, listening for sounds only he understood. She put her bed jacket back on and propped herself up against the pillows while he jotted down a few notes. Then he looked up. "You look very tired today. Are you taking the laudanum at night as I suggested?"

"No. I worry about becoming dependent upon it. Years ago I became addicted to Veronal. It caused me great harm. The withdrawal was very difficult. I don't want to ever put myself through that agony again."

"You must trust me when I tell you it's all right to take laudanum. Its tincture of opium relieves the pain so that you can sleep. I assure you, after the pain is gone, you will easily put the stopper on this lovely bottle." He held it up to the sun's reflection.

"And when will the pain be gone, Doctor? "

"I can't answer that," he said, wrapping his soft, warm hand around her wrist while he counted to himself. "Your pulse is weak, Mrs. Murry. You must promise me that you will get some rest. You can't afford another fever in your weakened condition."

Ida peeked in at the door. "Would you like a cup of tea, Doctor?"

"Yes, that would be quite pleasant. Thank you."

Katherine threw LM a sharp look when she returned with a tea tray holding three teacups. LM saw that look and only poured tea in two. She took the other one away and closed the door behind her.

When they were alone again, Dr. Sorapure said, "I've been studying your case to better understand why you first became ill in your early twenties and why you've become progressively more crippled with rheumatism."

"I thought the cause of my rheumatism was the same as my mother's rheumatic fever."

"I don't think that's accurate."

"No? What is your diagnosis?"

"First I need to ask you a few questions. Questions you might find unpleasant, even embarrassing. But I must ask before I can help you further. And know that what you tell me will not be written into any medical report."

"Patients have no privacy. What do you want to know?"

"When did your back and hip pain start?"

"After my surgery."

"Is the scar on the left side of your stomach from that surgery?"

"Yes."

"Will you tell me about it?"

Katherine, unaccustomed to being without words, fell silent when he opened his notebook and waited, pen in hand, staring at her. She reminded herself that he was there to help her and began.

"It was over nine years ago. Before Mr. Murry. I'd left my home in Wellington to return to London where I attended school. When I arrived in London, I fell in love with a young musician. His name was Garnet Trowell. We were to be married, but his parents broke off our engagement for reasons you needn't hear about.

"I married my first husband, George, to forget Garnet and made a bloody fool of myself. I realized I'd made a terrible mistake and ran out of the hotel on our wedding night before consummating our vows." Embarrassed, she held her gaze on the bedroom window and continued. "My mother whisked me off to Bad Wörishofen, a spa in Bavaria known for its cold water treatment cure for hysterical women. The patients were hosed with icy water and immersed in baths. She left me there.

"I was lonely. I met someone who was very kind to me. He helped me forget Garnet. Months later, when I realized I didn't love this man I returned to London.

"Without funds, I asked George to take me back. We'd only been living together a short time when I woke up one night with excruciating stomach pain. He took me to the hospital. I don't remember much after that except I had a most unpleasant doctor, not at all like you." She took a sip of tea before continuing.

"He told me that he'd have to operate immediately. I was only twenty. I didn't think to ask any questions. I woke up hours later, the pain was only a dull ache. The doctor told me the surgery was a success."

Dr. Sorapure wrote down a few notes.

"He didn't ask you anything else?"

"Yes, if you must know, he asked me several intimate questions that I found objectionable. I became angry and told him to leave me alone."

"I'm sorry but I have to ask you one more question. Did the surgeon ask you if you'd been sexually active outside your marriage to Mr. Bowden?"

Katherine hesitated before answering. "Yes, he did. But why are you asking me that now?"

"Because I want to find out the source of your illness so that I can help you. The surgeon, I'm sure, also wanted to help you."

"He lacked empathy."

"It's possible that a sexual partner ten years ago gave you an infection that has made you an invalid today. That surgeon probably tested a sample of tissue taken from the infected area and found out the source of your abdominal pain was gonococcal bacteria."

Katherine turned her gaze within as her mind filled with disturbing memories: borrowing money from LM to stay in an unaffordable elegant hotel; the itchy discharge; the missed periods; the burning pain; the smell; too poor and too embarrassed to ask for a doctor's help. In her mind she slammed the door shut and outwardly turned her gaze upon Dr. Sorapure.

"Doctor, did you ever read Oscar Wilde?"

"Yes, I believe so when I was at University."

"I read him when I was a child growing up in New Zealand. Every word he ever wrote. I had just turned sixteen when I read *The Picture of Dorian Gray*. The narrator said that *the only thing worth pursuing in life is beauty and the fulfillment of the senses. The only way to get rid of temptation is to yield to it.* Under Wilde's influence I came to London on my own at nineteen to pursue that life of beauty and the fulfillment of the senses."

She took a sip of water to clear her voice. "You asked if I was sexually active outside my marriage to Mr. Bowden. The answer is, yes." She was surprised not to see disdain in his face when he looked up from his notes.

"Am I to blame for my illness, Doctor?"

"No, Mrs. Murry, not at all. Unfortunately, women do not recognize the symptoms of gonorrhea, nor do their doctors. With men it's quickly diagnosed and treated before it infects their bodily organs. Because your infection was not diagnosed it spread. I'm sure the surgeon thought he was extracting the growing bacteria but instead it leaked into your bloodstream, infecting your joints and other bodily organs. I believe it is the source of the inflammation and pain you now have.

"I'm sorry to be the bearer of such bad news. But you mustn't blame yourself or your doctor. If he had known what we know now he would have first treated you with antibacterials and avoided surgery."

He reached for her hand and held it. "Now that I know the probable source of your infection, we can try injections of organic compounds to kill the bacteria."

"Will these injections also arrest the tuberculosis and stop this hacking cough?"

"That's not as treatable, at least not yet, but it might help. You have to be patient with us doctors. Even these injections are experimental." He released her hand and sat back in his chair. He smiled. "I could tell you to smoke less but I know you wouldn't listen. I could tell you to eat fruit and vegetables instead of beaten eggs and wine for lunch. I could—"

He was interrupted by her coughing spasm. He offered her another glass of water. She took a sip and then reclined against the pillows. He picked up the green Bohemian glass bottle and held out a spoonful of the amber liquid he'd mixed earlier. "Take this. It will help you rest." She opened her mouth and let the fluid slip soothingly down her throat.

"You're a strong woman, Mrs. Murry, but you can't will away tuberculosis. If we can give you relief from your crippling pain, at least you won't be bedridden. Isn't that worth something?"

"I hoped that by sequestering myself here, taking the home cure, my body would no longer be my enemy. It's been plotting against me all this time and I didn't even know it."

Katherine looked around at her room that she'd painted white. The flowers in their bowls. Her yellow writing table, now too painful to sit at. The fountain pen, now agony to hold.

"You understood my need to write. It is through my writing that I have had the will to go on living. I don't know how much longer I can go on if I can't write. Am I a fool to hope for a cure?"

"Nothing is incurable," said Dr. Sorapure. "It's all a question of time. The experiments of today may just provide that link that will make all plain to a future generation. Each person plays but a small part in the history of the world. What is incurable today will be curable tomorrow and you will have shared in that success."

"Does that have the same meaning as, there is the sky and the sea and the shape of the lily and then there is illness and death; there are parasites and bacteria that grow strong and kill and then are killed?"

"Yes." He smiled. "But I much prefer your more poetic description. We keep learning more about how to cure disease. First, Pasteur discovered bacteria, and now we are discovering the difference between good bacteria and bad bacteria and experimenting with how to destroy the bad bacteria without damaging the good bacteria."

Katherine saw LM slip into the room.

"Do you want me to arrange for your injections at the hospital?" he asked.

"What injections?" blurted LM.

Dr. Sorapure turned to her. "We have seen success with injections of organic compounds that kill bacteria. If it works, maybe part of Mrs. Murry's illness will be cured and she will be able to walk and write again without pain."

"*If* it works?" asked LM.

Katherine held her eyes on Dr. Sorapure and said, "Ida, it's all right. I trust Dr. Sorapure. Besides I am only a cog in the wheel. Right, doctor?" She weakly smiled. "These injections can't be any worse than those electrical treatments I've been taking for my rheumatism. Regardless, I expect to recover—one has to, you know—from everything."

Dr. Sorapure stood up to leave.

"Ida, after you've seen the doctor out, please come back and close the curtains. I want to sleep."

"But Mrs. Woolf is coming to see you. It's too late to send her a note."

"Tell her that I'm sorry but I'm not well today. She'll understand." Katherine heard her own voice fading. "I only want to see Jack."

Dr. Sorapure's tincture was drawing her away. She felt herself falling into its amber flow but felt no fear.

SHE AWOKE TREMBLING, still remembering the white-uniformed soldiers marching toward the precipice where she stood, teetering on its edge, off to the side, their hilted swords and medals reflecting the sun, empty grenade holders banging against their hips, hollow eyes beseeching her, enormous rough hands reaching out to her before each soldier dropped off the precipice into the dark sea below.

Her deceased brother approached carrying a newborn, bundled in sheets of handwritten paper, black ink dripping like melted ice onto her brother's pure white cadet uniform. He handed the newborn to her before stepping over the precipice to join his comrades. She held the newborn over the abyss. She always woke up before letting him go.

She knew to just lie there, breathing deeply, her eyes wide open, not moving a finger until the tremors stopped.

2

Autumn 1908

The Trowells—London

Oh—let it remain as it is—
Do not suddenly crush out this,
the beautiful flower—
I am afraid even while I am rejoicing . . .
Notebooks—KM

Ten years before . . .

ARRIVING IN LONDON, the Trowells gave her a warm welcome and called her by her childhood name, Kass. She found it quite natural to call them Father and Mother, surrogate parents who shared her passion for art.

After several visits to their Hampstead home, she realized Arnold, at age twenty, decidedly loved her, but as a sister. Resilient, she turned her attention to his twin, Garnet, a tall, slender boy who loved books almost as much as he loved his violin. And of equal importance, he was a Trowell, and she wanted very much to be a part of the Trowell family. She was far more successful with her new suitor. In only a few weeks they fell in love and talked of a future together as great artists.

The night before Garnet was to leave on a winter road tour with the Moody Manners Opera Company, Kass was invited to a farewell dinner. In the kitchen, as now expected, she helped Mrs. Trowell and their young daughter Dolly prepare the evening meal. Mrs. Trowell, unable to afford a domestic on her husband's music teacher salary, had been hesitant to ask the Bank of New Zealand's daughter to help. Kass swayed her opinion by telling her that she felt more like their daughter if she did her share of the work.

She peeled potatoes happily, while listening through the thin walls to Garnet playing the violin accompanying Arnold on cello and their father on piano. They were learning a new composition that Arnold had just finished writing. This is how I want to live, she thought, straightening her back and reaching for another stack of unpeeled carrots. This is my true family not the Beauchamps who consider wealth the only meaning of success. Here I'm among artists.

She looked up at Mrs. Trowell wiping her flour-covered hand across her perspiring forehead. "It's too stuffy in here," she complained. "Open a window and go set the table, Dolly. Tell the men dinner will be served shortly."

After dinner, Garnet came up and softly said, "Kass, let's go for a walk." She turned to invite Dolly. "No, just the two of us. I have something I want to tell only you."

He grabbed his brother's overcoat for himself and offered his own to Kass before they slipped out the back door. Under a streetlight, Kass said, "Look up, Garnet. See how the limbs of these two trees are stretching their limbs toward each other as if holding hands against the bitterly cold wind."

"Let me be your limb and protect you from that wind." He wrapped his arms around her. "Marry me, Kass," he whispered in her ear. "Marry me, my darling."

Her legs wilted under her and she leaned against him for support. He smiled down on her. "Don't say anything. Just nod your head, yes."

She nodded and he lifted her face up to his, gently kissing her mouth for the first time.

She looked through the window at the Trowell's sitting room, the golden tones of the wood-burning fireplace, the vacant seat on the couch waiting for her. "I'm so happy," she whispered. Garnet reached for her hand and they rushed back inside.

"For goodness sake!" exclaimed Mrs. Trowell. "What are you two doing outside on this chilly night? Come here my children. Get warm near the fire."

His cheeks glowing as deep red as his hair, Garnet burst out, "Kass and I are engaged."

Mrs. Trowell was the first to recover. She took both their hands. "Why this is quite a surprise." Mr. Trowell stood up and stiffly hugged both of them. Instead of offering congratulations he asked Katherine, "Does your father know?"

"No. Not yet. She laughed. "Garnet just asked me."

"Well do it right away," he said and left the room.

Arnold shook Garnet's hand, "Why you ole sneak. So this is what you two have been up to. Congratulations, ole man. I'll dedicate my new composition to you two lovebirds. Let's see what shall I call it. I know . . . *Clandestine Love*."

Garnet and Katherine giggled and holding hands plopped down together on the couch.

Kass saw Dolly sitting alone by the fire playing Cribbage, ignoring their happiness, but was too excited to go over and ask her if anything was wrong.

The next morning Garnet left to join the musical tour.

KASS CARRIED HER CELLO to the house several times a week for a lesson with Mr. Trowell and then stayed for dinner. After, she'd return to Beauchamp Lodge and write to Garnet sometimes two or three times in one day: *Beloved—though I do not see you, know that I am yours. Every thought, every feeling in me belongs to you—I wake up in the morning and have been dreaming of you—and all through the day, while my outer life goes on steadily, my inner life I live with you, in leaps and bounds.*

Anxiously, she'd await his response, disappointed by the long gaps in between even though Garnet had told her he only had time to write on Sundays when traveling by train to the next venue. On October 14th, her twentieth birthday, a month after their engagement, she opened a letter from him and out fell a plain gold wedding band. She proudly showed it off to the Trowells that evening.

Around this time she became good friends with Margaret Wishart who also lived at Beauchamp Lodge. Margaret's father took a liking to Katherine and invited her to join them in Paris for a family wedding. She said yes. Garnet wouldn't be home for a few more weeks and the time would pass much faster in Paris.

It was a fairy tale wedding. Fortunately, she'd brought one evening gown from Wellington. Katherine enjoyed herself and she also enjoyed flirting with the young men who gathered around her, asking her to dance.

On the train back to London, she began to doubt her future with Garnet. Looking up at the borrowed suitcase joggling with the motion of the train, she found it depressing to think of never wearing her green silk gown again. Now that she was marrying a poor musician, there would be no more elegant dances. Garnet had asked her to sing in the Opera's chorus so they could be together on his tours. But how can I sing if I'm draggled and poor, she thought. But in her notebook reminded herself that she had a splendid voice and that *Fine feathers don't make fine artists.*

By the time the Paris train had pulled into Victoria Station she had reignited her love for Garnet. The Moody Manners was a huge company with over a hundred performers working six nights a week, if there was no room in the chorus, they could certainly use her skills backstage. And when they were not working she could write stories about their adventures.

When Garnet came back from his tour, his parents asked him to stay home and take care of Dolly while they visited relatives up North. Up until then their lovemaking had been brief, his parents keeping watch over them ever since they'd announced their engagement. The day they left Kass moved into Garnet's room.

The next morning when she came out of his bedroom in her nightgown and saw the shocked look on Dolly's face, she came up with a lie. "Look here, Dolly, can you keep a secret?"

"Yes, of course I can."

"Garnet and I were secretly married. We didn't want to say anything until I wrote my parents but we can trust you, can't we, to keep our secret?"

"Kass, does that mean you are going to live with us and play Cribbage and read to me every night before I go to bed?"

Kass laughed and pulled Dolly close to her. "Yes, my dearest, yes."

The Trowells returned home and Kass returned to sleeping at Beauchamp Lodge. Garnet left again on tour promising Kass that he would ask the stage manager to find her a place in the chorus so next time she'd come with him. It was around then that Kass noticed a change in Mr. Trowell and wondered if she was the cause of his cold silence. He had yet to congratulate them on their engagement.

Kass and Mrs. Trowell often spent time together in the kitchen after Dolly went to bed having a last cup of tea before she returned to the boarding house. One night she asked Mrs. Trowell if she had done anything to hurt Mr. Trowell because he seemed so quiet of late.

"Oh, Kass. I didn't want to say anything but you're like a daughter to me so I can tell you. He's having financial worries. Mr. Trowell came to London with great expectations, believing he'd have many students because of his sons' reputations, but it hasn't worked out that way. The money the boys bring home isn't enough. We have to bring in a boarder or move into a smaller house or go back to Wellington."

"Oh, dear Mother, no. You mustn't leave London. I'd be lost without you. Why not let me be your boarder? I could stay in one of the boy's rooms and pay you the same rent I now pay at Beauchamp Lodge. And I'll talk to my guardian, my father's cousin, Uncle Henry. He's a teacher at the London Academy of Music and might know of some students for Mr. Trowell."

"Would you do that for us, Kass?"

"I'll do anything I can to keep you near me. I've never been so happy as during the time I've spent here with you and your family."

At first, living with the Trowells was having found a place in London to call home, where she could hang her hat on the back door. When Garnet had a break from the tour and came home, she'd sneak into his room after his parents retired. If Dolly saw her coming out of his room in the morning, Kass would put her finger to her lips, smile, and tiptoe down the hall to her own room. They both enjoyed the secret.

But Kass soon realized that a lodger at the Trowells was treated differently than a guest. She was often late on the rent, as she had been at the Lodge, unaccustomed to holding to a budget. But her tardiness at the Trowells strained their friendship. Too embarrassed to say she didn't have the money, she stopped having teatime with Mrs. Trowell in the kitchen and escaped to her room after dinner, missing out on previous family evenings by the fire.

Equally embarrassing was asking for an advance from her father's accountant, Mr. Kay, at the Bank of New Zealand's branch on Regent Street. She'd have to sit and listen to him lecture her on the value of a pound as if she was a child. He'd tell her to be more practical, and then insist on taking her to lunch, an invitation she felt obligated to accept.

She never told Mr. Kay that she was a lodger at the Trowells knowing whatever she told him would be reported to Mr. Beauchamp in the next post. She knew her father would never approve of her living in her music teacher's home. Nor would he allow her to marry the young musician whose musical education he had contributed to. She kept delaying the letter she had promised she would send to her father asking him to approve her engagement to Garnet. But why should she have to ask him? Wasn't she now an independent woman who could choose her own husband?

One morning, in a hurry to meet her old friends from Beauchamp Lodge for lunch, Kass handed Mrs. Trowell a wash basket filled with dirty clothes.

"Hold on, Kass. I'll have to charge you for this wash."

"But you've always offered to do it before."

"That was before you became our lodger. Besides, your fancy things need gallons of hot water and we can't afford it when you hold out on the rent."

"All right, M—" She started to say Mother but how could she with Mrs. Trowell glaring down at her as if she was a street urchin. She held her head up proudly and said, "Mrs. Trowell. I'll pay you when I come home."

"That's what you said about last week's rent. You're not the same girl we invited into our home. I don't believe you anymore."

Kass was deeply wounded by her words but proudly turned away. What was she to do? Get down on her knees and beg? She had frantically searched her room for coins earlier and had found only one shilling, which she was now rubbing between her fingers in her pocket. She needed that shilling for the omnibus from Hampstead Heath to the tube and from there to Regent Street to meet her friends. She had planned to borrow from someone for her lunch and then see Mr. Kay afterward for an advance on her allowance.

"I am seeing Mr. Kay this afternoon and I will pay you then." She tried to pass Mrs. Trowell but the older woman folded her arms over her apron and glared at her, blocking her passage.

Kass took back the wash basket and angrily said, "All right, Mrs. Trowell, I'll do my own wash." She stomped back up the stairs and threw the basket on her bed. In her hurry to leave, she almost knocked Dolly down on the staircase but didn't stop to apologize, slamming the door on her way out.

That night she paid Mrs. Trowell the overdue rent and without another word went up to her room. Dolly followed her up the stairs hoping for a bedtime story but her mother called her back down sternly.

When Garnet came home a week later, Katherine complained of the change in his parents' attitude toward her.

"Your mother doesn't want me staying here. I can't do anything right by her. And your father keeps looking in the post for a letter from my father. He even threatened to write him. I'm afraid to tell your father that I haven't."

"And why haven't you?"

"Garnet! I thought you would understand. I will not ask my father's permission to marry you. It's not his decision. It's mine. We can tell him after we're married."

"Kass, must I remind you that I'm dependent on my parents' financial help. I don't have an allowance like you do. I don't make enough money for us to move into our own home after we're married. We'll have to live here so you must find a way to get along with my parents. They've made tremendous sacrifices so that my brother and I could become musicians.

"If you were to write your father and receive his permission for us to marry, my parents would be very relieved. My father shouldn't be the one to ask your father. Nor should I. We don't want your father to think we are asking for a hand out. He's been more than generous already. I don't see why you have to be so stubborn about this."

It upset her that Garnet took his parents' side, but didn't say so. That evening at dinner she promised Mr. Trowell that she would write another letter as the first one must have been lost at sea. She wasn't sure he believed her. She continued her weekly cello lessons but their meaningful conversations about the value of art and the sacrifices an artist and his wife must make had stopped. She thought to stop her lessons.

Garnet was leaving again on tour for six weeks and had been unable to convince the stage manager to take Kass on. She didn't think she could bear the loneliness now that his parents had turned against her. And when she went out to have fun with her friends, Mr. Trowell would wait up for her, angry if she came in later than promised. He was acting like her father and she didn't like it.

On Garnet's last night, the family was sitting in their usual places in the sitting room, Mr. Trowell at his desk, Mrs. Trowell in the rocking chair, bookends on each side of the blazing logs; Dolly playing with her doll at her mother's feet. Arnold's chair was empty as he was on tour. Garnet and Kass shared the couch, both reading, his leg pressed against hers under the blanket. They hoped to make love on his last night, but his parents kept their bedroom door open now and they were afraid of being caught.

Dolly had been unusually quiet during dinner and now sat leaning her head on her mother's knee. Kass invited her to come sit between her and Garnet so she could read her a bedtime story. Dolly shook her head. "What about a game of Cribbage?" Dolly stood and crossed her arms in front of her chest like her mother often did and blurted out, "Why haven't you told them, Garnet! Why do you keep it a secret?"

"Tell them what?" Garnet asked.

"Tell them that you and Kass are married."

"What?" said Mrs. Trowell looking first at Garnet, then at Kass and then back to Dolly. "What are you talking about Dolly? They're not married. They're engaged."

"When you were away on holiday, Kass told me they were married but to keep it a secret until she'd told her parents."

Mr. Trowell looked up from the sheet music he was studying. Normally nothing interrupted him when he was working. He spoke very quietly. "Kass, is this true? Are you married?"

"Not exactly."

"What do you mean, *not exactly*. Are you and Garnet married or not?"

"Why don't you ask him?" She turned to Garnet who had pulled away from her on the couch. "Garnet, your father wants to know what I mean when I say we are *not exactly* married."

Mrs. Trowell stood up. The sock she was darning dropped on the floor. The ball of yarn silently rolled across the room stopping at Kass's feet. Kass stooped to pick it up and brought it over to Mrs. Trowell, giving Garnet a chance to speak, but he didn't.

"All right, if you won't tell them, I will. Garnet and I are lovers," she stated to the room at large.

Mrs. Trowell sat down at the same moment Mr. Trowell rose from his chair. "Kass, did you also lie to me about having asked your father's permission to marry Garnet?"

"I don't have to ask him. I can marry Garnet without his permission."

"Oh no, you cannot, young lady!" shouted Mr. Trowell. "How could you do this to us? We took you into our home and treated you as if you were our own child and in return you deceived us. The engagement is off. If it weren't for your father's kindness toward us, I would have you leave our house tonight."

He turned toward Garnet and said sternly, "I will deal with you later but you are not to have any further contact with Miss Beauchamp." Garnet was studying the floor and didn't look up. "Do you hear me, Garnet?"

Kass had expected him to defend her. To honor her. To defy his father.

He didn't look at her when she touched his shoulder.

Dolly burst out crying.

Kass wanted to take Dolly into her arms and tell her she was sorry for lying to her, but Mr. Trowell stood between them.

"Garnet and Dolly go to your rooms!" he commanded.

Kass watched Garnet run up the stairs with Dolly behind him. "Garnet!" she cried out. "Garnet!" He didn't look back.

She grabbed her coat and hat and rushed out of the house believing Garnet would come after her. She stopped across the street to wait for him but saw the lights go off. The house was closed to her. A drizzle became a downpour and the wet air pushed her down the street. A bus pulled up and she jumped on it.

3

Mr. Peacock

"Not at all, dear lady. I am only too charmed."
Mr. Reginald Peacock's Day—KM

HER OLD SCHOOL FRIEND, Ida, pulled her inside. "My poor dear. What happened? You look lost and you're drenched."

I certainly am lost, she thought, but was too miserable to tell Ida that she had lost her entire family and that Garnet had betrayed her.

"My poor dear," Ida said. "Come by the fire. I'll dry your hair." Ida helped her off with her wet clothes. Katherine curled up on the couch and her only friend in the world tucked her under an eiderdown.

Early the next morning, she opened her eyes upon a small box tied in a wide red ribbon. She'd forgotten it was Christmas week. Inside the box was a black and silver Egyptian shawl. She thanked Ida profusely and promised her a poem in return. She borrowed a few bob for the bus and hurried back to Beauchamp Lodge, expecting to find Garnet waiting for her, or at least a message. There was no message but there was a cheaper room on the ground floor. Not as private or as quiet as her previous room upstairs facing the garden, but she could ill-afford to be uppity without a shilling in her pocket.

Her Lodge girlfriends tried to shake her out of her misery but she kept to her new room, wanting to be there when Garnet came looking for her. She found solace writing in her journal about that awful night that continued to haunt her. Yes she had lied to the Trowells and that was wrong but when she did tell the truth—yes she and Garnet were lovers—why hadn't Garnet defended her? She understood the

Trowells' behavior but not Garnet's. How could he abandon her like that, obeying his father instead of protecting her?

After several days of keeping to her room, expecting every knock on the door to be Garnet and feeling another terrible letdown when it wasn't, she finally admitted that he wasn't coming.

Filling her pen, she started scribbling down sketches in her notebook and as she wrote, a story developed that she had started before leaving Wellington. A story about a poor girl named Rosabel who works long hours in a millinery shop and spends her evenings in a shabby unheated boarding house. Her drab room is even more dismal in contrast to the elegant shop where she spent her days serving the wealthy female clientele who come dressed in their finery to buy stylish hats and soft leather gloves. They're usually escorted by gentlemen who always pay the bill; a few nice ones flipping her a coin on their way out with a wink and a smile. Back in her room, tired, hungry, and cold, Rosabel falls asleep watching the rain stream down her window and dreams that a rich gentleman falls in love with her and they are soon to be married.

The words formed quickly in Katherine's mind and filled several pages before she came to the final paragraph:

So she slept and dreamed and smiled and once threw out her arm to feel for something which was not there, dreaming still. And the night passed. Presently the cold fingers of dawn closed over her uncovered hand; grey light flooded the dull room. Rosalind shivered, drew a little gasping breath, sat up. And because her heritage was that tragic optimism, which is all too often the only inheritance of youth, still half asleep she smiled with a little nervous tremor round her mouth.

Katherine also smiled, pleased with her completed work. She looked over at her neglected cello leaning against the wall, a painful reminder of Garnet's absence, and tears welled into her eyes. No more tears, she told herself and said out loud, "See what I can accomplish without you. I don't need you. I have all that I need right here on this table." She pointed her pen at the cello. "Someday I'll be as famous as my cousin Elizabeth. You'll see. Then you'll be sorry. You coward, Garnet!"

Before putting down her pen, she took a blank sheet of paper and wrote *The Tiredness of Rosabel,* and neatly placed it on top of her story. Now what? she asked herself. How shall I celebrate finishing my story? A hot bun at a teashop would certainly be delightful. She counted her change, a pence short. She walked over to the cello, plucked its out-of-tune strings, put it away inside its velvet case, and snapped the lid shut.

In her wardrobe chest, she looked at the frayed skirts, drab jackets and unfashionable hats. This will never do, she thought. An accomplished writer needs to make a good impression. She looked over at the cello case, took it by its handle, grabbed her coat, and went out.

She walked down the familiar Abbey Road. Often when needing an extra shilling for Abdulla cigarettes to share with Garnet or a concert ticket at Queen's Hall or a bouquet of fresh flowers or, like now, a hot bun at the teashop, she frequented the area's pawnshops and exchanged trinkets for treats.

She walked out of the second pawnshop without the cello. After stopping in the teashop for a hot bun, she entered a dress shop to buy the black evening gown in the window that she'd coveted for a week, plus a purple coat, burgundy velvet skirt, pale yellow silk blouse, and shiny patent leather shoes with bright green stockings. Fully satisfied with her afternoon purchases, she returned to Beauchamp Lodge and arranged fresh new flowers in a vase.

Her coin purse now empty and counting the days on her fingers before she could collect her monthly allowance from Mr. Kay, she sat down and wrote a letter to Mrs. Gladstone, a social hostess whose parties she'd attended. After Katherine sang along to accompany another guest who was playing the piano at Mrs. Gladstone's last party, as she'd so often done at her parents' parties in Wellington, the social hostess unexpectedly and discreetly passed her with an honorarium.

Mrs. Gladstone wrote back promptly saying she remembered Katherine fondly and invited her to a party she was giving the very next weekend.

The night of the party, Katherine put on her new velvet skirt and yellow blouse. Her Lodge friend, Margaret, accompanied her. Midway through, she sang to an appreciative audience and even followed it with a comedic skit, another talent she'd developed in her Wellington music room. The applause that followed and the shillings slipped into her hand by the hostess gave her a brief thrill of satisfaction.

The thrill passed too soon, and she sank down on a sofa next to Margaret and complained about her feeble attempt to place *Rosabel* with a publisher on the Strand. Even though she had already published several stories in New Zealand they still had shown her no respect. They told her to come back if she ever wanted a secretarial position and literally shut the door in her face.

"I want to write stories, but what if no one ever gets a chance to read what I've written? I will not humiliate myself again knocking on publishers' doors." She sank further into the sofa and meditated on the bubbles rising up in her champagne glass.

"Margaret!" she said, suddenly sitting up, the champagne sloshing. "I have the most wonderful idea. Why don't I *read* my stories to the public? I don't mean entertaining at parties though I could start there, but hiring out a hall and giving readings. It's never been done before."

"It'll probably be difficult," said Margaret, "but if anyone can do it, you can."

Katherine felt someone's eyes on her and glanced over at a well-dressed man in gray trousers with matching gray socks and black tie. He looked familiar and then she recalled he was the one who laughed and applauded the loudest after her skit.

"Do you know that gentleman?" she asked Margaret.

"No." She smiled. "But he's been leering at you all evening. Rather an old dandy, don't you think? Certainly too old for you."

Before Katherine could respond, he was standing in front of them, introducing himself. Margaret saw a friend enter the salon and left Katherine alone with Mr. George Bowden. Katherine found him a very attentive listener and before too long he sat down next to her and she enthusiastically shared her new idea.

"You have to imagine a softly-lit stage," she said. "Flowers everywhere—a shaded red-tasseled lamp—and there I am seated in a great high-backed oak chair wearing a simple but beautiful orange silk dress or perhaps what I'm wearing tonight." She spread out her velvet skirt that settled nicely on the yellow brocade sofa, sat up very straight and recited the first paragraphs of *Rosabel.* When she stopped, worried he'd lost interest, he said, "No, don't stop. What a beautiful voice. And how sympathetically you write about poor Rosabel."

Katherine blushed. "Oh, you're being too kind." She leaned toward him to speak softly, "Do you really think I possess the power to hold people's attention?"

"You certainly hold mine," he said confidentially. "You are a very talented and, might I say, charming young lady. I don't know any ladies who can sing, recite, and mime as well as you."

"I could do much better if I had a teacher. My voice needs refinement."

"Well, dear lady, perhaps I can help you."

"Really, Mr. Bowden. How could you help me?"

He pulled himself up very straight reminding Katherine of a peacock showing off its vibrant feathers. "I teach voice and elocution to vocal students at London University and I also have stage credits."

"Oh Mr. Bowden, had I known you're a professional artist I would have been too timid to perform for you. But now that I do know—you must tell me if it's quite silly of me to think there's a big opportunity for something sensational and new in giving readings to an audience."

He smiled down at her. "My dear lady, not silly at all and I would be only too charmed to teach you how to improve your voice, if you would let me."

"Let you? Why Mr. Bowden I would be honored. But do you have the time? I couldn't afford to pay you very much."

He laughed. "If you'll have dinner with me tonight we could discuss your lessons further. That is if you're available, Miss Mansfield?"

"Available?" She hesitated looking down at her barren finger, having only this morning removed Garnet's gold band. She smiled. "Yes, I am, Mr.—May I call you George? Mr. Bowden is so formal."

"I'd be only too charmed, my dear lady."

"And you must call me Katherine."

SHE NO LONGER WOKE UP in the morning hungry and lonely now that she had the evenings with George to look forward to. He escorted her to fashionable restaurants and told her to eat whatever she wanted. He also escorted her to London's fashionable salons where she never before had been invited. He seemed to know everyone and be adored by many women who were often his students and began to look upon Katherine with jealous eyes.

A bachelor, he gave her three lessons a week at his home in voice and elocution and told her to pay whatever she could afford.

He began each lesson instructing her to move her lips while repeatedly singing *moo-e-koo-e-oo-e-a* in front of a mirror. One afternoon tired of her girlish silliness, he said sternly, "Katherine I cannot teach you if you keep laughing. You need to train your lips to have more flexibility. Now stand up straight. You are quite petite and will be lost on the stage if you don't stand up tall. Okay now turn and face me. Don't be shy. Pretend I am your audience. Use your large deep somber eyes to draw me in. Don't be timid. You are a beautiful woman and you mustn't hide that beauty from your audience."

She did as she was told, still trying not to laugh but feeling quite self-conscious standing in his home singing into mirrors with him staring at her. Sometimes his arm brushed against her and she pulled back, but he was so patient and understanding that in time he gained her trust. And they were never completely alone. His ancient butler, Charles, often brought her a glass of water when her throat was dry from the exercises. And after her lesson, George would invite her to stay for tea and Charles would serve it in the pleasant sitting room. Katherine would linger, not wanting to go back to her lonely room and then he would invite her to dinner. When his flatmate, Lamont, a musical performer, came home late he joined them. She was most pleased when he told her that their flat was a far happier place to come home to when she was there.

With an allowance that barely covered her room and board, she came to realize that her life would be quite boring if not for George's entertainment. He gave her an escape from the harsh reality of her drab and limited existence.

Under his admiring gaze, she blossomed like the bouquets delivered to her boarding house each morning signed: "To my best student."

He started sending her passionate letters written on elegant hand woven stationery. At first she made fun of his flirtation, reading his letters out loud to her girlfriends at the Lodge. But in time George became more appealing. He was over thirty and she was barely twenty, but she liked being with a mature man who was more capable of taking care of her than Garnet. And though George was sophisticated, he never teased her for being a little Colonialist. He even gushed enthusiastically and showed her off when she gained a reputation of being rather eccentric in her behavior and took to dressing like a gypsy or a Japanese princess. With George by her side, prepared to defend her, she could act as she pleased.

He also introduced her to social hostesses who invited her to perform at their parties. She started to believe in herself again and felt she could fulfill her dream of becoming a famous artist.

When George returned from the hospital after having his tonsils removed, she took care of him, spent all day by his bed, helped him to eat and entertained him, performing comical skits and reading her stories.

A week later, in the middle of teatime, after having known him for only six weeks, she didn't laugh when he got down on one of his knees and said, "Dear Katherine, marry me. Together we will enchant the world."

"I don't know, George. We haven't known each other very long."

"Here let me show you how pleasant our arrangement could be." He took her hand and led her down the hall. "This will be your writing room. Charles has taken quite a liking to you and will take care of your every need so you can write without interruption and, when you're ready,

I'll introduce you to some publishers. Lamont, whose room is the furthest down the hall is in complete agreement with Charles and me that you should join us here. Please, Katherine, let us take care of you."

There was a single bed in the room and she thought to ask George if this would also be her bedroom, as she wasn't sure she would want to share his—at least not until they knew each other better.

As if he understood her thoughts, he said, "We've only known each other a month and I don't want to rush you. This can be your room for as long as you like. For now, think of yourself joining two bachelors as a flatmate. Our marriage will give our arrangement legitimacy and keep tongues from wagging."

What fun! she thought. It'll be like the three of us camping out. I'd like to see Garnet's face when he finds out! Yes, marrying George is the perfect solution and it'll keep me from running back to Garnet again and getting into more trouble than I already am. And George is right. It is impossible to work in a lodge filled with young female musicians practicing instruments all day and then there's the constant interruption of finding ways to make extra money. Now I can really be a writer and didn't he say he knows publishers?

She looked up at George's admiring gaze as he waited for her answer, and said, "All right George, I will marry you."

"Thank you Katherine. You have made me a very happy man." He gently kissed her mouth, but ever so gently, she thought.

Not wanting to make the mistake she'd made with Garnet's father, she immediately wrote to her guardian Uncle Henry, asking that he might meet her fiancé. She also mailed a letter to her parents announcing her nuptials, she just didn't give the date, seeing no reason for them to come.

Uncle Henry's daughter, Elizabeth, the famous author, had left her husband Count von Armin and with her five children had moved back to London. She was visiting her father when Katherine arrived with George for teatime. Katherine wished she had come alone so that they may have talked as Elizabeth took no interest in her or George 's nuptial plans. She politely excused herself and went out.

Elizabeth by now had published several books exposing the lack of feminine power in a male-dominated world. Katherine wished she too someday would have her cousin's financial independence acquired from her writing income but for now she must rely on George's promise to see her through. Hadn't he said that their marriage would further her emancipation, rather than in any way cripple it? Elizabeth would have applauded that.

Katherine let her uncle know that she and George were planning to marry in three weeks, on March 6th, and there would no time to arrange a reception or have her family come all the way from New Zealand to attend. It would be a simple ceremony at the registry with Ida as witness. She knew her uncle was shocked by her news and would cable her parents immediately but she also knew that there was nothing they could do to stop her.

A few days later at the Beauchamp Lodge breakfast table, Katherine stood up and clicked her spoon against her orange juice glass. Ten girls raised their heads to see what their flatmate had to say. She often amused them with wild stories of her adventures in London. They never knew whether to believe her or not. "Tomorrow I'm getting married."

The Lodge matron said, "Miss Beauchamp, you mustn't make light of such things." Several girls laughed. "But I am serious, Mrs. Tate. This is my last breakfast at Beauchamp Lodge. Tomorrow I will become Mrs. George Bowden." The girls, remembering how they had laughed at George's gushing love letters, continued to shake their heads and giggle in disbelief as murmurings spread around the table.

"Quiet, girls! If you leave this time, Miss Beauchamp, you won't be invited back," said Mrs. Tate. "I've put up enough with your shenanigans. You're on your own now. I can't have you coming and going as you please. This is a respectable lodge for young women." She stomped out of the dining room.

After breakfast Margaret came to Katherine's room. "You were just having a go at us, weren't you? You really don't mean to marry that old dandy, do you? "

"Yes, I do. He's offered to help me in my writing career."

"But are you in love with him?"

"No. But he told me that doesn't matter."

Margaret frowned. "Really? Doesn't matter! Do you think he's marrying you just out of the goodness of his heart? Oh, Katherine how can you be so naïve? He'll expect you to behave like a wife after you promise to "love and obey him." If you don't love him than why are you doing this?"

"I just told you. He's going to help me. He's promised to find someone to publish my work and he is going to help me find a venue where I can perform my readings—" Margaret's continual frown stopped her from listing any further benefits and she took another approach. "Look at it this way," she said. "It'll make good copy, material for future short stories." She laughed. Margaret didn't. "Oh Margaret, don't look so worried. It's just a lark."

"Marriage is not a lark, Katherine."

"I know it isn't. But I'm bored of being poor and lonely. I don't want to have to make an income anymore playing bit parts and kicking my feet up in chorus lines. I've already been in London for six months and look at the mess I got myself in with Garnet. I need someone to take care of me." She smiled. "And George is most entertaining. You must come for dinner very soon, then you'll see. He has a wonderful flat. He even has a butler named Charles. And the nicest flatmate. Yes, that's it. You must come to dinner and see how much fun the bachelors and me have. Why it's absolutely charming!"

Margaret's shocked face stopped her again from listing more of George's virtues. "I've given him my word," she said, bursting out in tears. Margaret put her arms around her and held her.

Katherine married George Bowden the following day with Ida and a Registry clerk as their witnesses. It was March 2nd, 1909, six weeks after they'd met.

4

July 1919

Virginia's Visit

Is there another Life? Shall I awake and find all this a dream? There must be—we cannot be created for this sort of suffering.

Letters—John Keats

AFTER COPYING KEATS'S WORDS into her notebook, she put down her pen and looked up at her bedroom. Everything in its proper place just like the furniture and ornaments she'd carefully placed as a child in her dollhouse. But her current dollhouse was also her cage and possibly her casket.

Dr. Sorapure had just listened to her crackling lungs. Before leaving, he simply said, "I warned you last winter that you should leave London but you chose to stay. This year you haven't a choice. If you stay, you won't make it through the winter."

The experiment had failed. The effects of weekly streptococci injections, which were supposed to rid her of the bacteria corrupting her body, had kept her languishing in bed with long periods of high fever. Her fingers still cramped when she tried to write with a pen. A cane was needed to hobble across the room. Worst of all was the shivering chill in her bones. It was what frightened her when she looked out her window at the trees and streetlights already shrouded in fog. The foreshadowing of the approaching winter made her hide under her eiderdown trying to get warm.

Laudanum brought her relief at night until it wore off, and during the day the books of Chekhov, Dostoevsky, and Shakespeare. But it was Keats, a consumptive like her, that she turned to for solace.

She'd reassured Dr. Sorapure that plans had been made to go to San Remo on the Italian Riviera, which her good friend Anne had written to suggest for sunshine and warmth. It would be the second time she'd leave Jack for her health.

Through the clear panes of glass, she looked down from the second floor at Virginia Woolf who was standing at the iron gate frowning at Katherine's home. The home Katherine and Jack fondly called The Elephant because of its tall grey walls. Virginia was more apt to call it a white elephant, too bulky, too tall, and in her eyes, quite ugly. She imagined Virginia telling her friends that the little Colonialist's choice of the Elephant expressed her lack of good taste, and concluded with "After all, one must remember, in fact it's impossible to forget, that Katherine's not English by birth. Her saving virtue is that she attended Queen's College at the impressionable age of fourteen." She knew of Virginia's gossip because there was little anyone said in the Bloomsbury group that didn't pass from mouth to mouth, finally reaching her ears.

Virginia drew in her parasol, adjusted her hat, and straightened her shoulders before opening the squeaky iron gate. She frowned again. Katherine remembered from her last excursion outdoors with Jack that the gate squeaked. She'd forgotten to tell LM to have it repaired. A woman who demands perfection of herself as Virginia did, would certainly frown over a squeaky gate. Virginia looked up before Katherine could hide behind the curtain, and waved.

She returned to the sofa and listened to the front door closing after the bell rang. She often played a game imagining what was going on downstairs when a visitor arrived. She imagined LM's oversized body, which had given her the nickname The Mountain by Katherine's friend Ottoline, filling the entry hall, dwarfing Virginia, who would look up and say, "Good afternoon, Ida."

"Good afternoon to you, ma'am," LM would reply, her timid voice belying her size. Then she'd curtsy like a delicate hippopotamus and, without taking Virginia's hat or parasol, awkwardly lead her upstairs before Virginia could politely enquire about Katherine's health.

Virginia's steps were light and tentative on the stairs, stopping at every step to look around, while LM plodded ahead. Virginia probably thinking that LM didn't behave at all like a proper British housekeeper and she'd be right. She wasn't one but hardly anyone knew they were old friends.

"You needn't rise," said Virginia walking into the room. She sank back down in the pillows piled on the sofa. Virginia's shock was evident. Though Virginia visited her often, the first expression was always the same. Katherine wondered what it was like for someone to watch her shrink in size and fade in color. She looked in the mirror too often to notice the progression, except sometimes she frightened herself when she didn't recognize her reflection in a window. She was certainly far removed from the young girl who used to practice her elocution in front of George Bowden's mirror.

Virginia, who seemed to want to look anywhere but at her, looked over at a bouquet of marigolds.

"How lovely," she said.

"Yes. Aren't they? I picked them from my garden this morning."

"Oh, then you do manage to get out."

LM pulled up a chair for Virginia, and asked, "Shall I bring tea?"

"Virginia?" Katherine asked hating the sound of her weak, raspy voice.

"Yes. Yes, that would be lovely. Thank you, Ida."

LM nodded and backed out of the room.

Katherine gathered her black Spanish shawl around her shoulders hoping its vivid flowers and birds embroidered in silk would cheer Virginia who was looking at her too pitifully. But at that moment the sun slipped out from behind a cloud and a ray of light fell cruelly on her pallid face exposing her to further pity.

"Forgive me for not dressing for your visit," she said, moving out of the sun's glare.

"I must say that you are looking quite marmoreal, my dearest."

Katherine smiled. "A white marble statue, yes, that's exactly how I mimic myself when I pose in the mirror." She raised her arms in a statuesque pose. Virginia laughed. "It surprises me that blood still flows through these veins." She dropped her arms. "But please don't turn me into a statue yet though I am one when I sit at my desk without writing anything of value.

"I had hoped to have something to read to you today but if I'm not helping Jack select submissions for the Paper I'm working against deadlines for my weekly novel reviews. The rest of the time I take to my bed, too tired for my own writing."

"How well I understand," said Virginia. "Just yesterday, in the middle of a sentence, I had to put down my pen, close the blinds, and retire before the spits of fire assaulting my brain sparked a headache."

Katherine hoped she'd say more about herself but she changed the topic. "I've heard talk that you are considering San Remo for the winter?"

"Ah, our dear friend Ottoline is never one to keep a secret, is she?"

"She didn't know whether Jack was going with you?"

"No. He won't trust anyone to carry on with the paper in his absence. You know well enough with your own printing press the urgency of deadlines. I don't know how it is for your Leonard but Jack's life *is* the paper. And nearly mine, too, what with giving him help and my weekly column. I don't know how you find the time to write reviews and novels. Look at that stack of books on my writing table waiting impatiently for me to plough through. By the time I've read two or three and written their reviews the week is over and I have to start reading again for the following week."

"Your reviews are very popular. Everyone is reading them, including me."

"That's what keeps me doing it. Unable to write my own stories at least I'm actively writing and someone is reading. I even had a letter from your colleague Lytton telling me of his pleasure in reading my reviews, and in the past, as you well know, he was not my admirer."

Though Lytton Strachey had encouraged Virginia to meet Katherine, having found her intriguing, she'd heard through the gossipmongers that he had also described her as having *an ugly impassive mask of a face—cut in wood, with brown hair and brown eyes very far apart—and a sharp and slightly vulgarly-fanciful intellect sitting behind it.* It was embarrassing that words said privately among this exclusive literary group somehow got passed around like delicious truffles. Many had been hurt by such vicious gossip but there was no stopping it. Katherine knew Virginia, a leader in the group, often made her own contributions to the fray and she must be careful of what she said in front of her.

"Have you read Lytton's *Eminent Victorians* yet?" asked Virginia. "It's caused quite a stir among those who wish to keep Florence Nightingale on a pedestal. He has brought her back to life in a way never before accomplished in a biography."

"I haven't read it but I hope I will be given a chance to review it. Unfortunately too often Jack gives the books I want to review to others on his staff, and leaves me with the "women stories," some of which should never have been published in the first place. He doesn't seem to realize women reviewers are just as capable of reviewing a male writer as well as the other way around."

"I would certainly have been disappointed if anyone other than you had reviewed my *Kew Gardens*. You understood exactly what I was trying to do."

"I only wrote the truth, Virginia. *Kew Gardens* is your best work so far. It was a pleasure to review. So modern. There is nothing out there to compare to it. Your writing came alive—" Katherine's cough interrupts her.

After she stopped coughing, Virginia said, "You know the seeds of that story came from our walks in the garden when you visited us at Asheham and you spoke of the need in our writing to break from the mold. Ah, but I'm not as courageous as you." She laughed. "I realized that on those late nights that I hand-set your *Prelude* onto our printing press. I studied your work letter by letter as the words under my tired hands came to life and told a marvelous story."

Katherine laughed. "Well your hands did a marvelous job too. I was very pleased with the results and quite proud that you and Leonard included me in one of your first publications on Hogarth Press with the likes of T.S. Eliot."

"We should have sold more of the three hundred copies we'd printed," said Virginia. "*Prelude* is a work of art and is worthy of far more attention than it received but Hogarth Press doesn't have the staff or for that matter the desire to promote what we print. But at least work like yours that otherwise might go unpublished has a chance to be at least read by a few discriminating readers. My work too would go unpublished if it weren't for my half-brother's Duckworth Press. But after this second novel, I will publish all my books on our press as I only need Leonard to edit and approve of my books before they go to print."

Silence filled the room, not uncomfortable, just thoughtful.

"You're not going alone to San Remo, are you?" asked Virginia.

"No, though I would if I was well. I love the excitement of traveling on my own. Once I traveled by train into the War Zone because I was passionately in love with Carco, a Frenchman. I also lived for a short time at his Paris apartment but returned to Jack, a far more sensitive lover. Later I used my adventures as copy in *The Indiscreet Journey*."

Virginia picked up Katherine's doll Rib, lying between them on the sofa and adjusted his silk kimono but not before Katherine saw her blush. Virginia looked up at her, "I have never traveled far alone. My parents would have never allowed it and now Leonard. Even today he tried to prevent me from coming to London on my own. He made me late and I wasn't able to bring the flowers I had promised you. I *am* sorry."

Katherine smiled, inwardly pleased at getting a glimpse into how Virginia's mind worked. Yes, Leonard would be her excuse for forgetting and how easily embarrassed she was about sexual references.

"Leonard sends you his regards and hopes you visit us again soon at Asheham. There is no one who entertains him as well as you do with your witty mimicries. I must say that he'll be most displeased to know that Jack is not escorting you to Italy."

"Oh no, dear Virginia, you misunderstood me. Jack is coming, at least for the first week or so. After I'm settled he'll return to London. Ida will stay on with me."

"Well that's a relief. But can't Jack stay longer?"

"I wouldn't want him to really. I need solitude to write and he's flourishing as editor of *The Athenaeum*—I wouldn't want him to stop because of me."

"Then how fortunate you are to have Ida."

"Yes, I am." She looked down at Virginia's satchel on the floor by her chair. "Have you brought something to read today?"

"Yes, it's the last chapter," said Virginia with a large smile. "I wanted to talk with you about it, before I let Leonard read it. Sometimes he doesn't understand what I'm doing. You see this is my second novel and—"

LM entered with the tea service, interrupting their conversation. She poured tea in their cups, passed the cream, sugar, and biscuits, and left.

"I envy your endurance to work on a novel," said Katherine. "My notebooks are filled with outlines and vignettes but I haven't been able to piece them together."

"I'm certain you'll find your way back to your work once you find the right place. You've told me how well you work when surrounded by nature, for me it's London. I miss my city walks where I get many of my ideas, but Leonard insists on us living in Sussex."

"I hope you're right. I don't know about you but I become quite anxious when I don't write and after the initial excitement of completing a story there is a terrible letdown. Do you experience something similar?"

She was baiting Virginia to speak about her well-known mental breakdown after completing her first novel. She wanted to know more about it, but Virginia's silence told her not to prod and she changed the subject to writing, a subject where they were both at ease.

"My characters don't breathe as deeply as yours do," said Katherine. "Their feelings are briefly stated and sometimes misunderstood by the reader."

"I don't agree with you. You have a special talent for economy of words that cut straight to the truth—as clear as glass—refined . . . even spiritual. My characters immerse themselves into their dense landscapes, their houses, their benches, before they speak."

"Not so with *Kew Gardens.* You discovered a new way of writing in that story that is what I try to achieve in my own work. That brief moment when the secret life is half revealed; then a wind blows again and covers it over with leaves and flowers. It's so terribly authentic. So real."

Virginia leaned forward in her chair putting down her teacup. "How did you know that I would read a similar passage to you today, carrying that theme further. Shall I read some of what I wrote?"

"Yes please do. I am going to lay back and rest my eyes but I am listening."

"Are you sure you're not too tired?"

Virginia looked so disappointed, Katherine had to laugh. "No, I'm fine. I will give it my full attention with my eyes closed. Your reading voice is melodic but I assure you that your words always capture my attention. I will not sleep."

Virginia reached in her satchel for the manuscript. "Oh, I almost forgot. I brought you a few packets of the Belgian cigarettes that we smoked last time I was here that you liked so much."

She opened the packet and lit Katherine's cigarette before lighting her own. She picked up her manuscript and read the last chapter finishing with:

Moments, fragments, a second of vision, and then the flying waters, the winds dissipating and dissolving; then, too, the recollection from chaos, the return of security, the earth firm, superb and brilliant in the sun.

Katherine had been listening, carefully weighing the words and their meanings. She hesitated, not wanting to offend her friend and then said, "If you're speaking of the end of the war as the return of security I don't think it's all that simple. We cannot forget what happened. Too many sacrificed their lives to preserve it. Our world, as we once knew it, will never be the same. I personally will never forget the loss of my brother Leslie. But perhaps you meant something different. My review will have to wait until I've read it from beginning to end. Certainly the words spoken flow beautifully, as always, you are a master of your craft, Virginia. Just be careful of being old-fashioned."

"Well, I certainly don't think of myself as old-fashioned but I'll take your warning into consideration. And you will certainly be one of the first to have a copy of *Night and Day*. I'm hoping you will review it in *The Athenaeum*."

LM came in to take the tea tray and seeing the full ashtray, held it at arm's length, and shaking her head dumped it in the waste basket before picking up Dr. Sorapure's cough syrup.

"It's time for your medicine," she said, holding a spoon in front of Katherine's face. She opened her mouth and swallowed the syrup that wet her dry throat. "Mrs. Woolf, please don't tire Katherine out too much." She placed the bottle back on the bureau and backed out of the room.

"Why does she leave the room backward?" asked Virginia.

They both laughed. "I don't actually know," said Katherine. "She's a most intriguing character. I find many of her gestures mysterious and often use them in my stories though she doesn't recognize herself unless I point it out. Shall we say, she is yet to know her own true identity." She smiled. "Perhaps because she spends too much time hovering over mine."

"How interesting that you mention identity. That's my concern with the main character, in my new novel," said Virginia. "I feel Katharine's true character is blocked by a shadow and I can't get a clear view of her."

"Katherine?"

"Not you, of course. There's no connection. I just like the name and I spelled it with an 'a'. If anyone, she's more similar to Vanessa than you."

"That's too bad! I would be most interested in your writing about my identity! As to your Katharine with an 'a,' I suggest you merge her true character with her shadow rather than be blocked by it."

"Why yes, of course. Why didn't I think of that? Though six years behind me in age, you understand the art of writing so well. It distresses me that there will be no one I can talk to with such ease when you're in Italy. I realized how important our talks are on that day I came to visit you last December. I arrived at the appointed hour, anxious to talk to you, and was told by Ida you were not to be disturbed. I was furious having come all the way from Sussex just to see you."

"Haven't I apologized enough for that? You know, like yourself, I have no control over when I am well enough for visitors. I thought you of all people would understand that."

"I do understand. And I forgave you when you told me later that you had been terribly depressed. You never told me what had happened to make you so miserable."

"Well I'll tell you now. I'd found a new doctor, the most wonderful Doctor Sorapure. Shall he say he lifted the veil on the source of my rheumatism. His diagnosis was enlightening but horribly revealing."

"And what was the source?" said Virginia, leaning forward.

She started to tell her and then just smiled before saying, "On second thought, I don't think I will tell you."

Virginia sunk back into her chair.

"I'm sorry, Virginia, but you can't expect me to trust you after the things you've said about me."

"What do you mean, Katherine?"

"Let's not discuss it now. I'd rather tell you the other news I've kept secret. Murry and I have lately discussed having a baby. And if so, perhaps we'll lease a cottage in Sussex, perhaps near Asheham. Then you and I can walk together in the park with our future children and later our grandchildren."

Virginia got up and walked over to the window suggesting that they should air the room of their cigarette smoke. Or does she mean my delusions, thought Katherine.

She changed the subject again. "Dr Sorapure has convinced me that I mustn't enter a sanatorium. Do you know the first rule of a rest cure is to remove your work? Do they think a writer will "rest" when there is no pen and ink in sight! No. We will write everything down in our heads and go mad. What imbeciles these doctors are!"

Virginia returned to her chair without saying anything other than to nod her head in agreement but that was all.

If only Virginia would be more forthcoming than so would I, she thought, waiting for Virginia to respond. I want her to tell me about her own experiences with doctors and sanatoriums but she just sits very poised, her eyes turned inward. Though I've never met anyone else with the same passion and dedication to writing, I'm disappointed that that's the only real love we share. She's proven to me that she sincerely cares for me with her endearing letters and lengthy visits but she never visibly shows her affection. Why is she so reticent when we embrace?

Katherine interrupted her own thoughts and said, "Can't you see us taking walks in the park with our children skipping by our sides? What do you want first, a boy or a girl?"

Virginia turned her head away without answering.

"Virginia, don't do that! Look at me? I need you to believe in my cure. I need you to believe that I will have all that I want, that I will again jump in the air, dance and run through the woods—" Katherine's cough prevented her from saying more.

Virginia handed her a glass of water. "I'm sorry. I only turn away because I'm unaccustomed to anyone speaking so openly about private subjects. But believe me when I tell you that we will rival each other for years to come. You must be cured or who will be my competition?"

Katherine reached for Virginia's hand and they held each other's gaze until Virginia looked down at her watch. "Oh dear look how late it is. I must go. Leonard is meeting me at Waterloo Station so we can take the train home together."

"You are a very fortunate woman to have Leonard." Katherine went to rise.

"You needn't see me out. Next week as usual?"

"Yes, please come. It does me good to talk to you. We have the same job, Virginia, you and I, and it's really very curious and thrilling that we should both, quite apart from each other, be after so very nearly the same thing? We are, you know; there's no denying it."

Katherine gripped the heavy, plush curtain for support, crushing it as she struggled to stand up and watch Virginia's departure from her window. Her eyes became Virginia's as she walked onto the street. She felt Virginia stand up very straight and reach out her arm to hail a taxi.

She followed her into the taxi, and watched her remove her hat, pin loose strands of hair back, and reach into her purse for a handkerchief to wipe away the burning, swelling tears. She felt Virginia's need to reach the train station and find Leonard and have him encircle her in his arms, protect her and take her home.

Katherine read again Keats's words that she'd blotted into her notebook just before Virginia's visit. She needed to find Jack. She couldn't wait until dinner; she must see him now. She felt the golden hour slipping away, but before she could call out to him the black hour gripped her and pulled her down into the abyss carrying her back into remembrances of things past.

5

London—1912

John "Jack" Middleton Murry

There was a child once.
He came to play in my garden;
He was quite pale and silent.
Only when he smiled I knew everything about him,
I knew what he had in his pockets,
And I knew the feel of his hands in my hands
And the most intimate tones of his voice.
I led him down each secret path,
Showing him the hiding-place of all my treasures.
I let him play with them, every one,
I put my singing thoughts in a little silver cage
And gave them to him to keep...

There was a Child Once—KM

SHE DECIDED UPON the shimmering dove-grey evening gown, a sensual fit around her petite body; draped a gauze scarf of the same color loosely around her long neck; pinned a single Christmas rose to her bodice, and wrapped a red silk turban over her short-cut hair. On her wide forehead she flattened down her chestnut bangs with a bit of spit. Pleased with the results, she smiled at her reflection. Quite suitable for a twenty-three year old author who had just published, *In a German Pension*, her first collection of short stories that were now the talk of London Town. She repeated what the top reviewers had said as if it was a Bowden lesson in elocution: *acute insight—unquenchable humor—realistic skill.* Yes, that's me, she thought, painting her lips bright red.

She admired her gown in the mirror once more before disdainfully covering it with her embarrassingly unstylish coat, but it was a chilly night, and it wouldn't do to catch another cold.

Arriving at the party flushed from being chased by a sudden gust of wind, she rushed into the dimly lit salon as if still being chased, profiting from everyone's immediate attention to her dramatic entrance. Walter Lionel George, her host, and writer for *Harper's Magazine*, pulled her over and pointed across the room at a young gentleman, nonchalantly leaning against the mantel as if alone in his own parlor, flicking ashes from his cigar into the fire. W.L. whispered in her ear, "That's John Middleton Murry. I'm sure you know he's going to publish your short story in his new journal *Rhythm* but did you know he's here tonight expressly to meet you. Being he's a stranger in town, perhaps you could help him feel more at home."

"He looks quite at home to me," said Katherine as they crossed the room.

"Hello," she said, "I'm Katherine Mansfield."

"Hello," he said, pulling himself up though not much taller than her.

How handsome! she thought, gazing into eyes, like two pale green pools separated by a distinguished alpine nose and shaded by thick black lashes and heavy brows. Unconsciously, he ran his hand through a mass of thick, wavy black hair, pushing back a few renegade strands that had fallen on his forehead.

"I'm John—"

"I know who you are. W.L. wanted us to meet. That's why I came over."

As they shook hands, one side of his mouth lifted up in response to her smile. A lovely but frightening mouth, she thought, raising her other hand as if to touch it, but dropping it quickly, telling herself to behave—he might be afraid of bold women.

As she turned away to meet the other guests, her gown brushed against her stockinged legs and, feeling his eyes roaming down her body, she shivered slightly, pleased she'd worn the high heels that showed off her small ankles and narrow feet.

She joined a group discussing Constance Garnett's translation of Chekhov's *The Cherry Orchard* currently playing at the Aldwych. Katherine, a passionate reader of Russian literature, enjoyed adding her opinion, though she hadn't seen the play, and soon forgot Mr. Murry's tempting green pools. But he didn't seem to forget her. She felt his eyes on her as he listened attentively to the discussion. He didn't join in. Hadn't he read Chekhov? she wondered. How could anyone not have read Chekhov?

At the end of the evening he approached her as she was waiting for her coat in the entry hall. "Miss Mansfield, before you leave, I want you to know how impressed I was by *The Woman at the Store.* I don't know of any other short story that honestly exposes the revulsion of life as you have, and I do hope you'll submit more stories like it to *Rhythm.* I strongly believe your original style matches my editorial mission to seek out the strong things of life—both in its purity and its brutality as you so realistically portrayed in *The Woman at the Store.*"

She smiled. "Thank you. Mr. Murry. It's always encouraging when someone recognizes what I'm trying to accomplish. My favorite readers are the ones who see my characters as, shall we say, 'real.' You must come to tea someday so that we can continue this most interesting conversation."

"I would like that very much. But how do I contact you?"

The maid approached with Katherine's coat, and without answering him, she draped it over her shoulders and rushed out the door.

A week later, she asked W.L. for Mr. Murry's address. But before she could send him an invitation to tea, she caught a cold that worsened into a serious lung inflammation, which made it painful to breathe.

Her pulmonary doctor diagnosed her second case of pleurisy and insisted she leave London immediately for a more favorable climate. She disobeyed him preferring to visit a girlfriend in Brussels rather than stay in a foreign hotel where she would be unbearably alone.

In early February she returned to London with a slight cough and was happily greeted back into the literary salons she had become so fond of. At one gathering, Jack Murry's name came up in an animated conversation centering on the radical content of his journal *Rhythm*. The modern artists the young renegade editor published had created quite a stir in literary circles. Katherine remembered his favorable opinion on her writing and sent him a note asking him to tea at 69 Clovelly Mansions, her London flat.

SHE SILENTLY FORGAVE HIM for being late, noticing that, like herself, he didn't wear a watch though that was no excuse as she was always on time without one. She led him into her sitting room and laughed when he said, "Where shall I sit, Miss Mansfield?"

"Why not the rocking chair?" she suggested, pointing to the only chair in the room besides the hard wooden one by her writing table. "And you needn't be so formal, call me Katherine."

"All right then, Katherine. And please call me Jack."

She stepped into the kitchen and returned with a tray laden with a teapot, bowls, brown bread, butter and honey. Recently influenced by Orientalism, the rage in Paris after the premiere of Dahgliev's Ballet Russe, she preferred bowls to teacups, particularly when she wore her red and yellow kimono that matched their polished glaze. She sat cross-legged on a blue and purple pillow, one of many brightly colored pillows on the straw-matted floor, put a cigarette between her lips and leaned toward her guest for a match. He lit hers then lit his own. They sat in silence enjoying their smoke.

She noticed that his pale green eyes, even more startling in the daylight, took notice of the embroidered white flowers on her silk kimono but he avoided looking directly at her, which was a waste seeing the amount of time she'd spent dressing for his visit. The tea brewed. London traffic hummed in the distance.

"I'm told you're a graduate of Oxford."

"Well, I'm not," he said, clearing his throat. "You see, I haven't taken my final exams."

"Oh. Why not?"

"It's rather complicated."

"I might not find it complicated and I like to listen to people tell their stories."

"All right, if you really want me to. Last year, I took a leave from Oxford to visit Paris. Since my return, I've been unable to study the works of Aristotle and Plato with any enthusiasm. They've lost their importance—at least from my point of view. And now with *Rhythm* requiring my constant attention I have neither the time nor the inclination to work toward my degree. I know this might sound quite foolish but I've quite the mind to pack it in."

"To the contrary I think it sounds quite necessary."

"You do?" he said, surprised.

"You simply have more important things to do then spend your days in a stuffy library. How could Oxford compare with a vibrant life in Paris or even here in London? And how much more exciting to create your own literary journal than to read Plato."

"I wish my father understood as well as you seem to," said Jack, leaning back in the rocking chair. "He made, shall we say, sacrifices, and now demands a return on his investment. I'm supposed to follow him into the civil service. He vehemently objects to my career as an editor and thinks *Rhythm* is a waste of my time. He laughs at me when I tell him I want to establish my career as a literary critic and develop my skills in poetry, essays, even novels."

"Your father sounds like a tyrant," said Katherine, handing him the ashtray.

He stomped out his cigarette just before the ashes fell on his seat or worse her pillow. She poured the tea and passed him a bowl.

Jack continued, "I tried to leave Oxford several times when I realized my studies were not preparing me for what I really wanted to do. I'm a déclassé student."

He looked so like her little brother Leslie when he was unhappy that she felt the urge to take him in her arms and comfort him as she would've her brother. "Déclassé? What do you mean by that?"

"I'm on scholarship. The other students have always looked down on me. They never included me. Even in sports, I've been left out."

"How awful. What are you going to do?"

"I don't know. I can't afford to live in London and I don't want to stay at Oxford. You certainly didn't have to go to Oxford to become a published writer, did you?"

Katherine laughed. "Need I remind you that women can't go to Oxford?"

"Regardless, you've proven that one can be published in *The New Age* without a so-called traditional education; you just have to write well, like you do. I want my paper to be as popular as *The New Age*. A.R. Orage has all the best modern writers. May I ask why you brought your new story to me instead?"

"He didn't like it. He prefers my more satirical and less sympathetic stories."

"Well it's his loss and my gain." She felt a far less sisterly desire to touch his lips when he half smiled as when they first met.

He stopped rocking and leaned toward her for another serving of tea. She handed him another slice of brown bread after spreading it with honey and then got up to wash her sticky fingers.

When she returned he was leaning against the mantelpiece cupping the smiling brass Buddha in his hand. The light from the two small windows fell on his finely chiseled face. She imagined him cupping her face rather than the Buddha's and felt a slight thrill rise up her spine. He turned to face her as if he knew what she was thinking and they held their eyes on each other for a brief moment, long enough for her to feel his interest in her was more than literary.

They both sat down again but this time he joined her on the pillows. "I see you found my Buddha," she said. "New Zealand is far away and I could only bring a few things with me when I left home. When I become a popular writer, I'll be able to fill my home with anything that aesthetically pleases me, as I once did with my dollhouse back at home."

"I bloody hell wish I had your confidence. I never really imagine myself as being successful. I waffle back and forth without moving forward. I'm too anxious to be decisive."

He fell back on the pillows, put the Buddha on his stomach, crossed his legs and closed his eyes, giving Katherine the pleasure of studying his face closely. His expression reminded her again of Leslie's expression when their father told him he couldn't have a piece of cake until he finished eating his vegetables.

"Life is like this, isn't it?" she said. "Anxious moments before plans are made. Actions taken without knowing what effect they will have upon us later. But I strongly believe it's well worth the risk to make your own independent choices, even if there is failure. Shall I tell you what I think you should do?"

"Yes, please do," he said, sitting up.

"Risk! Risk it all! Care no more for the opinion of others, forget about those censorial voices like your father's. Act for yourself alone, even if for the moment it is the hardest thing you've' ever done. Don't remain another day at Oxford. Come to London. *Rhythm* has respect on Fleet Street. You'll get work, I'm certain of it."

"Do you really think so?"

"I do," she said. "But right now I have my own work to do." She pointed toward the writing table neatly stacked with her notebooks. She handed him the last bite of honeyed bread. "Shall we meet again next week?"

"Next week then . . ." he said, standing up and stumbling toward the door while putting on his shoes. She hesitated, her hand on the doorknob, wanting him to kiss her. He seemed to want to, too, but he didn't and, disappointed, she let him out.

JACK MURRY RANG UP a few days later. His Oxford friend, Frederick Goodyear, wanted to meet her. He had read and admired her *New Age* sketches. How would it be if the three of them had dinner? They could dine cheaply at the Dieppe for one shilling, fifteen pence each.

She said, yes, but asked to go out and have tea with Jack before so they could continue their earlier conversation. Thoughts had been brewing in her mind about his future plans as well as her own.

When she opened the door to his knock, he didn't tell her how smashing she looked in the dark blue serge suit she'd chosen for their first evening out in London. Instead, the first thing out of his mouth was, "I'm employed!" He took a check out of his pocketbook and proudly unfolded it. "Look here. An advance of five pounds! I can buy you dinner."

"That's wonderful," she said, clasping his hands with the check between hers. "Come inside while I put on my hat and coat."

She led him into the entryway and while she stood in front of the mirror pinning a tiny bouquet of gay flowers on her straw hat he continued speaking excitedly about his new job as a reviewer for the *Westminster Gazette*, a small weekly paper publishing intellectual and literary reviews, sketches and short stories.

"Wait! Don't tell me now," she said putting on her coat. "Tell me over tea."

At the front door she paused, "I haven't shown you my flat, have I?" He followed her down the hall into the kitchen, which had a gas-stove, a table, two chairs, and a wide window that she opened. "This is my favorite view."

They looked out onto the chimney-potted roofs, with a tall grey church spire in the distance reflecting the late afternoon sun.

"It's very beautiful," he said. His green eyes looked at her long enough that she blushed and turned away.

"Here's the music room." Like the sitting room, its wallpapered walls were brown, the only furniture a grand piano and a divan. Earlier in the day, knowing he was coming, she had placed fresh lavender on the fireplace grate, its sweet fragrance filled the room.

She bent down and picked up a giant shell, which lay on a mat, keeping company with a green-bronze lizard bathing in a flat oval bowl, its long, tapered tail shimmering underwater. "I brought this Pawa shell from home." She turned the shell on its side to show the iridescent colors changing in the light.

"Here is the bathroom," she said standing in a short narrow hall where they could barely fit without touching. Across from it was a tiny bedroom—almost a cubicle—just large enough for a camp bed and chair. "And that's my bedroom."

She led him back out to the entryway. "Do you like my flat?"

"Very much," he said. "But isn't it terribly expensive to have extra rooms?"

"Yes, fifty-two pounds a year. But I believe it's better to spend money on the rooms and go short on other things? Better be hungry than miserable. No?"

"Well I don't know if I'd agree with you. I think I'd rather have food and live in one—"

"We must go. You don't want to keep your friend waiting and we haven't had our teatime."

AT THE ISOLA BELLA TEAROOM Katherine and Jack sat with their backs to the street window, alone except for the female server.

"Now," she said, after they ordered. "Tell me what happened. How did you come about acquiring this job so quickly?"

She listened as he described in detail all the small events leading up to what was really important—the check in his pocket. "When my Oxford mentor realized how determined I was to forego my exams, at least for now, he gave me an introduction to *Westminster Gazette*'s editor J.A. Spender who then offered me freelance work as a reviewer of English and German writings. Of course it's only temporary until *Rhythm* has enough subscribers so I can afford to work on it exclusively."

"Let me look at that check again." She turned it every which way before saying, "I don't think I've ever liked the looks of a fiver so much."

"I think in some way you are responsible."

"Me?"

"Yes. It was you who inspired me to make a move. If it hadn't been for your telling me to take risks and not worry a damn what people think—why I'd still be stuck at the crossroads not knowing which way to turn."

"I'd like to think I helped you," she said, briefly brushing her gloved hand over his.

"Listen Katherine," he said. "I know this is rather forward, but now that I'll be working in London, I wanted to know if you would help me with *Rhythm*?"

"Well, I don't know—how do you mean?"

"Not all the time. It's only a quarterly paper. You have your own work to do. But maybe you could read some of the submissions and help me decide which fit *Rhythm*'s mission to publish only the best modern work. I can't pay you very much but I thought you might start by reviewing that exquisite book of poetry I told you about, Neuburg's *The Triumph of Pan*. It's quite controversial and I'd like to have a review for our summer issue. By you." He smiled. "That's if Orage won't mind me kidnapping his best author. He has a reputation for being rather proprietary."

Katherine removed her gloves, reached into her bag for cigarettes and handed him one. They sat back in their chairs blowing rings of smoke across the room. "Please don't tell anyone this," she said, "but Orage and I are arguing over the new direction of my work. I want my readers to ponder over characters they can identify with, who are real to them. But he says 'Stay with the satire, that's where you write best and that's what suits *New Age*.'"

"I think he's wrong," said Jack. "What made *The Woman at the Store* exceptional was how you empathized deeply with your female character and in so doing you created an authentic, unforgettable person and you did it with such economy of words. You have a very special talent, Katherine. Don't let anyone tell you otherwise." He half smiled. "Even the extraordinary Orage."

Katherine was touched by his energetic passion for the art of writing and particularly her writing. He understood her. Few did. She knew right then she'd willingly share his mission, which she'd memorized after their first meeting—*to seek out the strong things of life—both in its purity and its brutality it shall be real.* It was a noble, modern vision. One that she could wholeheartedly contribute to. If Orage didn't want to publish her next stories, then Jack would.

"Yes, Jack, I would like to help you edit *Rhythm*." She looked deeply into his eyes and felt the sudden desire to embrace him, kiss his dangerous but beautiful mouth.

Embarrassed, she looked down. "Oh there goes the time again. We're going to be late if we don't hurry."

FREDERICK GOODYEAR was a handsome man with thick curly hair like Jack, but brown, much taller and, three years Jack's senior, more sophisticated, light-hearted and confident. His first words to Jack upon meeting Katherine were, "Where did you meet this ravishing woman?"

After a most animated dinner, shouting to be heard across the table in the crowded Dieppe, they stood outside. It was a lovely spring evening and nobody wanted to go home.

Katherine suggested walking to Piccadilly Circus. Freddie thought it an excellent idea, and, taking Katherine's arm in his, off they went with Jack following behind.

After racing around the fountain, they collapsed on a bench to have a smoke and enjoy the mild air, each in their own thoughts. Jack broke the silence. "It's going to be difficult finding a room in London for ten shillings a week but that's all I can afford right now."

Katherine leaped up and stood in front of them. "I have a marvelous idea."

"Yes, go on," said Jack and Freddie together looking up.

"I'll let you the music room in my flat. I'll have to move the piano to make room for a bed but I hardly ever use it after I stopped taking vocal lessons. We'll share the kitchen and the bathroom. And I won't charge you ten shillings, because I shall have two rooms and you've only one. Would seven and six be too much? I think it'll suit you better than anything you'll find for ten shillings."

Jack stared at her in disbelief. Freddie spoke up at once and said, "Don't just sit there like a fool, Jack. Say yes or at least nod your head so Katherine knows you accept her generous offer." Jack continued to stare. "Well I'll leave you two to sort this out," said Freddie. "May I say, Katherine, it has been a most wonderful evening and I hope to see you again quite soon." He kissed her on the cheek, shook Jack's hand, and called out good night as he walked away.

Katherine sat back on the bench and lit another cigarette. Jack took out his pipe and lit it before saying, "Are you really serious—about the room?"

"Of course I am."

The pipe ashes lit up as he took a long drag. "Then I should like it very much."

"Go—ood!" she said, imitating a flute. "When?"

"Well I don't know. What do you think?"

"I think next Monday—at teatime. Do you like eggs?"

Before he could answer, she gave him her hand and said, "Auf wiedersehen," and ran off across the Circus holding onto her straw hat.

On the designated day—April 11th—Jack arrived at her doorstep with two battered suitcases. Katherine was dressed to go out and quickly led him to his room. She didn't tell him the piano had been sold to cover her mounting debts. By the one window, she'd placed a table covered with a bright blue tablecloth. There was an empty cupboard for his books and clothes.

She handed him a ring with two keys and said, "I have an appointment. You'll have to make your own tea. I stocked the cupboard with provisions so you'll find everything there you need. I like to cook but don't have the time. Good-bye for now!"

The following morning Katherine set the table with brown bread and butter and honey and a large brown egg in an eggcup. She put a kettle of water on the stove and scribbled a note on a half-sheet of notepaper: "This is your egg. You must boil it. KM." She set the note between the egg and the eggcup. Counting out the coins she'd borrowed from LM, she dropped a few shillings in an empty sugar bowl and covered it with a second note that read: "Use when needed." She looked at her good deed and smiled.

On her way out to her appointment with Orage, she called out, "The flat is yours for the day. You'll find breakfast in the kitchen."

A week went on like this. They went out separately during the day or worked in their separate rooms. Jack paying his keep by writing reviews for *Westminster Gazette* and Katherine writing short stories and poems to be published in Rhythm's next quarterly issue in June. Then, at midnight, with Katherine in her kimono, Jack in his lounging robe, they would sip bowls of tea on her pillows and talk for hours about their plans for *Rhythm*, deciding on the contents of Rhythm's summer issue. To their great amusement before retiring they'd shake hands and say:

"Good night, Mansfield!"

"Good night, Murry!"

THE PLEURISY SHE'D HAD earlier in the year returned. But this time she stayed home. Jack would come and sit by her bedside but slip away with some silly excuse when she had a coughing spasm. He had a terrible fear of consumption that was known to start with a respiratory infection so anyone, even with a chest cold, made him cringe and back away.

Katherine asked LM to come in the afternoons to take care of her, as she had done many times before. She made hot broths, cooled her brow with wet cloths, puffed up her pillows and, sometimes kept vigil through the nights when Katherine was feverish and couldn't sleep.

In spite of the hard work Jack put into writing reviews for the *Westminster Gazette*, they were seldom accepted. He barely made a pound in the first two weeks and Katherine was being prudent with her hundred-pound annual allowance. To make ends meet, they lived on homemade soup or shared a greasy meat-pie from the corner shop. They'd drown the taste at the local pub, where the owner took a liking to this young couple. After they paid for one drink, she always insisted to stand them another.

On one of those evenings Jack said, "I never told you this but my job at *Westminster Gazette* was offered on one condition. I promised to take my finals at Oxford. I've been putting it off these last weeks as we've been so busy with *Rhythm*'s next issue but now that it's ready to print I think I should take those exams. If only to get my father to stop talking about it."

"Why didn't you tell me before?"

"I didn't think it was important."

"Well it is important that we are honest, not only in print, but between ourselves." They smoked their cigarettes in silence until Katherine put hers out and said, "I'll go with you."

"Really? You'd go with me to Oxford and stay until I've finished?"

"Why not?" She smiled. "It's not that far away and I've never been to Oxford. But won't they throw us out if we share a room?" she said, teasing.

"We can't stay together, Katherine. You must know that. I'll stay on campus and we'll get you a room in the village."

Not allowed in the Oxford library because of her gender, she and Jack studied in her boarding house parlor. He didn't graduate at the top of his class but he made Seconds and that qualified him to graduate.

On their way back to London, they stopped at his parents' house to give them the good news but his parents were quite out of sorts that he brought a female companion and were cold toward Katherine. Jack took her away promptly, forgetting to give them what he thought would please them most, his hard-earned diploma. He posted it from London and hoped his father wouldn't be too upset with the lower marks.

Upon their return they went to their pub and spent the evening celebrating his graduation. Returning home, they lay down on the purple floor pillows. Katherine got up from hers, turned down the gaslight and lit several candles. Jack relaxed on his back, his legs crossed, reminiscing about the afternoon he had first come to tea. Tonight he was far more comfortable. He propped his head up against a pillow and puffed on his pipe.

Katherine felt a strong urge to ask him why after all the nights they'd spent together he'd never shown any desire to make love to her like other men had. She felt unloved by Jack and it bothered her, immensely.

She blurted out, "Why not make me your mistress?"

"Katherine that isn't funny," he said sitting up. A few hot ashes from his pipe dropped on the floor matting and smoldered before going out. "My high respect for you would never allow me to do such a thing. Why risk destroying our friendship? Aren't you happy with the way things are?"

"No, I'm not." Katherine said, standing up. "Why must you be so damn proper? Is it because I'm still married to George? Is that what stops you? Or are you afraid I'll become another Marguerite?" Marguerite was a prostitute Jack had met in Paris. They became lovers and, misunderstanding his intentions, she asked him to marry her. Afraid to tell her that he didn't love her, he packed his bags when she wasn't home, slipped out, and returned to London. He felt terribly guilty about abandoning her but made no attempt to contact her after that.

He stood up and cupped Katherine's face with his hands. "You mean much more to me than Marguerite ever did."

She kissed him on the mouth. He pushed her away.

She went to her bedroom, slamming the door behind her.

The next morning she wouldn't talk to him. For several nights, she stayed at LM's house. She came home for a change of clothes and Jack was waiting for her.

He reached for her before she had taken off her hat and pressed her against the wall, kissing her mouth. They laughed as they fell down onto the pillows, rolling over each other across the floor. Every time they stopped rolling they kissed and then they would roll again, giddy with laughter. Their childish kisses turned to passion. Their childish laughter turned to cries of pleasure.

Later she wrote in her notebook:

And there we kissed and passionately
We clung together—all the past
Blotted from out my memory
I knew I had found love at last.

A FEW EVENINGS LATER they were at the kitchen table having their evening soup and bread when Katherine said, "Jack! Let's go to Paris."

"Paris?"

"Yes, let's go to Paris?"

"Paris? We're living on soup and bread? How can we afford Paris?"

"We can use my allowance. Now that *Rhythm* is launched surely there will be more money coming in. Oh Jack I'm so tired of being frugal."

"All right, if you think we can afford it, let's go." He half smiled. "We'll pretend it's our honeymoon."

6

September 1919

San Remo, Italy

Love! Love! You pity me so!
Chide me, scold me—cry,
"Submit—submit! You must not fight!"
What may I do, then? Die?
But, oh my horror of quiet beds!
How can I longer stay!
"One to be ready,
Two to be steady,
Three to be off and away!"

Covering Wings—KM

KATHERINE STUDIED THE CONTENTS of the well-worn traveling trunk to be sure LM hadn't forgotten anything on the packing list for the long "rest cure" in San Remo. She smiled as she imagined LM's anxious conversation with herself as she fastidiously handled Katherine's possessions as if they were her own and tried not to break anything.

I must be kinder to Jones, she thought. My dutiful, loyal companion who has never stopped believing in my full recovery. And Jack? I don't know what he really believes other than that I should go away. It is much easier for him to dream of our future when he doesn't have to hear me coughing.

She saw her Japanese doll, Rib, peeking out from between the folds of her black Spanish shawl in the trunk and picked him up. "No, Rib, you're not coming." She propped him up on the writing table. "I want you to be here to greet Jack when he returns in a few weeks to this empty house. He'll be pleased to see I let you stay behind to keep him company while I'm away."

Hearing Jack's hurried footsteps on the stairs, she walked over to the window and turned away from the door pretending to look for something in her writing case. She didn't want to show her impatience at his lateness, too soon she wouldn't hear his footsteps at all.

"Why, you've packed," he said, glancing at the trunk on his way over to her. "You're way ahead of me. I haven't started." He stood behind her and wrapped his arms around her waist, kissing the back of her neck.

"You're coming right back," she said, unable to keep the bitterness out of her voice. "You're only dropping me off. Remember?"

"Katherine, don't say it like that," he said, spinning her around to face him. "I'm hardly abandoning you. I would stay longer if I could but you know as well as I do that I can't leave the paper for longer than a few weeks. I'm as unhappy about this as you are. But there's nothing we can do about it."

"Then there is no justice in this world because it isn't fair that I have to go away from you or die and you have to stay to make money."

She felt the warmth of his arms enfolding her, pulling her close. She laid her head against his tweed jacket and listened to his heart that for a single moment beat only for her; a cherished moment that she'd recall when she was lonely and too far away for his arms to reach her. She looked up at him and smiled, "It's getting late. Let's take our last walk, shall we?"

"I don't know if you should," he said, kissing her forehead and letting her go. "There's a gusty wind stirring up the fallen leaves on the Heath."

"Dr. Sorapure insists that I take a walk every day regardless of the weather, even if only for a few minutes." Glancing in the mirror, she pulled her dark blue cloche down over her bangs and pinched her cheeks. "Did you know that women find it attractive to powder their faces to look as pale as I am? What kind of world is this, Jack, when to look like you're dying of consumption is fashionable?" She hobbled across the room to the wardrobe looking back at Jack's frown. "Don't worry, my dear, I'll wear my fur."

"Ah, yes your marvelous old coat," he said, helping her put it on. "Someday I must buy you a new one."

"But I like this one," she said, remembering back ten years when LM had surprised her with the coat, telling her that she wanted to protect her from England's raw winters. Had she a presentiment then, Katherine wondered, of how I'd come to dread the winter season even before the autumn leaves were stripped from their branches by the headwinds?

THE RAMBLING, WILD HAMPSTEAD HEATH welcomed their footsteps on its deserted paths and rolling hills. When she and Jack had moved to the Elephant she had expected to race up these hills. But today, only a year later, careful to cough into the discreet handkerchief hidden under her sleeve cuff, she had to stop several times along the way to catch her breath.

"Eight months! Jack," she called out in desperation. "I don't know if I can bear to be away from you that long."

"But you said yourself that you wanted the time to work without any distractions."

"I know, but eight months is a very long time without any distractions."

Jack picked a bench in front of an ancient, wide oak trunk that he thought would protect her from the wind. He did not notice that its broken hollow spine was a wind tunnel, the chilled air blowing on her neck. She hugged the fur and turned to tell Jack she was cold, but his eyes had turned inward, and even if she shouted, her complaint would go as unnoticed as the futile twittering of the swallow gripping the tree branch above.

Katherine recited to herself the lines from her poem *Covering Wings* published in *The Athenaeum* the week before:

Two bleached roads lie under the moon at the parting of the ways. But the tiny, tree-thatched, narrow lane, isn't it yours and mine?

Was it all false? She must know.

Jack's eyes refocused and he looked toward the descending sun and said, "I have a bit more work to finish before we leave tomorrow."

"I need to ask you something."

"Can't it wait until we're back home sitting by the fire in our parlor?" He locked his eyes on hers and half smiled in his usual charming way.

"No it can't. Do you really believe we will live in the Heron? We spend so much time furnishing it in our imaginations and talking about it."

"I have said it before and I will say it again now. I absolutely believe that after you are cured, we will find the Heron in Sussex and move there. Italy is the key to your recovery and to our future together. We must hold on to that belief. This isn't like you to doubt our future. You used to be the one who had a kind of overplus of belief that couldn't be shaken. Why not now?"

"I've lost my faith and I don't know how to recover it. So long the sport of circumstance, my dice are tired of being rattled and thrown."

"It won't always be this way. You must use this time to heal yourself, so that we can be together again come May. Don't work so hard—"

"What about the reviews for *The Athenaeum*?"

"I'm not talking about the reviews. You should of course continue writing them. They're a very popular supplement to the paper. That's not what's wearing you down. It's the story writing that must stop. There will be time for that later."

Katherine thumped her cane near Jack's foot. "You, of all people, should understand that the writing is what I must do above all else. That is why, thank God, I'm not in a sanatorium. It's the writing that keeps me alive and there won't be time for *later*." She coughed and reached for her handkerchief.

Jack waited until she could breathe again before rising from the bench and pulling her up.

"I love you terribly, Bogey" she said, clinging to him. "I'm too frightened to leave you."

"Katherine, please, I need you to be strong. Come the month of May you'll be cured. We'll come home together and never be separated again. But we'll only succeed if we remain firm with our plan."

She put her arm in his and together they walked home.

The following morning Katherine placed the notebook she had scribbled in through the night on top of a stack of other notebooks, the layered chronicle of her life, and snapped her smaller trunk shut. When first arriving at the Elephant, she had removed these same notebooks and placed them on her freshly painted yellow writing table in front of the window overlooking the Heath.

What expectations! In the first weeks, every morning, she sat at her table only to write brief sketches and return to bed exhausted. In the weeks that followed she was too weak to get up and instead arranged her writing materials around her bed. But in too much pain, she only stared at them.

And now, after sequestering herself in this house for a year, a cab would arrive shortly and take her, LM, and Jack to Victoria Station where they would embark on a noon train for San Remo.

She sat down and lifted her pen, dipping it in the ink holder, she wrote affectionately to Jack:

My darling boy,

I am leaving this letter with Mr. Kay just in case I should pop off suddenly and not have the opportunity or the chance of talking things over.

If I were you I'd sell off all the furniture and go off on a long sea voyage on a cargo boat, say. Don't stay in London. Cut right away to some lovely place.

Any money I have is yours, of course. I expect there will be enough to bury me. I don't want to be cremated and I don't want a tombstone or anything like that. If it's possible choose a quiet place, please do. You know how I hate noise.

All my manuscripts I simply leave to you.

That's all, but don't let anybody mourn me. It can't be helped.

As she stopped to refill her pen, the sunlight streaming through her window caught the sparkle of the blue-stone setting in the center of iridescent pearls that Jack had slipped on her finger on their "honeymoon" in Paris, promising to marry her once her divorce from George was finalized. It took seven years before he could keep that promise.

And when she married him on May 3rd 1918, instead of admiring a blushing bride, he saw a gaunt, pale stranger with circles around feverish eyes, unrecognizable as the girl he had first made love to at Clovelly Mansions.

She should have released him from his promise but didn't realize that until immediately following their vows, witnessed by David and Frieda Lawrence. She had a coughing spasm just as Jack leaned over to kiss her. He quickly pulled away but not before she saw the fear in those pale green eyes she so adored.

She finished her letter:

I think you ought to marry again and have children. If you do, give your little girl the pearl ring.

She folded the letter into an envelope and addressed it to Mr. Kay at the London branch of the Bank of New Zealand, enclosing instructions to give it to Jack upon her death.

She jumped at the loud knock on her door. LM ushered in a young taxi driver who lifted his cap to Katherine, smiled, and carried out her trunk on his back as if it weighed nothing. She handed LM the sealed envelope and asked her to post it.

Katherine gave the bedroom one last look and silently whispered good-bye. She'd grown quite attached to her bright, cheerful dollhouse before it became her cage. She gripped the banister and carefully walked down the stairs with the help of her cane.

At the bottom of the landing, she saw the taxi outside and excitement welled up in her as it had in the past whenever she left on a trip. A new adventure meant new possibilities and perhaps this time the cure. Her faith suddenly renewed, she wanted to tear up Jack's letter but LM had efficiently given it to the maid to drop in the post. It didn't matter. Jack would never receive it as it was only to be opened if she died and she wasn't going to do that, at least, not yet.

Jack stood waiting by the front door. His soft black felt hat shadowed his eyes but she needn't see them. It was that precious half smile of his that drew her across the entry. Together they walked out to the waiting taxi.

KATHERINE WAS RELIEVED at how comfortably the time passed on the train to San Remo compared to the trips she'd taken during the war. Now that the Armistice had been set in place and peace achieved, passing through borders was easier, though the wreckage from the Great War was apparent in the blurred bombed-out buildings they sped past.

At the hotel, LM registered while Jack and Katherine stood to the side with the baggage. Italians feared contagious diseases more than any other Europeans, particularly consumption. Any pale foreign strangers, particularly those with hacking coughs were immediately under suspicion. Katherine had avoided using her cane in the hotel lobby, leaning on Jack instead and kept her head down until they were in their rooms; a suite for her and Jack, a single adjoining room for LM.

Katherine told Jack she would eat meals in their room. She worried that the other guests would shun her or worse, decide she was contagious and tell her to go away as she was a threat to their families. Jack told her she was being silly and why should she care what they thought anyway? He never could understand how exposed she felt pinned under the public eye that microscopically diagnosed her, judged her, and spurned her.

"My god, Jack," she said, "I'm only *thirty* and I hobble around like an old woman." But he insisted. He wanted to show-off his famous wife, the celebrated writer.

She put on her best dress, covered the dark rings around her eyes with white powder that blended with her skin, painted her hollow cheeks with rouge, and drew ruby red lipstick across dry, chapped lips.

The other diners only glanced at her when she walked into the hotel restaurant before resuming their meals. That is until she coughed. Then all eyes were on her, pinning her under the light of the glaring chandelier. She barely touched her dinner. After that she ate in their room, only accompanying Jack to see the tourist sites of San Remo. Out in the open air, they relaxed and happily shared their holiday away from London, the responsibilities of *The Athenaeum*, and her convalescence.

Their happiness was temporary. A few nights before Jack's scheduled return to London, they were summoned to the office of the British hotel manager, Mr. Vince. He told them politely but firmly that guests were complaining about Katherine and her frail condition.

"I'm sorry but you'll have to leave," said Mr. Vince. "We can't take the risk of anyone becoming ill."

"What if my doctor sends you a letter reassuring you that my consumption is at a stage where I am not contagious."

He shook his head. "It wouldn't matter. If you don't leave, several of my guests will. Please try and understand my position and leave without any commotion."

"Leave?" said Katherine. "You are throwing us out? And where, Mr. Vince, do you suggest we go? We had booked your hotel for many months."

"I have considered that. I know of a small vacant casa near the village of Ospedaletti, three miles from here; a beautiful view, and very comfortable accommodations and amenities, such as indoor plumbing, that I know you'd appreciate."

Katherine didn't know if she was more furious at Jack for not taking a strong position against Mr. Vince or the additional charges added to their bill for fumigating their room as if she were vermin. She wanted to argue down the price but Jack advised against it. "Why embarrass yourself," he said. "Isn't it better to walk away with our pride and just a small hole in our pocketbook?"

"Whose pride, Jack? You must be talking about yours because I don't have any left. Why didn't you defend your wife when she was accused of being an unhealthy, dangerous vermin. And as far as the small hole in the pocketbook, it's my pocketbook and it's not a small hole."

"Now Katherine. Calm yourself. It would have been pointless to defend you against Mr. Vince's accusations. The guests had made up their mind. You know how ignorant people are about tuberculosis. Their fear is because of that ignorance. That's not something you can fight."

"The point is that by not saying anything in my defense you accepted his judgment of me and that's what hurts. You too think I'm vermin and that's why I no longer have any pride left."

7

Casetta Deerholm—Ospedaletti

It is on a wild hill slope, covered with olive and fig trees and long grasses and tall yellow flowers. Down below is the sea—the entire ocean—a huge expanse. It thunders all day against the rocks. At the back there are mountains. Many lizards lie on the garden wall; in the evening the cicada shakes his tiny tambourine.

Letters—KM

KATHERINE'S ANGER AT JACK was short-lived now that the stress of hiding in her hotel room was over and she would soon be staying in a private house. A few days later they were in a horse-drawn wagon that was carrying them and their traveling chests to Ospedaletti, a small village along the rocky Italian coastline.

"Look, Jack!" Katherine shouted as the wagon pulled up to a sign that read Casetta Deerholm. "How wonderful!" She wanted to run down the steps into the wild, blooming garden but, afraid she might cough and upset Jack, she slowly descended a pebbled path shaded by ancient olive and fig trees. LM directed the driver burdened with their baggage, toward a small pink villa hanging on a precipice over the ocean.

"What a stunning view," she said, standing on a large veranda, white frothy waves rubbing against the rocks below. A gentle wind tenderly caressed her face and above the sky smiled down warmly upon her. She took Jack's hand. "I feel my faith returning. I know I will get better here. And think of all the writing I will accomplish sitting on this veranda."

"Work, Katherine? Let's not talk about work—at least not yet."

She breathed in the soft, sweet Mediterranean air without feeling any pain in her lungs, and silently thanked Dr. Sorapure for keeping her outside the sanitarium walls. Only three weeks on the Riviera and already better.

She smiled at Jack and squeezed his hand. "Do you remember in Bandol when I read you Emily Brontë's poem *I Know Not How It Falls On Me?*"

"Of course I do. I remember everything that happened in Bandol from the chamomile tea sipped in the garden, to sitting by the fire at night reading, writing, and talking, to the wanderings by the sea and into the hills picking wildflowers. . ."

"Forgive me if I've shunned so long/Your gentle greeting, earth and air!/ But sorrow withers e'en the strong/And who can fight against despair," she recited. "Like in Bandol, I will fight against my sorrow and I shall win. I only wish you could witness my recovery instead of the Faithful One who you can be sure will take credit for it."

"I would wish nothing better than to send the Faithful One back to London and be your caregiver instead. Just the two of us here on our own, like in Bandol, I'd have the time to write that second novel I keep putting off and I haven't finished my book of poetry. But *The Athenaeum* won't go to print without me there. You know I must go back. Come the—"

"I know Jack. Come the month of May—"

A loud clatter from within was followed by cursing.

"Oh God, what has she broken now?" They followed the noise into the kitchen, to find a shattered teapot on the floor and a distressed LM picking up the pieces.

"I was holding it over the tap waiting for water and nothing came. I banged the tap and the pot slipped out of my other hand. Can you believe this? There isn't any water. How am I going to make tea?"

"It's all right," Katherine said. "I forgot to tell you that Mr. Vince said it would take a few days before we had running water. Until then we are to walk down to the village fountain. Jack will do it."

"But he leaves tomorrow! And look at this stove, if it is a stove. How do I light it?" Katherine looked over at the ancient appliance. "Look Jack," she said, not to be daunted by LM, "it's just like the one in Bandol." She found a matchbox on the kitchen counter and opened the stove's hatch to light it. Jack picked up a pail by the sink and said he'd be right back.

"Let's have that tea you promised out on the veranda before the sun sets," said Katherine, taking teacups down from the pantry shelf.

"But I can't. There isn't a teapot."

"Ida, please try and be imaginative. There must be something in this kitchen you can use as a pot. Look in the cupboards, you'll find something. If not, we'll skip tea and take a walk into the village to buy a new teapot. But please calm down."

THE DAY AFTER they had settled into Casetta Deerholm, Jack hung his floppy, velvet Felti on the entryway hat rack for his return in May. He kissed Katherine good-bye and with valise in hand walked out the door and down the street to a local bus stop that would take him to the train station in San Remo where he'd board a train to faraway London.

She pulled herself up the stairs to the bedroom window and grabbing a white chemise frantically waved, hoping he would see her and wave back, but he boarded the bus without turning back. She collapsed on the bed exhausted from pretending she was well and happy.

Later that day she ventured out onto the veranda and saw a basket chair in the garden under an ancient olive tree. She sat down to write her dear friend, K.K. Koteliansky, a Russian immigrant who had been introduced to her and Jack by the Lawrences when they were close neighbors in Chesham during the war. Later they were flatmates with a few other artists in London, all housing together to save money.

Mostly through correspondence and shared literary interests he and Katherine had developed an intimate friendship. Kot eked out a living by translating Russian literature and had recently asked her to work with him on the English translation of Chekhov's letters that *The Athenaeum* wanted to publish. He trusted her to smooth out his rough English grammar and fix any awkwardness in meaning.

A great admirer of Chekhov, she enjoyed reading Kot's translations, and today was moved to tears by Chekhov's anguish over knowing, as a doctor, that his tuberculosis would prevent him from completing his literary work. He believed that the work was what kept him alive.

She picked up her pen to tell Kot about the Casetta that hung on *a wild hill slope, covered with olive and fig trees and long grasses and tall yellow flowers.*

It was warm enough to stay outside. She finished Kot's letter and picked up her well-worn Shakespeare. LM often interrupted, asking ridiculous questions like "shouldn't you come inside" or "do you want company, dearie" or "do I know whom you are writing to." Irritated by these unnecessary interruptions, she added a postscript to Kot's letter:

It is not being ill that matters it is having to let people serve you and fighting every moment against their desire to share.

Her thoughts turned to Jack on the train. She imagined him tired and hungry, longing to sleep, wrapped in his overcoat, too cheap to reserve a sleeping berth. Rocking in her basket chair, she closed her eyes and imagined the Heron, a small thatched cottage, with two . . . no, three children playing in its garden, the little boy looking just like Jack, the same pale green eyes. She opened her own eyes onto the sun slipping behind the Mediterranean and wrote *twenty-eight weeks* in her notebook, marking the time until she and Jack would reunite.

Over dinner, Katherine mapped out a routine that she asked LM to follow. She was to be awakened promptly at ten with a breakfast tray. She was not to be disturbed earlier as she might be writing. Afternoons silent. She'd fix herself something for lunch, if she were hungry. She'd read or write on the veranda, or, if too tired, recline in bed upstairs as there weren't any downstairs sofas. The sitting room adjacent to the kitchen and the only room in the house other than the two upstairs bedrooms, she designated as her writing room. The door when closed would be a code to LM that she was not to be disturbed for any reason. She made up menus for LM to follow, suggesting her own recipes. LM was to avoid asking any questions that she could answer herself when it came to running the Casetta, including what to buy at the market, but know that there was little money for extravagant shopping.

"If you follow my instructions, through my writing, I can make enough income for us to remain here," she said. "I am under much pressure with deadlines and can't be bothered with domestic problems. That is your job."

"I understand, Katie. I will try not to bother you. But I thought you were to rest while we were here and not work. Isn't that what Jack said?"

"And what does Jack think we are going to live on? Need I remind you that the only income I receive from my husband is when I deliver the novel-reviews for *The Athenaeum*. We will be short of funds until I receive the advance from my next short story collection of which I haven't even chosen which stories to include and those will have to be reviewed carefully."

"Oh I do hope you include *Bliss* in that collection. It's my favorite right now and if I recall correctly you were paid very well for it."

"Yes I was." Katherine smiled. "Actually I am considering *Bliss* for the anthology's title." She'd heard that Virginia Woolf thought she had "ruined her reputation" with *Bliss* and she wanted to throw it back in her face when it sold far more copies than anything Virginia had published. No, it wasn't her best work but it was quite popular. Her readers had liked it well enough and so had the critics after its publication in the *English Review*. Virginia never would understand that there were some writers who had to earn a living at their craft and couldn't always offer the public their more serious work, not if they wanted an income. Virginia had the privilege of writing for herself or for the very few. Besides, she liked writing for the common readers.

* * *

IN THE FIRST MAIL she received a packet of four novels from Jack that he needed reviewed immediately to make *Athenaeum*'s deadline. She did as he asked but enclosed in the finished reviews a letter complaining that these novels ignored there had ever been a war and that was absurd. The war had changed everything and had to be confronted, not ignored. She wondered why he asked her to review these inconsequential books and then gave a new printing of George Eliot's *Middlemarch* to one of his assistants.

LM struggled in the primitive kitchen trying to make meals, but even the simplest meals seemed to upset her and often she broke her promise to leave Katherine alone. Katherine would hear her curses through the wall and often the crashing of yet another plate or glass and feel obligated to stop working to find out what had happened.

She wondered what LM's talents really were. She was an inept housekeeper, even struggled lighting the stove, was too embarrassed to ask for help, couldn't cook a tasty meal or deliver it on time, and was even tardy bringing the tea tray. Perhaps her large size and massive hands were her main assets as she did manage to carry large pails of water up from the village fountain. The expense of feeding her was making it difficult to adhere to a strict budget. Everyday LM was asking for more money to shop in the village or in San Remo for supplies. She said she was dieting and hardly touched her plate at their shared meals but then where did all the food go? LM was known to feed anything that breathed upon this earth that passed by her vision but there would still have been leftovers.

These were Katherine's thoughts as she watched from her bedroom window as LM struggled up the hill from the village with two full buckets of water sloshing back and forth. She didn't remember her being so clumsy and heavy when they were students.

LM HAD BEEN the first student she met at Queens College. When they arrived from Wellington, she and her three older sisters had been taken to their sleeping quarters. Katherine had rushed ahead and claimed the corner bed as rightfully hers. Why? her sisters asked. Because she would value the view from the bay window more than they would and they didn't appreciate watching the rain fall. Nor did they watch flowers bloom or stars fall from the sky. She'd rushed from her claimed bed through a door into a giant bathroom that for some strange reason contained to her delight a grand piano. Could it be that all houses in London had grand pianos in their bathrooms?

"Kathleen!" yelled her eldest sister Vera. "You're not being polite. Ida carried your trunk up three flights of stairs and is waiting for you to tell her where you want her to put it down."

"I'd prefer if you didn't call me by that name," she said coming around the corner. Her two elegant sisters stood dressed in plumed hats and floor length skirts in what was then the fashion in New Zealand. But what drew her attention was a very tall, large young girl plainly dressed in a dark gray blouse and skirt. Her long, fair hair was separated by a severe part down the middle and pulled back tightly, locks cascading down her back. If not so large, she could have been Brontë's Jane Eyre.

Ida stared back and then shyly looked away but not before Katherine had looked into the saddest eyes. I must sketch her in my journal, she thought. "Here. Bring my trunk here!" she demanded, pointing to the side of her bed. Ida did as she was told and then waited as if not knowing what to do next without instruction.

"Kass!" shouted her other sister, Marie, "Ida isn't your maid, she's the school monitor and was asked to show us our rooms and the College. I think you should apologize for your rudeness and thank her for bringing in your baggage."

Kass didn't like being told by her sisters how to behave and turned her back on them, quietly saying to Ida, "Thank you." Ida gave a deli cate curtsy, which was quite graceful considering her height.

She put out her hand. Ida shook it and said, "Hello, Ka—"

"No, don't call me Kass. Or Kathleen for that matter. Only my sisters do that and my friends back at home. They're childhood names. Here in London you can call me Katie."

"Hello, Katie."

"And what did you say your name was?"

"Ida. My name is Ida." This creature whose high-pitched childlike voice was so much smaller than her size surprised her again. Certainly a character worth writing about, she thought.

"Ida? Ida what?"

"Ida Baker."

"Hmmm. Would you mind if I changed your name? I don't think Ida suits you at all. I'm very good at giving people names. I do it all the time in the stories I write."

"You're a writer?" exclaimed Ida, showing the first signs of life.

"Yes, but I am going to be a professional musician. And you? What is your ambition?"

Ida blushed. "Ambition? I don't know if I have one. I study the violin."

"Excellent. My instrument is the violoncello. We can play duets."

"I'm not very good," Ida said softly, turning to leave.

"Now I know what to call you. It will be your stage name, too. Lesley. It is also my brother's name and I am quite fond of him."

"I don't know. I'm used to being called Ida. And if I was to change my name I would call myself, Katherine, my mother's name."

"Well that will never do. My nom de plume is Katherine. It would be confusing for both of us to have the same name, don't you think?"

"All right," said Ida. She got up to leave and turned back to say, "If you like, I'll come back when you've unpacked and show you the school."

"Why wait? I want to see everything now."

KATHERINE RECLINED BACK on the bed after watching LM climb up the hill to the Casetta and returned to the letter she was writing. She and Jack had promised to write each other every day. She started off by telling him that she wished it was him carrying the pails instead of LM, and that he was hiding a red geranium in his waistcoat pocket that he would give to her. Outside the open window she heard the waves whisper "Boge" each time they rolled over the rocks below and wrote:

My dearest Boge, you are more loved than anyone in the world.

8

October 1919

31st Birthday

Now it is Loneliness who comes at night
Instead of Sleep, to sit beside my bed.
Like a tired child I lie and wait her tread,
I watch her softly blowing out the light.
Motionless sitting, neither left or right
She turns, and weary, weary droops her head.
She, too, is old; she, too, has fought the fight.
So, with the laurel she is garlanded.

Loneliness—KM

HER THIRTY-FIRST BIRTHDAY arrived without fanfare. Jack sent a small delicate silver spoon for the future Heron. A letter from her father but he didn't mention her birthday. Katherine knew he gave money to her sisters on their birthdays and was hurt that he had ignored hers.

Propped up in bed, angry with LM for taking so long to bring the morning tray, she marked in her journal *199 days*, encouraging herself not to give up hope. *Stay firm*, as Jack would say.

LM entered beaming, "Happy Birthday Katie!" She proudly brought over a tray with a steamy pot of coffee, a mug, and a brilliant bouquet she must have picked from the garden.

"I thought you couldn't find any coffee beans in the village?" was Katherine's grumpy response. If she wasn't having fun on her birthday no one else was going to.

"I didn't say I couldn't find any, I said there were none to be had on your budget. But this morning I found a quaint little shop selling small bags at a bargain price."

"How much?

"Oh, not so much, considering how tightly the beans are packed in the bag."

"How much, Ida?"

"Ten lira."

"Why, that's almost as much as a doctor's visit. You know we can't afford it. You know that Jack and I are saving for the Heron. But what do you do to help? Not only do you break the Heron dishes I am collecting, but you frivolously use my money for your own pleasures. I'm deducting these coffee beans from your pay. Now take it away."

LM continued to grin from ear to ear like a pumpkin. "My aren't we the happy birthday girl. Deduct it from my pay, if you like, though I have no idea what my pay is. But now that I'm paying for it, I freely give it to you as a birthday present. Enjoy!"

Before Katherine could reply she left.

The fragrance steaming from a pot of fresh coffee was irresistible. She poured herself a cup. That was when she saw a small perfume bottle of Genet Fleuri, her favorite perfume, behind the flower vase. Oh Jones, how thoughtful. She took a sip from the mug. Oh how delicious. She dabbed her wrist with the perfume and thought, what a detestable person I am. Why does she stay? If not for me, she'd be married and starting a family. Why sacrifice all that for me? And worse, why do I let her?

She returned to reading a book that she kept putting down from boredom but must finish. She had to write the review, and send it out before *Athenaeum*'s deadline. Jack always sent the books at the last minute leaving her hardly anytime to read and review. He didn't seem to realize how long it took and how anxious it made her being under a strict, unreasonable deadline.

She was startled by a loud crash in the kitchen. "I will never get any work done as long as *she* is in my house," she said out loud, quickly forgetting the guilt she had just been feeling at her unkindness. She hurriedly dressed and went downstairs.

In the kitchen, LM was bent over, sweeping up shattered glass.

"What have you broken now?"

"It was just a silly brandy glass. Way too frail. It would never have been much use. I know that's a terrible excuse, but it's true. Oh, Katie, don't look so angry. You know how clumsy I am. You must give me more time to get used to this kitchen work."

"That's what you said in London. We don't have any more *frail* items for you to practice on. In one week you've broken the thermometer—"

"That's unfair. It fell off the bed table when I accidentally put down your milk glass on it."

Katherine continued. "A plate and a saucer."

"They were frail, too. And isn't it rather nice and homey when you occasionally smash a thing or two?" She giggled, getting up off the floor with shards of broken glass sparkling in her hands.

Katherine slammed the door and returned to her writing but not before thinking, if only that young, cheerful and petite village maid hadn't left us without notice. The two days she was here were peaceful. If she had stayed, I could send *her* packing today.

She'd just sat down at her writing table when LM came bursting in, another cardinal rule broken. "Have you no scruples," she shouted. "Can't you see I'm working. Please leave me alone!"

"Oh sorry Katie, I didn't realize you were working?"

"That is why the door is closed."

"I wanted you to know I'm going shopping. With your permission I'll purchase those muttonchops I saw in the butcher shop before someone else does and we need eggs. And wouldn't you like some figs, dearie, for your birthday?"

"You think I just write in this notebook and money magically appears. You just bought groceries. Where did that food go to, certainly not into *my* stomach?"

"Nor mine. Haven't you noticed how little I eat?"

Katherine knew she was lying. She didn't want LM to know it, but she had been spying on her and just the other day had seen her stuffing herself with an Italian bread loaf when she thought Katherine was sleeping.

SHE SPENT THE AFTERNOON reading on the veranda. When LM came out to check on her, she exclaimed, "Katie what's happened?"

"What do you mean *what's happened*?"

"Look at your legs."

They were vivid red and twice their normal size. "Oh my god, what is it?"

LM ran to the neighbor for help.

The neighbor took one look and said, "Pa-pet-e-chi-kos!"

"Che cosa sono pa-pet-e-chi-kos?" they both asked. He lifted his shoulders and shrugged. They heard him laughing as he left, amused by his foreign neighbors.

LM looked up the word in her Italian dictionary and read out loud to Katherine, "Tiny, invisible, deadly mosquitoes."

"What do you mean *deadly*?"

"I don't know but we must bring down the swelling. I'll get ice."

"Ida, we don't have any ice!"

"Oh right. Well, it's too late to go tonight but I'll go to the pharmacy first thing in the morning. Señor Mario will know what to do."

The following morning she awoke to lit candles on every surface in her bedroom and LM hooking a mosquito net around her bed."

"What are you doing? And why are the candles lit?"

"Señor Mario said to do this." LM took a bottle out of her bag and waved it in front of her. "He wants me to add this solution to your bath."

"What is it?

"I don't know. He spoke very quickly and I couldn't understand everything he said."

LM picked up a vase of fresh flowers.

"Where are you taking those?"

"He said no flowers in the house. The papetechikos feed on their nectar."

"Don't touch those flowers!"

"But Katie."

"Put them back instantly. What else did he tell you?"

"Keep your windows closed at night and sprinkle the floor with water though I can't understand what help it would be to wet the floor. And, oh yes, as best as I could translate, 'Bear up until after the fruit season.'"

"When is that?"

"A few months from now."

On the hot windless days that followed the pa-pet-e-chi-kos continued their assault, breaking through the netting to feast on her relentlessly.

IN EARLY NOVEMBER, a month after arriving at the Casetta, Katherine lost her faith in being cured. She became anxious and depressed. She'd depended on Jack's letters to keep her from entirely giving up, but there were too many days in between. Her loneliness was unheeded, he did not hear her cry.

In the afternoons, she'd sit at her writing table waiting for LM to return from the post office. The courier hand-delivered to the Casetta in the morning, but she'd hope Jack's letters got held up. Even after she heard the front door bang, she'd hold off calling out, watching the seconds click by on the clock until the strain was too much and she'd shout, "Ida, is there any mail?"

Too often the reply was, "Nothing today."

Sinking into dark, uncontrollable moods, she wrote letters to Jack about LM's stupidity, or wrote to her friends about Jack's thoughtlessness, lashing out at the two people that cared the most about her. Because LM was the one present, she got the worst of it, but even Jack who had previously managed to avoid her sting, was now the targeted victim of venomous letters that Katherine couldn't hold back though she knew she should.

Late one afternoon, waiting for LM's return from the post office, she was correcting Chekhov's last letter in Kot's packet, a letter to his wife in which Chekhov was trying to explain what it felt like to be a consumptive:

My mind is weakened by illness and I am now like a child: now I pray to God, now I cry, now I am happy.

Tears came to her eyes as she read words she could have written herself. She knew it was the consumption that made her so uncontrollably moody but what was she to do about it? How could she control these black moods that came upon her at all hours. She was desperate for sleep. The last drops of Dr. Sorapure's laudanum were gone.

She raised her pen to respond to Jack's last letter filled with complaints about his cold. She copied out a Chekhov catchphrase:

People love talking of their diseases, although they are the most uninteresting things in their lives.

She continued in her own words:

You see my darling that is why I don't tell you when I'm feeling badly, because it is boring. So please don't bore me with telling me about your illnesses either. We have far more interesting things to consider such as next week's edition of the A. or whether you have yet found the Heron—are you even looking or are you feeling as discouraged as I am today that this house we so wish for is not possible because of that boring thing I choose not to speak of today.

The doorbell clanged again and again. "Ida!" she screamed.

"I'm coming. I'm coming." Heavy footsteps followed, like horse hooves clomping down a wooden ramp.

LM ushered Mr. Vince into Katherine's writing room. "Good afternoon Mrs. Murry," he said, stopping to wipe back the perspiration from walking up the hill from Ospedaletti. "I was in the area and thought I'd come by to see how you two were getting along. Is the water coming through the taps?"

"Yes it is. And we are most grateful for our baths. Now if there is nothing else—stop by the kitchen on your way out and Ida will give you a drink of water."

"Well Mrs. Murry actually there is something else."

"Oh, do you bring news about Augusta? I was worried about her. She seemed happy enough but she only worked for two days and then abruptly left without notice. Is she ill?"

"I told her to explain to you . . . but she was too embarrassed and asked me to tell you."

Katherine waited but when he said nothing she said, "Yes?"

"It's your illness, Mrs. Murry. There's been gossip. You know how it is in these small villages. Her mother told her she couldn't work for you. Augusta was disappointed, but young girls must obey, mustn't they? But it is regrettable. I was a bit worried about your welfare living here the way you are, just the two of you, I thought this might be a good idea."

He brought out a revolver and placed it on her writing table with a box of bullets.

"What's that for!" asked LM, stepping back.

"I worry about you two women being here alone and what with the war ending the way it did and the bad feelings here about us English, and what with Mr. Murry away and you being, well, you know—sick—I think you need protection."

"Have you had trouble, Mr. Vince?" He had lived in San Remo before the war, and then returned after, but he was still an Englishman, a foreigner, and for four long years the enemy.

"Goodness no, Mrs. Murry, not in San Remo. There are so many of us there. It's a regular old British colony. But here in the countryside, well one never knows when one might need protection in these isolated parts. I thought it would be a good precaution."

Katherine picked up the revolver, handled it, feeling its weight. She sensed terror and fascination simultaneously and put it back down.

"Thank you Mr. Vince for your concern. It is true that the doorbell has been ringing late at night but no one answers when we call out. I haven't paid it much mind."

"Just what I suspected. These Italians don't realize that we're no longer the enemy. Our presence is a strong reminder of their defeat. They do not realize that we don't want to occupy their country. We just find it pleasant to live here. Anyway, I'll feel a lot better myself knowing you have this. May I show you how to use it?"

"Why, certainly."

"Katherine! You would use this gun?" said LM, shocked.

"Mr. Vince would never have introduced us to this revolver if he didn't think we might have to use it." She picked up the gun again. "Is it loaded, Mr. Vince?"

"No. I was going to show you how and give you a little target practice."

"Really," said LM. "Is that necessary?"

"Shall we, Mr. Vince?" said Katherine leading the way outside. "Coming, my dear? You could use a little practice, too."

"No thank you. My father taught me how to use a gun in Rhodesia. I know more than I want to know about guns."

In the garden, he loaded the gun for Katherine and brought her arm up, showing her how to pull the trigger. She practiced shooting after he was gone and liked the sensation of power it gave her and the pleasure of knowing it bothered LM. She put it away in the hallway table drawer, near the front door, unloaded, but with a box of bullets nearby.

The next morning LM brought Katherine's breakfast tray and then said she was taking a bus to San Remo to visit a few friends. "Are you sure you don't mind being on your own for the day?"

"No, actually, I look forward to it."

WHY DOESN'T LM put anything back after she uses it? Katherine asked out loud, as she stood in the garden after almost tripping over a rake.

She sat down in her basket chair to enjoy the warm air, like silk against her skin. Down below, the clear waters of the Mediterranean made it possible to watch the arms and legs of swimmers paddling underwater.

Sailboats and steamboats glided past reminding her of Wellington where she'd viewed the port from her bedroom window. In the distance, slivers of white shown across the horizon each time a wave rose and fell. That distinctive white light, that moment of truth, subtle but enlightening is what I want to express in my writing, but when? she asked herself angrily. Every hour was occupied with the novel-reviews, the Chekhov translations, and the revisions to her short stories for the anthology. She wasn't writing anything new. The ideas crammed in her head or scribbled in her notebooks were not being used.

She settled back in her basket chair to read a letter from Kot. Tears filled her eyes when she got to the last paragraph:

Your indomitable will has kept you alive this year. I am absolutely sure you will get well and grow into your dream of achievement.

Katherine brushed away the tears and looked out to the sea for comfort, deeply breathing in the warm, soft breeze and letting it linger in her mouth with the pleasure of a vintage wine. The drifting sun slipped briefly behind a white cloud and came back out again to shine down on the blossoming rose-red geraniums and her.

She took out her pen and wrote with a revived strength she didn't know she still had in her:

Yes, Kot, you are right. I will be healed here in this fairy-tale house in Ospedaletti. In spite of having to share it with Ida, my albatross. And I will start to write again soon.

She put down the pen pleased with the feeling of renewal Kot's generous words had given her. And, she thought, the next story I write I will dedicate to my dear loyal friend Kot who hasn't forsaken me like the others. Her new optimism carried her back to the house and to her writing table.

That night her optimism turned on her. She awoke in her netted bed believing she was being eaten alive and screamed for help before hiding under the covers. LM came running. The moonlight reflecting on the white cotton headboard lit up a fat-bellied mosquito resting after a meal. Katherine peeked out from under the covers to see LM catch the monster in her big hands, and walk over to the window, open it, and fling it out.

"You let it go free? You didn't squash it?"

"The poor thing. I couldn't kill her, Katie," she said as she shut the window. "Did you know that she must bite to fertilize her eggs."

Katherine got out of bed and re-opened the window. "Then let's leave it open so she and the rest of the maternity ward can feast on me. We certainly don't want to wipe out their population because of my ungodly selfishness. What a shame, my dear Griselda, that your blood does not whet their appetites, as I'm certain you would be far more willing to sacrifice yourself for their progeny than I am."

"Now, Katie, you are getting into one of your silly moods again. You must calm down. We don't want a fever, do we? It's true that I would prefer if they attacked me instead of you, but they like you better. Certainly a few tiny bites are no reason to kill her, are they, my dearie? Get back into bed and let me cover you with the net."

Katherine grabbed her bedside drinking glass and threw it at LM. "Get out! And don't speak to me again until I give you permission. Don't think I don't see through your pitiful self-sacrifice. I know what you want—you're just like them, you want to eat Me! You think I'm stupid don't you. You don't think that I know you're the Albatross coming back for revenge. I took your life from you and now you've come to kill me. Admit it. Albatross! But I won't let you do it. I have a gun now to protect myself with. Mr. Vince didn't know that the enemy was within my house not outside."

"Katie. Stop! It's not you saying these horrible things. You'll be sorry later."

"Get out! And don't call me Katie. I'm Mrs. Murry to you. You hear that? Mrs. Murry."

Katherine banged her fist against the pillow. "Jack. Damn you too! Why have you abandoned me in this god-forsaken place with this monster? You care more about that damn journal and your ambition than you do me. That's the truth."

Overcome by a coughing fit she reached for the water glass forgetting she had thrown it at LM and got back into bed with a parched throat.

In a dream she stood in the garden, raised the handheld gun for target practice and turned it on a grinning LM walking toward her with a tea tray. She pulled the trigger and glared down at LM's blood and tea-stained body, transformed into the white-feathered, bulbous body of an albatross, its broken wings spread across the pathway.

She woke up thinking that would never do. The dead body of a woman the size of LM would be too difficult to dispose of. Too heavy to drag through the garden and drop into the sea. But oh how she would like to get rid of her somehow. But then how would she survive without her?

9

November 1919

I am sitting in the dining room. The front door is open, the cold salt air blows through. I am wrapped up in my purple dressing gown and Jaeger rug with a hot bottle and a hot brick. On the round table is a dirty egg-cup full of ink, my watch (on British time an hour slow) and a wooden tray holding a manuscript called "Eternity" which is all spattered over with drops of rain and looks as though some sad mortal had cried his pretty eyes out over it. There is also a pair of scissors—abhorrèd shears they look—and two flies walking up and down are discussing the ratification of the Peace Treaty and its meaning re our civil relations with Flyland.

Letters—KM

KATHERINE PUT DOWN HER PEN, closed her notebook, and walked out onto the veranda to watch what in the last few days had transmogrified from a sun-drenched, turquoise pool into a dark, treacherous sea. Yet another thunderstorm preparing its attack. Casetta Deerholm was no longer the paradise she'd hoped for. The frigid wind beat against her and the unprotected precipice she stood on. She was under-dressed in her purple dressing gown but she didn't care. The only one who did care, LM, had gone out to meet a Dr. Bobone at the bus stop.

Any doctor, Katherine had told her, any doctor with a stethoscope hanging from his neck will do. Not because Katherine was feeling terribly ill, to the contrary she was feeling much better since leaving London, but because she needed medical evidence of her well-being. She needed confirmation that being locked up with LM and deprived of Jack's company were worth the cost—that she really was better. In the past, too often she had imagined herself better only to be disappointed.

She wanted medical confirmation that her disease was inactive, even gone; that there was a future for her and Jack, that her belief in a cure this time was not a false optimism, not a further putting off of the truth that she was dying. And she needed Dr. Sorapure's tincture to keep away the night terrors and soothe her cough. The medicine bottle, his gift to her, was empty. She laid awake at night without it.

DR. BOBONE pressed his stethoscope against her chest. She listened to him listening. Was it the log in the stove or was it her lungs crackling? He said nothing.

She asked him again if he didn't want to review her medical records before giving his opinion.

He replied offhandedly, "Not necessary. My ear hears everything. The apex of your left lung is affected, Fräulein."

Katherine looked into the marble red eyes of an ox about to charge and pulled back in fear of being trampled.

"That's what must be cured, Fräulein," he said. His two fingers tapping on her chest felt like the ox's stomping hoof. "Rest. Sunshine. I warn you. If fever. You die."

She turned away from him so that he wouldn't see her terror and put her under jacket back on. "I'm out of the tonic my English doctor gives me to sleep. Can you mix a bottle for me?"

"If you mean laudanum, no, I cannot," he said, taking a small ugly bottle from his medical bag before snapping it shut. "We must heal the underlying cause of your illness then you'll be able to sleep. Swallow this, Fräulein, make your lungs strong."

"I must ask my doctor if it is safe. " She read the label.

"Not to worry, Fräulein. It won't harm you. Make you feel better or it does nothing."

Katherine put her purple dressing gown back on and paid him what she thought was way too much.

She ran out on the veranda after he left. Her dressing gown buffeted by the stormy wind, she gripped the railing and imagined she was on a ship carrying her home to New Zealand. Dr. Bobone was only an ox-like character in a bad dream.

In the distance, a boat sharply bobbed against the cloudy white horizon like an ink spot on a white sheet of paper. She felt a piercing stab in her right lung where the ox had just stomped and knew that the black spot in the distance was the indelible black spot on her lung.

The storm thundered and bolted throughout the day. Katherine took to her bed and wrote Jack asking him to see Dr. Sorapure immediately and to send her the herb. She'd have the pharmacy mix it. She gave him the name of Bobone's tonic saying she wouldn't take one spoonful without Dr. Sorapure's assurance.

She put her pen down and looked up at the sparse bedroom. The small coal stove hissed and sputtered; barely keeping her warm. She shivered. The little house hanging on the precipice shivered. She wrapped the Jaeger rug tighter and dug her feet down into the fur hand muffs, but still felt the wind penetrate the Casetta's crumbling walls and grip her in its chilly arms.

LM came in holding a glass of warm milk on a tray. After a few days of silence Katherine had given her permission to speak.

"This might help you sleep," said LM, putting down the tray on the bed. "Oh my, don't tell me you're cold, dear Katie. You just have no fat on that petite body of yours. I gave the stove the last of the coal an hour ago. Are you really that cold?"

"Yes, I'm *that* cold," she said, her teeth chattering.

"Let's take your temperature. We can't be too cautious, can we? Remember what Dr. Bobone said about 'no fever and no die.'" LM giggled at her German accent but stopped when she saw Katherine wasn't amused. "Oh my, your hot-water bottle is frozen. I'll put it near this nice fire to warm it up."

LM forced the thermometer between her pursed lips. In the fading twilight, Katherine stared up at LM's wide fat arms like giant flailing wings, the wide-spread black beady eyes, the tiny blind breasts, the baby mouth . . . the bulbous curved beak of an albatross. Was that not a mariner's breadcrumb or two on the corner of its orange beak?

I'm becoming a fiend, she thought, and I have no control over it. She shut her eyes blacking out the albatross image of her caregiver.

LM removed the thermometer. "Thank goodness. No fever. But we'll have to move you downstairs where it's warmer and you have the wood fire to keep you warmer."

"Need I remind you that there is nowhere to lie downstairs," said Katherine, glaring at LM.

"No, you needn't remind me. I'll get Mr. Vince to move the bed downstairs. Now drink your milk while it's still warm."

Katherine looked at the offered glass and imagined LM in the kitchen dripping drops of arsenic into it. She said, "Would you please taste it first. I don't want to burn my tongue."

LM drank down half of it and handed it back saying, "It's warm and delicious."

A FORTNIGHT WENT BY before she received Jack's response to her letter. Dr. Sorapure's herbs had arrived that morning in the same packet and LM had taken them and the emerald green medicine bottle to the San Remo pharmacist to prepare the tincture.

Jack said her last letter had depressed him. She mustn't trust that stupid quack, Dr. Bobone. He advised her to take courage as he had done when obligated to attend yet another dreary party without her. She laughed out loud at his courage wishing she too could "suffer" at a dreary party. Poor, poor Jack!

She turned to writing a review for his precious *Athenaeum* until the clanging doorbell interrupted her. Walking by the side table drawer that held the revolver, she hesitated, reasoned with herself that the gun was unnecessary. It was the middle of the afternoon and murderers and thieves only come in the dark of night. Besides she was already half-dead and she had nothing worth stealing.

The door opened on a small, stooped-over man who leaped inside like a bright-eyed cat. Shocked, she pulled back. "Vous desirez?" she asked hoping to be rid of him quickly.

"Dr. Ansaldi," he said tipping his straw hat. "Here at your request, I believe, but does not appear so."

"Oh yes." She'd forgotten Mr. Vince's offer to send her a specialist in respiratory diseases, before she had found Dr. Bobone.

Dr. Ansaldi suggested he examine her in the warm kitchen. She watched him bend down and add wood to the kitchen stove. He turned to her, "You must stay warm during this unusual frigid winter on the Italian Riviera. Isn't what you expected, is it? Not the weather promised in the tourist brochure that bring you English here."

He drew a very modern stethoscope out of no less a purse, more sophisticated than Bobone's, and a percussion hammer. Without being asked, knowing too well what was expected of her, she removed her Jaeger and several layers of sweaters and scarves she'd been wearing.

"That's good. Dress warmly," he said, looking at the woolens now piled on the floor. He asked her to breathe slowly in and out while he listened and then tapped on her back with his hammer. He read over Dr. Sorapure's medical report, studied the charts, and jotted down notes in a journal similar to the one Dr. Sorapure carried. She began to trust him. Over a cup of tea he gave his opinion.

After he left, she added a log to the already roasting fire and poured herself another cup of tea. She held off writing Jack so that she could savor Ansaldi's news for herself alone. But too excited to wait another minute she picked up her pen and wrote:

My bad lung is drying, there's only a small spot left at the apex. The other lung also has a small spot at the apex but it's improved. She sipped her tea and ate a fig just to stretch out feeling the good news a little longer:

Ansaldi says 'It will take two years to cure me but that I shall be a great deal better by April.' Yes, Jack! Dr. Ansaldi said I could be normal.

Remembering Ansaldi and Bobone's warnings to stay warm, she asked Jack to send her one of those long blankety woolen scarves to wrap around her neck several times to keep out the chill.

After dressing for bed, she stood at the window looking out at the starry night and shivered, not from the cold, but an unfamiliar thrill of joy. And more unfamiliar was the sudden irresistible urge to leap into the air, something she'd been afraid to do for quite some time. What if I fall? What if Dr. Ansaldi hadn't told me the truth? What if my heart stops? She ignored her voice of doubt and walked to the center of the room, stood perfectly still, took a deep breath, closed her eyes and jumped once. And then jumped again much higher.

Her heart beating fast, she stood in front of her mirror to see if she looked any different and peeked at a very bright, lively face that she hardly recognized as her own. Climbing into bed and propping up her pillows she wrote to Jack:

What is the Present when the Future is removed, when life is haunted, not by Death in the fullness of time, but by Death's fast-encroaching shadow? But I now say, 'away with that shadow and come no more.' I will live in the Present and no longer fear the Future. Five months and a fortnight, my dearest, and we will never be separated again.

LM came in holding Dr. Sorapure's emerald green bottle in her hand and waving a spoon. "Look what I have, Katie."

"I shan't need more than one spoonful." she said, knowing there would be no terrors that night.

SHE RECEIVED NEWS from her father that after his long stay in London with her sisters, before returning home to New Zealand, he'd promised to visit his cousin at her winter villa in Menton, France. Katherine wrote to tell him that Ospedaletti was just on the other side of the border from Menton, a simple day's excursion. Anxious that he might not visit her, afraid of becoming infected, added: *Please come, Pa, I am much better. I no longer cough.*

She was surprised and delighted when he wrote back accepting her invitation. He would bring his older cousin with him, Miss Connie Beauchamp, and her long-time companion Miss Jinnie Fullerton. The two women now retired had managed a nursing home in London and now invited their previous English patients to Villa Flora, their villa in Menton overlooking the sea, for the winters.

Katherine's wish for a sunny day on their visit was answered. The Casetta looks less rundown under its golden brilliance, she thought, standing on the veranda waiting for her father's arrival. A fancy white motorcar rolled up the hill driven by a uniformed chauffeur. She rushed to the gate.

"Pa. I'm so glad you're here. Come in. Come in. Hello Connie. Oh! You must be Miss Jinnie. Welcome! Welcome to Casetta Deerholm." Two matronly women, one stout and one tall, in their fifties or, perhaps much older, and her robust father, who in his finely tailored Bond Street suit reminded her of King Edward, followed her into the entryway that hardly fit her royal guests.

"Why it's a dollhouse!" exclaimed Jinnie. Seemingly charmed by the sitting room, they looked around for a closet to hang their furs and shopping bags. Finding none, they were plopped in the corner. The only other surface, the writing table, had been set for lunch.

No one but Katherine seemed to notice the too thickly cut onions or the burnt potatoes or the overcooked roast. LM glowed when Jinnie thanked her for the delicious meal and complimented her on the lovely table setting. "Why you have such a colorful variety of china," said Connie. LM had used every cracked and chipped dish found in the cupboard.

Her guests had stopped along the route to buy knick-knacks and had been particularly amused by a shop selling reading spectacles. They'd each bought several pairs that they now modeled and passed around for everyone to try on. Katherine's only pair remained in her pocket. As if she knew, Connie gave her a pair of her grandfather's horn-rimmed specs, saying they were very special. Katherine was touched by her thoughtfulness.

Her father suggested a car ride and she was bundled up in a fur rug and seated next to him. She rested back against the velvet cushions, snuggling up against his fur coat. In her desire to be independent she had run away from his opulence, finding it suffocating, but now it seduced her. Let the car drive on forever, the motor purring, and his arms around her, sheltering her from the harsh world.

He told a story about having his wallet stolen on Bond Street in London. He said the loss of ten pounds was nothing compared to the embarrassment of being made a fool of.

Katherine thought to say, "Ten pounds! What you think 'nothing of' I could have lived on for a month,'" but she had learned to curb her tongue when her father made thoughtless remarks, as she did with Jack. They both had no idea how she struggled to keep a budget that excluded spectacles and motorcar rides. And she preferred it that way rather than humbling herself by describing the paucity of her life as if expecting a handout. She would never admit to either one of them that she felt abandoned by both of them in Italy, out of sight, out of mind.

Mr. Beauchamp amused the ladies by speaking into the limousine's horn to the chauffeur in Maori, the native tongue of New Zealand, which he was sure the Italian driver would not understand. The colonies were far away from here and no Maori had ever set foot on Italian soil or so he thought. The driver stopped at the top of the hill so they might admire the cliffs. Connie and Jinnie took a short walk. Pa pulled off his fur-lined leather gloves and slipped then onto Katherine's bare hands. He spoke softly, calling her by her childhood name.

"Kass, I am very worried about you. You look much too pale for someone recovering from illness." Like Jack, he never called her disease by its name. "I hardly recognized you when you greeted us. You're too thin."

"You needn't worry. I'm better. I told you what Dr. Ansaldi said."

"I do worry. You told me that you had to leave London or you wouldn't survive another winter but where you're staying now seems to be as damp and as bitterly cold as any London winter. Your Casetta is completely unprotected from the wind and so are you. Nor is it insulated for winter." He didn't give her time to reply.

"I've never understood Jack's lack of duty toward you. But certainly he would never have abandoned you here if he'd seen these harsh living conditions. And such isolation. What would happen if there was an emergency?"

"Oh Pa, you're exaggerating. I'm not entirely alone. Ida is here." She didn't mention the gun Mr. Vince had given her for emergencies. "And Jack did see the Casetta and wholeheartedly approved of it. As far as the isolation, I prefer writing in remote natural settings. Now that I am feeling better and really I am, I have much work to do on my own. I only wish it wasn't so expensive to keep the Casetta heated. And then there's Dr. Ansaldi's fee."

"But why isn't Jack here?"

"He has promised to come for me in May and then we will move into a Sussex cottage where we will live most comfortably. I just have to make it on my own through the next five months and get well."

"Kass, this is all wrong. A husband shouldn't leave his wife, particularly a wife in your weak condition, in a foreign country where you have neither family nor friends. There is something you are not telling me. I ask you again, why isn't Jack here?"

"He must consider his career. Certainly you can understand that. It would be unwise for him to leave his new editorial position at *The Athenaeum* and I wouldn't ask him to do so. Why should both of us suffer for my illness? Besides we have no choice. My stories are selling, but there are medical expenses."

Her father turned away and looked out at the sea. She hoped that once he considered the escalating costs to keep her well, he would offer to increase her allowance.

He turned back to her and said, "If you were my wife I would take you away from here today. Jack is way too self-absorbed. I've always thought so. He takes no responsibility for you as if he thinks you can live on mulberry leaves like a silkworm. Where is that man's sense of duty?"

"He does his best," she said, giving him back the gloves, keeping her hands warm under the blanket, resigned now to knowing her father will never increase her allowance until Jack supports her. He called out to the chauffeur to take them back. Jinnie and Connie, seated behind them, filled the awkward silence with chatter comparing their wonderful Menton to Ospedaletti: "How lovely this view is but wait until you see ours. You must come soon, and stay with us, Katherine."

Back at the Casetta, her father's exuberance returned. He admired the garden and picked a bouquet of daisies and one lily and gave them to Katherine. The invitation to move to Menton was repeated. Ida was invited, too.

Before leaving, he said, "I cannot tell you what to do, Kass, I never could, but I do hope you accept Connie and Jinnie's invitation and leave here very soon. This is a dangerous place for you and the sooner you get away the better. If there is anything I can do, please write me."

"You've done more than enough, Pa."

He took her in his arms, "My precious. Get better you little wonder. You're your mother all over again."

Katherine promised the ladies she would visit in the spring and, after waving them all off, she admired her father's bouquet that she put in a vase and displayed next to his gift of five Three Castle cigarettes, which he had left on her writing table. She had been touched by his unusual affection toward her. Now a widower perhaps he had a better understanding of loneliness and the longing for an absent loved one.

COME THE END OF NOVEMBER, she hurried to get a letter off to Jack before the post office closed. She picked up her pen and wrote:

Jack you will find this hard to believe but I have gained five pounds by daily eating bowls of macaroni soaked in butter and fresh vegetables and fruit. I weighed myself on the drugstore scale as I do every few weeks and I have gone from 97 to 102 pounds. Isn't that wonderful? It bodes well for our future at the Heron. Also, the tonic has had a most superb effect. Très potent! She looked over at Dr. Sorapure's bottle. *Strongly effective. Even on stormy nights.*

Her mood shifted when she felt her silent, empty room and, suddenly weakened by sadness and yearning, wrote, *I do wish you were here, Jack. I don' t know how long I can continue on this journey alone.*

Her eyes filled with tears as she walked out into the garden to be consoled by the late- blooming flowers and to breathe in the sweet air. The unpredictable sea was now calm, not even a wind to dry her cheeks.

She left Jack's letter on the hall table for LM to post and climbed upstairs reciting the poem she'd written when she and Jack had been together in Bandol:

We might be fifty, we might be five
So snug so compact, so wise are we!
Under the kitchen table leg
My knee is pressing against his knee.

10

December 1919

The New Husband

Someone came to me and said
Forget, forget that you've been wed.
Who's your man to leave you be
Ill and cold in a far country?
Who's the husband—who's the stone
Could leave a child like you alone?
The New Husband—KM

At midnight on the first of December, gale-force winds shook the Casetta's foundation. Katherine gripped onto the bedpost in fear of being dragged out into the turbulent sea where not even Dr. Sorapure's tincture would save her from being sucked into the abyss.

By morning, the storm had passed and the grateful sea returned to its calm self. Katherine put on her Jaeger coat and drew her chair to the window to look out on the calm, blue Mediterranean gilded over by a wide, wide pale yellow sky.

If one were not alone here, she thought, then the cold would not matter. Ospedaletti is so simple and unfashionable that no parasitic life can exist as there is nothing for the greedy to feed upon. This is quite the most beautiful place I've ever been, even more beautiful than Bandol but there Jack was with me. If he were here now to see this beauty he would give up London, give up *The Athenaeum,* and return to his own writing. Together, here, we could accomplish so much.

* * *

A FORTNIGHT LATER, as promised, Dr. Ansaldi examined Katherine a second time. After he left, she paced across the veranda. All lies. Fever and melancholy and rage, how well they feed each other, she thought, bringing her cold hands up to her flushed cheeks, and how well I know the signs. Afraid of a chill, she returned inside hoping by writing to Jack she'd gain control over the dark mood coming over her.

She dipped the dry pen into the inkwell and wrote:

Dr. Ansaldi was here today and I will not be cured in two years. In truth, I will never be cured. Do you hear me, Jack? There will be no Heron for us. Never. The truth is that my lungs are in the same or worse condition than before I left London. Nothing has changed for us. The other truth remains the same. You cannot leave the A. to attend to your invalid wife and I would die if I came to London.

Ansaldi is a charlatan. After groping me with his stethoscope and beating me up with his hammer, he told me emphatically that I could not winter in England next year or the year after, that I must have sun and warmth. Can you imagine the polite smile with which I listened?

I asked him if it was consumption that brought on the melancholia that not even Dr. Sorapure's tincture could keep at bay. He said, "Yes, melancholia is part toxin poisoning from your disease, but also because you are alone wiz nobody near to love and 'sherish' you. Where is your husband, Fräulein?"

She put down the pen. The Terra Cotta stove was steaming but the chill deep within her could not be melted by fever or fire. Where was the shawl that Jack had promised? The shawl he had bought for her to wrap around her shoulders until he could keep her warm himself. He said he'd sent it weeks ago. Where was it?

She wiped the leaking nib across her brass pen wiper in the shape of a pig with threaded hairs on its back, her father's gift before she left Wellington and wrote:

Why don't I adopt a baby boy? A nurse could care for us both at the same cost, she wrote. *Would you mind if I did that, Jack? Of course I would be responsible for all the costs.*

I can't be left on my own like this ever again. I haven't written any stories since I left London. I have no one to talk to, no one to hold me. But if there was an adopted child for me to cherish and play with I could live alone.

Writing to Jack had not calmed her. The dark mood she'd tried to hold at bay was pressing on her, pushing her toward the abyss but she kept writing.

It is loneliness that is weakening my heart and crushing my breath. You only live with me in the future when we will have our fairy-tale house, The Heron. It's cruel to make such plans as they will never come to be. It's false of you to pretend. You must face the truth that I will never be well enough to live with you in England. We must make other arrangements. Yes there must be future plans but not built on fantasies. Truth between us is what is needed now.

If I have to spend next winter abroad, I can't spend it alone. And no, Jack, I don't want you to quit the A, borrow money from my father and come here to replace Ida to care for your invalid wife. It's not in your character to be a caregiver. It would destroy us.

Goodbye darling, I am ever your own . . .

She reached for a sheet of blank stationery:

Someone came to me and said
Forget, forget that you've been wed . . . .

Her pen began to scratch across the paper as more verses rushed forward:

I had received that very day
A letter from the other to say
That in six months—he hoped—no longer
I would be so much better and stronger
That he could close his books and come
With radiant looks to bear me home.

The only other sound besides the scratching pen was the waves rubbing against the rocks below her window. As she hurriedly wrote more verses, the gurgling in her lungs, the gnawing ache in her hips, and the loud beating of her heart became silent, even her loneliness seemed to hush:

Ha! Ha! Six months, six weeks, six hours
Among these glittering palms and flowers . . .

She stopped and looked up thinking she heard footsteps but no one was there:

So I became the stranger's bride
And every moment however fast
It flies—we live as 'twere our last!

Exhausted, she put down her pen. The verses that had been shifting in her mind ever since her father's visit now put to paper.

She enclosed the poem in Jack's letter, requesting that he put it safely into her deposit box until she had time to review it before publication. After leaving the envelope on the hallway table for LM to post, she went upstairs to bed.

The following morning LM found Katherine trembling uncontrollably under heavy woolen bedcovers. She rasped, "Find me a doctor! But not those charlatans, Ansaldi and Bobone. A real doctor, not an idiot. Or send me to the Devil."

Just then the doorbell clanged and LM ran downstairs. It was Ellen Turner, one of many wealthy Englishwomen who had taken up residence in San Remo and occasionally dropped in on Katherine out of curiosity to see how a famous writer lived. After LM told her how sick Katherine was, she rushed off, returning with her own physician.

"Your left lung is seriously diseased with tuberculosis. Your right lung is quiescent," said Dr. Foster, after carefully packing away his tools in Katherine's bedroom. "But there is good news, Mrs. Murry. It's not galloping consumption that gave you a high fever. You have a mild case of bronchial pneumonia and can be cured with bed rest."

She whispered hoarsely, "How do you know tuberculosis didn't cause my fever?"

"The stethoscope. Bronchial pneumonia clogs the airways of your lungs. A quite different sound than the crackling of active tuberculosis. Once I knew this, it was simply a matter of tapping your lungs until I found the infection, which was when you cried out. An infected lung is filled with pus and painful. Fortunately only one lung has a bacteria infection."

"I'm not dying?"

"No, certainly not, though you probably feel like you are." He looked down at his notes. "Your complaints were the symptoms of pneumonia or influenza. If you stay in bed, stay warm, drink hot liquids, and eat well you'll get better. I wish there was something I could give you but there is no prescription yet that can kill bacteria. At least not yet." He smiled at the pack of Abdullah's on her bed table. "Mrs. Murry, you smoke my favorite brand. I haven't seen those for a while."

He turned to LM hovering by the door, "It would be a good idea to move Mrs. Murry downstairs. She must stay in bed until she's out of danger, and this room is chilly." Before departing, he took her hand and while he checked her pulse looked into her eyes. "In a week or so you will feel much better. I promise."

MR. VINCE CAME and with a neighbor's help they put Katherine's writing table in the kitchen to make room for her bed in the sitting room.

Four days later her temperature dropped. Her body had not given up on her; it wasn't her enemy; she would revive; she would have more time to write, to continue her work. She heard LM puttering in the kitchen and called out for a cup of tea with breakfast.

"I was saving these until you felt better," said LM, handing her a packet of letters. "There's a wire from Jack and several letters from friends. You see, my dear Katie, you are not alone. And you always have me, too." She set the tea tray in Katherine's lap.

"Please let Mr. Vince know that we would like to have the bed put back upstairs so I can have my writing room back."

"I don't know if that's wise. Your fever just broke—"

"Ida, do as I ask . . . please." LM shook her head and went back to the kitchen.

Katherine first opened Jack's wire:

8 December 1919: WILL COME FOR WEEK OF XMAS.
STOP. LETTER EXPLAINS. STOP. JACK

"Oh no!" she called out. Now look what I've done. I should never have sent that letter and that poem. I'm so sorry, Jack.

"Ida!" she shouted. "Bring me my pen and writing paper. Why didn't you give this to me earlier?"

She asked him to remember when they lived with D.H. Lawrence and he had one of his tuberculosis "rages" brought on by fever. She'd had a fever when she wrote him and was afraid it was galloping consumption, after what Dr. Ansaldi had told her. But she wasn't afraid anymore. It had turned out to be a mild case of pneumonia. Not to worry. LM was taking care of her.

She ended with:

I've driven you to this. I won't be such a vampire again. We must stick to our plan. In May I shall be better. All will be different. Above all there is no need for you to come now. DON'T COME; DON'T COME.

Worried he wouldn't get her letter in time she sent a wire:

9 December, 1919: IMPLORE YOU NOT TO. STOP.
WRITTEN. STOP. DISMISS IDEA IMMEDIATELY. STOP.
GREATEST POSSIBLE MISTAKE. STOP. BETTER TODAY.

Afraid he wouldn't believe her she wired again:

10 December 1919: URGE YOU MOST EARNESTLY NOT
TO COME. STOP.
UTTERLY UNNECESSARY. STOP. ENTREAT YOU TO WAIT
TILL MAY. STOP. LETTER SENT EXPLAINING.

Four days passed before Jack's letter arrived with his explanation. LM brought it upstairs to Katherine. Her bed had been restored to its proper place and she was resting. She tore it open:

12 December, 1919

My own darling,

I got your Thursday letter and the verses called "The New Husband." I've wired you today to say I'm coming out for Christmas. I feel there is not much more I can say.

I don't think that at any time I've had a bigger blow than that letter and these verses—more like a snake with a terrible sting.

Her heart was beating so fast she had to put down her pen and rest her head on the pillows before she could go on.

She waited until LM brought the tea tray and then read Jack's entire letter. It was terrible—half was an account of what she had done to him and the other half about his debts. She forced herself to get out of bed and go downstairs to her writing table. A log sputtered in the Terra Cotta. She added another one before sitting down. She decided to respond to one paragraph at a time otherwise it was too overwhelming.

After accusing her of being a snake he said:

But it's kind of you to tell me you have those feelings: far better, for me anyhow, than keeping them from me. You have too great a burden to bear; you can't carry it. Whether I can manage mine, I don't know. We'll see when I get out to you.

She replied:

However ill I am, you are more ill. However weak I am you are weaker—less able to bear things. You make me out so cruel that . . . I feel you can't love me in the least—a snake I am not. Are you fair in punishing me so horribly? I will not receive your dreadful accusations into my soul for they would kill me.

She read his next paragraph:

What is certain is this can't go on—something must change. My faith at present is that my coming out for a little while will put you right. But I don't see why it should. I feel that everything depends upon me; that I have to do something quite definite, very quickly. But I don't know what it is . . . I wish to God I were a man. Somehow I seem to have grown up, gone bald even, without ever becoming a man; and I find it terribly hard to master a situation.

She replied:

The truth is that until I was ill you were never called upon 'to play the man' to this extent—and it's not your role. When you once told me that you ought to be kept, you spoke the truth. I feel it. Ever since my illness this crisis I suppose has been impending, when suddenly in an agony I should turn all woman and lean on you. Now it's happened. The crisis is over—You must feel that. It won't return. It's over for good. I will not lean on you again.

She stopped to watch the sputtering fire before picking up his letter again to read:

At present I'm trying to clear up the remains of last year's debts. Until they are cleared I shall stick to the A. That's callous, I suppose, but I can't help it. You know my position as a previous bankrupt. I dare not leave our debts unpaid. Once we're straight—and if things were to go moderately well I shall be straight by April—I'll do anything. But I know that to cut with little money coming in and heavy debts would mean inevitable disaster.

I had no idea, she thought, before picking up her pen:

Jack, why have you kept me in the dark? Have your creditors come down on you? What are these terrible debts? I must be told them. You hint at them and then say I lack sympathy. You're not a pauper. You have £800 a year and you only contribute to my keep—not more than £50 a year at most. You write as though there were me to be provided for, yourself, and all to be done on something like £300. I know you have paid my doctor's bills and that my illness has cost you a great deal. IT WILL COST YOU NO MORE. *I cannot take any more money from you ever and as soon as I am well I shall work to make a good deal more so that you have to pay less. But your letter frightens me for you—I think you have allowed this idea of money to take too great a hold on your brain.*

And yes I know your previous position as a bankrupt. Need I remind you that we used my allowance to pay those debts.

Reading his next paragraph she felt his anger replaced by resignation.

If I felt certain that my being there would really make things right until May, then nothing would matter. But now I can't pretend to a certainty I don't feel. We just have to leave it and see.

Her falling tears stained the ink of his letter. She brushed her tears aside.

Why must he wrench my heart? No, I will not feel sorry for him. Not this time. Angrily, she underlined the *I*'s in his letter and asked herself how anyone could write a letter with fifty-five *I*'s. He'd piled delicate agony after delicate agony as if he was writing a tragedy, documenting himself as the martyred hero for future publication, after she was gone.

She thought about how to end her letter. What did she really want from him? There was no clear answer. But what she did know was that without Jack, she had no one to love. A barren, lonely life was unlivable. She wouldn't be able to bear the emptiness. Faced with this truth she wrote:

Let us bury the past—and go on and recover—We shall. Our only chance now is not to lose Hope but to go on and not give each other up. Your devoted—yours eternally, Your wife.

She wanted to believe what she wrote would make a difference, that their marriage could be saved, but she couldn't shake the fear that something was deeply wrong between them and it might be irreparable no matter how hard she clung to him.

She scribbled onto the envelope of the letter he had sent, *You have killed something within me and I no longer fear death.* She enfolded his letter and put it in her drawer to be filed later with the others. Her letter she sent to the post office with LM hoping it would arrive before he left London but maybe it was better if he did come after all.

Jack did not respond to her first telegram but after receiving the second one he wrote a short letter:

It's no use you know: I've made up my mind to come.

He went on to say that he bitterly regretted what he had written on 12 December and asked her to *Forget it, Burn it. It's got nothing to do with me, but only with a me that was harassed and inclined for a moment to throw up the sponge. But once the decision was taken, I've been a changed man. I've thought of nothing but the sheer happiness of being with you.*

11

I Shot the ALBATROSS

And a good south wind sprung up behind;
The Albatross did follow,
And every day, for food or play,
Came to the mariners' hollo!

In mist or cloud, on mast or shroud,
It perch'd for vespers nine;
Whiles all the night, through fog-smoke white,
Glimmer'd the white Moon-shine.

"God save thee, ancient Mariner,
From the fiends, that plague thee thus! —
Why look'st thou so?" — With my cross-bow
I shot the ALBATROSS.

The Rime of the Ancient Mariner
—Samuel Taylor Coleridge

THE HOUSE WAS TOO SMALL for the three of them. LM slept in nearby San Remo at the house of a new friend she had made on her shopping excursions. In her absence, a maid was found by Dr. Foster after he squashed the rumors in the village that the Casetta was a dark, foreboding house of contagion, inhabited by two women, one a giant and the other a consumptive.

One evening a storm kept LM at the Casetta and she cooked a special dinner from one of Katherine's recipes. Even Katherine thought she did an admirable job and hoped Jack might say something kind. But he had been suffering all day from neuralgia, and couldn't see past the shooting pain in his face and hands.

"Oh you have no idea how intolerable this is, I am in agony," he cried out at the table. LM rolled her eyes at Katherine as if to say how he could possibly not know that Katherine was an expert on agony.

Katherine said, "Let's go sit by the Terra Cotta and play Demon. That will help you forget and it will be warmer for all of us."

"You have no sympathy. Neuralgia is extremely painful and no card game is going to distract me from it," he said sinking his head into his hands and moaning.

"I'm just trying to help you feel better. I know for myself that distractions relieve pain. Pain only becomes unbearable when one has no escape. You'll see what I mean when we play."

LM got up to do the dishes. "No Jones, please play with us. As I recall you once played Demon with Jack and beat him to his great discontent. He wanted to prove to us that he could win by being thoughtful and therefore was indecisive with his moves, and you beat him with your spontaneous quick plays and sheer boldness. Let's see if you can take him on again tonight and still be victorious."

"That's unfair Katherine of you to tease," said Jack. "You know I can't take on any such challenge when I'm ill."

"Oh come on, Jack, at least try." She and LM exchanged smiles.

Katherine and LM set out the three decks of cards and unwillingly Jack played. He lost every game and finally threw in his cards and retired to the spare bedroom.

LM slipped into Katherine's bedroom after she heard Jack's snore and arranged her blankets and pillow in the customary corner easily going back to sleep.

Katherine didn't want Jack knowing LM slept in her room. She didn't like to admit to him or anyone else, including herself, how much she now relied on LM for everything. Lying in bed, listening to LM settle down in her bedroll, she reflected on one major difference between her two caregivers. LM ran to her when she coughed, offering a glass of water or a clean handkerchief; Jack found excuses to leave the room. LM had an overzealous curiosity to know her symptoms every day; Jack never asked about her health or discussed her illness, not even naming it, as if it was a taboo subject between them. She smiled to herself as she slipped off to sleep thinking perhaps there was no perfect caregiver.

The pleasurable hours during Jack's visit were when she pretended not to be ill. On those days, seated cross-legged on the floor like children, they rebuilt their life together. As steam wafted from the Terra Cotta sizzling with burning logs, Jack sketched the Heron's floor plan outlining the library and Katherine's writing room. In this dollhouse of their shared illusion, she arranged the china, furniture and knickknacks they'd both been collecting for their future life together—once she was well.

They sat up late into the nights discussing Dostoevsky, Chekhov and other writers and they discussed each others work and what they wanted to accomplish in the coming year. Jack was writing notes for a book on the style of writing and she planned to write many stories and start her novel again. She couldn't have this kind of discourse with anyone in Ospedaletti other than when she imagined Virginia joining her for chamomile tea.

Dr. Foster had allowed Jack to take her on short walks because her lungs were considerably better and they'd visited the antique and curio shops. But on the afternoon Jack departed for London, sixteen days after he'd arrived, Katherine returned to her bed exhausted from playing the role of a strong woman just to keep Jack at ease. Honesty should be prized above everything but afraid of losing him, she'd joined in the masquerade and pretended that her illness wasn't that serious. Their relationship was now based on a lie and in her darkest hours she knew their love would not survive.

On one of those bad nights, she watched from her bed as the sun became shrouded in dark clouds, the thunder raged, lightning struck, and the wind bit down hard on the roof, carrying off some of its tiles.

The crashing of the surf against the rocks made sleep impossible. She locked the windows, drew the heavy curtains against the siege and hid under the eiderdown.

When she awoke the next morning she was relieved she could lift her hands because before dawn she had awoken to someone crying out for her but she couldn't help. Her legs and arms were bound in ropes. Her mouth gagged.

Stretching out on her bed in the sunlight she knew it had only been a dream, but the physical sensation of being entrapped, unable to save someone calling for her help, haunted her throughout the following days as she kept asking herself who needed to be saved? Who tied me down and then let me go? Or worse, I am going mad.

The melancholy she had kept at bay while Jack was there now washed over her and, too weak to resist she fell over the precipice into even darker moods. She knew the reason.

The only writing she accomplished was the weekly novel-reviews for *The Athenaeum*. That required hours of reading, and except for a few, should never have been published. She decided that reading for the vast majority—for the reading public—was not a passion but a pastime, and writing, for the majority number of modern authors, was a pastime and not a passion. A reprieve came when Kot sent her more translations of Chekhov's notebooks for her to edit. In the packet was also Kot's personal letter encouraging her to be hopeful. He was one of the few who still believed in her.

Chekhov's writings also encouraged her. In spite of his consumption, as a doctor he continued to administer to the sick, and as a writer he continued to write and publish his work. Chekhov quoted from Daudet of whom she was also reading:

"Why are thy songs so short?" a bird was once asked. *"Is it because thou art short of breath?"*

The bird answered, *"I have very many songs and I should like to sing them all."*

That, she thought, would have been Chekhov's response and hers, too.

In his notebooks, Chekhov gave a simple diagnosis of his own illness. If there was no fever or cough and, if one continued to gain weight, the tuberculosis was quiescent. Chekhov also said it was not a death warrant if there were bloodstains on your handkerchief, so she stopped checking every time she coughed. He coughed up blood for years before he died and it never stopped his work. He was determined to go on while he could, to value every living hour regardless of his fate. Yes, she thought, out of this nettle, danger, we pluck this flower, safety.

And that's why I should stop these novel-reviews for Jack's paper. They drain what spirit I have. So what if Lytton Strachey said my column was well written or Jack said that the paper would lose subscribers if I stopped. What about my own work that I have to push aside? Is this what I want to be remembered for? A reviewer of novels. Heavens, no. I only do it for the money and for Jack. My own work I should be making income with, far better income than these measly checks from *The Athenaeum.*

She picked up her pen and wrote in her journal:

Can I not make myself felt as a real personal force? I have had experience unknown to others. Surely I do know more than other people. I have suffered more, endured more. I know how they long to be happy and how precious is an atmosphere that is loving, a climate that is not frightening. I must cultivate my garden and do it now. I am the one who needs saving and only I can do it.

One morning, excited to have ventured to the village drugstore on her own, without LM and without her cane, she weighed herself and saw another pound added. With a lilt in her step she headed back to the Casetta but stopped when an idea for a new story filled her thoughts. Without her notebook to scrawl it down, she hurried home.

At her writing table she wrote a quick sketch about a young, courageous woman who has just found out she's pregnant. Before she'd been afraid but now that it was certain she felt quite joyous, felt part of the stream of life. She knew it would be difficult but had the conviction to see it though. But she knew her boyfriend, Roy, wouldn't feel the same. Oh yes, he'd told her enough times he'd marry her if she'd have him, but she knew he didn't mean it. She decided not to tell him. The doctor agreed to lie for her and tells Roy that she's just tired and needs a stay at the seaside. Yes she can eat caviar sandwiches and drink champagne—the danger has passed.

Now that she was writing again, Katherine asked to be left on her own. LM made plans for an excursion to San Remo, promising to return that evening but, at the last minute she hesitated. Katherine had to push her out the door, saying, "Don't worry. I'll be fine."

She worked at her writing table all afternoon on her new story, and had just written its title sheet "Last Spring," when she became conscious of her heart's loud thumping. She pressed her hand against her chest to slow it down. Her eyes searched the room for the brandy. Upstairs. She pulled herself out of the chair, gasped for air and rasped, "Jones! The brandy."

She reached the staircase. Her heart raced ahead. She felt herself falling over the abyss.

She awoke to a blurred face looking down at her. She whispered, "Jones?"

She didn't know why she was on the floor but couldn't move. Her heart ached more than her back. Yes, she thought, my heart.

She felt herself being scooped off the floor and strong, sturdy arms carried her upstairs laying her on the bed. Covers gently pulled over her, she was tucked in. "Mother, is that you?"

"Everything's going to be all right. Sleep, my dearest."

"Please don't go," she called out as the gentle hand cooling her brow was removed.

"I must go to the village to telephone Dr. Foster in San Remo."

"Why? What happened?" she said, trying to raise her head but had no strength.

"You fainted. Now rest. I'll be right back."

"Please don't leave me alone. Am I dying?"

"Heavens, no." LM poured a glass of brandy and held up Katherine's head so she might take a sip.

"My feet are so cold."

"I'll fetch your hot-water bottles," said LM, putting down the empty glass. Katherine grabbed her hand.

"I promise, Katie, I'll be right back."

She drifted off, awoke to her feet being gently massaged. Normally she resented LM touching her but now it gave her comfort. LM placed her feet over the hot-water bottles. "Thank you, Jones. I don't thank you enough, do I? What would have happened if you hadn't come home? I don't know why you stay with someone who treats you so cruelly. I've been a fiend."

"It's the illness that makes you act like that. I don't take it personally. And what with these storms every night and not being able to sleep, they bring on those dark moods. Why you just haven't been yourself. Can I call Doctor Foster now?"

"No! Please! I'd like another brandy and have one yourself. It must have been a fright for you, too."

"Let me just go downstairs to fire up the Terra Cotta and get some heat up here. The fire must have gone out after you fainted. Then I'll join you for a glass."

Jones only wants the best for me, she thought. Like Coleridge's Albatross who *every day for food or play* loyally followed the Ancient Mariner's ship. And the Mariner shot him down. I will suffer like the Mariner if I don't change my thoughtless ways. If not for Jones, I'd still be lying on that floor and soon dead if no one found me.

LM joined her under the covers like they used to do in school and after their brandies Katherine drifted off to sleep.

In the early morning light, she awoke. LM must have gotten up earlier to light the fire and bring the tea as she'd done at school. Katherine smiled, remembering when she first asked LM to be her friend at Queen's College.

SHE WASN'T HER FIRST CHOICE. She made other school friends and only spoke with Ida, when they practiced their instruments in the music room. She found her to be a sullen, slow-thinking girl and wondered how she'd ever managed to win the highly competitive President's Scholar award that helped pay the Queen's College tuition.

Ida was born in England, but was raised in Rhodesia, where her father was a doctor. When the family returned to London, she and her sister May attended Queen's College as day students. Their home was nearby. The two sisters would walk to school together. Ida's sister, crippled from polio, would lean against her for support.

At fourteen Ida's mother fell suddenly ill with typhoid fever. Ida nursed her through increasing stages of delirium and fever until her agonizing death a month later. Immediately after the funeral, Dr. Baker, her father, locked up the house and took May and their brother to live in their country home. He said he couldn't bear staying in London where memories of his loving wife were too vivid. He arranged to have Ida moved into Queen's College as a boarding student. Inconsolable, she withdrew from her school friends and kept to herself. Then she met Katherine who was just arriving from New Zealand.

One afternoon coming back from class, Katherine found Ida in her room, reading a poem she had left out on the bedside table. Ida jumped when she came in and quickly put down the paper.

"Sorry I came to deliver a letter and—"

"It's all right. I like to have my poetry read."

"You wrote this?"

"Yes."

"It's very good."

"Thank you. Are you a poet, too?"

"Heavens no. I can't write anything but I very much appreciate those that do."

After that, Ida would visit Katherine in her room in the evenings. They sat together on the floor while Katherine read. Ida was an uncritical listener.

But she wasn't always so shy and acquiescent. They were both on the debating team and Ida was very good at arguing a case and often won the debates, even against Katherine who was an excellent debater and also not accustomed to losing.

Queens College girls took chaperoned walks in Regents Park and followed the strictly enforced rule of staying in a crocodile line, which meant you were not to break out of line or you'd get in trouble.

One day on their walk, Katherine was feeling those deep-seated emotions that came upon her when she was in Nature, and wanted desperately to run freely under the trees. She was surprised to see the usually compliant Ida chasing leaves falling from a giant oak, shaken by a sudden gust of wind. As the gilded autumn leaves fell, she reached out for them with her large clumsy hands and gently held them to her breast. She saw Katherine watching her and smiled for the first time that Katherine could remember. She hadn't expected Ida to share her joy in the fleeting beauty of Nature.

Katherine waved to Ida to join her when the girls stopped to rest on park benches. Ida hesitated. "Come on, silly. Come and sit with me." Ida sat down, still holding the captured leaves.

"Let's be friends," said Katherine.

Ida shrunk back and then said with dignity, "Friends don't happen just by saying it, Katie. Friendship is a very serious matter. Friends are something you become in time through loyalty and consideration."

The crocodile line was reassembled for the march back to school and Katherine didn't mention her request again, feeling rather slighted by Ida's response. Several students had already found her too bold with her emotions and excused her strange behavior by calling her the Little Colonialist from New Zealand. But she had thought Ida would have welcomed her friendship.

She waited until she was seated across from Ida during afternoon tea before saying, "Well now that we've taken a walk together and shared a pot of tea, can we be considered friends?"

Ida giggled. Then reached for Katherine's small hand, covered her large hand over it and said, "Yes, friends. Friends forever!"

* * *

LM BROUGHT IN the morning tray. Late, but Katherine bit her tongue rather than complain. LM puffed up the pillows and helped Katherine sit up.

She watched the dark clouds release their own tears that streamed down her window. Hearing Dr. Foster climbing the stairs, she dried her tears on her handkerchief and sat up, she greeted him with a smile as he arrived out of breath.

After his examination he sat down on the bed and took her wrist in his hand to check her pulse against his pocket watch. "Your heartbeat is still weak."

"I'm not surprised. It's exhausted. I don't ever want to hear my heart thump like that ever again. You know, I was afraid I was dying."

"People often say heart palpitations feel like that. To us doctors we see them as dire warnings to our patients to take better care. Your attack was brought on by acute nervous exhaustion. The truth is, Mrs. Murry, you're too isolated here and these winter storms are too harsh on a woman in your weak condition. You've fought a good fight but you don't have much strength left. You need people around you who care about you. Ida can't do it all. She's worn-out too and could become ill herself."

"But didn't you say I wasn't contagious?"

"Yes, and if she hasn't been infected already there's little chance of it but there are other diseases besides consumption."

"I am well aware of that Doctor."

"How long has Ida been in your service?"

Katherine laughed. "She's not in my service. We've been friends since our school days sixteen years ago. After I was diagnosed a consumptive, she moved in with my husband and me as my companion and housekeeper. That was a year ago. Even before then she took care of me when I was ill, but never as my servant."

"You are quite fortunate. There are not many Griselda's in this world willing to dedicate their lives to serving others without financial reward."

"Ah, you've read Chaucer."

He smiled. "Yes, but a very long time ago." He pulled up a chair next to her bed. "Mrs. Murry. You need to seriously consider moving to some place where the weather is more moderate and where you can receive excellent care."

"Do you mean a nursing home, Doctor?"

"Yes, I do. You must have complete rest until your heart is stronger."

"A tuberculosis clinic?"

"No, it needn't be. For now I'm not worried about your lungs. It's your heart that's at risk."

After he left, Katherine wrote a letter to Connie and Jinnie in Menton asking for their help. A few days later she received their response. L'Hermitage, a nursing home in Menton, had a room available. It wasn't too expensive and it was very near their own home, Villa Flora. And there was a position for Ida in another nursing home nearby that would help defray expenses. Ida could stay with them at Villa Flora and once Katherine was feeling better she could join them.

In the same post was a letter from her sister, Chaddie, with news that upon their father's return to Wellington, he'd married Laura Kate Bright, their mother's best friend. She wondered why he hadn't spoken of his intentions during his visit. He must have known his plans then. She wasn't surprised at his marrying again. Since her mother's death the previous year, he had been miserable living alone. She expected the same of Jack. Once she was gone he too would quickly find someone else to take care of him.

She envisioned Laura standing on the Wellington dock as the ship pulled in and as he stepped off the gangplank she could feel the warmth and safety of his arms embracing her.

She scribbled down a sketch on a similar dock. But it would be the wife returning and the impatient husband waiting on the dock. The ship delayed because . . . .

* * *

AFTER DR. FOSTER'S NEXT EXAMINATION, he said, "Your pulse is still weak. Have you thought more about what I said about leaving Ospedaletti?"

"Yes, I have. My cousin has found me a nursing home in Menton. She and her companion reside in a villa nearby."

"Excellent. You're a decisive woman. With Ida and your cousin there to take care of you, and the professional care of a nursing home I think you will see a full recovery."

"A full recovery, Doctor? My lungs, too?"

He hesitated. "I don't believe in giving my patients false hopes. As you well know, there is no cure yet for tuberculosis but, just like there is no drug for pneumonia. Until then, my job is to encourage you to leave here and your job is to rest until your heart regains its strength."

SHE'D AVOIDED TELLING JACK about her palpitation attack or her plan to leave Ospedaletti as soon as her heart was strong enough to travel. She wanted to avoid what happened the last time when she confessed the true state of her health and emotions and he jumped on his white horse to rescue her. She picked up her pen after Dr. Foster left and carefully considered before writing:

Now, my precious, please forgive what I am going to say. And do not think you came here all for nothing or anything dreadful like that—It's just my peculiar fate at present which won't leave me—I must tell you, but there is no action for you to take—nothing for you to worry about in the very slightest. I don't ask your help or anything & God forbid I should make you work harder. Just go on as you are and I shall manage what I have to manage.

She told him about the nursing home in Menton and that LM would be traveling with her. And then she went on to explain briefly what happened after he left:

It is not feasible to believe—She was away one day this week—I was alone. It was evening. I had a heart attack in my room & you see there was no one to call . . . Now don't think that means I regret you are not here now. It does not—All it means is that I must not be alone.

12

Griselda

There is no thing, and so God my soul save,
That you may like displeasing unto me;
I do not wish a single thing to have,
Nor dread a thing to lose, save only ye;
This will is in my heart and aye shall be,
Nor length of time nor death may this deface,
Nor turn my passion to another place.
Canterbury Tales—Geoffrey Chaucer

THE MONDAY BEFORE THEIR DEPARTURE, at the end of January, a postal strike was announced, which would delay mail between Italy and Britain. Italy was demonstrating its resentment against the Allies for not giving them what they asked for at Versailles—the Adriatic Coastline—and for not treating the Italian Prime Minster with respect during the treaty negotiations. Italians started taunting English tourists in the streets.

The morning of the strike LM was sneered at on her return from the market by several Italian men yelling, "You'd better pack up your traps and go. We don't want any more of you English here. We're going to clear you out."

If only they knew how soon and with what delight Katherine accepted their orders to 'pack up your traps and go' and with what great anticipation she planned her exodus. What she couldn't anticipate is how Jack would respond to her leaving Ospedaletti before May. That is not what they'd planned together.

In bed that night she thought about the letter she'd carefully crafted to Jack about her heart attack and her pending departure. It made her anxious that she'd censored her true feelings so that he might not suffer for her sake. But why should she have to suffer alone? Unable to sleep, she propped her blond wood writing case on her lap and took a pen from its compartment and wrote what she'd held back from writing to Jack: *These are the worst days of my whole life.*

She blew out the gaslight and sank into her pillows hoping to escape into sleep. But an idea took hold of her and as her mind developed it into a story, she heard characters speak and saw details come into view until the night turned into daylight.

The moment she heard LM stirring, she called out, "Jones, bring me my morning tea," forgetting to add "please."

Throughout the day she wrote on her writing case in bed, stopping only when LM brought the afternoon tea and egg sandwiches and pushed the work aside, insisting that Katherine eat. Late that night she crossed out *The Exile* on the cover sheet and changed it to *The Man Without a Temperament.* The story was now about the husband and not the wife. She placed the title sheet on top of a stack of written pages that told the story of a husband who took a two-year leave of absence from his profession to go into seclusion with his wife in a hotel in southern France while she recuperated from a severe illness. The wife knows she's a burden and tries not to ask him to do things for her, but her illness has made her an invalid and needy of his care. The husband can't accept the pale, emaciated woman she has become and turns away from her to dwell in the past, when she was his beautiful, passionate wife. The other hotel guests find his trance-like state inhuman and his distant eyes reptilian. The children are afraid of him. Only the wife forgives his lack of compassion.

Exhausted from her work, Katherine tried to sleep but the stormy night shook the Casetta and the sea howled. She searched for a match and relit the gaslight to write in her journal notebook:

I have made it a rule of my life never to regret and never to look back. Regret is an appalling waste of energy, and no one who intends to become a writer can afford to indulge in it. You can't get it into shape; you can't build on it; it's only good for wallowing in.

She wrote this down to keep herself from slipping into the dark pool of her own regrets that led down into the secret life she had tried vigilantly to avoid but when she closed her eyes again . . .

She found herself standing in front of the familiar Bavarian pension, her hand on the doorknob . . . "Don't open that door!" she warned. Her stomach cramped. Her hands felt the damp sticky sheets. She screamed out, "No!"

LM heard Katherine screaming and came running to her bedside and, as she had so often done before, held her, rocking her until she stopped shaking and the night terror slipped away, forgotten.

Katherine awoke to LM bringing in her morning tray of tea and toast with jam. "I can't bear another day in bed. If it's warm enough outside I want to spend it on the veranda finishing my story. Don't look at me like that. Get me my cane."

"Didn't Dr. Foster tell you to stay in bed?"

"I didn't say I was going for a walk. I promise to take tiny careful steps."

She sat in the basket chair until a brisk wind forced her indoors. At her writing table, next to the warmth of the crackling Terra Cotta, she wrote the story's end.

As tired as she felt, she refilled her pen in the inkpot, wiped it against the hairs of the little brass pig standing on her tabletop and wrote to Jack:

I am sending to Arts and Letters by post registered this day a story called "The Man Without a Temperament." The MS I send is positively my only copy.

She had decided if A&L didn't want it, she would ask them to send the MS to Jack. If they did want it then send original MS and the proofs to Jack so he could compare them and correct any errors before the story went to print.

She asked Jack to have the original MS professionally copied at her expense as she did not have *so much as a shaving or a paring of it wherewith I could reconstruct its like. I hope I do not exaggerate. If I do—forgive me. You know a parent's feelings—they are terrible at this moment. I feel my darling goes among lions. And I think there is not a word or comma I would change or that can be changed.*

THE DOORBELL CLANGED incessantly. LM in fear of the recent Italian hostilities against the British was sleeping in her day clothes. She rushed to the window, peeked out and reported back to Katherine that there were several men stumbling around down below. Even though the night was well lit by the full moon, she could only see their silhouettes. The bell kept clanging over their raucous laughter.

"Why don't they stop?"

"Because they've nothing to fear," said Katherine. "We have no phone and even if we screamed for help the neighbors are too far away. They have us!" She whispered, "Get the gun."

LM hesitated, shaking her head violently. Katherine whispered again, "Get the gun!" LM tiptoed out of the room and returned gripping the gun stiffly in her hand. At the window she called out a warning, "Go away before I shoot." The bell stopped clanging. The men argued below. The clanging returned and the laughter. LM aimed the gun out the window. A shot rang out followed by shouts and running footsteps fading into the night.

Katherine stared in wonder at LM's large figure standing at the moonlit window in her day clothes at midnight with her finger still on the trigger. She burst out laughing.

"Katie, this is not funny. What if I've hurt someone and they're injured or dying?"

"I doubt that. But you certainly scared the living daylights out of them." She started laughing again. "Oh Jones, I do wish you could have seen yourself pull that trigger. You were fearless. You saved us from god knows what."

LM raised her empty hand to her mouth and started to giggle.

"I think we should have a glass of brandy after your heroic deed," said Katherine.

LM put down the gun timidly and poured two glasses. She joined Katherine under the eiderdown and both enjoyed a peaceful moment after the jarring noise and commotion.

Katherine broke the silence, saying, "I must confess to you that in this mad place and in the mad state I've been in, I've recently imagined you were trying to kill me. Even poisoning my milk! Seeing you defend me like this tonight, certainly makes such imaginations ridiculous."

LM again shook her head but not violently. "How could you ever think me capable of such a crime. I would rather kill myself first than harm you. What could I have possibly done to make you think otherwise?"

"You seem to relish my fevers as if they were a blessing, a sign that I'm closer to death and you're nearer to being freed from bondage. Of course you would never leave me of your own free will."

"It is difficult to know how to act around someone so critical of my every gesture, but I certainly don't relish your fevers." LM got up to pour another brandy. "Whether I'm silent, or cross, or pleasant, you scrunch up your eyes and give me that accusing look as if I'm guilty of having wronged you. No matter how hard I try to please you it comes out wrong, wrong, wrong. My only desire is to make your life as comfortable as possible so that you can continue with your work—"

LM was unaccustomed to speaking with such fluidity and had to stop and catch her breath before taking another sip of brandy and slipping back under the covers

"I'm sorry, Jones. It must not be easy to help someone who wishes she didn't need help. Dr. Foster said something that made me realize how poorly I've been treating you. He was under the impression that you were my servant. I set him straight of course but he must have his reasons for thinking so. Please forgive me. If only you would speak up when I treat you unkindly. When he found out you weren't my servant he told me I was lucky to have Griselda caring for me."

"Who is Griselda?"

Katherine smiled. "I'm sure you were introduced to Griselda in school. We all had to read and recite *Canterbury Tales*. Chaucer created Griselda. She was the king's wife. She devoted her life to him and was even willing to sacrifice her children if it pleased him.

"Everyone, but me, sees how devoted you are to me. There's no one as constant as you my dear Jones. No matter how awful I behave you stand by me, just like Griselda stood by her husband. He even brought another woman into his castle and threw Griselda out, but she never weakened in her resolve to remain faithful to him."

"How wonderful that Dr. Foster sees me as Griselda. There's no one I would rather be."

"Oh no! You misunderstand me. Chaucer was warning women not to follow the way of Griselda:

Nay, follow Echo, that holds no silence,
But answers always like a countervail;
Be not befooled, for all your innocence,
But take the upper hand and you'll prevail."

Katherine reached over and slipped her small hand under LM's much larger one. "I want you to take the upper hand. I don't want you to be my Griselda. You are not my wife, you are not my servant, but my dear loyal friend, as you promised to be when we were students."

"It's you and Chaucer that don't understand Griselda or me," said LM angrily, getting out of bed again. "I have always given myself to others. I consider it my art, my profession, as perhaps Griselda did. I grew up taking care of my sister and then my mother when she became horribly ill and after that my father needed my devotion. If I hadn't left him on his own in Rhodesia he might not have taken his own life." She gasped and turned away.

"Jones, I'm sorry I never knew that was how your father died. You never wanted to talk about it."

LM turned back to her with the same sad eyes that had first drawn Katherine to her at school. "If I wasn't taking care of you, I would be in the service of someone else. This is what I do. I am not independent like you. It's you who must try and understand me better."

"Please come back to bed. You're shivering." LM sat on the edge of the bed and Katherine put the eiderdown around her and gave her a hankie.

"I'll try to understand you," Katherine said. "But I don't believe anyone should sacrifice their own life for someone else. It isn't right that I ask that of you just so I can be free to do my work."

"But your work is far more important than anything I could possibly do. You see—it's my destiny to help you."

Silence filled the room before Katherine spoke again. "Do you dislike Jack? You're very critical of him and the way he behaves. Sometimes I imagine you would prefer he and I remain apart."

"Well Jack is JACK! Thoughtless and terribly self-absorbed, now isn't he?" said LM curtly. "He distracts you from your work and thinks his own more important. Now that's the truth." She was embarrassed by her outburst.

Katherine laughed. "Yes, that's true, but he is also my husband and I accept his faults as I ask you to accept mine. Someday, when we are all living at the Heron—"

"I thought you didn't want me to join you when you move into the country house," interrupted LM. "That's why I have never felt comfortable here at the Casetta, never even unpacked my trunk. I know any minute you'll be sending me off."

"Oh dear, I am heartless, aren't I? But consider that to be in the past. I ask you to share my present minuses in the hope that you'll always be able to share my future pluses. After what's happened these past few weeks, I couldn't imagine you not staying with me. You will come, won't you?"

"Yes, Yes. Of course, I'll come," said LM, without hesitation.

"But you must try to get along with Jack, if only on my behalf." She paused and smiled. "But feel free to beat him at Demon anytime. It does him good to be knocked around a bit."

SHE PUT HER WRITING CASE in order and packed her notebooks, ink and pens. She left her traveling companions, the laughing crocodile nutcracker and brass pig pen-wiper for last. They would all take the long taxi ride across the Italian border into Menton, France.

She sat down to reread a few of Jack's letters before putting them in the trunk. The tone of the letters disturbed her. She opened up her notebook and wrote to herself:

I know now that I can only write when I am in the Present and my writing is what matters, nothing is more important. I must write. But how to make Jack understand that if he cannot live in the Present with me then it is best that we remain separated.

Returning to her own work had filled her with new hope. It was the absence of work, the meaninglessness of her existence that had brought her to the abyss. Writing was the cure. It always had been. She opened another notebook and wrote:

An old woman sits in her living-room window knitting. She looks up at a funeral march passing her window. She's surprised and rather frightened when they stop. A man jumps out of the carriage and walks toward her door. She drops her knitting in fright thinking there must be some mistake.

The sketch completed she put down her notebook with a sigh, confident she would continue with it once settled in Menton. Oh, Menton, she thought, how can one word sound so wonderful?

She wrote Jack one last letter and posted it before they left, hoping it wouldn't be held up too long by the postal strike.

My dearest Bogey:

Ever since you left here this time—since this last 'illness' of mine—my feelings toward LM are absolutely changed. It is not only that the hatred is gone. Something positive is there which is very like love for her. She has convinced me at last, against all my opposition, that she is trying to do all in her power for me—and that she is devoted to the one idea which is (please forgive my egoism) to see me well again . . . My hate is quite lifted—quite gone; it is like a curse removed. LM has been through the storm with us. I want her to share in the calm—to act Marie's part for us in our country house. Do you agree? I feel I cannot do without her now. It was only when I refused to acknowledge this—to not acknowledge her importance to me—that I hated her. Now that I do, I can be sincere and trust her and of course she, feeling the difference, is a different person. Her self-respect has all come back.

You must realize that now that we are at peace I am never exasperated and she does not annoy me. I only feel 'free' for work and everything.

After finishing the letter to Jack she wrote another to his brother, Richard. Richard had sent her a bound leather copy of her story *Je ne parle pas français* that he had helped set on Jack's home printing press for publication under their small publishing house, The Heron. She wanted to thank him for the beautiful job he had done on the illustrations.

She told him how much she looked forward to leaving the horrible days and nights spent in the unpleasant climate of Ospedaletti behind her, but ending with *Yet there are moments you know, when after a dark day there comes a sunset—such a glowing gorgeous marvelous sky that one forgets all in the beauty of it—these are the moments when I am really writing—Whatever happens I have had these blissful, perfect moments and they are worth living for. I thought, when I left England, I could not love writing more than I did, but now I feel I've never known what it is to be a writer until I came here.*

13

January 1920

L'Hermitage—Menton, France

A gulf of silence separates us from each other
I stand at one side of the gulf—you at the other
I cannot see you or hear you—yet know that you are there.
Often I call you by your childish name
And pretend that the echo to my crying is your voice.
How can we bridge the gulf—never by speed or touch.
Once I thought we might fill it quite up with our tears
Now I want to shatter it with our laughter.

The Gulf—KM

SHE OPENED HER EYES upon cornflowers, jonquils and rosemary sprigs arranged in a crystal vase on her bedside table. Outside her open window morning birds sang and a soft warm breeze carried the faint fragrances of tangerines with just a touch of nutmeg. Under the cuddly warmth of a lambskin blanket, she ran her hands along the fine linen sheets that had held her sore and tired body through the night. *I must be dreaming*, she thought. Hearing a soft tapping at the door, she sat up against the fluffy pillows.

"Come in," she said, expecting a fairy godmother to appear. A young girl stepped lightly through the doorway wearing a golden yellow uniform with a starched white apron tied around a tiny waist. She curtsied and said, "Bonjour Madame. Bienvenue à L'Hermitage. Je m'appelle Marie. Would you like breakfast in bed this morning?"

Katherine looked in wonder at this wingless angel. Marie set down a white basket tray with a blue china teapot, matching china piled high with toast, a pot of honey, a thick slab of butter, and a bouquet of violets. Katherine thanked her and asked if she could see a British newspaper. Marie curtsied again and said she'd see what she could do.

Katherine's eyes flitted like a butterfly over the huge room, taking flights of fancy from the floral couch to the needlepoint chairs to a large writing table with a cut-glass inkstand that she longed to sit at soon.

She squeezed her eyes shut and opened them again to be certain this wasn't a dream. Yesterday I was an impoverished woman in distress being carried downstream in a raging river, and look at me today, she thought. If I can't be cured here, I will never be cured.

The startling juxtaposition from Ospedaletti to Menton brought to mind a camping trip she had taken at nineteen, just before leaving Wellington for London. She'd camped out on the hard ground and played with the Maori children. She asked many questions and scribbled the answers down in her notebook. The quick sketches of the rough, impoverished lives of North Island's inhabitants she later used in *The Woman at the Store*, the story that had brought her to the attention of Jack. He had published it in his literary journal *Rhythm*. The camping trip had been a grand adventure but she'd been relieved to return home to Wellington, as relieved as she was now to find herself surrounded in such finery after roughing it at Casetta Deerholm.

On the bedside table stood an electric lamp under a gold, silk shade. She flicked it off and on, laughing with pure joy. No more lighting gaslights with a match she could never find when she wanted to read.

Slipping out of the bed she carried her teacup over to the wide-open windows that let in the warm breeze that had awoken her earlier with the fragrance of tangerines. The first window she stood at looked out upon olive groves, the sea in the distance. She called it "blue view" and slowly crossed over to the other window and christened it "green view" as it looked over the mountains forested with pines. The sky had never been a deeper blue. She felt too fragile to step out on the marble balconies but knew she'd like it when she did.

She'd just gotten back into bed when she heard another tap at the door and turned to see two fairy godmothers make their stage entrance: Jinnie Fullerton, tall and regal, and Connie Beauchamp, stout and matronly; both elegantly dressed, effervescently charming, and motherly.

"Welcome, dear child. How are you? Do you need anything? No don't get up."

Katherine smiled, reclining on the pillows. "Much better thank you. Ida didn't come with you?"

"She is settling in at the health clinic where she will be employed while you are here. She's very pleased with the arrangements and asked me to tell you that she came by last night but found you asleep."

"We thought you might like something to read," said Connie, placing a few English magazines and two Christian pamphlets with embossed gold crosses on her quilt. The pamphlets didn't surprise Katherine. Her father had forewarned her that they would try to convert her to Catholicism.

"How did you know those are my favorite flowers?" she said, looking over at Jinnie arranging a bouquet of budding yellow jonquils in a crystal vase.

"A little angel told us." They said and giggled simultaneously at the same time.

"We won't stay too long my dear. You mustn't be anxious or worried about anything for the next several weeks. Let your heart heal. If there is anything you need, tell Marie, and we'll bring it on our next visit."

"Well, there is one thing," she said, and smiled. "Please tell me this is not a dream. You really are standing here with the sunshine streaming behind you. Tell me I will not fall back asleep and wake up in my bed at the Casetta. Have I truly escaped?"

"Yes dear. You're safe now with us."

"This is all too wonderful."

After they left she used the bed tray to write Jack the good news. There'd be no more miserable letters written with her pen.

After a week of bed rest, she ventured downstairs to eat with the other nursing home guests. The pretty dining room with all its elegant trimmings could not hide the pain and suffering of the people slumped at the tables. Many had private nurses spoon-feeding their lax mouths with green pudding that slipped down on to their clothes and remained there. Other guests sunk down in their wheelchairs seemed to be half alive. The ones with hacking coughs were quarantined in a corner where a seat had been reserved for her and marked with a name card. She wanted to say there was some mistake, she was here to heal her heart not her lungs, but then had a coughing spasm and remembered she was here for more than one illness.

She stared down at her plate through dinner, unable to bear looking into her companions' sunken eyes, eyes that had the feverish glints of consumption. Do I look as mad? As emaciated? As old? Or is this what the final stage of my disease looks like? she wondered, willing her hand to pick up a fork and eat.

After two weeks at L'Hermitage she was cheered to return to her room after lunch and find a stack of mail that had been forwarded from Italy and another stack that included letters addressed to Menton. She immediately opened a letter from Jack.

In her first letter to him from Menton she had listed the many expenditures she was forced to make at L'Hermitage and told him how terribly hard up she was. She told him she was even willing to sell her new story collection outright for £20 as long as she would receive the cash immediately. She found it too humiliating to ask for his help directly but hoped he would consider it on his own, though Jack was never quick to open his wallet to anyone. How ironic that the only two men she could appeal to for financial help, Jack and her father, were both renowned misers. Whereas LM, who had far less income than either of them, was always generous.

How abominably selfish, she concluded reading his letter through a second time, it's all about his walk through Sussex. *A day's sheer happiness—Drunken with the magnificence*—has he no understanding of what life is like here living with the very ill and wondering when I will be one of them? The last line in his letter is the most inexplicable: *How's money—let me know, please.* Didn't he read my letter? How much clearer must I be without humiliating myself?

As the days passed, she became more wretched and bitter toward him. But she held off writing him, hoping a more compassionate, understanding letter would arrive soon.

One morning she was looking out at the "blue view" waiting for the mail. Marie tapped on her door and entered again with empty hands. After she withdrew, Katherine grabbed her pen and paper and set to writing Jack the letter she had written in her head several times but hoped never to send:

PLEASE READ THIS ALL THROUGH she wrote in thick ink across the top of the page.

My dear Bogey, you have hurt me dreadfully—if you reflect for one moment you will perhaps realize how your 'how's money?' struck me. Did I not tell you the expenses I had coming here—the bills to settle, the hire of the motor, the theft of my overcoat, the more expensive room, the extras such as goûters, frictions and LM to look after. Yes, I have told you all these things. I imagined you would immediately wire me £10. I imagined you would have written, 'It's gorgeous to know you're there & getting better. Don't worry. Of course, I shall contribute £10 a month towards your expenses.' But no nothing at all.

In addition I counted on your loving sympathy and understanding, and the fact that you failed me in this is the hardest of all to bear. I really wonder Bogey if you even read my letters.

So now I will be direct . . . I ask you to contribute £10 a month towards my expenses here . . .

It is so bitter to have to ask you this—terribly bitter. Nevertheless I am determined to get well. I will not be overcome by anything—not even by the letter you sent me in Italy telling me to remember AS I grew more lonely SO you were loving me more. If you had read that in a novel what would you have thought? Well, I thank God I read it here and not at the Casetta.

I've nothing to say to you, Bogey. I am too hurt. I shall not write again.

Your Wife

Their letters crossed in the mail. The next day she received a second letter from him and she felt a rush of guilt when a check for £20 dropped out of it. That was until she read the letter and learned the check was not an expression of her husband's generous love. To the contrary, he was offering it, like a book agent would, as an advance on her next short story collection. He would get it back, and probably much more for her, as soon as he negotiated a deal.

His letter rambled on about another trip to the '*breathtakingly lovely country*' of Sussex and how he would '*beat the country thoroughly*' the next weekend searching for their Heron.

A third letter quickly followed. He wrote: *though things are tight, I will send you another cheque for £20 tomorrow, if you will repay me when you get the money for your book.* And then in the evening mail he withdrew his offer, writing that he could only manage ten.

She stood at the window looking out at the boats tossing back and forth at sea and wondered where he spent his thousand pounds a year salary because he certainly wasn't sharing any of it with her.

She sat down at her writing table and wrote:

As regards the advance money I would rather wait and receive it for my book than that you should lend it to me. I MUST have it for my overcoat, fare home, etc., and I certainly do not want to borrow it from you. Perhaps I did not make clear that I BOTHER you for the £10 a month—I mean, NOT as a loan.

If you can agree to allowing me £10 a month for my expenses while I am here I shall look upon this cheque as the first 2 months installment. I would perfectly understand your money is tight had I NOT consumption, a weak heart & chronic neuritis in my lower limbs.

As far as her not writing more often:

It's no good my writing every day. I can't. I simply feel you don't read the letters—I try and do my own work instead. There's a much better chance that you'll read that one day—though why you should I don't know.

She reminded him that she must now correct the proofs of *The Man Without a Temperament* as he was living at such racing speed, she didn't think he had the time to do a good job himself. Anxious that her story might go to print without her seeing the proofs, she wrote:

Every word matters. I can't afford mistakes. Another word won't do. I chose every single word. Please answer this request when you next write.

THE CONSTANT NOISE of patients, nurses, and servants clattering back and forth in the hallway made it impossible to work. She complained and was moved to another room but it was just as bad. In three weeks her residence in L'Hermitage had proven to her that she would never get well in a sanatorium because she'd never get any work done. The voices and words and half visions were driving her mad.

She was behind in her novel-reviews and the short story that she wanted to include before her second short story collection went to print wasn't finished. She had titled it *Second Helping* and thought it a good title for the collection. Usually she would ask Jack's opinion, as he was always helpful when it came to her work, but she no longer trusted him. How could she when he had withdrawn so from her? His mind was only on his own financial worries and the paper and his "torturous walks" through the countryside searching for the Heron that she would never live long enough to see.

After weeks of bed rest, she was still unable to walk beyond the garden at L'Hermitage. On her own she at least took a few short steps into the garden, enjoying the winter blooms of pale violets, and particularly the lovely palm that she often watched from her window. Its friendly fronds waving to her. Ah! To fall in love with a tree.

She returned to her room determined to finish *Second Helping.* Only the writing would relieve her melancholy. At the end of the day she had finished and, quite pleased with herself, opened to a blank page in her notebook and wrote:

Work will win if only I can stick to it. It will win after all and through all.

Jack's next letter gave her some relief as his response clearly showed he had read every word of her last letter. If she would send *Second Helping* he would type it himself and she would see "without fail" the proofs for *The Man Without a Temperament.* He would read it before sending it to her but would not change a word.

He still asked her to write every day. She sat down and wrote a letter speaking the truth from her heart not caring anymore if he would suffer from her honesty. She must tell the truth:

My darling, I can't write every day—I love you but something has gone dead in me—rather—no, I can't explain it. Explanations are so futile—you NEVER listen to them, you know—I shrink from trying anymore. Give me time will you? I'll get over this—I get over everything but it takes time. But darling, darling, that doesn't make me love you less—I love you—that's the whole infernal trouble!

After sending these anguished words, she had a few bad days of nervous headache. The doctors at L'Hermitage insisted she stay in bed but she no longer trusted their medical advice. They became angry when she had refused the sleep-inducing Veronal but she'd withdrawn from its addiction in Bavaria and had sworn never to touch it again.

Several days later she received Jack's response and before opening it she sat down at the open window, looked out on the "green view" and prepared herself.

She searched for the passion that his letters had once evoked but he was still playing the part of a book agent, informing her that Constable had agreed to the £40 advance. His coldness gripped her heart. Has he forgotten why I am in the south of France and not at home with him? How else could he only discuss business? Why compliment *The Man Without a Temperament* saying it was *amazingly good, no one can write like you-but it's also extraordinarily beautiful?* I don't want your compliments. I want you to read the story and maybe understand us better.

He finished off his "agent" letter by reminding her to make up her mind which stories were to be included in the soon-to-be published second collection. There was no lover hidden between these lines. You'd think he was writing to a client. "Where is my husband?" she asked aloud, looking around her lovely but lonely room.

Why hadn't he written to say, "Dearest, I cannot bear to be away from you another moment when I know how you are suffering from isolation and loneliness and illness." How she would have willingly flown into his arms and forgiven him everything, but this?

The only warmth she could wrap around her chilled shoulders was his sign off: *Your own, Boge.*

She cried out in her notebook:

It was a question of sympathy of understanding, of being the least interested, of asking me JUST ONCE how I was.

She sent a wire with the pretense of requesting to hear a response from their cat "Wing," as she couldn't bear another letter from Jack:

> THURSDAY LETTER CAME. STOP. TELL WING WIRE IMMEDIATELY. STOP. YOUR COLDNESS KILLING ME. STOP. WIG

"Wing" responded:

> WIRE RECEIVED. STOP. ALL WELL. STOP. HE LOVES YOU DESPERATELY. STOP. HE CAN'T DO MORE. STOP

A few days later she received another letter from Jack:

I've waited a minute. Lit a cigarette. I must be calm. For somehow in spite of myself our destiny has come to tremble on a razor's edge. Hitherto I have written desperately, and made the wounds I have inflicted on you worse. I must be calm.

Darling my own heart the very me. I feel tonight at the end of my tether. Some blind force is crushing the hope out of me. For I swear to you as my lover and my wife that all I have done since I came back from Italy has been with a single thought—love of you. Instead of bringing us nearer it has driven us apart.

There is, Wig, a certain amount of real insensibility in me. I think that has been proved now. I must just accept it: I hate it, and try to kill it. But the fact remains that I never realized how much you were suffering in Ospedaletti, nor how great would be your anxiety about money in Menton. Both those things you had a right to expect of me as your lover and, there's no doubt in my own mind that I failed in them both.

You see my darling it's wrong for us to be apart. That is what it comes to at the last. You can understand my harshness, blackness, my habit of silence when you are near me, and make allowances; but when we are so far away that is impossible yet it is more necessary than ever.

The only thing is for you to get well. Get well my darling, and let's put an end to this time of torture. Your voice is sweet, but mine is harsh when we call from so far away.

Let me hold you in my arms. Let this ghastly nightmare go. Your own Boge

Katherine let out a sob. Finally he had heard her cry. Finally she could feel his arms around her again. Her writing case propped on her knees, she wrote:

Your Saturday evening letter has come with the 'explanation.' Don't say another word about it. Let's after this put it quite away. Yes, I felt in Ospedaletti that you refused to understand and I have felt since I have been abroad this time that you have turned away from me. Withdrawn yourself utterly from me.

Let's get over all this. What has been—has been. Not being an intellectual I always seem to have to learn things at the risk of my life—but I do learn. Let's be wise, true, real lovers from now on.

Let's enter the Heron from today—from this very minute and I shall rejoice in you and if it's not too great an effort—dear love—try and rejoice in me.

It's lunch time. I'm in bed, I must fly up. My nib will not write—It must write that I love you and you only world without end amen—

14

February-April 1920

Villa Flora, Menton

Today Jinnie arrived with a carriage and fur rugs and silk cushions. Took me to their villa . . . a chaise longue in the garden—a tiny tray with black coffee out of a silver pot, Grand Marnier, cigarettes, little bunch of violets. Their villa is a dream—Spanish silk bed coverlets, Italian china, stillness, maids in tiny muslin aprons flitting over carpets . . . .

Notebooks—KM

JINNIE AND CONNIE WRAPPED HER IN FUR RUGS for the first visit to their home, Villa Flora. LM, who lodged nearby, joined them for tea in the salon. Katherine was shown a silver bedroom with a balcony view of the sea. She wanted to move in that day.

"We want you to come here and live here with us. It's dead quiet. You can be alone all day if you like. We're sure you'll get well here under our care. This is what we have wanted since our invitation in Ospedaletti," said Jinnie, looking terribly concerned. "But we must consider our other guests. We mentioned your coming to Mr. Davis, who has been most generous to us, and he was quite concerned, being of weak health himself, that your illness might be infectious. We wouldn't want him to leave on your account, now, would we, dear?"

"Certainly not. But if Dr. Rendall gave a favorable report on my condition could I come?"

"Nothing would please us more than to have you safely in our home and under our care," said Jinnie, warmly hugging Katherine. "We will pray that Dr. Rendall will find you on the mend."

A few days later a letter came from D.H. Lawrence with a packet of mail. They'd had their turbulent moments in the past but she still considered him one of her closest friends and, not having heard from him for quite some time, she hoped he was writing to renew their friendship.

She burst into tears reading:

I loathe you. You revolt me stewing in your consumption. You are a loathsome reptile—I hope you will die.

In her empty bedroom she cried out, "Lawrence! Why? Why do you turn on me like this?" She stood on the balcony for several minutes until her tears dried trying to understand why. What have I done that you have such a low opinion of me to want me dead? I can forgive you if you wrote this in the middle of a TB rage. That I might be able to understand having said vile things I never should have said during my own fevers. Yet I've never said anything as vile as this!

She returned to her writing table and wrote Jack what Lawrence had said, including he had called Jack a "dirty little worm." She asked if he were her man to not befriend Lawrence or review his work in *The Athenaeum.*

Be proud! she wrote. She thought to tell him to hit Lawrence the next time he saw him when there was a knock at the door. "Come in!" she shouted angrily, swinging her own clenched fist.

Dr. Rendall walked in carrying his medical satchel. "Hello Mrs. Murry, are we feeling a bit cranky today?" He smiled.

"Forgive me Doctor Rendall. I've had some bad news."

"I'm so sorry. Shall I come back later?"

"No. I'm all right. It's just a question of pride." She smiled. "Please come in."

He set down his satchel. "And what can I do for you today?"

"I've been invited to Villa Flora by my aunt, Miss Beauchamp, and her associate, Miss Fullerton, but only if, after your examination, you can tell them that I am not infectious."

"Let's have a listen, shall we?"

After watching him put away his stethoscope and hammer, she anxiously waited while he wrote his notes.

It seemed forever before he looked up and said, "You still have a low fever but that's normal for your condition. Your cough is infrequent and dry and your air passages are clear. I'll let Miss Beauchamp know that you are not a threat to their other guests at the villa."

Katherine could have hugged him at that moment but he was very English and would have been uncomfortable with such an emotional display. Even in leaning toward him she could feel him pull back. "Thank you. It will be such a relief to move to a quiet home where I can work uninterrupted. But now I need to know when you think I can go home?"

"Home?"

"Yes. You see my husband is buying a house in Sussex where we can live together through the English winters instead of living apart half the year."

"England? Does your husband understand the risks you'd be taking?"

"He believes a house in Sussex, which has the most moderate temperature in England and the most sunshine, will be safe once my heart is strong enough."

"He's wrong. With your chronic rheumatism, I'm afraid in a wet climate, like England, you might not be able to walk and your tubercular lungs would not remain quiescent for long immersed in its damp winters. I don't recommend such a move."

Katherine, embarrassed by her tears, stood up and walked over to the balcony.

"Mrs. Murry, are you all right?"

She returned to her seat.

"Forgive me. It's just that my husband needs to hear I am cured and if I told him what you just said he would despair. You see he will accept nothing less than a cure. His happiness depends upon it and therefore mine."

"Doesn't he know that you are chronically ill?"

"I try not to complain to him too much. He only wants to hear that I'm well and coming home."

"I see. Perhaps there is another solution. Did you say Mr. Murry was also a writer?"

"Yes. Why?"

"Perhaps he could leave London temporarily and work here where the climate is the most beneficial for your health."

"How long is *temporarily*?"

"Probably two years."

"Two years! No. That would never do. He'd be most unhappy. Will it always be like this?"

"Mrs. Murry, I can't predict your future. I can only give you my medical opinion. May I be direct?"

"Yes please. I must know the truth."

"With bed rest your heart will get stronger. Your tuberculosis is quiescent in your right lung, but the left lung is permanently damaged. The bacteria lodged in your lungs could become active again at any time. You only breathe out of one lung and it puts a tremendous strain on your heart."

She got up again and walked over to the balcony, wiping away her tears. Not wanting him to think she was stewing in her consumption. She took a deep breath and turned to him, "Thank you, Dr. Rendall. You've made things very clear for me. I don't think I've ever understood my situation so clearly. But for now I think I should keep this from my husband. I fear he suffers too much already and won't be able to bear the truth."

"Perhaps your husband should consider your health more than his own."

After he left, Katherine sat on the edge of her bed and reached for her cane and leaned her chin upon it. It was the one possession she had of her mother's, given to her by Pa after she died. There were days when her mother had kept to her room after she contracted rheumatic fever, as Katherine did now, but her husband and family and close friends were nearby.

Who do I have, Katherine lamented to herself? LM? Jack? Certainly not Lawrence who finds me revolting. My only companions are a packet of letters and the characters in my stories. I can't wrap my arms around them.

THE FOLLOWING MORNING Jinnie rushed into her room. "Sorry to burst in on you like this but we couldn't wait another minute."

"What is it, Jinnie?" Katherine said, pulling herself up on the pillows and straightening the covers tossed askew during the night.

"I've come to take you home. Dr. Rendall has just told us the good news. I feel so much better knowing I can be at peace about you, my darling. You will be safe with Connie and me and the Good Lord looking after you. Connie would be here with me but she's preparing your room."

Katherine was overcome as she looked upon this kind, generous woman whose only thought was her welfare. Jinnie handed her a lilac-perfumed lace handkerchief.

"Thank you but I shouldn't use your hankie."

"Not to mind, darling. It's yours now," she said, raising her eyes to the ceiling and pressing her hands together, "The Lord has delivered you into our hands and please be God's will to cure you." She returned her gaze upon Katherine, "I'll go ask Marie to help with the packing. We must hurry, the carriage is waiting."

Katherine looked over at the stack of notebooks that she had hardly opened since her arrival at L'Hermitage and said what she wouldn't say in front of her new benefactors: "I need my work to cure me, not God."

* * *

AT VILLA FLORA, Katherine settled comfortably into the luxurious life she had known as a child in New Zealand. Everything was done for her and her heart grew stronger. She was so seduced by their generosity and gentle kindness, the carriage rides in the hills above Menton, the champagne picnics and elegant accommodations that she began to take the idea of becoming a Catholic seriously. Even telling LM she was going to do it, but so embarrassed at the idea, she told her in a letter rather than face her and made her promise not to tell anyone.

She knew she needed something to believe in and had attended Mass, read the Bible, and listened to Jinnie's persuasive words. To encourage her further, Jinnie gave her *The Imitation of Christ* to read. But when Katherine read "It is a very great thing to be in a state of obedience, to live under a superior, and not to be one's own master" she scribbled *Nonsense* in the margin.

One evening, returning from an elegant picnic on the hillside and a tour of Monte Carlo, Connie and Jinnie invited her into their drawing room for a glass of champagne before retiring. Katherine sank into their yellow silk sofa and watched the bubbles rise and pop in her glass.

"Do you think you would like to speak to our priest?" asked Jinnie softly. It was the first time she had directly brought up Katherine's conversion.

Katherine put down her champagne glass on the mahogany table. "You have both been so dear to me. It's because of your loving kindness that my despair has been lifted and I am filled with new hope. For this reason alone I have been tempted to join your faith. But I cannot do so."

"But my dearest," said Jinnie, taking her hand in hers, "You won't have us to take care of you. There will be dark hours. With faith you will see the light and not be afraid."

"Yes, I have come to realize that I do need faith. But it can't be in a personal Deity."

"Not a Deity who loves you very much and waits patiently to hold you in His arms?"

"I have trouble believing that, Jinnie. It's difficult to trust in a God that brings such evil into the world. After the war, many lost their faith in such a God that allowed so much pain and death. For many of us who survived that war, He is now gone."

"Katherine!" said Connie. "I fear for you when you say such things. You must learn to open up your heart to Him so that you might see His Way."

"I'm sorry but it's not God that I should open up my heart to. It's mankind."

She sat forward taking them both in with her eyes, wanting them to understand what she had come to realize these past few months. "I want to live by the spirit of Love. I want to see into things so deeply and truly that I can love all things. You see, we must love and we must carry our weakness and our sin and our devilishness to somebody, but not to God as he's no longer there for us. Love is to be found in each other. We must feel that we are known, that our hearts are known as God once knew us. I don't mean love in the usual manner. Love today between "lovers" has to be not only human but also divine. Love each other for everything and through everything and your love becomes your religion. It can't become anything less. Even affection can't become less supreme because it's an act of faith to believe in each other."

"Oh Katherine," said Jinnie, visibly disappointed. "You are truly a challenge to God. The Virgin Mary, too, is trying to forgive you."

Katherine was taken aback. Had they not heard anything she just said? She sunk back into the couch, resigned to not being heard. "What did I do to the Virgin Mary?"

"It's how you described her in that story you wrote. I don't know if your stories are all like that one but I couldn't really make much sense of it. Why do you write such blasphemy?"

Katherine picked up her glass and took a sip rather than rudely laugh. She had written the first draft of that story when the war was never out of her mind and everything was poisoned by it. That story was her cry against corruption. A cry that came from a deep sense of hopelessness, of everything doomed. The story's cynical character expressed that sense of doom. She looked back up at her gracious hostesses waiting for her to respond.

"Do you mean the line from *Je ne parle pas français?*"

She recited: *"One would not have been surprised if the door had opened and the Virgin Mary had come in, riding upon an ass, her meek hands folded over her big belly."*

"Yes, Katherine, that's it," said Connie, shifting uncomfortably. "I must tell you that I discussed that story with your father. I found it too uncomfortable to read, but after Jinnie and I discussed it, I asked your father if he had read it. He said he didn't think it was clever and chucked in the fireplace."

Katherine felt her heart quicken and, not wanting them to see how hurt she was by this news, she returned her gaze on the bubbles rising and popping in her champagne glass. She'd given her father copies of all her stories. He never mentioned them. Although he had encouraged her to be a writer, she suspected that of a celebrated writer like his cousin, Elizabeth, and not the maverick literary writer she had become. Now she knew why he never said anything about her stories and the truth hurt terribly.

"I'm feeling rather tired," she said. "I'm sorry if I've disappointed you. I wanted to join your faith but I can't if I don't believe in your God. But you needn't give up on me yet." She pulled herself up from the chair. With as much dignity as she could muster leaning on her mother's cane, she said, "Thank you for the champagne, it was most delicious."

ON APRIL 27, after three weeks at the L'Hermitage and two months at Villa Flora, she and LM left Menton to travel by train to London. She and Jack had made plans for her return but he hadn't been able to spare the time to come to Menton to get her.

He had found the perfect cottage in Sussex—the Heron that they dreamed of having someday. The current tenant wouldn't be vacating for a year so she'd decided there was no point in discussing what Dr. Rendall had told her. There would be time enough for that when she reached home. And she could always hope that Dr. Rendall was wrong.

Connie and Jinnie were moving to another villa across the bay from Villa Flora, and perhaps not giving up yet on her conversion, had offered, come October, a long-term lease on a smaller independent villa on the property. Katherine had fallen in love with Menton and didn't hesitate to say yes. LM would return with her.

Katherine hoped that Jack would join her but she only wanted him to come if he did it for himself and not for her. If he came as a man without a temperament, sacrificing his own life to take care of his invalid wife, it would destroy their love.

15

May 1920

The Elephant House—London

Just wait till I get home, that's all the best. And we shall be alone & all the house ours and a perfect table & the new cups and saucers with their flowers & fluting. And the windows shall be open—you in your old clothes, I'll be in fair ones. Our cats Wing & Athy there—fruit in our Italian dish—HAPPINESS, happiness. I'll be able to pick up your hand—look at it—kiss it—give it back to you. I'll say BOGE my own; you'll say, yes. We'll look at each other and laugh—Wing will wink at Athy and pretend to play the fiddle. Oh I love you. Je t'aime. Wig

Letters—KM

"JACK! JACK! I'M HOME." Katherine called out, opening the front door of 2 Portland Villas. Violet, their housekeeper, rushed toward her.

"Mrs. Murry. Can this truly be you? Why—why you look—wonderful. Here let me take your coat. Mr. Murry didn't know when to expect you. I'll call him at the office. So glad to have you home again. And, you too, Miss Baker!"

"No. Don't call him," said Katherine. "I want to rest before I see him."

"The weather couldn't be pleasanter for your return. I think you'll be most pleased with the garden." Katherine noted the marigolds set on the entryway table along with a stack of mail. "Nothing there for you ma'am," Violet said. "I put your mail up in your bedroom just like I used to."

"Thank you, Violet. Did Mr. Murry cut these flowers?"

"Oh no, Ma'am, he never has time for anything but the paper. I've been tending the garden."

"I'd like to plant some vegetables this summer. Perhaps you'll help me." Violet smiled and walked away carrying their coats.

The soft gray wallpaper she'd chosen for the stairwell welcomed her home, encouraging her ascent. "I'll be all right," she said, shrugging off LM's offered arm.

"I don't remember this hallway being so dark," she thought, pausing in front of her bedroom door.

"Shall I bring tea?" asked LM.

"Not yet. Wait until Jack comes home."

"Are you sure you don't want me to help you undress? Unpack your—"

"Ida! I'm not a child! Let me be."

She turned the knob and stepped inside, relieved to see the room was untouched, as she left it. A few letters were tossed on the floor because Violet had aired the room and left the window open. She stooped down to pick them up, noting the addresses: Kot, Lady Ottoline, and even a letter from Virginia. She put them down on her bureau, the loyal correspondents that followed her from place to place.

She brushed her gloved hand across the bright yellow writing table where she had written her will eight months ago, now safely locked away in her bank deposit box with instructions not to be opened by Jack until . . . "Don't be afraid to say it," she thought, "until my death." She placed her notebooks on the table, making a promise to sit down and write something original every day, if only a few words.

She reread Jack's last letter from before she left Menton:

It's the place where we can be together: where all my hatred of life will depart from & all the blackness you hate in me (& I hate too) will be dissolved away; where we can live as we are meant to live. All day long I think about it, simply because I can't help it. It brings me near you & holds us together. I shut the door & we are in each other's arms. Your husband, Boge.

After a month at home, it became painfully apparent that the hopes she'd formed from Jack's letter and the plans they'd made when they reunited "come May," including a holiday in the countryside, were just really false expectations.

Now, May had come and gone, and tonight, like every night, she listened for Jack's footsteps on the stairs. She lay back on her pillows, very still, but her mind raged uncontrollably. I must face the truth, she thought, he's unreliable. I can't depend on him at all.

Yes, the weekly *Athenaeum* deadlines demanded his full attention during the day but the evenings, too? And there were other distractions. While she was gone, he'd taken up tennis with their mutual friend Brett.

Brett had written to Katherine about the "orgies" she and Jack frequented. Offended by the unsavory details, Katherine had written to Jack and warned him about drinking too much wine. He'd replied that Brett had exaggerated. They weren't "orgies," just insufferable parties that he had to attend as *Athenaeum*'s editor. He dragged Brett along to keep him company.

She heard his footsteps, flipped on the reading light and reached for the nearest book.

"Are you still up?" he asked cheerfully.

"Why are you so late?"

"Sorry. Didn't I tell you? I stayed at the office to finish an article before tomorrow's deadline. What did you do today?"

"Nothing."

"Well, that's a shame. Listen, I had an idea on my way home tonight," he said, sitting down on the edge of the bed. How handsome and happy he looked, she thought. "Why don't you start writing a monthly fiction column for *The Athenaeum*?"

"But the paper doesn't publish fiction."

"Not yet, but as its editor I can change that. There weren't any novel-reviews either until you started writing them. And look how successful that is. It will have to be limited to one column but I think our subscribers will be pleased. It will probably increase our subscriptions, but more important, it will give you a home to publish your stories."

She felt the warmth of his hand gently covering hers and her anger melted along with her fear of being a jilted wife. "All right. I'll start on a sketch tomorrow."

"Good." He bent down and brushed his lips against her cheek. "Good night, my love."

"Aren't you coming to bed?"

"No. I mean yes. Actually I've been meaning to say something about that. I think you'll have a better rest if I sleep over there." He pointed to the alcove sofa. "I'll still be right here if you have one of those dreams. By the way, that was certainly a bad one last night."

"I don't remember," she lied.

She woke up the next morning with LM standing over her with the breakfast tray. "Where's Jack?" she asked.

"Brett came by earlier and they went off to play tennis. Didn't he tell you?"

"Yes, of course he did, I just forgot."

She finished her breakfast and sat down at her writing table to write down a sketch she'd been developing in her mind. To her satisfaction she had completed *Revelations* by late afternoon, in time for *Athenaeum*'s mid-June issue. How right Jack was to suggest this, she thought. And having deadlines will help me. How could I have doubted his love?"

One afternoon, Jack invited her to come to the office. "You're such a strong influence on the decisions I make at the paper, I want everyone to meet you. And wouldn't it be nice to get out of the house for some fresh air? You're looking way to pale, my dear. I don't want anyone to ever think I'm not taking good care of you. Come, let's put some color in those pretty cheeks."

She hesitated. It was true she needed to get out and it would be nice to share a carriage with Jack. Just this morning she'd looked out of her bedroom window at the brilliant violets in her garden and thought, what a beautiful day for a ride.

"All right, Jack, let me get my hat and coat."

"She looks worse than I expected" was written on the faces that looked up when she walked into the *Athenaeum* office. They tried to recover saying "Mrs. Murry, how good to see you. My you are looking well," but she knew what H.G. Wells, who was working there, and the others were really thinking: "Poor Jack. What a saint he is putting up with a dying wife."

After the visit to *Athenaeum*, she seldom went out again and asked her friends to come to the Elephant if they wanted to see her.

Her first story, *Revelations,* was an immediate success and Jack asked her to write another story for July. To relieve the cramps in her fingers she got from writing with a pen, he loaned her his Corona typewriter, a small black model with round keys that acted like hammers. It made writing easier not to have the fingers cramp anymore and she was able to write her short stories and keep up her novel-reviews.

When not working in her room, she came downstairs to see invited visitors such as Virginia who came for precious two-hour conversations about writing, telling Katherine how much she missed their talks. Neither mentioned Katherine's critical review of Virginia's novel *Night and Day*.

She gave a dinner party for T.S. Eliot, whom she'd wanted to meet, and his wife Vivien. She didn't think Eliot liked her and she didn't like Vivian.

She had hoped that she and Brett, who lived nearby, would renew the friendship that had developed through their correspondence, but Brett seemed quite occupied.

Brett had been introduced to her and Jack at Garsington, Lady Ottoline's 1500 acre estate outside London. Lady Ottoline, though not an artist herself, supported the arts and invited artists to reside in various cottages on the property. It was an oasis from bombed-out London. She enjoyed having parties that mixed the "underground" artists like Katherine, Jack, and D.H. Lawrence, with the Bloomsbury group, wealthy middle-class intellectuals who didn't have to make a living by their art alone.

Hon. Dorothy Brett, nicknamed Brett, was a Bloomsbury member with the proper credentials; her father a barrister and legal advisor to the Queen of England. But she, like Lady Ottoline, leaned toward the more bohemian life style of the "underground" and like Katherine and Ottoline, had a special friendship with D. H. Lawrence. Later, she would follow him to his artist colony in New Mexico.

What Katherine and Brett had most in common was their passion for impressionist art. Katherine felt her stories were fragments, sketches and small forms influenced by impressionistic paintings. Brett, schooled in the art of impressionism, painted still-lifes and portraits that pleased Katherine's eye.

Brett, five years older than Katherine, was nearly deaf the majority of her life. She carried an ornate brass ear trumpet named Tobey wherever she went. Katherine would shout her ideas, often interrupted by coughing spasms, into Brett's trumpet and Brett would respond by shouting back, "What?" "What?"

One afternoon, Brett arrived for teatime just as Katherine was finishing *Escape*, her story for the July edition. The writing had gone well and she was excited to talk about it. Losing patience while waiting for Brett to unpack her trumpet and place it next to her ear, she shouted, "When you paint apples don't you feel that your breasts and your knees become apples, too?"

Brett's face flushed in response so Katherine was sure she had heard her and went on.

"You think I'm speaking great nonsense, don't you?"

Brett responded by shaking her head, no, quickly.

"Well, I'm sure it's not. When I write about ducks I swear I'm a white duck with a round eye, floating on a pond fringed with yellow-blobs and taking an occasional darting look at my reflection, which floats upside down beneath me. In fact the whole process of becoming the duck is so thrilling that I can hardly breathe, just thinking about it. For although that's as far as most people can get, it's really only the 'prelude.' There follows the moment when you are more duck, more apple, or more Natasha than any of these objects could ever possibly be, and so you create them anew."

Before Brett could reply, Jack arrived, apologizing for being late for their scheduled teatime.

Brett and Jack sat across from her. She poured the tea. Jack mentioned their last tennis game and Brett put down her trumpet and launched into an enthusiastic description of how they'd beaten their opponents. Katherine felt excluded, and relegated to the role of observer. She noted Brett's blush when Jack leaned close to her ear to make sure she heard him say, "It was your strong serve that won the match."

Several days later Katherine happened upon an open letter sitting on Jack's desk. Recognizing Brett's handwriting she read it just as she might have read any of the letters Jack carelessly left around the house. They had always been quite open about each other's correspondence.

Sinking down in the nearest chair, she thought, Why Brett has come unbalanced! What on earth is she talking about? *Rush into the cornfield... he must smack her hand*—threatens to cry over him until he's all wet. Poor wretch! She's thirty-seven, hysterical, and says he's *awakened her*. Dear God!

She avoided speaking to Jack about the letter, believing the affair was one-sided. Jack would soon put an end to Brett's foolishness. And, if not, she would not play the role of the jealous wife. Early on in their relationship they had agreed to not hold each other back from having other relationships. Jack was as free as she was to have affairs. But with Brett? That seemed utterly ridiculous.

COME SEPTEMBER her return to Menton neared. Her health, as Dr. Rendall had predicted, had worsened in wet London and she feared the autumn chill. Connie and Jinnie had kept in touch and informed her about the splendid small villa that awaited her. Their continued exuberant warmth toward her filled a place in a heart that had not much tenderness in London. Jack was determined to stay in London and keep the paper running.

She and Jack had just finished their last discussion about the submissions for *Athenaeum*'s next edition. Since their days as young editors at his magazine *Rhythm*, he had always counted on her advice. Satisfied with their work, they sipped their tea.

"I can't believe you're leaving so soon," said Jack. "I'll certainly miss your advice. You've been a great help to me."

Katherine smiled. "It won't be any different than last time. We'll correspond over the submissions and I'll send you the novel-reviews and the sketches for my fiction column."

"Yes, of course, but it's not the same as having you here with me. You don't realize how large and empty this house is without you, and what a huge responsibility. The truth is I don't think I can bear another winter here alone. I was thinking of renting it out."

"But where would you live?"

"Brett has come up with a practical solution."

"Brett?"

"Yes. She's invited me to come and stay with her. There's a spare bedroom."

"Am I to understand this is nothing more than *l'amitié pure?*"

"I have no feelings for Brett if that is what you're inferring."

"Then why have I seen you linger when you kiss her cheek or touch her arm?"

"It's only natural with a dear friend who sympathizes with my situation. My relationship with Brett is a convenience that I expected you, more than anyone, would understand. If I took her up on her invitation, I could lease the Elephant and relieve myself of the financial burden."

"Why discuss it with me if you've already decided," she said, putting down her teacup.

"Brett asked me to."

"Brett? Did she? How thoughtful of her." She swallowed the bitter taste in her mouth. "You can tell her not to worry. Our marriage has never prevented you from living freely."

"As you have also," Jack retorted. "Before we met, you were never one to hold back. But there's no need for us to discuss our past, is there. What's important is Brett's feelings."

"Oh yes, of course we must think of Brett's feelings."

"Don't be snide Katherine, it doesn't become you. She wants you to be comfortable about this arrangement. You're a close friend and she wouldn't want you to think badly of her for coming to my rescue. Will you continue to be nice to her?"

Katherine pushed herself up from the chair, held onto its arm, and willed her legs to gather strength under her so that she could cross the room. On her way out she turned and said, "Tell her *the arrangement* is fine with me."

Alone in her bedroom, she sat at her writing table and fumed. "Nice to her! He's asking me to be nice to her."

She scribbled quickly in her journal:

I suppose one thinks the latest shock is the worst shock. This is quite unlike any other I've ever suffered. The lack of sensitiveness as far as I am concerned—the selfishness of this staggers me. This is what I must remember when I am away. He thinks no more of me than of anybody else . . . . I must remember he's one of my friends—no more. Who could count on such a man! To plan all this at such a time and then ask me to be nice to Brett. How disgustingly indecent! I am simply disgusted to my very soul.

BEFORE LEAVING LONDON she invited Jack's brother Richard to see the Russian Ballet at the Royal Opera in Covent Garden. During her absence, they had become close correspondents. He was only eighteen but they shared a passion for art and Katherine often wrote to him about her love of nature and the joy she found when she picked up her pen to write. He arrived in a carriage and carefully escorted her to the theater.

They returned home to a dark, cold house that seemed even drearier after the bright cheery lights of the concert hall and the inspiring, uplifting music they had enjoyed so much.

"Where's Jack?" he asked.

"Oh he's probably at the office. He often works late."

Richard lit the logs and joined her on the couch, watching the fire build. The crackling flames warmed Katherine's feet but she felt a chill on her back. Richard saw her shivering and said, "Where's your shawl?"

"It's up in my bedroom but you needn't get it."

He ran up the stairs and returned, gently wrapping the shawl around her shoulders. He added another log to the fire.

"How different you are from your brother," she said. "He never notices when I'm cold." She laughed. "But then again, I'm always cold."

He turned to Katherine and said, "It shames me to see how unfairly my brother treats you. When you cough, he hides his face with his fingers as if it is unendurable. There's just something missing when it comes to him being sensitive to anyone other than himself. I'm embarrassed about him. He's always been like this. But that doesn't excuse him from moping around with that dour look on his face as if he's the one who's sick and not you."

"It's not that he's without feelings—he's just not in touch with them."

"That's just his excuse. He's self-absorbed, Katherine. He never bucks you up at all. You're so strong in every other way I don't know why you put up with it."

"Please, Richard, let's not spoil a wonderful evening. I'm quite tired. Thank you for joining me tonight. We must do it again."

"May I help you upstairs?"

"No, I can make it on my own. Please leave a light on for Jack."

SHALL ONE EVER BE AT PEACE with oneself, ever quiet and uninterrupted—without pain—with the one whom one loves under the same roof? Is it too much to ask? she wondered, alone in her bedroom. Richard can't understand. Jack is everything to me. I can't let our love die. But the only way I can keep it alive is by finding a cure. He cannot love a consumptive.

16

August 1920

There are always these moments in life when the limits of suffering are reached and we become heroes and heroines.

Revelations—KM

"WELL, THAT'S A SURPRISE!" Katherine said looking up from her letter at LM. "Elizabeth has accepted my invitation to tea." Katherine was reading her afternoon letters.

"That's nice, dear. Shall we get those special scones for the occasion? A little expensive but if you have a very special guest coming . . . . Who is Elizabeth? I can't remember."

"My father's cousin. I wonder why she accepted my invitation? I only invited her because Pa asked me to. She's had a rather miserable time of it, he says, since her divorce from Earl Russell. Pa thinks she was mistreated and needs someone in the Beauchamp family to lend her support. Or perhaps my recent short story reviews have been printed in the New Zealand papers and he's read that widowed, divorced and disenfranchised women are consoled by them."

"Well I don't know about being consoled but I've certainly felt an affinity for the women in your stories. I consider them now to be my friends. Katie, do you not want that piece of bread and butter?" She shook her head and continued reading a letter. "Then I'll take it, if you don't mind," said LM, reaching out for it and continued chattering. "Earl Russell? Isn't that Bertrand Russell's brother? Oh yes, I met Bertrand when I came to fetch you from those Bloomsbury gatherings at Virginia's. He used to come around to that flat you shared with several other bohemian artists in Bloomsbury . . . during the war, wasn't it? You'd shoo me away so you could be alone with him. What was that flat called?"

Katherine dropped a sugar in her tea. "The Ark, Ida, the Ark. And you needn't mention Bertrand or his brother when Elizabeth comes for tea."

"Of course not. You know how well I keep your secrets. It must be a long time since you last saw her because I've never met her and I thought by now I'd met all your family. When did you last see her?"

"Good Heavens! It's been ten years! At a tea given at my uncle's house to introduce George and announce our engagement."

"She met George Bowden? How unfortunate for her."

"George wasn't so terrible. It was my fault marrying him."

Katherine felt LM's eyes on her when she poured another cup of tea. Stare all you want, she thought, just don't start up again about George or Jack for that matter.

Katherine's thoughts turned to the famous Elizabeth. She'd grown up listening to her father talk about how extraordinary she was, a cut above all other women. Not only had Elizabeth become an extremely popular author in her early thirties when she published *Elizabeth and Her German Garden*, reprinted twenty-one times in the first year, and translated into several languages, but she'd also married a wealthy German count and given birth to five children. Katherine had fallen short of Elizabeth's achievements. Jack was certainly not a count and though they still spoke of having children, she was childless. And she was not rich from what she considered her meager body of work.

Elizabeth's taxi pulled up at #2 Portland Villas, ten minutes late to Katherine's masked irritation. Katherine found her cousin's light grey wool skirt and jacket and matching grey plumed hat enviable. Wishing she had taken more time with her own dress, she quickly covered its drabness with her multi-colored, embroidered Spanish shawl and stood up tall to greet her.

As she pulled back from Elizabeth's kiss on her cheek, she saw the familiar shocked look on her face. The look that was on all the faces of those who'd heard she was ill but didn't understand *how* ill. But in Elizabeth's face she also saw authentic concern and felt moved by it. "I was surprised to hear back from you," said Katherine, offering a chair and then sitting herself. She preferred the sofa but didn't want to limp across the room in front of Elizabeth.

"I've been planning to visit but, as you well know, being a writer yourself, there is never enough time to write, and when one does find the time everyone and everything is forgotten."

They looked at each other for a long moment before Elizabeth said, "Your Pa has kept me informed about your illness and tells me how hard you've fought against it. He's very worried. I told him I would help anyway I could. All you need to do is ask me." Katherine heard no pity in her voice just an honest appeal to be friends and she liked her for it.

LM brought in a tea tray laden with scones. Katherine poured the tea and was relieved that her hand didn't embarrass her and cramp.

"I wish my stay in London was longer so I could visit you more often," said Elizabeth, "but I'm leaving next week for my châlet in Randogne, Switzerland. Perhaps someday you will visit me there. Many Londoners come to the Alps to take open-air cures."

"Yes, an open-air cure has been suggested to me but I have a terrible fear of the cold. That's why I go south to the Riviera, but perhaps someday I'll change directions."

"Your father tells me that you're an ardent admirer of gardens. If you visit next summer you will have an opportunity to admire mine as I have had the privilege to admire your novel-reviews in *The Athenaeum*."

Katherine looked down at her teacup rather than show her blush.

"Your husband was very clever to add your review column. Or was that your idea? I find them well thought out and often quite amusing. I have read several books based on your reviews and skipped several others for the same reason."

Katherine looked up at her cousin. "Thank you Elizabeth, you're most generous with your compliments."

"Your husband, too, has gained much respect in the literary world as a brilliant young editor with modernist views. But perhaps you are the one to be congratulated. Am I right in thinking you instrumental in his decisions?" She continued without waiting for Katherine to answer. "From what I've read of your work, I can tell that you are a modern woman with very strong opinions. But why haven't I been able to find any of your new stories? Are you not publishing?"

"There is my new fiction column in *The Athenaeum.*"

"Ah yes, I read *Revelations.* I couldn't get my heart around that one like I did with that brilliant masterpiece *Prelude.*"

"Thank you. I'm planning to write several new stories this winter that take place in New Zealand as *Prelude* did. But I have so little time to work here. I'm most anxious to return to France for this reason and am leaving in a few weeks myself."

"Yes, one must write mustn't one? How else can we writers enjoy life?" she said, and smiled.

Katherine's eyes lingered on Elizabeth's. They were the same deep brown as the cup of tea she lifted to her lips and as unreadable.

"Please tell me about yourself, Katherine. I want to get to know you."

"I don't have much to tell. My stories tell much more about me than I ever could."

"Yes. I can see that. Your stories about women are quite believable. Your characters unforgettable, I might say, even haunting. You are a far more serious writer than I am. Your stories go beneath the surface. Mine are far more superficial."

"Yes but you have achieved great popularity. Pa admires you. It influenced his decision to let me come to London on my own. He thought I might follow in your successful footsteps. So far I've disappointed him. Brief sketches compared to your novels."

"Oh but you could write a wonderful novel. Have you ever considered it?"

"Yes . . . often. Started several times. Notebooks filled with scenes and character sketches. I even have a title for it, *Karori*—my childhood home. The story takes place there and in London." For a moment she submerged herself in the landscape of *Karori.* She awoke to Elizabeth's curious stare. It had only been a brief second but she felt in that moment that her cousin had shared a foreigner's landscape that separated them from ever being authentic Englishwomen. A separation they were both proud of.

"You must accept my invitation to Châlet de Soleil in Randogne. I've written my best novels there. It's remote . . . quiet . . . There's solitude. The pure alpine air will revive you as it does me. Listen to me," she laughed. "I sound like an advertisement in the *Times* for open-air clinics. Sorry, but know that my enthusiasm is authentic and so is my invitation. If you come in the spring or summer, we can spend time together working in the garden."

"I think I might just do that, Elizabeth. Thank you for asking me."

They spoke further about the books they were reading: Katherine—Shakespeare, Elizabeth—more current work. Some Katherine liked, others she didn't. She spoke of her concern after reading so many after-the-war novels that ignored how the war had changed the way they lived. How writers wanted to continue telling stories as if the war had never happened. New ways must be found, particularly for female writers to not tell us how the world had changed for them but show us and in showing us reveal the truth. Yes, show the beautiful leaf but do not ignore the worm underneath it. That was Katherine's challenge and should be every writer's challenge who cared passionately about their art. Elizabeth spoke of the novel she was now working on that she hoped Katherine would someday review. All of Elizabeth's books were protests against female frailty in a man's world.

They then spoke of their linked family, the Beauchamps, and when the clock on the mantelpiece chimed five times both were surprised how late it was.

"Oh dear, I always forget the time. I must leave. I have a train to catch. You needn't get up, my dear, I can find my way out."

"Thank you for coming Elizabeth. Unfortunately, very few members of my family find their way to Portland Villas at Hampstead Heath and it has been a special treat having you here. Perhaps because we are both not truly English, that I feel an affinity with you that I don't feel with my English friends."

"Do you ever think of going back home for a visit?" asked Elizabeth.

"Oh my yes. But with Jack's position as *Athenaeum's* editor he hasn't the time to go with me and I'm not well enough to go alone. But as soon as I'm better."

Elizabeth stood up to leave, put on her plumed hat, and adjusted it in the mirror over the mantel. "Please tell your husband I was sorry he wasn't here for us to meet, but I did enjoy our time alone. Men too often interrupt honest conversations between women with their need to express their importance on all matters. I look forward to longer chats in Randogne. I believe we have much in common."

After she left, Katherine felt dreary. Elizabeth's cheerful affirmation of life had been so brilliant that the parlor sagged without her. Perhaps an open-air cure in the Alps is a good plan, she thought.

THE MORNING she and LM left for the train station, Jack was under a deadline at the paper and couldn't see her off. They had both avoided discussing his move to Brett's, and kept their conversations about the paper. As long as she didn't know anything about it, Katherine had decided she didn't care about his ridiculous affair with Brett.

I don't love Jack less, she thought, just differently. My love for him has become a cannonball tied to my feet, when I am already trying not to drown. If he could only, for a minute, serve me, help me, give HIMSELF up! I never could get well with him. I must go it alone. It's the writing that will see me through. That's where I must focus all my attention.

After her trunk had been taken downstairs to the waiting taxi, she turned back at the bedroom door to say good-bye. Stripped of its props, the room became an empty stage. Its main actress, the heroine, was traveling on to another play, another story that would be far more joyous.

And I can't write it here, she thought, putting a new notebook in her traveling case to use on the train. Until I'm cured, it's better for both of us that we live separate lives.

She closed the curtains on the windows that looked out on the park, switched off the gaslight, and firmly closed the door behind her.

WHEN SHE AND LM stepped off the train in Menton she felt she'd come home. The familiar sweet air touching her face, the brilliant sunlight, the small quaint station with only a few people, the silence. A porter found them a carriage that transported them and their luggage to her new home that Connie and Jinnie had prepared for her—Villa Isola Bella.

"Can this truly be the place?" whispered LM, when they pulled up on a leafy lane thickly overhung with lush green plants. "Look. There's Connie's maid, Annette, waving at us."

Katherine was too tired to enjoy the garden. She requested that Annette bring her immediately to her bedroom. Before retiring she stood on the balcony and listened to the cicadas, the frogs and someone playing notes on a flute. She felt tears of joy blur her eyes and whispered, "Let the new play begin."

The next day before allowing Annette to bring her breakfast she sat up in bed and guiltily wrote the novel-review that she promised to send from Paris. She'd been too tired on the train. After sending LM to the post office, she finally allowed herself to breathe deeply under the shade of a giant date palm. Her eyes took in a vast budding magnolia and a tangerine tree covered in green balls. Her thoughts turned to Jack and how happy he would be here. She went inside to write him her first impressions while fresh in her mind:

A real little salon with velvet covered furniture and an immense dead clock and a gilt mirror; and two very handsome crimson vases which remind me of fountains filled with blood. It has 2 windows. One looks over the garden gate, the other opens onto the terrace and looks over the sea. The dining room is equally charming in its way & has French windows, too. Upstairs are four bedrooms with balconies overlooking the sea and are carpeted all over & sumptuous in a doll's house way.

I do not know what it is about this place. But it is enough just to be here for everything to change—I think already of the poetry you would write if you lived such a life. I wish you were not tied. I have always at the bottom of my deep cup of happiness that dark spot, which is that you are not living as you would wish to live.

17

October 1920

32nd Birthday

When I first saw her, October 15, 1920, Patient had been suffering from lung troubles for three years, and at the time was complaining of bad attacks of coughing, especially morning and evening, of much stiffness and pain in the right hip joint and muscles round and also in the spine, and of palpitations in the heart on the least provocation.

History: After an attack of peritonitis in 1910 at age 21 (very likely from gonococcal origin previous four months of white discharge), left Fallopian tube was removed. Has been more or less troubled ever since, suffering from rheumatism, in various muscles of the body, hip joints and small joints in feet.

Dr. Bouchage—Menton, France

KATHERINE HESITATED SENDING Dr. Bouchage's medical report to Jack. Not because of the "origin" of an earlier illness first explained to her by Dr. Sorapure that Jack already knew about, but the detailed report described a chronically ill invalid.

What was not described in Dr. Bouchage's report was the happiness she'd found on her walks in the verdant garden, her reflections from her balcony watching the gilded sunset over the sea, the delicious food prepared by her new cook and housekeeper, Marie, and the pleasures found in her dollhouse villa where she could write freely without interruption. In the one month she'd been at Isola Bella she'd kept up with the weekly novel-reviews and written what she called her hallucinatory story, *The Young Girl,* for *Athenaeum*'s fiction column, and worked on a new story for the next issue.

"I'm not dead—at least not yet," she said out loud, quickly rising from the bed. She walked without limping over to the travel chest she carried from retreat to retreat, filled with letters from family and friends, comforting knowledge that she was alive for other people, too. If I exist for them, she thought, even during these long lonely absences, then I exist.

She insisted to Marie and LM that all decorative items remain where she placed them because they represented stability in her impermanent life. Each vase, bowl, even the medicine bottles, had been placed to create a balance, a flow. Like each comma in her stories, they were not arbitrary decisions but well thought out. She didn't want Jack or any other editor removing her commas and she didn't want anyone changing her ornamental placements. Her personal belongings were rooted around her and she was writing again. She was no longer a weed without purpose. She transformed into a seed, planted in the soil—not random—but useful, purposeful, enriched.

"Katie!" LM called up to the Juliet balcony from the terrace below. "Teatime. I've been to the post office. Wait until you see the stack of letters."

"I'm coming down." She briefly looked in the mirror, pleased to see the silk buttons of her dressing gown straining against the recent gain in weight. She smiled at her mother's cane sitting in the corner, unused, and descended the spiral stairs to the black and white marble entry, stopping to smell the fresh bouquet of jonquils on the table.

Out on the terrace was a tray holding fresh bread and jam, and the letters. She settled back into her wicker chair to read Jack's letter first and LM poured her a cup of tea. She sat up abruptly, almost knocking over the full cup. "Oh no!"

"What's wrong now?" asked LM calmly, accustomed to Katherine's outbursts when reading Jack's letters.

"Floryan is back in our lives again. Why can't he leave me alone?"

"Who?"

"Don't you remember the man in Bavaria who helped me recover, the man who—"

She was interrupted by a coughing spasm.

"Now calm yourself, my dear," said LM, handing her a glass of water. "Of course I remember, but you asked me to never mention his name again so I don't. In all honesty I remember him quite well. I didn't like him. An insidious pest who shows up whenever things are going well for you like right now. Remember! Need I remind you that I was the one who forced him to leave your cottage in Runcton where he had comfortably settled down to live off you. *Rhythm*'s owner had run off with the assets and the secretary and left you and Jack bankrupt. You had to give up your lovely cottage, return the leased furniture, and move into that hovel in London. The creditors were on your back until you insisted on paying the overdue printing costs off with your allowance and you and Jack then ran off yourselves to Paris, hoping for a fresh start. It was just before the war and—"

"All right, Ida! You do remember. I only hope I outlive you so that my sordid past will go with you to your grave."

"Katie! What a thing to say though I do hope I die before you as I would be too lonely without you. Now tell me what does Floryan want?"

"He wants forty pounds for the letters I wrote to him ten years ago."

"Forty pounds! That's absurd."

"He tried the same thing with Bernard Shaw but Shaw told him the letters had no value."

"Well perhaps you should follow his example. Why pay forty pounds for some foolish love letters sent by a lonely young girl who had lost—" LM was stopped by Katherine's glare and asked instead, "Must you agree to it?"

"I don't want a scandal. What if he gave them to the press and they're published? It would give the Bloomsbury gossips too much fun. I don't want that period in my life revealed to anyone. Jack writes that Floryan must have found out about the advance Constable offered for my story collection as he asked the same amount. But I won't get paid that advance until the stories are delivered and Floryan wants the money now. I can't ask my father for an advance on my allowance and asking Jack is just as humiliating. You know what misers they both are. Jack would try to negotiate a lower figure and that would only make Floryan angry."

LM put down the bed jacket she was mending. "Let me help you, Katie."

"No, Jones. You've helped me out enough."

"I won't have you worry over this. Your health is far more important to me than forty pounds. Please I insist. It'll be your birthday present."

"Thank you, Jones, I couldn't ask for a more generous gift but I'll find some way to pay you back."

Katherine wrote to Jack asking him to settle with Floryan, telling him that LM would pay the blackmailer's fee.

Please take Floryan to a solicitor and get his sworn statement that he will never threaten me again. Don't trust him Jack. Recover those letters before you pay him. Once you have them, destroy them."

A week later she received a telegram from Jack:

LETTERS IN MY POSSESSION. STOP. AND FLORYAN'S SIGNED DECLARATION. STOP. POSTING THEM TO YOU IMMEDIATELY. STOP. YOU MUST BE THE ONE TO DESTROY THEM IF THAT IS YOUR WISH. STOP. LOVE, JACK.

A week went by and the letters didn't arrive. Katherine found it difficult to work. She wrote to Jack asking why the letters hadn't been sent.

SORRY. STOP. FORGOT. STOP. SENT THE PACKET TODAY. STOP. JACK.

She was furious. How could he forget something that was obviously so important to her as those letters?

When the packet did arrive, she carried it up to her bedroom. She feared reading words written during her "Oscar Wilde" period, when she risked all for the experience. There were about ten letters tied together with a pink ribbon. On the envelopes she recognized her quickly scribbled handwriting, which had not changed, she thought, but she wondered who had thought to tie the letters together with pink ribbon? Was it hers from long ago that Floryan had kept as a souvenir? Or had Jack read the letters and retied them with a pink ribbon? She hoped not. Her instructions were to destroy not read. He knew too well that she wanted to leave as few traces of her camping ground as possible after she was gone.

"Annihilate the past," she said, holding up the packet. Under Oscar Wilde's influence she had once believed that was simple to do. But it wasn't. Remembering the slight gesture of someone lighting an Abdullah cigarette brought back . . . .

The flame swallowed each letter she fed to it. One by one, words to ashes—a ceremonial cremation of a secret past.

ON HER 32ND BIRTHDAY, she polished the silver spoon Jack sent to Ospedaletti on her last birthday. His forgetfulness on this birthday was a painful reminder of how estranged they were now and how thoughtless he could be. Her only birthday present was Dr. Bouchage's weekly experimental iodine injection to relieve rheumatism. But the injections only effects were mood swings, fever, and headaches. Illness was so tiresome and relentless.

The candles lit, she sat down and sipped cream of mushroom soup from Jack's delicate spoon. A fairy spoon she'd been saving to place in the Heron's cupboard. Jack didn't speak of their dream cottage in Sussex anymore.

A few days later propped up in her bed she scribbled in her notebook, *Jack wishes me dead.* The ink bled onto the page and she got up and walked over to her writing table to blot it. The brass crocodile's smile always tickled her humor but tonight it sneered at her. She sneered right back and said, "Do you, too, think Jack wishes me dead?"

More depressing thoughts started to fill her head as she looked down at Brett's letter written in green ink on willowy stationery. Jack's letter lay next to it and the envelope they came in, addressed to her. "Why else would he send me her letter?" she asked the crocodile who glared back at her with his reptilian eyes.

"Oh so that's what you think? He's asking me to rescue him from a hysterical woman? That this is not his fault. That he didn't encourage her? The truth is she flattered and got him! She listened and didn't criticize and sat at his feet and worshipped and asked for the prophet's help. His vanity and self-absorption delivers him into the arms of countless INFERIOR females and when they become inconvenient he wants me to get rid of them because he doesn't have the courage to do it."

She imagined Jack and Brett's laughter in the Elephant's parlor, sharing an intimate evening amusing themselves by reading her love letters to Floryan. Is that why he didn't send them immediately? she asked herself. She had never believed him when he said he'd *forgotten.* Was the pink ribbon Brett's?

Oh why didn't I put a stop to this affair long ago? That's my problem. I don't deal with unpleasantness when it occurs. I don't confront the situation. I bury it within.

She reread Brett's paragraph about wanting to peep under Jack's shirt and her schoolgirl threat to be severe with him.

He asks me if I resent her letter? Is that not a horrific question to ask his wife?

She picked up her pen and wrote:

I do resent it most deeply. I feel violently physically sick.

* * *

IN HER BATH she thought if she could buy Isola Bella she would, but if that was not possible she hoped Jinnie and Connie would accept her offer to lease it for another year. She knew she had disappointed them by not converting to Catholicism but hopefully they wouldn't let that influence their decision.

Submerged under the warm water, her arms at her sides, her legs straight out, and only thirty-two, she thought, this is how I shall look, this is how they will arrange me in my coffin. She pressed her shiny wet toes against the end of the bath. They look so gay, so unconscious of their fate. They seem really to be smiling all in a row—the little toe so small.

"No not yet," she said aloud, throwing her sponge at an imaginary row of distinguished white-uniformed doctors leaning over her, stethoscopes swinging from their necks, hammers in their hands.

"Fooled you, didn't I?" she shouted. "You said two to three years. Four years on the outside if I checked myself into a sanitarium. Ha!" Her laughter shattered their apparitions. The stethoscopes hung briefly above her, reflecting the moonlight, and then were swooped into the night.

She slipped out of the tub, wrapped her dressing gown around her shoulders and stepped out onto the moonlit terrace. The sea's white caps glistened under the full moon. The mimosa's fern-like leaves whispered gently to her, "You're going to be all right. Don't worry. You're going to get well."

Dr. Bouchage wasn't lying when he told her she was better. Even if I'm never cured, she thought, I can accept being an invalid as long as I'm given the time to continue writing for years to come. Not two—but many. I must be given more time, there is much still to write.

Ideas started to form for a new story and she returned inside.

At her table she wrote a quick sketch about a seductress who jilted one man for a younger lover and was now about to jilt him for someone else. She felt no remorse. Promiscuous love affairs lack true emotions.

The title came quickly to her and she scribbled down: *Poison.*

LM found her still working when she brought in the morning tea.

ONE OF THE MANY PLEASANT AFTERNOONS she and LM shared at Isola Bella found them seated on the cobblestone terrace sipping chamomile tea under a giant umbrella that half-shaded them from the bright sun. The late autumn breeze was brisk but while the sun shown they could stay outdoors comfortably.

An ancient brick wall protected them from the eyes of curious passersby and allowed only a breeze from the Mediterranean to pass over the wall onto the terrace. The drifting puffy white clouds provided a changing landscape to Katherine's tranquil mood. She closed her eyes and felt the breeze on her face. On days like this she never wanted to return to London or the literary salons that Jack now found so seductive.

Stretched out on a cane longue, she picked up an old notebook from 1903, the year she and LM had first met at Queen's College in London.

She was amused by how little LM had changed since they were students. *A giant body with a little voice.* So much wanting to please others that she had made it her life's ambition. So afraid to give her own opinion that she didn't have one. So shy that when she expressed herself, she looked down and mumbled incoherently. Incapable of making the slightest decision without approval.

"Do you remember Queen's College fondly?" Katherine asked.

"Why, my dearest, for such a brilliant woman you ask very silly questions. We wouldn't have become such good friends, would we, if not for Queen's College? I wouldn't be sitting here now, so, yes, I remember it fondly."

"There's something I have always been curious about. Why didn't you ever boast about your prestigious scholarship prize? I only knew about it from the other girls. If it had been me, I would have shouted the news from the courtyard."

"Oh, it wasn't that important!"

"Not important. You got the highest marks in our class. You could have succeeded in so many ways. Musician? Scholar? Instead you're taking care of me."

"It's what I want to do, and besides, you're much easier to take care of than my father. After my mother died his grief was really inconsolable. He looked at me with such disapproval and scorn I thought he held me responsible. The smallest task I accomplished displeased him. I tried to take charge of the household but he argued against all my decisions down to the smallest detail. If I bought one pound of flour I should have bought two or if I bought two I should have bought one. And always the cost. I had to budget every penny but he still thought I was extravagant."

Katherine laughed. "He sounds like me!"

LM blushed. "Well, yes, you do have similarities, but he was far more of a tyrant than you could ever be. And you're not cruel."

Oh yes I am, thought Katherine.

"At the end of each month he would call me into his dark, clammy study to go over the accounts. Even with the fire blazing there was a chill. He'd thump his cane on the stone floor." LM's usual canary voice turned loud and gruff as she humped over and imitating her father said, "I told you not to make any purchases without my permission." She hit her fist on the table, rattling the teacups. "Do you hear me, young lady!"

Katherine laughed at LM's mime.

"I swear there were times when I walked by and he stuck out that horrid cane to trip me intentionally. My mother's sudden death had cut out his heart. I was terribly afraid of him and afraid for him at the same time."

Katherine poured them both another cup of tea, and thought back to the winter before in Italy. "You weren't afraid when you shot those prowlers with the revolver."

"I had to. They might have hurt you."

"That night I realized how much you cared for me and I've felt very safe ever since. Truthfully, I don't think I could live here without you. Here at Isola Bella I've had the best working conditions I've ever known and you have a lot to do with that. You leave me alone and keep others from bothering me."

She looked into LM's smiling, blushing face, a face that could pass for a grinning pumpkin but there was no laughter in the eyes. The eyes were dark holes, without any light illuminating from inside. "You were so sad at school and so quiet," said Katherine. "Even Professor Lester, the kindest of our teachers, couldn't get you to speak above a whisper in his writing class. He gave me such encouragement to become a writer."

"He encouraged me, too," said LM, unexpectedly defensive.

"You? Were you interested in writing? Wait I do remember one night when you came to my room gripping sheets of paper you wanted to read to me. You were so excited. I had just put down my pen after writing a story for Lester's class. I read first. I remember you were quite moved by it. I think you cried. I don't remember what the writing assignment was. Do you?"

"Yes I do," said LM. "We were to write a story about someone in our lives that had profoundly influenced us. I wrote about my mother."

"Was that the story you were holding in your hand? Why didn't you read it?"

"Not after you read yours. Your story was so much better than mine. You wrote about your mother, too. She came alive when you described her coming to your room at night to tuck you into bed and how you felt safe knowing she was there. She smoothed things over, kept all your lives in order. You see, you were describing my mother, but doing a much better job of it. I'm afraid that was the end of my writing ambitions."

The setting sun cast shadows across Katherine's longue. She would have gone inside sooner but it was so seldom LM talked about herself.

"I'm so sorry I didn't hear your story that night," she said. "I'm sure it was quite good."

Katherine enjoyed a few puffs from her newly lit cigarette, and said, "You were such a mystery to me and the other students. You hardly ever said a word but then in debating class you came alive. You were a very powerful debater. I was often angry when the girls voted for your argument instead of mine."

"I argued for what they had been taught to believe. What they already understood. You were full of original ideas that we English girls found shocking. You were foreign, even exotic. You spoke differently. Dressed differently. We were unaccustomed to seeing such boldness in a fourteen-year-old schoolgirl. Even the way you walked expressed a confidence we didn't have. The other girls teased you and called you the Little Colonial."

LM stood up. "You're shivering. Shall we go in or shall I get you the eiderdown?"

"The eiderdown, please. I'd like to watch the sunset."

Katherine brought out her notebook. She wanted to write a story about two sisters. She'd call one sister Constantia, as constant as LM was.

She saw the story opening with the Colonel, their father, dead a few days. The two daughters suddenly liberated from his tyranny didn't know how to behave. Never given the opportunity to mature, to develop their own ideas, they'd sacrificed their youth serving their father.

The story captured her full attention for several days. She was late on the novel-reviews, but she dedicated her every hour to *The Daughters of the Late Colonel*, her longest story since *Prelude.*

18

December 1920

Villa Isola Bella

And now I'll be personal, darling. Look here you ought to have sent me your Corona! You really ought to have. Can't you possibly imagine what all this writing out has been to a person as weak as I damnably am? You can't or a stone would have sent it. You knew what a help it was to me in London.

But oh dear I don't mean to accuse you—because I can't bear, as you know, to make you feel unhappy. But what you could have saved me—I can't say! Isn't it awful that I have not dared to add to your burdens by reminding you before?

I must remind myself that the hole I might so easily trip into is far bigger—far blacker than your troubles.

Letters—KM

DR. BOUCHAGE PRESSED THE STETHOSCOPE to her chest and up close she saw what she had missed before—his burning eyes. All consumptives have that same glow. The inextinguishable fever.

"Your right lung is still inflamed but quiescent," he said after his examination." She thought how tedious it had become hearing about her condition that never changed. "But your inactive left lung is pressing against your heart. That's why it's painful and belaboring to breathe, even on short walks or climbing a few steps. Your heart is exhausted from the strain of keeping you alive. It needs complete rest. Your life will be shortened if you don't cut back on your work."

"I can't do that! It's my writing that keeps me alive, not my heart! I might as well be dead if I don't write."

"Calm down, Mrs. Murry," he said gripping her hand. "Listen to me. Your life is in danger. Limit your writing to a few hours a day."

She looked again into his fiery eyes. "Am I right in believing that you have a personal understanding of what it's like to be a consumptive? Can you stop your work?" she asked.

"You are an astute diagnostician, Mrs. Murry. Yes, I am a consumptive but I find it better in my practice not to mention it and, no, I continue my work, but I'm careful."

"I'm sorry you're one of us but could you help me understand why one moment I feel very alive and full of promise and the next moment I'm suddenly drowning in despair. Is it me or the illness?"

"It's most likely the fever brought on by your illness. Melancholia is not unusual for us and, in your case, even hysteria. When one has suffered as long as you have one has a different sense of reality, a heightened sense. The world can appear awful at one moment and quite beautiful the next."

"You make it sound like I'm going mad."

"No, you just experience life differently from those who are unconscious of death's approach." He put his stethoscope in his bag and pulled out an amber colored tincture and a needle.

Katherine pulled away. "No more of those iodine injections. They make me too tired and bring on headaches."

"But isn't there less pain in your hips, less cramping in your hands?"

"No, not really." She smiled. "I need a typewriter more than I need iodine."

"Is that so hard to find?"

She laughed. "It shouldn't be. I've asked my husband to send me his and I'm waiting for his response."

"Certainly he'll say yes."

She smiled again. "I hope so."

He stood up to leave and then changed his mind. "Mrs. Murry do you believe in God? Or do you have some other belief or religious faith?"

"Nothing formal or anything that I practice. I'm not one to get down on my knees and pray to a merciless god if that's what you're asking. What I do believe is that if I could accept Death, submit to the inevitable rather than try and escape from it, my days would be far more bearable, even peaceful. But when Death lurks in the shadows, watches me, waits for me . . . I'm terribly afraid.

"When I sleep, he guides me in my dreams. In one recurring dream I embark with him in a little boat that enters a dark fearful gulf and I cry out—'put me on land again.' But it's a futile cry. The shadowy figure rows on. I want to uncover my eyes to see the mystery before me . . . but I wake up screaming."

"Is your husband coming for the Christmas holidays?"

"I've asked him not to. You see, I don't know what I want. At times I plead with him to come immediately but that's when I'm feeling despair and loneliness. Then there are other times when I'm writing and don't want to be disturbed by anyone, not even Jack. Then I cling to my solitude and search within for Truth in the comforting silence. These are the brief moments when I glimpse reality but then a veil covers my view and I can't see clearly anymore."

She realized she was gazing out at the sea and returned her gaze upon him. "Doctor, do you understand what I'm talking about or does all this sound ridiculous? Jack tells me it does. Am I going mad?"

"No, Mrs. Murry. It's quite understandable. Thirty-two is a very young age to come to terms with the pain and fatigue that two diseases are forcing your body to bear every day. Suffering that is untreatable with anything I have here." He patted the satchel sitting in his lap.

"You know there are moments when I believe my suffering is a rare privilege and just like in my dream I should stop resisting it."

He pulled out his pocket watch. "Oh dear, look at the time." He snapped his satchel shut and stood up to leave. "I must hurry. Other patients are waiting for me. I'll be back in a few days to check on you."

His abrupt departure left her in despair, cut off from everyone and not even her doctor, a mutual consumptive, could help her. If not for her writing, she'd be lost.

She sat down at her writing table and wrote Jack.

It is with the most extreme reluctance that I am writing to tell you that Katherine can't go on. She will review the last two books you sent and can do no more.

She looked out her window at the arc of the rising new moon.

I am not dying. If I were I would have you come immediately. It's a question of shortening my life if I keep writing the reviews and I can't do that. I do not want to die because I have done nothing to justify having lived yet. I must keep alive until there is a modest shelf of books with K.M. backs.

A WEEK LATER, she received Jack's reply and before opening the envelope she anticipated a sympathetic, loving response. But instead it was a confession—*Thinking about my lies this evening, I discovered that if I had told you the whole truth from the beginning, I should not have been corrupt . . .*

In one week, he'd considered sleeping with a tart but took her to dinner instead, impulsively kissed their close friend Anne, took Brett in his arms, caressed her and, revolted, pushed her away. A few days later he'd shared a car with Princess Bibesco and impulsively kissed her on the cheek. He was afraid that these women would think from his sudden intimacy that he wanted to make love to them, but he didn't. What he really wanted was to be held gently and comforted and though he didn't come right out and say it she knew he felt it was her fault because she was ill and unavailable to him.

Too angry to write back she sent him a wire:

> STOP TORMENTING ME WITH THESE FALSE DEPRESSING LETTERS. STOP. AT ONCE BE A MAN OR DON'T WRITE ME.

Later, after calming down she wrote to him:

I told you to be free—because I meant it. What happens in your personal life does not affect me. I have of you what I want—a relationship which is unique, but it is not what the world understands by marriage.

She hesitated. Was that really the truth? Did she want him to be free? But was it fair for her to ask him to be faithful to an absent wife?

That is to say, I do not in any way depend on you, neither can you shake me. Nobody can. I do not know how it is, but I live withdrawn from my personal life. (This is hard to say.) I am a writer first. In the past, it is true, when I worked less, my writing self was merged in my personal self. I felt conscious of you—to the exclusion of almost everything, at times.

But now I do not. You are dearer than anyone in the world to me—but more than anything else—more even than talking or laughing or being happy I want to write. This sounds so ugly, I wish I didn't have to say it. But your letter makes me feel you would be relieved if it were said . . .

She quickly sealed the letter and asked LM to take it to the post office before she changed her mind.

Two days later the pain she felt from cutting Jack off was far worse than anything he had done to hurt her. She felt sure he wouldn't be with her for the Christmas holidays. She shuddered thinking of the cold, colorless, and friendless life she would have without someone to love. No, she must find a way to forgive him, even share the blame for his infidelities. Wouldn't she have turned to someone else out of loneliness if he had been ill and constantly separated from her? Years ago, *she'd* been unfaithful and he'd forgiven her. The truth was, as far from perfect his love was, he did love her, and she needed to be loved by someone. And there was no other "someone" but Jack.

She sent him a telegram:

> PAY NO HEED MY LETTER. STOP. ILLNESS EXASPERATED ME. STOP. ARE YOU ARRIVING TUESDAY. STOP. IF SO WON'T WRITE AGAIN. STOP. FONDEST LOVE. STOP. REPLY.

* * *

SHE PUSHED AWAY HER WRITING CASE and got up from her bed, laughing and shouting, "It's finished! It's finished!"

"Katie! What's wrong?" shouted LM, awoken from her sleep.

"Why must you always think the worse has happened when I call out? Look at me," she said, grinning like a Cheshire cat. "I called you to come celebrate my happiness with a cup of tea."

"Celebrate? Tea? It's three in the morning."

"My story is done." She waved a thick stack of pages. "It came very quickly, with hardly a break or correction." She coughed. "*The Daughters of the Late Colonel* is my best story ever and it all came together in a few days. Tea, Jones! We must have tea."

LM returned with the tea tray and they sat cross-legged on Katherine's bed and sipped from their well-sugared teacups.

Katherine burst out with, "Did you know that I've always had a longing to heal people and make them whole, enrich them? Not just in my writing, I want to do it in life, too. I imagine, if you were free of me, you would save the entire world."

As if on cue, LM leaped up and swung out her large hands cupping a mosquito that she threw out the window.

"Don't you want to do more than protect me from mosquitoes?" she called out, but LM, standing at the window, didn't answer.

Katherine joined her and put her hand on LM's shoulder. "My God, you're my age. You should marry and have children."

LM turned to her, "I have no desire to marry. And your stories are my children. Or at least I'm their godmother. I have all the happiness I need right here with you."

"Jones, I won't always be here to give you such happiness," she said quietly. They both looked out at the moonlit sea.

LM spoke first, "Katie, please don't talk like that. For me you'll always be alive."

Katherine grabbed her arm and swung her around. "Listen to me. I'm trying to warn you. Know that someday I'll either be cured, or

I'll be gone and you'll be independent, and when that happens please don't waste the rest of your life believing I'm alive in the next room." Seeing the fright reflected in LM's moonlit eyes, she changed her tone and said playfully, "To be sure you don't, I'll send you a small matchbox with a coffin's worm in it to remind you where I've gone."

"Stop saying gone. You're not going anywhere. And no more talk of morbid things—worms in matchboxes, where do you get such ideas!"

LM set the teacups back on the tray and seeing all was in order said good night.

After she left, Katherine sat up in bed and watched the morning sun reach across the sea until it touched her balcony. She put the writing case on her knees and wrote in her notebook:

I simply can't afford to die with one very half-and-half little book and one bad one and a few stories to my name. In spite of everything, in spite of all I know and have felt—I have this longing to praise Life—to sing my minute song of praise, and it doesn't matter whether it's listened to or not.

In dawn's early light, she jotted down a sketch about a maid who chooses to remain with her mistress after being sorely tempted to leave with a man who has asked her to be his wife.

ON THE SCHEDULED DAY, December 20th, Jack arrived at Villa Isola Bella. LM showed him upstairs explaining that Katherine had been too tired to come downstairs that day.

"Oh Boge, is it really you?" Katherine called out hoarsely, peeking out from under the covers. "I thought I'd frightened you away."

"You will never frighten me away. It's more like I was frightening you away," he said, putting his Felti on the bureau and leaning over to kiss her lips. He sat on the edge of the bed and together they watched the crackling logs spark and sputter in the fireplace.

"I know I've hurt you Katherine and I am very sorry. I don't want to cause you any further suffering. Will you forgive me?"

"I've been lying here, waiting for you," she said calmly, "planning what I was going to say to you. And now you're here so I can tell you that I've come to the conclusion that suffering can be overcome. I don't mean physical suffering. The pain of my body and lungs I can control. It's child's play compared to emotional suffering.

"Last year in Italy I thought one more shadow would mean Death, but suffering is boundless. It's unavoidable. I mustn't fight it any longer. It's better to accept it."

"Don't say that. You mustn't give in to it. I've always thought you had the strength to fight it and overcome it on your own, or at least deny it and that I was the weaker one. And then I've only made things worse by confessing my indiscretions to you, not realizing how much I would hurt you. You will suffer no more on my account, Katherine, I promise."

"Quiet, Jack. Let me have my say while it's fresh in my mind. There's nothing to learn from suffering if you do not accept it fully—make it a part of Life. Everything in Life that we really accept undergoes a change. So suffering must become Love. This is the mystery that I've been afraid to see. Now I know what I must do. I must give to Life what I once gave only to you. I must put my agony into something—change it—transform sorrow into joy. I must pass from personal love, which has failed me, to greater love."

"Katherine our love has not failed."

"Yes it has. Accept the truth, Jack. The fearful pain I felt from your last letter—I will now gain strength from it. I will learn the lesson it teaches. These are not idle words, nor the consolations of the sick. This present agony will pass. As in the physical world so in the spiritual world—pain does not last forever. I know that now."

"Oh Katherine!" Jack cried out, reaching for her.

She pushed him away. "No, Jack don't move and don't say a word. This is difficult enough to confess without your interrupting. I must finish and you must listen." She raised herself up straight, her head off the pillows. Her eyes looked deeply into his.

"It's hard to make a good death. And your claim not to suffer anymore on my behalf was hurtful. It was base in its selfishness."

"Katherine it was wrong of me to say that. When I'm separated from you I feel completely desperate and terribly lonely and I do foolish things but I never stop loving you. Please listen to me. None of those women meant anything to me. It was only a distraction—a selfish way to escape from my own suffering. I don't desire any woman but you."

Jack looked at her so plaintively that she couldn't resist pulling him toward her. His head on her breast, her hands combing his hair, she whispered tenderly, "I still love you Jack. I will always love you." And in that moment she found the compassion to forgive him and the courage to risk everything, if only to be with him again.

He was essential to her. For all their differences, they were two sides of the same medal. She had wanted to become independent of him but now that he was there, she could never let him go.

On Christmas Day he surprised her with the Corona typewriter and her doll Rib that she had left in London to keep him company. As long as they were together Rib didn't need to stay in London. In the weeks that followed, Katherine's weak condition improved and she was certain it was because Jack was with her and her depression had been lifted. She came downstairs and took short walks with him in the garden.

LM moved into a nearby pension so they could enjoy their intimacy. Marie, now in charge, enjoyed setting the table for candlelight dinners and serving delicious meals to such a loving couple. She enjoyed being near their happiness so much that they had to find excuses to send her away so they could make love. They drank champagne afterward late into the night and made plans to travel the world, chasing the sun forever.

They decided he should resign from *The Athenaeum* in April. After all his Herculean efforts the paper's circulation hadn't reached his expectations and was losing money. It was going to be merged with the younger paper, *The Nation*. Now that he had achieved fame as a well-respected critic he would be paid for writing articles for *The*

Athenaeum/Nation and other intellectual publications and Sir Walter Raleigh had commissioned him to give six literary lectures at Oxford on *The Problem of Style.*

It promised to be Villa Pauline in Bandol all over again five years later. Sharing books. Sharing ideas. Sharing the writing table. Sharing the fire. Sharing the bed.

Jack returned to London in January to complete his obligations. Ten days later Katherine took a turn for the worse and he came rushing back. He stayed with her until she recovered from a high fever and then returned to London to resign from *The Athenaeum* two months earlier than he had planned and gave a farewell party for the staff and his friends. He wanted Katherine to come with him to London but Dr. Bouchage said it would endanger her recovery. What recovery? she later asked herself. After Jack left she spent most of the time in bed.

At the end of February he took up permanent residence at Isola Bella with Katherine, both acknowledging that the England where they had worked together to build their literary reputations was no longer a desirable shelter for their marriage and they would never separate again.

19

March-April 1921

> *I am not in despair about my health. But I must make every effort to get it better soon, very soon . . . I was not born an invalid and I want to get well . . . I feel every day must be the last day of such a life. I must escape.*
>
> Notebooks—KM

SHE PUSHED HERSELF OUT OF BED when she heard Jack calling, "Katherine!" She wanted to be on the terrace when he returned from his afternoon walk but she'd fallen asleep. The scarf hanging on her bedpost reminded her of what she had to do that day and the reason why Jack was calling out her name. At the mirror, she hid her swollen neck with the scarf and put on her cloche.

If only I could've put off this surgery until LM returned from London, she thought, staring at her reflection. LM was in London to sort through, store, give, or throw away most of her and Jack's possessions that remained at the Elephant. Katherine would have preferred waiting until she came back but the pain in her neck was interrupting her work and Dr. Bouchage said the only way to give her relief was to puncture the infected gland pressing against her artery. She would just have to trust Jack to care for her in LM's absence.

"We're going to be late. Did you order a car?" she asked. Jack was standing in the entry hall watching her walk stiffly down the stairs.

"A car? Wouldn't the walk do you good?"

"How can I walk there when I can hardly make it down the stairs?"

"Right. Silly of me," he said half smiling.

After the surgery Katherine felt faint and leaned on Jack to climb back in the hired car. She reached for her purse to pay the cabbie but Jack told her not to worry he'd take care of it. "That's nice of you," she said, and leaned her head on his shoulder.

He helped her upstairs to bed. She didn't see him again until that evening when she woke up to the sound of his pen scratching at the writing table.

"Water please. My throat is parched," she said hoarsely.

"Are you feeling better?" he asked, pouring a glass from the pitcher.

"Yes. Only tired and a little sore." He had returned to the writing table before she finished drinking. "Are you working on your lectures? I don't think I could listen right now but I'd like you to read to me later."

"Actually I'm going over our budget, trying to put things in order. I have a few questions for you."

"Right now?"

"It'll only take a few minutes."

Her heavy eyelids shut as he listed their expenditures since he joined her in Menton. She drifted in and out until she heard "your share of today's cab fare" and looked over at him, pulling herself up on the pillows. "Today's fare from the clinic?"

"Look here, no need to get upset, you don't have to pay me right now. Tomorrow will be fine."

"Take it from my purse on the armoire. Take it all!"

"Katherine you'll irritate your throat shouting at me. I never know when it's a good time to discuss our money affairs. I'll let you rest."

She watched him count the money from her coin purse and then slip out the door.

How can I possibly rest now? she thought. She sat down at the writing table and angrily stacked the papers he'd carelessly left behind. She pulled out a blank sheet from her own stack and wrote to LM who was waiting for answers to detailed, irritating questions about what to do with their things left behind at the Elephant. She went on to tell her about the meanness of Jack over the taxi fare and how much his stinginess with money reminded her of her father. She also told LM how she missed her thoughtful care. Jack was inept at handling the domestic distractions and her writing had fallen off. She asked her to move back into the villa.

Katherine was reading the morning mail on the sunny terrace when she suddenly shouted, "Ida! Where's Jack?" LM rushed out, dishtowel in hand.

"He went for a walk."

"That was hours ago. Did he see the post before he left?" Katherine demanded angrily.

"No, I think he'd already left. What is it Katie? Why are you so angry?" Katherine waved an envelope in her face.

"Hold still," said LM. "I can't read it. Bi-bes-co? Who is that?"

"Madame la *Princesse* Bibesco. Come listen to how she scolds me about *her* Jack."

"*Her* Jack?" LM sat across from her but Katherine got up and paced the terrace as she read the letter like an official document:

20 March 1921

Dear Mrs. Murry. I cannot let Jack suffer any more because of your selfishness. How dare you keep a hold on him when you are incapable of performing as his wife? You can't make him happy when you are living in France and you have told him you won't come back to London. Even after he made a home for you there, you left.

Katherine's cough stopped her. She held the letter out to LM who continued to read it out loud but not as formally:

I regret that you are ill. But this is not Jack's fault though he feels it is. I can't believe it is your intention to use your illness to keep a hold on to him. No one could be that cruel. You must realize, the observant writer that you are, how the man suffers from loneliness and lack of affection.

He wants to be free of you but every time he tries to tell you this he says you faint or have one of your coughing spells. Not wanting to be the cause of your condition worsening, he sacrifices his own happiness. It's so good to hear him when he foolishly laughs instead of being so anxious and worried.

He has told me that you are a wonderful, sensitive woman but I find that hard to believe by your actions. Understand that Jack can't go on like this. Your hold on him is killing him. He needs to be loved and caressed. I can give him what he needs. He knows that but his guilt keeps him from me. He is embarrassed to even kiss my hand. I beg you to let him loose. Please Katherine, I beseech you.

Sincerely, Princess Bibesco

"Oh my," said LM. "Who is this woman?"

Katherine laughed harshly. "This is not the first I've heard of the Princess but he promised to put an end to it."

She was folding up the letter when Jack walked in. "I've just read a letter from your Princess Bibesco."

LM said she had work to do and backed out of the room.

"Shouldn't you have left it for me to read, my dearest?"

"It wasn't addressed to you."

"Why would she write to you?"

"That was what I was going to ask you, Jack."

"I have no idea. I've only met her and her husband a few times socially and there was that time I impulsively kissed her in the carriage. But I told you about that." He sat down across from Katherine and poured himself a cup of tea.

"Then why does she tell me . . . here let me read it:

He wants to be free of you but every time he tries to tell you this he says you faint or have one of your coughing spells.

"Oh, balderdash!" said Jack.

"Such a sweet clever writer your Princess. Why didn't you tell me you arranged personally to have one of her short stories published in *The Athenaeum*?"

"This is ridiculous. Let me see it." He snatched the letter from Katherine's hand.

While he read, Katherine watched, hoping for signs of guilt or culpability or at least embarrassment, but he showed no emotion at all.

He folded it up into small pieces all the while shaking his head. Katherine grabbed it back before it disappeared inside his jacket pocket.

"What are you going to do about this?"

"Why do anything? It's bollocks. Ignore it. She won't write again."

"Really are you so sure of that? I'm not. She sounds extremely confident about your affections and seems to think she's better suited to take care of you than I am. Perhaps she's right." She unfolded the letter. "How did she so politely put it? Oh yes here it is:

I can't believe it is your intention to use your illness to keep a hold on to him. No one could be that cruel. You must realize, the observant writer that you are, how the man suffers from loneliness and lack of affection.

"Katherine, she's hysterical. There's not a bit of truth to what she's saying. Why I hardly know her."

"Really, Jack? I think she knows you quite well. But she doesn't know me."

"What are you going to do?"

"First tell me what *you* are going to do. Don't you think this letter requires some formal declaration on your part to rid us of this woman?"

"Yes . . . I could write something I suppose."

"Never mind. I'll do it myself. I'll tell her never to write to my husband again as long as we are living together under the same roof. I will also scold her for considering a liaison with a married man when she was already married herself, and suggest she turn to her husband for a lesson in etiquette."

Jack laughed. "Yes that should do it. Good idea. She's more apt to believe it coming from you. You know what a pushover I am. She talks as if we were lovers though I promise you I kissed her only once."

After sending her letter, Katherine never heard from Princess Bibesco again. But she confided to LM that she doubted it would be the end of Jack's affairs with other women and predicted Jack would marry Brett after she was gone. "Brett gives him exactly what he needs from a wife," she told her, "flattery, reverence and adoration."

Katherine was too ill to offer any of these things any longer nor would she want to if she could.

DURING A FREEZING MARCH, the splendid view of sea and garden from her bedroom balcony began to irritate her. Her writing had reached an impasse. Jack continued with his. After he finished writing the six lectures for Oxford, he was thinking about writing a book of poetry or finishing the novel he had started in Bandol now that he was no longer obligated to *The Athenaeum.*

She thought Dr. Bouchage was bored with having to continually pierce her swollen neck glands and had given up on curing her after a coughing spasm spurted blood. The only good piece of advice he'd given her lately was that the hot, humid summer would not be good for her rheumatism or her lungs. Also, Connie and Jinnie had reneged on the year lease on Isola Bella they had promised. Katherine thought it was because they'd given up on her conversion to Catholicism and had another tenant who would be more agreeable to their faith. She now became convinced she had to leave Menton but where to go and how to convince Jack it was the right thing to do?

She remembered her conversation at the Elephant in London with her cousin Elizabeth who had recommended the Alps for a tuberculosis cure. She opened "Tubercle" a British magazine she subscribed to that advertised the most recent treatments, cures, and miracles, including testimonials from cured patients—a magazine she hid from Jack who didn't believe in miracles or anything else without scientific proof. Her attention was drawn to a full-page advertisement for a tuberculosis clinic in Switzerland. It was the same clinic Elizabeth had mentioned at their teatime.

Her heart skipped when she turned the page and read an article on Dr. Spahlinger, a Swiss microbiologist, who had discovered an anti-tuberculosis serum—a serum produced from infected horses with tuberculosis. She knew better than to get her hopes up. There had been more than a hundred miracle serums or other fake cures for tuberculosis, but the British government was financially backing this one.

She calculated the travel and living expenses in Switzerland and wondered how she could afford it. She had the income from *Bliss & Other Stories,* which was selling way beyond expectations after excellent reviews but it would be several months before she was paid royalties. Maybe with her allowance it would be enough. If she had to, she could ask friends for help. She would never ask Jack or her father who she had stopped writing to after hearing from Connie that he resented giving her an allowance when she had a husband to provide for her.

Once her mind was set, she invited LM into the drawing room to join her for afternoon tea while Jack was on his walk. She'd asked her earlier to pick up some pastries at the local patisserie and LM brought in a tray with several delicious morsels.

Settling down in facing armchairs they both stared at the brewing teapot. Katherine spoke first. She told LM how difficult the London move must have been and how much she appreciated all her work. She couldn't resist adding, "But you did ask an overwhelming number of questions. I didn't expect you to ask my approval on every item in the house."

"I'm sorry, but what if I'd thrown out something you really cared about?"

"You needn't have worried. Everything I need is here—my pen and writing materials and a few souvenirs. The rest is superfluous. What need have I of gowns and evening wear when I have no interest in returning to London?"

"Oh Katie you say such silly things. You'd never give up the art galleries, or the Ballet Russe or concerts at Queen's Hall or your London friends. You'd miss Kot and Ottoline and Virginia as I'm certain they must miss you. You're having one of your dark moods, aren't you?"

"No, Ida, I'm not having one of my *dark moods*." she said hotly. This conversation was not going the way she had planned. She changed her tone, "I think the tea is ready now. Shall I pour it?"

"No Katie. Let me do it. But shouldn't we wait a few more minutes? You know how upset you'll be if it's too weak."

"It's fine," she said and got up to close the door, peeking out in the entryway before doing so. She sat back down and said, "I wish to speak to you before Jack returns. I want to leave the Riviera. I must see Dr. Spahlinger in Geneva as soon as I have an appointment."

"Leave? Spahlinger? Geneva? What on earth are you talking about?"

"I'm sorry I'm getting ahead of myself. Have another of those delicious cream puffs while I read this article to you."

"'The British government has definitely decided to acquire the rights for making the anti-tuberculosis serum which Henry Spahlinger has discovered after research and experiments lasting more than ten years. His father's mansion has been converted into experimental rooms, while the grounds are largely used for stabling and keeping horses, cows, donkeys, goats and other animals needed for extracting serum . . . Hitherto Spahlinger has never received remuneration, direct or indirect, from his patients.'"

Katherine looked up from reading. "I have asked for an appointment to see him but so have thousands of other wandering consumptives seeking cures. I know Jack's against me going because Spahlinger's not officially a medical doctor. He wants us to stay here. I had to ask him several times to ask his associate, Sullivan, who knows Spahlinger personally, for his help in getting an appointment."

Katherine returned the clipping to her tuberculosis-labeled folder and looked over at LM. "I'm most encouraged but I must say you look rather disappointed. Are you like Jack? Don't you think I have a chance? Don't you believe in miracles?"

"It's just I'm rather surprised," LM told her. "I thought you'd finally found the perfect place to settle down until you got better."

"Ida, we've been here since October. When I get a little better, I only relapse soon after. Am I really getting any better? No. Didn't you hear what I just read? Spahlinger is offering a cure. I must find out for myself if he's authentic." She poured them both another cup of tea to give LM time to get used to the idea of leaving.

Katherine watched LM's vague, inexpressive face and hesitated before making another effort to rally her to her cause. "Jones, we must pin all our flags on Switzerland."

LM awoke from her stupor. "Yes! Of course. Certainly. It's just a lot for me to take in. Serum . . . cures . . . leaving . . . It all seems so sudden. But you know I'll do whatever I can to help."

Katherine reached out and gripped LM's hand in hers. "Thank you, my dear loyal friend. I couldn't make this trip without you.

"First you must go to the train station and see about tickets . . . and find out about accommodations. We might be there for a considerable time. Perhaps we should stay in Montreux instead of Geneva. It's less convenient but Geneva will be too expensive and we must consider the costs."

Katherine looked up thinking she heard Jack's footsteps and lowered her voice and said hurriedly, "Just you and I are going. Jack is going to lecture at Oxford and he doesn't know his plans after that, but I can't wait.

"And there's something else we need to talk about. Hear me out, Jones, and don't interrupt before I'm finished. From now on I want you to look on me *not* as a friend who needs looking after but just as a friend. I mean that in all its implications. Do you understand?"

"No, I don't understand. What implications? Katie, speak in plain English?"

"What I'm trying to say is that I don't want you to *hover* over me as if I'm a wounded bird that can't fly without your assistance. You've been my nursemaid for too long. I want you to be my companion. Allow me to take care of myself. Otherwise, it won't work. We must be independent of each other if our relationship is to continue. Each pursuing our own interests."

"But you are my interest," said LM, getting up and walking over to the window. Katherine waited. Finally LM turned back and said, "All right, I'll try to do as you ask."

"Good. It'll be better for me to have to make do without your help. But for now," she laughed, "would you brew another pot of tea? Jack should be home soon. Let's have a piece of that lemon cake, too. Or did you eat all of it?"

"I haven't touched it, Katherine. You know I'm dieting."

A MONTH LATER, seated at her writing table, Katherine wrote a few letters to her sisters, and friends in London, telling them not to write her in Menton as she was moving to Switzerland. She'd heard from Spahlinger's associate and she had a confirmed appointment the second week of May. She still couldn't write her father after what he'd said about resenting her allowance.

Jack had left that morning for London. He'd finally come around to understanding her desire to leave Menton was not impetuously foolish. If Dr. Spahlinger's cure were a fake, she'd try the open-air cure in the Alps. They'd made plans to meet there, after his lecture tour, and find a châlet for just the two of them with a housekeeper—not LM. This was Jack's idea and she knew it wasn't fair to LM, but she had to hold on to LM until she was certain Jack would come. She fantasized going alone but she realized that was no longer an option.

20

May 1921

The Swiss Alps

I see a small white châlet with a garden near the pine forests. I see it all very simple, with big white china stoves and a very pleasant woman with a tanned face and sun-bleached hair bringing in the coffee. I see winter—snow and a load of wood arriving at our door. I see us going off in a little sleigh with huge fur gloves on, and having a picnic in the forest and eating ham and fur sandwiches. There is a lamp—très important—there are our books. It's very still. The frost is on the pane. You are in your room writing. I in mine. Outside the Stars are shining and pine trees are dark like velvet.

Notebooks—KM

ARRIVING AT THE CLARENS-MONTREUX TRAIN STATION, Katherine took a room at the Hotel Beau Site and awoke the following morning to a corner view of the Alps. LM had checked into a more economical hotel in nearby Blonay.

After unpacking her notebooks and setting up her writing table, she opened the French doors onto her fourth floor balcony and breathed deeply without pain or cough. The crisp alpine air felt pleasantly cool as it passed down through her inflamed lungs. She was right to leave Menton.

A tap on the door and a large muscular Swiss maid in a starched white apron entered carrying a tray laden with a silver coffee service, croissants, butter and confiture. Katherine asked her to put the tray out on the sun-heated balcony. After breakfast, she dressed quickly. She didn't want to be late for her appointment with Dr. Spahlinger. LM offered to go with her but Katherine felt strong enough to meet Dr. Spahlinger on her own.

Before their meeting, she was given a tour of the converted-barn laboratory where she saw well-fed donkeys, cows, horses, goats, and sheep. She was shown in the laboratory the various tubes of growing bacilli cultures and told they were injected into the horses and then after the horse built up immunity to the bacteria their serum was injected into the tuberculosis patients. The scientific process was fascinating but arduous. She was revolted by the idea of a horse's blood mixed with hers but she was determined to try anything if backed by science. She wished Dr. Sorapure were there as he would have appreciated the evolving science of microbiology and would have encouraged her to offer herself as a guinea pig for this new cure.

Spahlinger's assistant told her that Dr. Spahlinger had squeezed her into an already overbooked day and ushered her into his examination room. She'd expected a much more mature scientist than the youthful, robust man looking up at her from his desk. His Swiss mountain climber complexion didn't look like someone who had dedicated his life to growing bacteria cultures. He might even be younger than her thirty-two years.

The exam was quite brief. Moments later she was seated across from his desk anxiously waiting while he reviewed her medical file that he had obviously not read before.

He looked up. "Yes, Mrs. Murry, I can cure you but you'd have to be patient. My methods take a very long time because we must find the right combination of cultures that can destroy your particular tubercular bacteria. And of course there are no guarantees."

"The word 'patient' has a double meaning, of course," she said. "I've found it ironic that I am a patient but when it comes to saving my life

I am not patient. You're offering hope to thousands like me who've been without hope, but it's difficult for any of us to be patient."

The phone rang.

After a long-winded conversation in German, he said, "Yes, now where was I," he said.

"We were talking about patience, Doctor," she said, showing her irritation.

"Oh yes, sorry about that call. I'm terribly in demand and we're understaffed. What I was going to say is you would have to live here in Geneva where I can monitor your progress closely after each inoculation period. It can be a very long process."

"How long?"

"Oh, perhaps a year or longer. But once we find the right serum, then the restoration period can be quite short, for some of our patients only a few months and they're cured. The vaccine is quite effective."

"I see. May I ask the cost of your method?"

He looked insulted. "Cost? I don't expect a fee from you, Mrs. Murry. My remuneration is adding you to the list of patients I've cured."

She was suspicious of a doctor that didn't charge a fee. In fact, the British government was considering a large investment in his discovery and if his list of cured patients grew many other countries would also invest tremendous amounts of money to produce his serum in large quantities.

He looked back down at her file and scribbled a few notes. She felt his diagnostic mind at work, appraising her chances of being added to the cure list. I'm right, she thought, he needs me, but do I want to be one of his guinea pigs?

"I see you were diagnosed with tuberculosis in 1918. That makes your cure more difficult than newer patients. You also have a weakened heart from the strain of breathing through your damaged lungs. And rheumatism. This would be a particularly difficult case to take on."

Katherine put away her notepad and stood up to leave.

"Mrs. Murry, I said difficult but not impossible. You're very young so there is hope. But as I said, I can only help you if you're willing to remain in Geneva. Our staff can help you find comfortable accommodations."

"Thank you Doctor. But I have my mind set on moving up into the mountains. I'm a writer and it's very important for me to continue my work while I'm being treated."

"I see. Well, then let me make another suggestion. There is a famous tuberculosis clinic a few hours from here up in Montana run by Dr. Theodore Stephani. I highly recommend his open-air cure. He's had excellent results with TB patients. If you like, I'll call him."

"Yes, please do." She put on her gloves. "I won't let this TB patient take up any more of your valuable time." He didn't argue.

Deep brown bovine eyes looked up from their meals of grass and tracked her departure. She shuddered at the thought of horse or cow blood coursing through her veins or any other blood but her own and turned her eyes toward the white alpine mountains.

Without consulting LM, or writing Jack, she contacted Dr. Stephani and requested an appointment. Why not go to the top? She smiled up at the Matterhorn that she could see from her balcony.

She was surprised by his quick response suggesting they meet in Sierre, the village below his clinic, in two days time. In an act of rare spontaneity and without thought of cost, she hired a motorcar to take her up the mountain to Sierre.

Driving through the brisk pure air, she arrived refreshed at Hôtel Château Bellevue where Dr. Stephani met her in a private salon. She found it difficult to listen to his English spoken in a heavy northern Swiss accent. So taken in by the lofty, gilded ceiling of the salon with teardrop crystal chandeliers, she almost forgot why she was there. But came to attention sharply when his icy stethoscope pressed against her chest.

He examined her far more thoroughly than Dr. Spahlinger and took more time writing notes. She dressed and sat across from him on the divan but was again distracted, this time by the beauty of the sunlight glimmering on a pair of bees spinning in the air. I must live for the moment, she thought, I know that now. It's a divine day and that's all that matters.

In the distance, she heard Dr. Stephani's voice pulling her back. "Mrs. Murry?"

"Yes, sorry, what did you say?"

He'd read her medical report and was repeating what other doctors had said about her condition. She wanted to respond with, "Yes all that's true, but do let's listen and watch the bees instead. I've never heard such bees. And do you see that delicious plant growing outside the window? It reminds me of Africa."

Her heart and lungs had become such a frightfully boring subject she couldn't imagine why he or anyone else could bear to talk about it. But that is why I'm here, she reminded herself. She turned her attention away from the beauty surrounding her and onto the serious mature face of Dr. Stephani. "You're a young woman of great courage to come here on your own, considering your poor health. Many consumptives give up early on, not only physically but also emotionally and spiritually. You seem to have managed to rise above your illnesses. I read here that there are several."

"I have faith in miracles, Doctor. I believe I'll find a cure."

"I must tell you that I don't believe in miracles but I do believe in science's ability to find cures or at least increase survival with proper treatment."

"Do you think I have a chance to recover at least partially if I'm treated at your sanatorium?"

He scanned her medical history. She held her breath.

"Yes I do. I have known patients with lungs as compromised as yours who have recovered. I have no idea how long it will take or how long you will live, Mrs. Murry, but our open-air cure can increase your survival if you're strong enough to tolerate the cold air."

"Thank you for your honesty, Doctor. With your permission, I will make arrangements to move to Sierre and start your program immediately."

"My, you are quick to decide."

"You and your clinic have an excellent reputation. I think I'll be safe under your watch. And I already feel restored just being in these gorgeous mountains."

"Good. I will arrange with Dr. Hudson to supervise your case. He's an Englishman, like yourself, and a very qualified pulmonary specialist. We work as a team and he will report back to me on your progress."

Katherine thought to tell him she was actually a New Zealander but decided it was irrelevant.

"Our sanatorium is at the Palace Hotel in Montana, a short trip from here on the funicular but fifteen hundred meters higher in elevation. Until a room becomes available you can start treatment right away at any local Sierre hotel as long as there's a full service restaurant that offers the same menu as at the clinic, which several do as many of our patients live in this village, and a balcony large enough to accommodate a chaise longue.

"Don't all balconies in Switzerland accommodate chaise longues?"

He laughed for the first time and removed any last doubt she might have had about his character. The only doctors she trusted were capable of a good laugh.

Very pleased with Dr. Stephani, for the return trip she settled down comfortably in the velvet cushions of the hired car. But her mood descended as the car descended the mountain road back to Montreux. She had wanted Dr. Stephani to say: "Six months at the very most and you'll be cured."

To shake her sudden despair, she had the driver stop on the side of an avenue with poplars. In the bright green corridor dabbled with sunlight she watched wooden carts pass filled with families. The market square ahead was hung with garlands. People were dancing to musicians playing instruments. Most of the women carried huge bunches of crimson peonies, flashing bright. Villagers were buying and selling farm animals. There were more people in the cafés under the white and pink flowering chestnut trees and at the windows of the houses there were pots of white narcissi and girls with orange and cherry handkerchiefs on their heads looked out. She was tempted to join the festivities but the driver continued down the mountain.

That evening she wrote in her journal:

It's an infernal nuisance to love life as I do. I seem to love it more as time goes on rather than less. It never becomes a habit to me—it's always a marvel. I do hope I'll be able to keep in it long enough to do some really good work.

From her writing table she looked up at the full moon beaming down on the surrounding snow-capped Bernese mountains. I must start making plans to go back there right away, she thought.

The following morning at breakfast she excitedly told LM about her meeting with Dr. Stephani and enjoyed seeing LM's shocked face. "See, I told you I could do things on my own." She asked her to find out if rooms were available at the Hôtel Château Bellevue in Sierre. She didn't want to stay anywhere else. "Montreux is so ugly compared to the villages I passed coming down the mountain yesterday."

She spent the afternoon on her balcony's chaise longue following the pamphlet instructions Stephani had given her on the open-air treatment program, feeling rather foolish buried up to her neck in every blanket she could find in her hotel room and giddy from the elevation.

SHE MOVED INTO HÔTEL CHÂTEAU BELLEVUE with LM a few days later. She wrote to Jack giving their new address and told him it would be his address, too, after he finished the Oxford lectures. She thought this was a good moment to tell LM that Jack might be joining them in a few weeks but held off. What if he changed his mind? Besides LM had taken so well to the Alps. It suited her own mountain-size shape, and she went off happily on daily mountain climbs leaving Katherine to her "treatments" on the balcony.

In Montreux she'd received a packet from her father but had yet to open it. Knowing now that her father resented giving her an allowance she feared the worse and even dreamed that the packet contained news that he was cutting off her allowance.

Without her allowance she would not be able to afford Dr. Stephani's open-air cure. Each time she thought to open it, she panicked.

It would lessen the blow if Jack opened it first and told her what was inside.

Jack, she wrote, *I feel certain this letter from Father contains that Blow I am always expecting. Will you open it & read it & wire me what result?*

The packet was returned with a letter from Jack informing her that it was only her bank deposit book. Mr. Kay from the bank had accidentally sent it to her father and he was returning it to her. Jack told her she'd been foolish. Why would her father ever stop her allowance?

Relieved, she picked up her pen to finally write to her father with the news of her move to Switzerland and Dr. Stephani's open-air cure. But too much time had transpired since her silence and she felt an explanation was necessary as to why. She still felt terribly hurt knowing he chucked her stories into the fire.

She put down the pen and stared at the blank page. She feared the consequences of telling the truth. She would write later when her recovery was imminent and she could tell him that she and Jack were planning that long-overdue return visit to her home in Wellington.

21

June-November 1921

Châlet des Sapins

There was a tremendous fall of snow on Sunday night. Monday was the first real perfect day of the winter. It seemed that the happiness of Bogey and of me reached its zenith that day. We could not have been happier; that was the feeling. Sitting one moment on the balcony of the bedroom for instance, or driving in the sleigh through the masses of heaped snow. He looked so beautiful, too, hatless, strolling about, his hand in his pocket . . . Then I came away after a quick but not hurried kiss.

Notebooks—KM

JACK AND KATHERINE WROTE heartfelt letters during their two months of separation. At Oxford finishing his lecture series he wrote:

Trust me as though I were part of your own heart. I am part of your heart. And now I have you in my arms my wonderful wife. You will be there always till I come in July.

She replied:

I have never loved you more than I love you now. This must be our Indian summer, I think.

His arrival was a joyful bright moment in an otherwise dull routine. They moved into Dr. Stephani's Palace Hotel in Montana to continue the open-air cure she'd started on her hotel balcony down below in Sierre.

She was restless at the sanatorium after one week. Montana was too taken up with pomp and circumstance for her simple taste. It was a resort where well-to-do consumptives, transformed by disease into desperate patients either hobbled on crutches or were pushed around in wheelchairs, a too-visceral vision of her own dreaded, unspeakable future.

And there were rules. Dr. Stephani insisted that stress encouraged tubercular bacillus growth and therefore complete rest was necessary to benefit from his open-air regime. Rest made Katherine nervous. No good would come of her lying around idle. The pure, elevated air had improved her breathing and appeased her cough so, yes, she accepted reclining all day on a chaise longue five thousand feet above the sea but she needed a notebook on her writing case and a table waiting nearby, complete with paper and ink.

With Jack by her side she saw no reason they shouldn't move into a châlet where they could work together as at Chez Pauline in Bandol or Isola Bella in Menton.

Dr. Hudson, assigned to her by Dr. Stephani, suggested they lease his mother's remote châlet, which hung on the edge of a precipice near Montana like the houses Katherine had admired when she first arrived.

Châlet des Sapins was perfectly situated. It was only a thirty-minute alpine walk down to cousin Elizabeth's Châlet du Soleil in Randogne and, in the other direction, a short carriage ride to Montana where she could continue her check-ups at Stephani's clinic.

LM was taken aback at first by Jack's arrival but took it with her customary resilience. She was now fond of the Alps herself and found a nursing job and accommodations at one of the tuberculosis clinics in Montana. She told Jack and Katherine they could call upon her when needed to run errands in the village.

They hired Ernestine to do the cleaning and cooking and moved into the small châlet. There were three stories, plenty of room for each to have their own study. The ground floor had a sitting room with a fireplace so massive that Katherine shivered just thinking of the chill that would make such a fireplace necessary. The weather was so moderate in the summer it was hard to imagine the harsh winter.

They adapted agreeably into a routine—work in the morning, meet in the afternoon for a picnic or a walk, more work in the late afternoon. After supper they read to each other from what they'd written that day and from other books they were reading and played games of chess and card games in front of the fire.

Only thirty-two, Katherine thrived that summer in this magical châlet on top of the world. She still walked with a limp, but her heart was stronger and she could take walks in the woods with Jack. On mild days she could even walk to Elizabeth's Châlet du Soleil for afternoon chats. They saw no one else except LM when she brought requested items from the village and stayed for teatime.

Katherine's mild cough didn't keep Jack awake and they slept together in the bedroom on the middle floor, which had the largest bed and a heating stove.

One such evening they were seated cross-legged on their bed drawing designs for the châlet they planned to build nearby. That afternoon Jack had taken Katherine riding in a horse-drawn cart. They were thrown back and forth on the rough road until they found a picnic location on a grassy knoll overlooking the snow-capped Weisshorn. They lifted their champagne glasses and toasted their decision to never return to England. The Heron châlet would be built right here. Why not? Where else could they be happier? And, cut-off from the world below, it felt like they had unlimited time to accomplish their work.

Elizabeth had warned them that it was natural for newcomers to the Alps to become invigorated by the pure air and the high elevation, the magnificent mountains and the beautiful weather. It could go to their heads. The air was intoxicating. It aroused passions. Their response to her warning was, "Let it happen!"

Jack having finished his Oxford lectures for publication had started his second novel, late to be titled *The Things We Are.* Katherine was writing every day. The stories figuratively flew out her balcony window to various publishers in London. None were rejected and from her friends' correspondence she learned that she was well spoken of at the salons. To pay for their bliss in the sky, she had picked up a lucrative contract to write a bi-monthly story for the British newspaper, *The Sphere*. And Jack, now one of London's most popular critics, contributed with payments from his essays and reviews.

On their bed that night they imagined their Heron—the pine forest at their back door, the Bernese-Ober blocking the icy wind blowing from the north, and, like Châlet des Sapins, two wide balconies facing out on the massive Mont Blanc and the Matterhorn, with the green Valais valley stretched out below. The vision made them both giddy and they fell on the bed laughing. He took her into his arms and made love to her.

"Let's call it Châlet Content," said Jack afterward, his voice muffled in the feather pillow. And then, groggily, "Let's not talk anymore. I need to sleep."

She looked around their bedroom and smiled. On every shelf or ledge she'd arranged bouquets of alpine flora, discoveries Jack had made on his mountain climbs. Many flowers were pressed between the pages of books filling the shelves and stacked on the floor against the walls. Enough books to keep them busy for the many years to come.

She closed her eyes to hold in her happiness. Jack mumbled, "Certainly not more than two floors and a large open fireplace." He put out his arm and she snuggled up to him. Bound together they gazed out at the quarter moon in the center of a multitude of glittering stars.

She whispered in his ear, "What about bees?"

"Most certainly bees, and I aspire to raising a goat." She laughed. She couldn't imagine her lazy bookworm husband out early in the morning milking a goat.

"Thinking about goats and bees makes me hungry," he said, sitting up. "You too?"

"Oh, yes, terribly."

"I'll go downstairs for a plate of Ernestine's lemon cake and you warm the milk here on the stove."

Wingley, curled at their feet, awoke and applauded their plans with purrs and smacking lips. LM had brought him back from London on the train in a basket after Katherine had mentioned how much she missed him.

11 SEPTEMBER 1921—Snow still lingered like linen hung out to dry on the rocks and on the tips of pine trees, she wrote in her notebook. She'd been contemplating the high ridge in the distance. Covered in blankets and lying on her chaise longue on the balcony, she watched the sun peek over the ridge. She had worked at her writing table through the night in a nine-hour pulse to finish one of her longest stories, *At the Bay*, and it felt good to stretch the legs and feel the rapture that came after a story's completion. She was particularly pleased with this story as it fulfilled the promise she'd made to write about family love and her childhood after her twenty-one year old brother died in the war.

She thought to wake Jack but he was not one to appreciate the early morning hours, particularly ones with a chattering wife. I must talk to someone, she thought, and lifted her pen to start a letter to Brett—a painter who understood the satisfaction from the results of practicing one's art. The breach between them during Brett's misguided affair with Jack had been mended and they'd kept up a steady correspondence since her move to Switzerland.

The pleasure of all reading, she wrote, *is doubled when one lives with another who shares the same books. But I would be lying not to say there is one thing one does miss here, and that is seeing people. One doesn't ask for many, but there come moments when I long to see and hear and listen—listen most of all.*

The only listening to be heard this morning was Jack's deep breathing in the bedroom below.

She tapped the pen against the paper, blotted the ink stain and continued:

I've just finished my new story. I've been at it all night. It's about sixty pages. I've wandered about all sorts of places—in and out—I hope it is good.

It is as good as I can do. All my heart and soul is in it— every single bit. Oh God, I hope it gives pleasure to someone. I must tell you that it is so strange to bring the dead to life again. I felt I was saying to them, 'You are not dead, my darlings. All is remembered . . . you may live again through me in your richness and beauty.'

What a thrill it was reawakening her own little people. She compared it to strokes across the canvas that draw forth an image, a memory of something once felt, something once seen, until those remembered thoughts come alive again on the canvas.

Wingley interrupted her letter, leaping off the windowsill onto the balcony to stretch out his long, plump body on the first patch of morning sunlight.

The last edge of the night sky had made way for a new day. Is there really an unseen stage manager running the show who just now lit the stage, she wondered? Seated on her perch, she could almost believe in such a God when witnessing Nature waking all around her to a new day.

No, we certainly won't be back in England for years, she wrote Brett. *You will have to visit us here.* A mist filled the valley shrouding the sun's burst of light. She shivered and brought the eiderdown closer to her. *But you must dress warmly.*

Finally admitting to herself how exhausted and chilled she was, she went downstairs and slipped under the covers next to Jack.

IT WASN'T UNTIL after she and Jack celebrated her 33rd birthday that dark clouds blocked out the sun, a harbinger of winter's approach. The exhilaration from the pure air and elevation stopped working its magic in a châlet that was never quite warm enough despite the big fireplace on the ground floor and heated pipes hissing all day.

Katherine had been initially pleased with her two stories *At the Bay* and *The Garden Party.* Now she felt they could have been much better. Jack disagreed telling her it was her best work. But she felt something lacking. She didn't know what it was but knew she could find the answer as long as she kept writing. She started another story, *The Doll's House,* which also took place in her childhood home in New Zealand.

After the first blizzard her hacking cough returned and she slept on the colder third floor so that she wouldn't wake Jack. More frequently during the day he escaped into the woods where she couldn't follow, climbing craggy peaks in pursuit of never-before-seen plant specimens or skiing down slopes with Elizabeth and her friends.

She never asked him to stay home, but became anxious when she heard the front door slam followed by a heavy silence. What if she were to have an attack like she did in Italy? Ernestine only came upstairs if Katherine called her. It could be hours before she found her. Besides, Jack was sloppy with his things and dropped them wherever he happened to be. His clothes were draped on every chair. He assumed that she would order the food, plan the menus, and take care of the accounts. This wouldn't do. She was weak from her disease and exhausted from the addition of domestic cares to her writing schedule with no time left to take the daily open-air cure out on her balcony.

She asked LM to tea. LM, who had resigned herself to living alone in the village, had made new friends and often told Katherine how content she was with her work at the sanatorium. Katherine wasn't sure how she would respond to her request to return as a paid aide and companion.

"What about Jack? Can't he help?" asked LM.

"Oh you know Jack. He has a way of disappearing for hours, and when he's home he's distracted or working in his study. I would only ask that you bring me lunch and serve us at teatime and tidy up things a bit and keep me company when he's away."

They both looked around the sitting room that was quite out of sorts. LM didn't answer right away and Katherine said,. "Do you want a few days to think about it?"

"No-no," said LM. "I'm just a bit confused. You told me that you and Jack were getting along so well that it was best that I leave you on your own, not be a third party as it was. But of course I'll come if that's what you want. I'll have to change my hours at the sanatorium. But won't I be in the way of you and Jack?"

"You needn't worry about that," said Katherine.

"Then I'll start tomorrow." She picked up the sweater Jack had tossed on a chair and hung it in the closet on her way out.

AFTER COMPLETING *The Doll's House*, Katherine wrote in her notebook:

Words cannot describe how cold I feel, and it's not even winter yet. We have central heating that never goes out, but I must remain outdoors at least six hours of the day and even buried in blankets my fingers turn to icicles.

At night, she and Jack huddled by the fire in the downstairs sitting room where they read all of Jane Austen's novels to each other. They had finished *Emma* and were now on *Mansfield Park*.

It was around Christmas time that a packet arrived from Katherine's previous editor and close friend, Alfred R. Orage. She wondered why the packet was addressed to Jack. Orage and Jack had never really been friends. At one time they had both competed for Katherine's work to be published in their journals.

She watched Jack open the packet and frown at what he found inside.

"Has he sent you a book, Jack? How curious. What's the title?"

"*Cosmic Anatomy*. Why on earth would he send me a book with such a title?" He read the enclosed letter and looking up at Katherine, said, "He wants me to write a review. Is he trying to be funny? He knows I have no interest in theosophy or mysticism or, as the author Dr. Wallace says here, the 'will to believe.'"

He flipped through the pages shaking his head, slammed it shut and left it on the table. When they got up to go to bed, Katherine picked it up.

"What are you going to do with that?" Jack asked, sneering at the book in her hand. "Certainly your mind will be better nourished reading Chaucer or Shakespeare than that hocus pocus."

"Why are you having such a violent reaction to this book that you only spent five minutes glancing at? Orage wouldn't waste your time with a book that didn't have value."

"Well, I would rather you didn't read it."

"Why Jack?"

"We are happy here. I don't want any theologian quack to convince you otherwise."

A FEW NIGHTS LATER, she reached for *Cosmic Anatomy* on her bed table and opened to the first page. An hour later she was still reading. The writing was difficult to understand and she was left with many unanswerable questions but she felt a strong interest in Wallace's explanation that reactions to certain causes and effects always have been the same throughout time.

Jack came in to say good night and sat on the edge of her bed. "So you're reading that book. I'd prefer if you didn't."

"Why Jack I think you're jealous. You've always resented my relationship with Orage but I've never known you to censor my reading material. This book is fascinating and perhaps helpful. Dr. Wallace is an educated theologian and quite knowledgeable on what you insultingly refer to as 'occult doctrines.' They're really religious ideas. Alternative approaches to experience could make for an interesting discussion between us. It might do us both some good to see things from a less lofty intellectual plane."

"My integrity as a skeptic would never allow me to consider theological thought as having any value. That's why I won't review that book. When I came in just now I thought I heard you mumbling something in voodoo."

"Oh, Jack, not voodoo. It's an Upanishad verse. *Om, krato smara, klibe smara, kritam smara.*"

"What does it mean?"

"I don't know yet."

He shook his head.

"Jack, do try and show some tolerance. It's most unbecoming on your handsome face when you look so stern. Look, it's not the only book I'm reading." On her bed lay Shakespeare's *Antony and Cleopatra* and the *Bible*."

"Interesting collection, my dear." He kissed her on the forehead. "Don't read all night. I'll wake you with tea in the morning before I go skiing with Elizabeth."

After he left, Katherine picked up her notebook and wrote: *I feel there is much love between us. Tender love. Let it not change.* But laying in bed unable to sleep she wondered how it could not change if he was repelled by her pursuit to find alternative ways to being cured.

She sat up and pulled out the original draft of the letter she had sent Orage last year from Menton and reread it:

This letter has been on the tip of my pen for many months.

I want to tell you how sensible I am of your wonderful unfailing kindness to me in the "old days." And to thank you for all you let me learn from you. I am still—more shame to me—very low down in the school. But you taught me to write, you taught me to think; you showed me what there was to be done and what not to do.

My dear Orage, I cannot tell you how often I call to mind your conversation or how often in writing, I remember my master. Does that sound impertinent? Forgive me if it does.

But let me thank you, Orage—Thank you for everything. If only one day I might write a book of stories good enough to "offer" you . . . If I don't succeed in keeping the coffin from the door you will know this was my ambition.

We have come full circle, she thought. When she first met Orage she had argued against his theological beliefs. And when she had met Jack and stopped writing for Orage's *New Age* she became even more critical about theological books, stating in Jack's *Rhythm* that mysticism was a passionate admiration for that which has no reality at all and leads to the annihilation of any true artistic effort.

That was before she became desperately ill. Now lying in her bed looking out at the snow-capped mountains reflected in the moonlight, she wondered for the first time if she could annihilate her physical disease without the help of science or medicine. *Cosmic Anatomy*'s author believed that the mind could control, transcend and even survive the body. Could hers? If she mentioned this idea to Jack, he would only laugh. But with Orage they could discuss her questions about *Cosmic Anatomy* through the night. She closed her eyes and saw Orage standing over her in his felt hat as if it had just been yesterday and not the twelve years she just counted on her fingers.

IN FEBRUARY 1910 he'd published *The Child-Who-Was-Tired,* the short story that had launched her career. His intellectual weekly literary paper *New Age* was about literature and the arts, politics, spiritualism and a supporter of women suffrage. It was a haven for modern writers and artists who emerged just before the war. At twenty-one, Katherine was the youngest on his roster. It gave her immediate respect and instant notoriety to be added along with the likes of Ezra Pound, George Bernard Shaw, H.G. Wells and G.K. Chesterton.

She remembered back to the first day she climbed the stone steps to his office. What a very handsome man, she thought, when she first saw Orage. As they shook hands he looked directly into her eyes, challenging her, and she in turn gazed into his hazel eyes without flinching though she had to tilt her neck up he was so tall.

She thought he would just ask her to drop off her three stories, like the other publishers, but instead Orage asked her to sit down and wait while he read them. As his long feline fingers flipped each page, he crossed and re-crossed his legs several times. His lips moved silently reading her words. Uncomfortable, she wanted to look away but stood her ground, focusing her eyes on his flame-colored tie. Her mind seeking respite imagined a field of orange tulips.

He startled her when he jumped up quickly after reading the third story and said, "This one is just what I've been looking for—drama arising from bad sociological conditions. What's the title?" Without waiting for her response, he flipped back to the cover page: *The Child-*

Who-Was-Tired. I like it. Bring me more stories like this and I'll publish them, too. I'll even give you your own column—*Bavarian Babies.*"

She wished he'd chosen a different story. She'd written it in Bavaria after Floryan had introduced her to Anton Chekhov's short stories. She had written it more as an exercise in learning his style and had used a similar Chekhov story to write from.

Orage was writing down some notes and didn't notice her worried look. "Do you have a nom de plume, young lady?"

"Katherine Mansfield."

"All right, Miss Katharine Mansfield," he said, writing it down incorrectly. "I'm not interested in these other stories you gave me but when can you bring me more satirical stories like this one?"

She didn't have any more stories like that but she didn't tell him that. At that time she wrote sentimental stories, even mawkish stories, hoping they'd be popular with women readers and she would be paid well. She looked around the scruffy, dim room. There was only space enough for the two chairs they sat in, their knees almost touching. His boots were more worn than hers. "Perhaps I can bring more," she said in her best mimic of a sophisticated woman of the world. "May I ask how much you pay your writers?"

New Age had a reputation for not paying their writers. The magazine had over thirty thousand subscribers but it barely turned a profit. She must have caught him on a good day. He threw back his head and burst out laughing, while reaching up with his hand to toss back a long tuft of brown hair that fell down over his forehead, a gesture she would get to know well and fondly. He said, "I'll pay you ten shillings for this story right now and the same for each additional one you deliver and I accept."

Orage did more than publish her stories. He took her under his editorial protection for two years and encouraged her to write serious pieces and stay away from being overly sentimental. With his encouragement and excellent editing abilities, she gained the confidence to reinvent the short story and, with a passion for technique, create a unique style of condensed sentences full of meaning and truth. With a "special prose" that was neither poetry nor prose in an early method of stream of consciousness she entered the minds and souls of her characters which would come to have a strong influence on the writings of Virginia Woolf and other modern writers.

After she met Jack, she flipped her loyalty from *New Age* to Jack's journal *Rhythm.*

Orage was furious. He considered it a betrayal after all he'd done for her and gave her an ultimatum: You write for *New Age* or you write for *Rhythm.* When it came to her work, she didn't like being told what to do by Orage or anyone else. She swore never to submit her work to him again telling Jack, *"Orage is too ugly!"*

Though estranged for years, she'd never forgotten her indebtedness to him. And now he was the person she most wanted to talk to about *Cosmic Anatomy* and other spiritual matters.

22

December 1921

Dr. Manoukhine's Cure

Congestion is quite simple. The lung becomes full of blood, and that means the heart beats too fast and that means one has fever and pain and one puts oneself to bed.

Letters—KM

HER CONSUMPTIVE FEVER kept her in bed for days. One morning upon waking she coughed into her handkerchief. She impulsively hid the bloodstained cloth when Jack, bursting with robust health, came into the room carrying her morning tea.

"How are you today?" asked Jack, looking down at her with his half smile that still touched her deeply. "You look a bit tired. I hope you didn't stay up all night working."

"No." She held back from saying she spent it coughing. "And you?"

"I'm feeling rather restless to get outside. After that blizzard last night there are several feet of fresh snow so I thought I'd walk over to Elizabeth's. She offered to give me a few skiing lessons on some of the easier slopes. Do you mind if I go off for the day?"

"No. Go ahead. LM will be here later. Have a wonderful time. Send Elizabeth my love."

After he left, the vision of Jack and Elizabeth, twenty years older than her own thirty-three years, racing down the slopes together made her jealous. She was angry with herself for not telling him the truth. His absence hadn't mattered when she was occupied with her writing but now that she was ill again she needed him there with her. But if she told him that, he would get depressed and make her feel worse. Wasn't it better that he was oblivious to her sufferings?

She picked up the English newspaper off the tray. The Russian writer Maxim Gorky had gone to Italy for health reasons. He had tuberculosis. The world press interviewed him.

Her interest increased when Gorky said that a Dr. Manoukhine, a fellow Russian, had "at last discovered the remedy" for tuberculosis. She realized that he was the same doctor Kot had suggested she contact a month ago. Gorky went on to say that Dr. Manoukhine had brilliant results irradiating the spleens of hundreds of Russia's tuberculosis patients and that he had brought his patented X-ray machine to Paris where he was now receiving new patients.

When Kot had mentioned Dr. Manoukhine, she had been feeling quite well and hadn't wanted to consider another treatment that would take her away from Jack. But, as always, her circumstances had changed. Now she was snowbound, bedridden, and coughing blood.

She immediately wrote to Kot asking him to send Dr. Manoukhine's address. She assumed Jack hadn't read the article or he would have mentioned it and decided not to tell him. He would only argue that Dr. Hudson had said it could take a year or maybe two of Stephani's open-air cure before her lungs was cleared of the bacilli. She no longer believed that was true.

Jack didn't understand what it felt like to write a story as fast as possible for fear she'd never finish it. Unaware of her ticking clock, he leisurely wandered the mountains and spent his afternoons visiting Elizabeth and her guests at Châlet du Soleil. In the evenings, he returned home, bursting with health, unaware that hers was fading.

Kot sent Dr. Manoukhine's address. Two weeks later he responded. She hid the letter from Jack and opened it after he left for the day. Wingley sat up on his haunches and watched her open the envelope, joining her on the bed while she translated his French out loud: "Yes I think I can help you. Come to Paris as soon as possible. After I examine you, I'll know if you are strong enough to tolerate radiation treatments. If so, we can start immediately."

She lost Wingley's attention to a ball of yarn and read it again to herself. Too nervous to stay in bed, she reached for her robe and stood at the window watching the falling snow. I've come to hate snow, she thought, particularly snow that never ceases piling up layer after layer of white upon white. How delightful it will be to walk among the floral shops in Paris.

Thank you for your letter, she wrote back. *Unfortunately, I cannot leave here until the end of the month. I will have my assistant call your office to set an appointment when I am free to travel. Thank you for giving me hope. Warmly, KM*

DOCTOR HUDSON SAT AT HER BEDSIDE. "You must eat more, rest more, and work less to bring down this constant fever," he said sternly, waving the thermometer in front of her face.

But what good did it do her to be the good patient if she was to be an invalid bound to her bed and forbidden to write? She mustn't stop now. Was Dr. Manoukhine her last chance? Or did Dr. Hudson, with all his tools inside that fancy leather satchel, know the answers she sought?

She buttoned up her bed jacket, sat up against the pillows and waited for him to finish packing his satchel and snap it shut before she said, "Doctor, I need to speak to you privately. Would you mind closing the door?"

He returned to his seat and waited while she drank from a glass of water to soothe her hoarse voice.

"I have written to a Dr. Manoukhine who claims to have found a remedy for tuberculosis and asked to take an appointment with him at his Paris clinic. Have you heard of him?"

"No, I haven't." He laughed. "I wouldn't have time to take care of my patients if I tried to keep up with every new remedy that came along for tuberculosis. As you know, there are many who claim they've found a cure. Some are even experimenting with elephant serum. No one has proven to extend the lives of consumptives as much as the open-air cure we practice here."

"From what I've read, Dr. Manoukhine thinks radiating the spleen triggers the immune system to build up antibodies that kill the tubercular bacteria."

"Oh, wait a minute, I have read about Dr. Manoukhine's use of radiation. The anecdotal reports have been excellent, but really I can't advise you on this because I don't know enough about it. But I can tell you that the radiation would be most taxing on your already weakened condition."

"I think it's worth the risk. Dr. Manoukhine might be my last chance."

"I must disagree with you Mrs. Murry," he said, his pudgy hand wound around the stethoscope. "I have just listened to your right lung and it's practically healed. And the other is a great deal better."

"Really? Then why are my lungs burning and why do I have to force myself to get up in the morning and why am I losing weight and why do I have a constant fever and I certainly don't need a stethoscope to hear my heart beating so fast. I don't have any strength left to fight this disease. I can feel it consuming me each day. Not to be vulgar but I feel I'm being eaten alive." She stopped to catch her breath.

"Please Mrs. Murry. Quite honestly, it's your heart that's most worrying. It's being overworked because your diaphragm can't expand because of your damaged lungs."

"But you just said they're better."

"They 'sound' better but they're permanently damaged and there's nothing we can do about that. I would say that a lower elevation might be kinder on your heart. If the remaining tubercular bacilli in your lungs *can* be destroyed through radiation, at least one of your lungs could do a better job of expanding your diaphragm.

"I'm confused, Doctor. Are you advising me to go to Paris?"

"I think it could be a good idea as long as you're careful and do not exhaust your heart. How long would you have to be away?"

"Just a fortnight. Long enough to meet with Dr. Manoukhine and see a dentist about my rotting teeth. After my examination at his clinic, if he convinces me that he can help, I would return to Paris in May. That is unless you think it is urgent that I be treated right away."

"No. Not at all. It's the trip to Paris that worries me. Do you think we could use Dr. Manoukhine's method here at our clinic? We are well equipped with the latest in X-ray machines. And if he was to instruct us on what to do . . ."

"I will write and ask him."

"Splendid." He got up to leave.

"I have another favor to ask before you go. Please sit with me for a minute longer?" she asked, extending her hand out to him.

"Yes, Mrs. Murry?" he said, sitting back down, resting his hands on his portly stomach.

"I would prefer if you did not discuss my plans with Mr. Murry." She smiled. "I'm afraid he does not believe in miracles."

They both watched him twirl his thumbs. He looked up at her. "Well this is an unusual request. I make it a practice to keep the spouse informed, but in your particular case, I will agree not to say anything if you promise to inform your husband as soon as you've heard from Dr. Manoukhine."

"I will Doctor. I promise.

Dr. Manoukhine did not respond favorably to Dr. Hudson's suggestion of collaboration. She would have to come to Paris. His patented X-ray machine was specifically made to his calculations and he would have to spend hours personally training anyone else to operate it.

A few days later her fever lifted and she asked LM to make the travel arrangements.

That evening after dinner she and Jack settled in next to the fire to read the end of Jane Austen's *Mansfield Park*. Before he started, she said, "Jack, we need to talk."

He looked up over his horn-rimmed glasses. So handsome and still so young, she thought. "Must we now, my dearest? I've been waiting all day to know the ending!"

"This is far more important. I read in the *Times* about a doctor in Paris, at the Pasteur Institute, who has excellent results with tuberculosis patients. Many claim to have been cured by his new scientific methods including Gorky."

"You read Gorky's interview, too? I was interested to read that he was a consumptive. But it sounds like a hoax to me. Radiate the spleen? How absurd. You didn't take it seriously did you?"

"At least you could have brought it to my attention, Jack. Not only was it about Gorky, but also it was about a cure for my disease. And, yes, Manoukhine radiates the spleen and, no, it's not a hoax. Kot recommended him and sent me his address in Paris. I've written him and he's responded. Jack, he says he can help me. I must go to Paris and find out for myself."

"Oh Katherine, let us not move again. Stay with Dr. Stephani's open-air cure. Dr. Hudson says you're making marvelous progress. Everything has gone so well for us here. Look at the work you've accomplished. And might I add your best work so far. Are you going to give that up for yet another miracle cure? Why is it whenever we settle down somewhere you decide to move? This time I really can't let you go."

She felt divided. Her resolve weakening but she stuck to her plan, which also meant telling him the truth. "Jack look at me. Really look at me and tell me I'm getting better when you know I'm not. Even my teeth are falling out. I cough so often you can't share the same bed with me. I cough up blood. I'm scared, Jack. I'm scared for us. What if Dr. Manoukhine can help me? Isn't it worth the risk to find out? It might be our last chance. I have to go."

Jack looked at her so pitifully that she sank back in her chair, but she'd told the truth and it had to be said whatever the consequences. She waited.

He stood up and came over to her. "So you went ahead and made plans without consulting me? Without asking my opinion? Don't I have a say?"

"You would have only tried to talk me out of it."

"No, Katherine, I wouldn't have. If you believe Dr. Manoukhine might help you, you're right, you have to go. But I'm upset you didn't talk to me about it."

"I'm sorry. Our happiness these last months has been so perfect. I don't want anything to change that. I dread our being apart even for a short time."

He kneeled in front of her and reached out for her hands warming them between his. "My dearest. That won't happen. Nothing will come between us. Do you want me to come with you?"

"No, I want you to finish your novel. I don't plan to stay longer than a fortnight and I'm only staying that long so I can have a dentist take care of my teeth. If Manoukhine offers to take me on as a patient and you and I think it's a good idea, I'll schedule the treatments in May after I've sold several more stories to *The Sphere*."

"And don't count me out. By May I should be able to help out, too. I'll have several more articles published by then and maybe I can get an advance on my new novel, if I have the time to stay here and finish it."

"Thank you Jack but I think I'll be able to pay for it on my own and if not we'll talk about it then."

"I don't like the idea of you going to Paris alone."

"Jack you're too funny. I do wonder how you ever became The Critic of London when you miss what's right in front of you. Do you really think I'm well enough to travel on my own? I've made plans with LM to accompany me there and back."

Later that night he came upstairs to her room. "Katherine, I'm sorry you felt you couldn't talk to me about this. I've been caught up in my own work and I've neglected you, haven't I? I'm sorry. I didn't want you to go to sleep without knowing that I love you very much and if you need me to come with you I will."

"Don't worry. I'll be all right. When you see me again I'll have filled these ugly gaps." She made a silly face that made him laugh.

"You will always be my beautiful girl with or without teeth."

The next morning there was a knock on her door and LM walked in and poured a glass of water. Handing her the glass, she said, "Are you sure you're up to taking this trip? You haven't been out of the house since that first blizzard and that was over a month ago. Does Dr. Hudson approve of your going?"

"Yes. He's thoroughly researched Dr. Manoukhine's radiation treatment and they've corresponded about my case. I must go to Paris."

"If anything happens to you, Jack's going to hold me responsible."

"Jones, you haven't changed your mind have you? I can't do this without you."

"No, we're going. I picked up the train tickets this morning. As long as you're up to it, we leave Monday morning."

That weekend Katherine straightened out her affairs. She called it making a clean sweep of her camp, leaving no mess behind. She wrote a few letters telling her family and friends her plan to go to Paris but kept putting off writing to her father. Even after finding out his last packet was just the return of her bankbook she had still been unable to write him though he'd kept her informed on his life in Wellington as a banker.

She'd excused herself from writing him for twenty-one months because of illness and not wanting him to know how depressed she'd been. But the real reason for her silence was because cousin Connie had told her that her father begrudged giving her an allowance. After his visit to Ospedaletti she'd believed the allowance was an expression of a father's love. A gift to see her through, knowing it was highly unlikely she would live very long and consumption was a terribly expensive illness for her to pay for on her own. When she found out the truth she felt he'd pushed her away and said, "I don't love you anymore." The loss of his love was unbearable and knowing it was her fault.

That evening she timidly approached her fear of being rejected by him and hesitated, her pen trembling over a blank sheet of paper. But as with Jack she realized that in order to heal the divided self she must tell the truth regardless of the consequences.

She pressed the pen down onto the paper and asked his forgiveness for having been an extraordinarily unsatisfactory and disappointing child. Her last words were: *Father don't turn away from me, darling. If you cannot take me back into you heart believe me when I say I am your devoted deeply sorrowing child Kass.*

After sending this letter off, she went through her letters and notebooks, pleased to destroy much of it. Before her departure she wrote a last note in her journal:

Whenever I prepare for a journey I prepare as though for Death. Should I never return all is in order.

23

January 1922

Paris

The great thing to remember is we can do whatever we wish to do pro-vided our wish is strong enough. But the tremendous effort needed one doesn't always want to make it, does one? And all that cutting down the jungle and bush clearing even after one has landed anywhere it's tiring. Yes, I agree. But what else can be done? What's the alternative? What do you want most to do? That's what I have to keep asking myself, in the face of difficulties.

Notebooks—KM

MONDAY MORNING SHE AWOKE GASPING for air and pulled herself up on her pillows. "I can't breathe any better than a fish in an empty tank!" she rasped, waking Wingley who leaped off the bed, fleeing out the open door.

In her mind she covered the deep snow beyond the window with a blanket of new spring grass and set herself down on a bed of yellow and white wildflowers. Today she was leaving for Paris and a new spring. Not even a blizzard could stop her.

This Last Chance is the miracle I've been seeking—the Last Chance for Jack and me, she thought. My days of a wandering consumptive are over. Dr. Manoukhine will cure me. No more medicine bottles. No more sleepless nights. No more nightmares. No more breakfast trays.

As if on cue LM walked in with the morning tray and Katherine laughed. One last tray.

"Katie why aren't you dressed? We have a train to catch. Let me help you."

Jack saw them off at the funicular, which took them down to the flatlands. LM checked in the baggage and joined Katherine in their cabin. The train whistled and the wheels began to curl down the tracks as they pulled out of the Geneva train station.

LM was gripping onto her travel chest. Katherine smiled over at her but LM spoke harshly, "This is our trip from Bandol to Paris in 1918 all over again."

"No it's not. I'm a bit tired but I haven't coughed all morning." She could see her trusted companion was still unconvinced. "The journey we took from Bandol was held up first in Marseille and then in Paris because the German's were dropping bombs on us. There was a war on, Jones. Look at the peace outside our window now. No soldiers anywhere."

They both turned to look at the white, mountainous landscape backdropped with a deep blue, cloudless sky.

"You should have waited until after the war to marry," said LM. "You were safe in Bandol."

"Yes, but you know my aversion to safety. If we had remained in Bandol, we wouldn't have had those thrilling moments in Paris down in the hotel basement dodging German bombs."

"I could do without such thrilling moments. What I remember is how angry you were with me for not finding us passage to London. As if it was my fault that the Germans were dropping bombs."

Katherine laughed. "Oh dear Jones, you're so right. I do drag you into terrible situations. But isn't that part of the fun of being my traveling companion, not knowing what might happen?"

"Not really. The *fun* as you call it is knowing I can protect you from danger, and right now I'm not having any *fun*."

Towering over the attendant, LM paid for the tea service. Katherine noted the generous tip and stopped herself from saying anything. She had promised not to criticize LM for her generosity to either mosquitoes or humans. This was to be an enjoyable train ride and LM was so sensitive to her criticism that a few words could have her pouting all the way to Paris.

When LM sat back down and poured the tea, Katherine said, "Please don't be cross with me."

"I'm not cross with you, I'm cross with myself. This is risky business going to see another doctor who's filled your head with miracles. Too many times I've brought you home and seen the disappointment on your face when a doctor didn't do what you thought he could. You may be jeopardizing what health you have on a fool's journey."

"Jones don't say that. I need someone to still believe there can be a miracle in my life."

The Victoria Palace Hotel that her painter friend Anne Drey had recommended was more than satisfactory. Her writing table was in front of a window that looked out on a narrow tree-lined street below. Across the street a woman could be seen feeding her caged canaries on a sunlit balcony.

The following afternoon, Tuesday, Katherine and LM left the hotel for Dr. Manoukhine's office. Though a chilly winter's day, she convinced LM that a walk through the streets of Paris was not only economical but a needed exercise after the many cramped hours spent on yesterday's train.

"This must be it," said LM with confidence. They turned into a narrow street that ended at a brick wall.

"I thought you knew where his office was?" said Katherine, irritated. Having slept poorly and woken with a headache, she didn't need to be lost and late to her appointment in addition.

"I never said that. You rushed out of the hotel and I followed you. You know very well that I have no sense of direction. You're the one who knows Paris so well."

"Don't get haughty with me, Miss Ida. As you're of no help to me, you should return to the hotel. I'll find my own way."

"You can't possibly get there on your own. Look at you. You can hardly breathe. You left so quickly you even forgot your cane. Here, lean on me."

"No. I don't need your help." Katherine straightened herself up as best she could and walked off. She felt LM's eyes drilling through her back even after turning the corner but she didn't look back and for once LM didn't follow. She hobbled down one street and then the next. She recognized the street name, but without knowing the number, it took knocking on several doors before she entered Dr. Manoukhine's reception area and collapsed in a chair.

"Êtes-vous bien?"

Katherine looked up at a tiny prim girl in a nurse's uniform looking down on her with great concern.

"Yes, thank you," Katherine answered in French. "It was a long walk from my hotel and I got lost. I have an appointment with Dr. Manoukhine. He and I have corresponded."

"Why you must be Madame Murry. We were expecting you. I'm Sonja, his assistant and translator. It's wonderful that you speak French as my English is not very good."

Katherine coughed.

"Oh dear, here I'm talking away. Let me get you a glass of water." While she sipped water, through the open door she heard several men speaking Russian at once, like a chorus, with one distinctive countertenor rising above the others. Was that resonant voice Dr. Manoukhine? She hoped so. She wondered what Dostoevski, Tolstoy, Turgenyev, Pushkin and other Russian writers had sounded like when they spoke. I must learn Russian, she thought so I can read my favorite literature in its natural tongue. And I must have a child and name him Anton.

Her thoughts turned to Chekhov. He and so many other Russian writers had expressed such an outpouring of passion for their country, their culture, and their people. It was à propos that she should find her miracle among the Russians whose literature she so admired.

Sonja ushered her into Dr. Manoukhine's office. His bulky size startled her. She had hoped for someone taller, thinner, more like Dr. Anton Chekhov. Without any introduction, he stiffly pointed to a chair in front of his desk and she obeyed but found his brusque manner disappointing and out of character for what she expected from a Russian doctor. Dr. Chekhov would have understood so well her circumstances, having been a tuberculosis patient himself.

"Please remove your jacket and blouse, Madame Murry." Sonja translated his Russian into French.

She was so close to him when he bent down to listen to her lungs that she could see new hairs sprouting under his goatee. His eyes were unreadable. She closed her own and breathed in as told.

After the exam, he gestured with his short arm for her to sit down. His rotund figure was less imposing seated behind an enormous desk, a buffer between them. Sonja stood next to him. He leaned back in his chair, turning his pen in his pudgy fingers for what seemed like a hundred times before he spoke.

"You are a sick woman, Madame Murry. You have tuberculosis in the second degree—the right apex very lightly engaged but the left apex is full of rales." Sonja's guttural French r-r-r-r-ales made vivid the death rattle he must have heard, her left lung full of crackling tubercular bacteria. "But your condition is better than third or fourth degree when both lungs are full of rales, patient has a higher fever and more severe symptoms than you presently have. Your time in the Alps has done you good."

He explained that his radiation equipment was explicitly built to his specifications. "No other X-ray machine like it. Doctors from around the world have come to study its use and they leave very impressed." He commented that Dr. Hudson's offer to give her treatments on a common X-ray machine was almost laughable. His arrogance was disagreeable. Sonja's French accent was difficult to understand and his Russian was spoken too quickly for her to make any sense of it. If only Jack was here, she thought, holding back her tears. She looked down at her worn boots, feeling tired and discouraged. Why did I come here alone?

Dr. Manoukhine suddenly stopped promoting himself and in a softer voice said, "I can cure you." She looked up into his eyes and repeated, "лечение". She had learned the meaning of "лечение" from Kot when they translated Chekhov's letters. "Are you certain?" she asked. He stroked his goatee and gave a long answer in Russian. She was impatient to hear Sonja's translation.

"Yes, I can promise to cure you—to make you as though you had never had this disease. It will take fifteen séances—once a week—perhaps more often depending on your body's toleration of radiation, then a period of repose preferably in the mountains for two, three, perhaps four months. Then you should return to Paris for ten more séances. After the first series you should feel perfectly well. The last ten are to prevent any chance of recurrence."

"I was planning to wait until May."

He pulled again at his goatee and studied her. "Madame Murry your answer surprises me. Why wait? It would be much better for you to start now. Your condition is favorable. But, of course, it's your decision."

Before she could respond, he spoke curtly to Sonja and got up and left. Katherine got up, too, believing her interview must be over and had gone badly. "Wait," said Sonja. "He had to make an urgent call. He's coming right back."

He returned and leaned against the desk in front of her, "Please do not misunderstand me, Madame Murry. I do not insist on your beginning now. I do not say you will be greatly harmed by waiting. The great advantage in starting now is that you are here, that's all. If you wait until May it would mean being in Paris for the summer. The weather here is not good for you in the summer."

Outside in the reception, Sonja and Katherine sat together on the couch. She told Katherine about the miracles she'd witnessed while working for Dr. Manoukhine. She'd traveled with him from Kiev where he had treated thousands of soldiers at the Red Cross Hospital.

While Sonja answered a phone call, Katherine argued with herself over Dr. Manoukhine's question—'why wait?' Isn't this what Jack and I have been waiting for? Now when I'm so close to a cure, why do I hesitate? Because half of me thinks this very expensive doctor is a charlatan. There is something most unpleasant about him. But what does that matter if he can cure me?"

Sonja opened up her calendar book. "Why don't you start tomorrow?"

"Tomorrow?" said Katherine, her resolve shattered.

"Yes. You are fortunate. There's been a cancellation."

"And when must I pay?" she asked.

Sonja explained the fees. Katherine added up a hundred pounds in her head from her savings. How many stories must I write to earn an additional hundred pounds?

She told Sonja she must have more time to decide.

On the drive back to the hotel, her head ached. Her thoughts were divided. Was it worth the risk to be separated from Jack for several months?

When she arrived at the hotel, she sat down and wrote to tell him her *desire was not to stay. Why? Because of our life. I feel I cannot break it. I fear for it.* She asked him to make the decision for her or if that was too hard to at least advise her. *But don't forget that above all I love you.*

The next morning when she awoke her first thought was optimistic. She must meet with Dr. Manoukhine again. She added to Jack's letter, *I feel this morning perhaps we forget a little what a difference it's bound to make to us both if I was well. And to wait for that longer than we have waited is perhaps foolish.*

She sent a note to Dr. Manoukhine's office by courier asking for a second meeting but this time with his French partner, Dr. Donat, who could speak to her in French, which would avoid any misunderstanding in translation. She received an immediate response: "Come to the clinic at five."

Dr. Donat and Dr. Manoukhine greeted her at the door. The clinic was much larger than Manoukhine's office and was impressively equipped with sophisticated, new equipment. In contrast to Manoukhine's short, rotund appearance, Dr. Donat, was a handsome elderly gentleman with kind, trustworthy eyes and dressed in a doctor's white coat and skullcap.

They showed her the radiation room where she would lie down under the X-ray machine for two hours at each séance. She asked Dr. Donat to explain the process thoroughly so that she might understand the risks and the benefits.

"Dr. Manoukhine's radiation acts like immensely concentrated sunlight. What the sun does in a dissipated way this machine does more quickly. There is no risk but there is a cure. He recently healed an Englishman in the third degree. After twelve séances he had no more bacillus in his sputum. We can do the same for you."

She stared at the daunting apparatus. She imagined it healing her as she laid beneath its rays.

"You've been ill for a long time," said Dr. Donat. "One has not an endless supply of force. The air of Paris and the rays of Dr. Manoukhine will make you well. Of that I am confident. But I don't want you to think this will be easy. The X-rays are concentrated onto your spleen. The first five weeks of séances will be most uncomfortable. After that you will feel better."

"I am well versed in discomfort, Doctor."

Returning to her hotel, she wrote Jack:

I have just returned from meeting with Dr. Manoukhine and Dr. Donat to find out more about their X-ray treatments. After my meeting I am confident that the radiation of my spleen is without risk. Dr. Manoukhine has discovered that the spleen is the spot where the blood changes and if the spleen is fed with X-rays the blood is likewise fed. He has experimented on so many animals and so on and found such and such results. It is the latest thing in science. I felt at their clinic that I was in the presence of real scientists—not doctors. I imagine Pasteur's Institute would be of similar quality and professionalism.

If through these difficult months they kept to their aim for her to be cured then their separation would not damage the renewed love they'd found at Châlet des Sapins. But they must remain calm.

Thursday morning Jack's telegram arrived:

> YOU MUST DO WHAT M. SAYS. STOP. BEGIN THE TREATMENT NOW. STOP. CRIMINAL FOR YOU TO COME BACK. STOP. YOUR LOVING BOGE

She was relieved. Jack had decided for them both. She called Dr. Manoukhine's clinic and made an appointment for her first séance. The following day at two o'clock, Katherine arrived at the clinic. LM had offered to come with her but she wanted to go alone. She was reading in the reception while waiting her turn in the radiation room when she looked up to see Dr. Manoukhine walking quickly toward her. He gripped her hand and said, "Vous avez decidé de commencer avec le traitement. C'est très bien!" He then rushed past her out of the room turning back to say, "Bonne santé! Tout de suite."

I'll never forget his act of kindness, Katherine later wrote Kot*, the act of someone very good.*

Friday evening, exhausted from the first treatment she returned to her hotel and from bed wrote to Jack with her writing case propped against her knees.

She told him that after she had received his wire she had her first séance. She confessed to Jack her own doubts and wrote *Even though I had a great confidence in Manoukhine—very great and yet . . . I am absolutely divided. You know how, to do anything well, even to make a little jump, one must gather oneself together. Well, I am not gathered together. A dark secret unbelief holds me back.*

She hoped he would come to Paris, if only for a few days. She didn't ask him directly because she wanted him to make the decision on his own. She wanted him to say he couldn't imagine being anywhere else but with her.

His response came several days later:

I hope, darling, you won't think this very cold and calculating. But I feel that if I don't work now, I never shall; and that if I don't break the back of my year's work, it will drag on and on. I am deep into writing my book. If I leave now, I'll never get it done. But I'm not so much in love with my own idea that I can't believe in a better one. I mean, if you would rather I stayed in Paris now, say so straight out.

His letter kept her awake all night. He was relieved to have her gone. No mention of coming, even for a few days. He spoke of "fetching" her in May.

Katherine didn't write back. She was quite weak after the first séance and needed to conserve her strength. Corresponding any further with Jack or even thinking about him made her violently agitated.

He wrote to her again. He wasn't sure he had made the right decision and asked her to tell him what she wanted him to do. When she didn't respond, he sent a wire asking her if he should come.

Please do not come here to me, she replied. *It's no good. I now know that I must grow a shell away from you. I want—I 'ask' for my independence. At any moment in the future you may suddenly leave me in the lurch if it pleases you. It is a part of your nature. Finish your book. What does it matter that this is one of the most important moments of my life. Come in May and hopefully I'll still be alive to welcome you.*

But there will be no *fetching,* she said to herself angrily.

He wrote again insisting on coming.

I would rather stay here alone, she wrote back. *I have seen the worst of it by myself i.e. going alone to Manoukhine, having no one to talk it over and so on. I want now intensely to be alone until May. Then IF I am better, we can talk things over and if I am not I shall make some other arrangement. Let us be independent of each other till then—shall we?*

Jack had disappointed her for the last time. She must not depend on him.

I must heal my Self before I will be well, she wrote in her notebook. *Yes that is the important thing. This must be done alone and at once. I have given up the idea of true marriage (By the way what an example is this of the nonsense of time. One week ago we never were nearer.).*

It's true I cannot bear to think about the things I love in him . . . little things. But if one gives them up they will fade. I am not complete as I must be. It is at the root of my not getting better. My mind is not controlled. I idle, I give way, I sink into despair.

To be sure he wouldn't come, she sent a wire:

DO NOT COME HERE. STOP. SENDING LM. STOP. SHE WILL "FETCH" WHAT I NEED AND RETURN.

He wrote back that she was *an upsetting soul.* He felt she was sending the same inverted message that had come so often before when he had made the terrible mistake of not hearing her cry:

I want to make quite clear that I have, of my own free will and in my right mind, calm as ever I hope to be, decided to come to Paris till your fifteen séances are over. I suppose you beg me not to come because you imagine that I am doing something that I don't want to do myself, for your sake. Well, I'm not. I have realized that I shall be intensely miserable here by myself so far from you, that I shan't be able to work, and as I explained that my first burst of feeling that I could be a hermit doing eight hours a day was simply due to the fact that I hadn't yet realized that you were gone. Boge. There's not much love in this letter, but there's plenty in my heart.

24

Spring 1922

Paris Séances

JOB-in-the-ashes. Manoukhine says in eight days now the worst will be over. It's such a queer feeling. One burns with heat in one's hands & feet and bones, then suddenly you are racked with neuritis, but such neuritis that you can't lift your arm. Then one's head begins to pound. It's the moment when if I were a proper martyr I should begin to have that awful smile that martyrs in the flames put on when they begin to sizzle! But no matter it will pass . . .

Notebooks—KM

JACK ARRIVED AT HER HOTEL with a suitcase in one hand and a letter in the other that he asked her to read before they spoke. He waited in the doorway while she read:

When I knew you were going to stay in Paris, I shirked it. The day after I told you I wouldn't come I knew it was impossible for us to be apart. I began to be anxious every hour of the day: I had lost my mate.

I wasn't claiming any freedom; I don't want, never have for a year now even dreamed of wanting 'freedom'. I was just shirking, shrinking from being uprooted. The last four years have taken away what little courage I had—and I never had any. That is a ghastly confession to make for a man who is well, to his wife who is ill. I am utterly ashamed. But what can I do? I fight against it. But when the moment comes I'm just petrified with fear. I can't move. And I forsake you.

She felt a tender feeling in her heart and a longing for him when she looked up from the letter and saw the fear in his eyes, a reflection of her own fear. She could not give him up. Not while there was still hope of her getting well. His half smile, which had drawn her to him when they first met, melted what resistance she had left. She opened up her arms to him and he reached out for her.

Jack's arrival presented a problem. What to do with LM? She and Katherine shared adjoining rooms and Jack would now need LM's room for his sleeping quarters. Katherine's nights of insomnia and coughing spells were too fitful to share with anyone.

LM should return to their châlet in Switzerland. She could rent the vacant rooms, which would cover her expenses and also pay the châlet's rent.

In her correspondence with Elizabeth and Brett, Katherine told them how wonderfully well she and Jack were getting along in Paris; how supportive he had been, taking her to the clinic each week and bringing her home afterward. How they had found an agreeable routine. Jack did the shopping, brought home bread from Ferguson's, petits fours from Conte, and the most wonderful teas that they would share in their cozy room above the crowded, noisy streets of Paris. After their work, they played chess or acted out the parts of a Shakespeare play. She wrote that Jack completely ignored her in a good way, in a way that's necessary when one is a writer. He's there and not there. That was something LM could never do.

She let her family and friends know of the early success of Dr. Manoukhine's radiation, and said she and Jack were floating together on a new optimism.

The reality was that the side effects of radiation brought on a torrential downpour of headaches, pain, and fatigue. In spite of this she managed to write "spasms" of stories during the days spent in bed between séances. The income from these stories published in *Sphere* went to pay for the expensive séances. Jack spent his time in the adjoining room finishing his novel, *The Things We Are.*

Several of her stories written at the châlet were published in other magazines. *The Garden Party* had been serialized for three weeks in the *Westminster Gazette* and excellent reviews had come out on her new short story collection under the same title. The Pinker Agency, which had previously turned her down, now requested more stories as her popularity increased.

Come late March, as promised by Manoukhine, the worst of the séances were over. Her appetite returned, her heart quieted down, and she could take short walks with Jack in the nearby Luxembourg Gardens. She moved slowly and if she became dizzy Jack was there to lean on.

Timidly at first, but with mounting evidence that she was better, she and Jack began making plans for the months ahead, even projecting into the years ahead. She kept up a correspondence with LM that included plans for returning to the châlet in May. She felt caught between her plans with Jack and those with LM. She didn't want to let either go, but only needed one of them at a time and for now that was Jack.

She came up with a solution that she hoped would please everyone. She would live with Jack for six months of the year in England and the other six, October to March she would invite LM to join her anywhere warm, perhaps the south of France or Italy. *You know by that,* she wrote to LM, *I mean they will be my working months but apart from work—walks, tea in the forest, cold chicken on a rock by the sea and so on we could share.*

The problem, she told LM, was how to afford it? She suggested she could cover LM's expenses during the six months they were together but what about the other months? Would it work for LM to manage a teahouse in England six months out of the year?

In her next letter a few weeks later, she told LM that if the séances succeeded she and Jack would spend the coming summer in Germany, visit Elizabeth in Randogne, and then return to Paris for the final ten séances in the fall. They had even spoken of a future sea voyage back home to New Zealand, to Wellington.

She reread what she had written. Had she said all that there was to say? "Tell the truth," she heard the canaries chirp from across the courtyard, and wrote: *We three can never live together again. That is impossible. For we must be happy. No failures. No makeshifts. Blissful happiness.*

She finished the letter telling LM about a French psychotherapist, Dr. Emil Coué, who cured his patients through autosuggestive psychotherapy, popularly known as Couéism. Coué prescribed a mantra instructing his patients to repeat it as fast as possible, from morning to night, and so to keep bad thoughts out of their minds. She wrote it out for LM: *Day by day, in every way, I am growing better and better.*

And then she gave her the same advice she gave herself: *The great point is—if you can—think of happiness, work for happiness, look for it.*

She sent off the letter with trepidation hoping LM would understand and accept the new arrangement that temporarily excluded her.

BESIDES READING DR. WALLACE'S *COSMIC ANATOMY* for clues to becoming one with her mind and spirit, she read other books that offered ways to become a whole person. She would try and discuss what she considered now her spiritual quest to heal her "divided" self with Jack, but conversations on what he considered the "occult" always ended in arguments. His mind was closed to any mindfulness that couldn't be proven medically or scientifically.

He withdrew from any discussions on free will or on taking responsibility for one's actions or the idea that what we cause to happen will ultimately have an effect. When she said her little mind was enlarged by reading *Cosmic Anatomy*, he just looked down at the chessboard and made his move in silence.

But he wasn't silent about his feelings toward her old mentor Orage. He never stopped cursing him for sending *Cosmic Anatomy* and blamed it on the growing breach between him and his wife. She now turned toward Orage—the only one who understood her need to heal her divided self.

One afternoon when she was in the middle of practicing a Coué mantra, "I am hap-py, I am hap-py" over and over, Jack rushed into her room, all white in the face. "I've lost my wallet!" Before she could ask him where he lost it, he rushed back out and made a terrific banging noise in his room.

She walked in on him dumping out the wastepaper basket on the floor. He pushed past her back to her room and shuffled through her papers, banged doors, pulled the bed apart and shook everything but her. He finally gave up and sat down.

It was at times like this that she really wished she could manage on her own. Jack was too exhausting, and LM never left her alone. She tidied up the mess he'd made on her table and tried to return to her work, but after several minutes of him sitting in utter despair, she went off to his room to look for his wallet.

"No, it's no use," he shouted. "It's gone. I've looked everywhere. It's hopeless."

Minutes later, Katherine returned, waving his wallet in the air. "I found it."

BEFORE HER LAST SÉANCE in May, Katherine had a major setback. She was writing one of her "spasms" at her table when she suddenly pressed against her pounding, palpitating heart with one hand and gripped the table with the other. "Jack!" she called out. He helped her into bed and then called Dr. Donat who came immediately. After listening to her heart, Donat told her they would have to postpone her last séance. He assured her the palpitations were not caused by the séances but rather by the last vestiges of the tubercular infection that remained in her lungs.

Even after her heart calmed down, Katherine was still frightened. She and Jack decided it was safer to repose in the Alps until they returned to Paris in the fall for the last series of séances. They put away the brochures advertising destinations in Italy and cruise ship voyages on the Pacific. Because of her weakened heart, they chose Randogne, not as elevated as Châlet des Sapins and nearer Elizabeth, whom they had both grown quite fond of during their stay in Switzerland.

Katherine hurriedly wrote LM with the new plan and asked her to look for new lodgings for her and Jack in Randogne. No longer needed at the châlet, LM decided to go back and carry out her plan of opening a tearoom in Brighton, England.

On her way there she burst in on Katherine in her Paris hotel room almost knocking over a beautifully arranged bouquet in her excitement to see her. "Oh how lovely, Katie. Did you arrange this yourself?"

"So you're going to go ahead with the tearoom?" Katherine asked, after they were comfortably sipping their tea.

"Yes," said LM, biting into a tea biscuit. "Yes, that's my plan for now, or at least I think so unless—"

"I think a chocolate shop *and* a tearoom would be best. I believe there's an awful lot to be made out of a good tearoom at the seaside, with morning buns after bathing and so on. But I'd make it very original, very simple, with a real style of its own. The great point is to be 'noted' for certain specialties and to make them as good as possible."

"My partner Susan Suchard would surely agree with you. She's most enthusiastic about specialties. She's found a seaside room in Brighton and is waiting for me so that we can sign the lease and get started. I hesitate to do that."

"Do what?"

"Sign the lease. I don't know if Susan will find it acceptable if I only obligate myself for six months so that you and I can travel together the other six."

Katherine could hear the canary though the open window across the courtyard. "Tell the truth. Tell the truth." Yes, she thought, I must do that . . .

"I've been meaning for us to have a chat about that. I must first tell you that I had a peculiarly odious dream about 'us', and though that didn't change my feelings, au fond, it made me feel that perhaps I'd been premature in speaking so definitely about the future . . . Perhaps you felt that too?" She didn't wait for an answer when she saw LM's rosy cheeks drain of color.

"We cannot live together in any sense until I am stronger. I am simply unworthy of friendship, as I am. I take advantage of you, demand perfection of you, crush you."

LM took out her handkerchief from her purse.

"Jones, please don't cry. I'm not saying we are to live apart for all our lives from now on. I just think it's best to leave the earth alone for a bit. Do you know what I mean? Let it rest as it is and leave what's there to either grow or die down or be scattered or flourish. By the earth I mean . . . the basis . . . the foundation of our relationship . . . the stable thing that it is. Let it rest!"

She looked over at LM's muddled face and realized she would have to be far more direct.

"In the host of indefinite things there is one that is definite. There is nothing to be done for me at present. And Jack can help out when needed. Not that he can do all that you did."

She stopped speaking to study LM's face to be certain she understood her meaning. She saw that LM still didn't. "I'd far rather take care of myself than have it done by you. You see, it's a false position between us. You deserve to have a life of your own.

"You would have been married by now if you hadn't been taking care of me these past five years. You must start living independently. That's only fair. Whatever happened to that young man you introduced us to? Have you kept in touch?"

LM blushed. "Katie, that was five years ago."

"No, is that possible? Well, you'll meet someone else once you're free from your obligations to me."

"I don't want to be free, Katie."

"I know that. You are truly my Griselda. I bought these cream puffs for you, I know they're your favorites." She remained silent while LM ate.

She continued, "Now that I'm being well paid for my work I want to offer you an income to help you start your new business. Do you know to this day I still don't know how you manage, what you live on. I can't afford very much but I was thinking maybe five pounds a week."

"I don't need your money. I've been more than paid for my services."

Katherine reached across the table and put her hand on LM's.

"I don't see my way at present, I confess, but perhaps in the future I could pay the travel expenses for a visit to Rhodesia to see your sister."

"You needn't do that." LM looked down at her watch, releasing Katherine's hand. "I must go."

She quickly put on her hat and coat.

Katherine handed her an envelope she had prepared earlier. "Please take this. It will help pay your travel expenses to London and help you get settled."

LM shook her head.

"Jones, please accept this gift from me. A token of our friendship. I'll be most upset if you don't take it."

LM stuffed the envelope in her coat pocket. Katherine kneeled down to say good-bye to Wingley who LM had brought along with her in his traveling cage. He was napping and opened his eyes and stared into hers. For one moment she thought to keep him but no that wouldn't do. That was as impossible as her keeping LM.

Katherine called out to her as she stood waiting at the lift. "I know your tearoom will be a great success. Write me. Let me know how you're getting along."

"I will, Katie."

"And please depend on me. I'm just the same whatever is happening even when I don't write."

The lift door opened and LM stepped inside. She didn't return Katherine's wave.

It was a strain to keep writing moneymaking "spasms" for *Sphere* magazine. She felt no loyalty toward them, only distaste. But there were still ten more séances to be paid for in the fall. And didn't her readers like the *Sphere* stories even if she didn't? She received many letters from them. Women who had fallen under the spell of men. Lonely women. Women betrayed. Men helpless. But there had also been criticism from the likes of Virginia, who expected more from her, and assailed the stories for their lack of originality, a step down from her earlier writings.

She slammed her pen down on the table and got up, restlessly walking over to the window to watch the canaries flit from one perch to the other in their limited space. The room seemed so empty without Jack. A perfect time to write. What was stopping her?

Since her last setback she was feeling much better. It was just her invisible heart that still gave her trouble.

Dr. Manoukhine said to be patient. Her heart would grow stronger during the break between séances. Until then he warned her not to walk more than ten minutes a day. He was confident that the radiation to her spleen had put a stop to bacilli growth in her lungs and that the séances in the fall would clean them out permanently.

She looked forward to leaving Paris and returning to the healing powers of Nature. The more she saw of life in Paris the more certain she felt that the people who live remote from cities are the people who inherit the earth. She imagined the early summer flowers on the sloping grass hills of the Valais valley.

She repeated, "Every day in all ways I am getting better," twenty times, stopping to smile at herself in the mirror, blow out her cheeks and pinch them until they were a healthy bloom. A smile was on her face when she heard Jack open the door and shout, "I'm home. Where's that girl of mine?"

25

June 1922

Return to the Alps

Timidly timidly she lifts her head from her wing.
In the sky there are two stars
Floating, shining . . .
O waters do not cover me
I would look long and long at those beautiful stars!
Oh my wings—lift me—lift me!
I am not so dreadfully hurt.

The Wounded Bird—KM

PACKING WAS CHAOTIC AND HECTIC. Though their train to Lausanne was a night train, with plenty of time to pack, Jack kept forgetting where he put things and anxiously repacked. He forgot to hire a cab and Katherine feared they would miss the train. Somehow they found a porter at the train station who hurried them on just before the whistle blew. The money she had given Jack to manage the travel expenses was lost when he overpaid the porter and gave him fifty francs instead of five.

The train was overcrowded with travelers heading for a summer event in Lausanne. There were no available seats left. A gentleman finally offered Katherine his seat. He must have noticed how pale she was. Jack commented after the trip that he was surprised the passengers treated Katherine as if she were an old woman, or, better yet, a wounded bird. Yes Jack, she thought to say, they see me for who I really am.

She was surprised and relieved when they arrived intact the next afternoon at the Hotel d'Angleterre in Randogne. Well, not entirely intact. Jack had managed to lose his only fountain pen as well as Katherine's traveling clock, a clock she'd coveted through all her journeys.

Her first impression of Hotel d'Angleterre was not favorable compared to the elegant Palace Hotel in Paris. But within the first week she came to appreciate the simplicity of the sparse furniture and the raw beauty of the bare wood floors. And the view from the balcony was just what she had hoped for when she stood at her window in Paris looking across the way at the woman tenderly tending her singing canaries.

In spite of her joy in returning to the Alps, her health immediately took a turn for the worse. She left Paris with the beginnings of a cold and then caught a chill on the train when Jack couldn't find any blankets. She ended up with pleurisy, which kept her in bed with a fever and a cough. D'Angleterre's proprietors, an elderly woman and her sister, did everything they could to make her comfortable, bringing her tea and soups. She and Jack were their only guests. The season was over and the sanatoriums and hotels were mostly vacant.

After a week of bed rest she was on the mend and she woke from a nap to the sound of cows shaking their cowbells as they headed down the mountain pass after a day of continual munching and sunshine. She opened the door leading onto her balcony, stepped outside to take in the pure air and stunning view of the Valais valley, and vowed to never be a city dweller again.

On the grassy slope covered in wild flowers and clover, the cows, goats, sheep, and their herders jauntily strolled toward her. The cows stopped under her balcony and looked up at her with concerned maternal eyes. In her imagination the farm animals danced, pranced and played together for their pleasure and hers, their music a symphony of bells ricocheting against the mountains. She was tempted to run down the stairs and join in her own fantasy.

She managed to dress herself although it took an hour without LM's help. In the mirror, the jacket and skirt she had filled out in Paris now drooped on her. The weight she'd gained, a manifestation of Dr. Manoukhine's healing powers, was being shed daily in spite of the kind efforts of her landladies who provided her with an endless supply of fresh bread, milk, cheese and butter.

She considered all the doctors she'd seen in the past four years and decided they were all charlatans except the indifferent Dr. Sorapure, the only one who didn't promise a cure. She cursed the time wasted as a wandering consumptive searching for a cure outside herself when all along the real cure was within. If only Jack could understand that, and share her new quest with her.

She sat at her writing table but didn't lift her pen. Though behind in the "spasm" stories promised to *Sphere* magazine, she felt no enthusiasm for it. Too tired. Just getting up and getting dressed in the morning was wearing her down.

When Jack was not working on his novel, he escaped to the outdoors, hiking, fishing, collecting flowers and butterflies, and visiting Elizabeth at her châlet nearby. At night he returned, robust from nature's blessings. She tried not to resent his youthful vitality that illness had stolen from her. In her notebook she wrote:

Why, just because I am bedridden, should he not be able to enjoy the vibrant Life surrounding us? But I will never get any work done if things continue the way they are.

She needed LM. She couldn't depend on Jack to take care of her and she was too weak to take care of herself. She hesitated, and then lifted her pen and wrote two letters.

The first letter asked LM straight out to return, explaining that she was ill and couldn't write and take care of the daily chores. The second was a draft of a letter Katherine wanted LM to put in her own handwriting and sign. It was a request to return in the capacity of Katherine's companion-secretary, explaining that things hadn't worked out with the tearoom and she needed a position at six pounds a month. This way Jack would not be held accountable.

LM responded immediately and Katherine showed the letter to Jack who agreed that they must help her after all she'd done for them. Katherine sent money for a train ticket and warm wool socks. The following week LM moved into L'Angleterre. They booked her in a room on the same floor but way down the hall so they could still have their privacy.

Under LM's care, Katherine returned to her work and started *The Dove's Nest,* a story she hoped to develop into a novel.

One evening Jack returned from dinner at Elizabeth's and interrupted Katherine who was in the middle of chanting Dr. Coué's mantra: "Every day, in all ways, I am getting better and better."

"Katherine, darling, you're not starting up with that again, are you?"

It angered her that he'd interrupted her but worse he was scolding her.

"And why not?"

"Because I find it quite shocking that a woman of your vast intelligence would consider such hogwash. There is no scientific or medical proof that you can use your Will to heal yourself. The only person who can cure you now is Dr. Manoukhine, an acknowledged medical expert. Why would you consider anything other than his proven methods?"

"Jack, look at me."

"Oh there you go again. Don't be silly about this."

"Please do this for us." She sat up on her pillows so that he might have an even closer look and pulled his hand to her face. "Take a long look at the real me. Not how you see me in the future or in the past but now. Feel my scarecrow hands, see my burning eyes, touch my white white skin and feel my hollow cheeks." He turned away. "No. Jack. Don't turn away. Stop denying the truth. You must do this for *us*." He held his gaze on her. "Now tell me if you truly believe those body-burning treatments I suffered through in Paris have cured me like Dr. Manoukhine said?"

"Well . . . certainly not cured but you are better. It takes time. You just need to rest—You need some sun on your face—that's it. I'll take you on a picnic tomorrow. Wouldn't you like that?"

"Jack, haven't you noticed that I can hardly walk across a room let alone go outside without my cane?"

"Then I'll carry you."

"Orage has written me—"

"Orage! He's a fool. Why do you continue to communicate with him?"

"Because I need someone to talk to about my desire to find peace within myself."

"Peace? Don't you think that's a misuse of a larger concept that has to do with war?"

"Not at all. I'm at war within myself."

"Stop this silly prattle. This is his influence. You never used to talk like this. He speaks of things he knows nothing about and fills your head with them. Don't follow him, Katherine. It will only bring you harm."

"That's what you said about Kot, after he suggested I go to Dr. Manoukhine for his cure."

"That's different. Kot at least recommended a legitimate doctor. Orage only sent that ridiculous book by that witchdoctor. They've caused a breach between us."

"Isn't that rather extreme calling Dr. Wallace a witchdoctor?"

"A doctor of theosophy is not going to cure you."

"No? I disagree. This book that you find so detestable, though you've never read it, has helped me through some very difficult days. It has helped me to come to terms with my illness. I asked you to read it, but you won't, even though I want to discuss it with you."

"Discuss what? Free Will? You really think you can focus your conscious mind on your illness and make it go away?"

She looked up at him. Perhaps he had read it.

He knew what she was thinking. "No I haven't wasted my time with that foolery and you shouldn't either. At one time you agreed with me about Orage. There was a long period when you wouldn't speak to him because of his relationship with that woman Beatrice. Have you forgotten the horrible things they said about you and me?"

"I impulsively judged him unfairly. It's a bad habit of mine."

"So now you judge me unfairly. Perhaps you would prefer Orage was here instead of me?"

"Jack stop sounding like a lunatic. Orage helping to answer my spiritual questions doesn't preclude my relationship with you."

The door slammed behind him.

KATHERINE'S HEART PALPITATIONS and difficulty breathing did not improve. She decided to move down the mountain to the village of Sierre, which had a lower elevation of fifteen hundred meters.

She told Jack she wanted to keep up the daily writing schedule established in Paris and needed to be alone to do so. She lied. She couldn't write. She kept that a secret and pretended she was working when anyone came into her room. She was counting on the lower elevation to quiet her heart so that she could resume her work.

Elizabeth offered Jack a guestroom at her châlet. He told Katherine he was very content with the new arrangement as he would also work and come down to her on the weekends.

Before she left, Elizabeth came to say good-bye.

"How strange that it took us so long to become good friends," said Katherine after they had settled back on the divan with their teacups. "Do you remember when I first met you at your father's house in London? Probably not. I hardly said a word. I was so in awe of you I was afraid of saying anything that might make me appear stupid. Pa was so proud of you. You are his brilliant star. I thought by becoming famous, I would earn his love, too."

"And haven't you?"

"No." Katherine smiled. "He's never respected my work. I've heard through my family that he doesn't even read my stories. In his letters he tells me how proud he is of my sisters and their children."

"Your father knows nothing about literature if he doesn't recognize your valuable contribution. Your work is on a much higher level than mine, and you're over twenty years younger! I've envied the originality of your modern literary fiction. I'm afraid I'm just a simple storyteller."

"You're a wonderful storyteller. Both Jack and I couldn't put *Vera* down until we finished it. And what an ending! That was certainly an original piece of work, and it's far more popular than anything I've written."

"What are you saying my silly cousin? Look how many printings your short story collections have had. Look at the reviews praising your genius. You're in great demand. Why I don't know anyone who hasn't read your stories in the *Sphere*."

"Ah yes the *Sphere* stories. I write those two-thousand-word 'spasms,' often in a day, to pay for Manoukhine. They don't challenge me but they do entertain my readers. Perhaps that's enough. But if my father thought to increase my allowance to cover my medical expenses, I would spend my time on more challenging work."

"Why don't you ask him to pay for Dr. Manoukhine's séances? He can certainly afford it."

"No. I won't humble myself. It would be saying that I've failed as a writer. Success to him means financial independence." She gazed into Elizabeth's eyes searching for understanding. "He'll never offer to raise my allowance. He's like Jack that way. They're both miserly in spirit. With Jack I understand better. He grew up with very little and holds on tightly to what he has earned. With my father it's propriety. Yes he's enormously rich but he doesn't want my allowance to make life easier for Jack."

"Do you agree with your father? Should Jack be your main provider?"

Katherine laughed. "Heavens no. I'd be wearing rags. He's given me money occasionally but he expects me to pay him back. He even asked me to share the fare when I was recovering from a lanced gland and we were coming back from the clinic in a cab in Menton!"

Katherine laughed at Elizabeth's look of horror.

"I would never have put up with that."

"I'm not as good at leaving men as you are."

Elizabeth blushed. "Now wait a moment, that isn't fair. My first husband died. It was only my second husband that I divorced."

"Besides I would never leave Jack. I still love him very much in spite of his miserliness, self-absorption, and indifference." Katherine had meant it as a joke but it came out differently.

"Then it's true, isn't it? *The Man without a Temperament* is Jack. You, too, sometimes turn to autobiography for your material. I certainly did in *Vera*. Fictionalizing my husband's dark side helped me through a miserable divorce."

Katherine smiled and took her time pouring them both another cup of tea before saying, "That story was a message to Jack. But he read it as a tribute to his great love for me, which I found curious. Now I understand that he'll always delude himself and anyone else he can influence into believing he sacrificed his life and career to care for his dying wife."

Elizabeth put her hand over Katherine's and looked into her eyes. "You've made many compromises, haven't you? Women do, you know. Perhaps you are no longer willing to do so?" Elizabeth released her hand.

"No, I still believe in our happiness. It's only recently, with my relapse, that it's become difficult for us to be together as we no longer agree on how I can be cured. I'm now pursuing a spiritual path that Jack doesn't want any part of. He doesn't believe me when I tell him that this new path will reunite us after I am healed."

Katherine put down her teacup.

"Elizabeth, please know that our conversations have been wonderful for me. It's very comforting for me to be able to speak my mind to you."

"Oh my dearest Katherine, is there anything I can do to make things easier for you?"

"You already have. It's much easier leaving Jack, knowing he's with you."

"He's a pleasurable guest. Never dull. His intelligence challenges my own in a way you don't often find in society."

"Yes, it's true, he has an extraordinary mind. He's a brilliant critic. In fact, he's now considered *the* Critic in London's literary and intellectual circles. But in his intellectual pursuits he forgets to smell the roses along the way. He needs me to remind him.

"Yes, I've noticed that," said Elizabeth. They both laughed.

"But let's not talk of Jack anymore," said Katherine. "Tell me about your new love. Are you happy? You certainly look happy when you're together."

"Oh yes, very. But sometimes I worry he's becoming bored with me. We're isolated here on our mountaintop and except for the occasional visitor we're often alone, and he is much younger."

"I wouldn't worry about that Elizabeth. You're extremely entertaining and quite ravishing. I've enviously watched the way he looks at you. I doubt you sleep in separate rooms."

Elizabeth laughed. "Separate rooms? Certainly not. Do you and Jack sleep in separate rooms?"

"Yes. At least while I'm ill."

They both studied the tealeaves in their empty cups until Elizabeth looked up and said, "I'm curious about something. Do you think you would have become a writer if you hadn't been a *femme malade*?"

"I've reached the conclusion that I'm a writer in spite of my illness but my suffering has given me the opportunity to see clearly what others might miss. It's enlarged my vision. I'm searching now for a more honest way to express what I've learned so I can help others to see." She hesitated and then said, "I need time to accomplish this."

A knock on the door brought them both to their feet. LM announced that it was time for Katherine's nap. Katherine, touched by Elizabeth's moist eyes, was brought to tears herself.

Katherine watched from her window as Elizabeth climbed the trail back to her châlet. Her heart tightened with the sudden fear that she might never see her cousin again.

26

July 1922

Château Bellevue

I must confess that there does seem to me something sad in life. It is hard to say what it is. I don't mean the sorrow that we all know, like ill-ness and poverty and death. No, it is something different. It is there, deep down, deep down, part of one, like one's breathing.

The Canary—KM

KATHERINE ENTERED THE MASSIVE GLASS DOORS of the Château Bellevue in Sierre. Coming in from the bright sunlight it was as dim and chilly as an empty church. Stephen, the smiling, hospitable bellboy, remembered her and set her at ease. She'd stayed there at the beginning of Dr. Stephani's open-air cure. It was hard to believe it was only a year ago.

"Hello Madame Murry and, ah, yes, Madame Baker isn't it? Come in. Come in. We've been expecting you." He grabbed the bags and led them up the hotel's spiral stone staircase, lit by the sun pouring in through the stained-glass windows.

Several steps up, Katherine took off her gloves and rubbed her hand against the broad, worn balustrade, an excuse to catch her breath. Stephen, kept talking cheerfully, oblivious to her several stops. At the top of the first landing, she asked him if there were mosquito nets over the beds.

"You won't need nets here," he said, surprised by her question, then touched his face and laughed. "Oh these. I was camping in the mountains this weekend and got attacked. As you noticed, they like my blood."

"Yes I see that," Katherine said and smiled. "They like me too, that's why I asked."

"Not here at the château. You needn't worry."

Stephen stopped at a heavy dark mahogany door, #12, and unlocked it with a large brass key. "This is your room, Madame Murry. I hope you find it to your taste."

Katherine was overjoyed. The rich green-paneled walls welcomed her. Floral-brocaded drapes held back by brass hooks framed deep-set windows, which looked out over a sun-gilded landscape of fields with the ever-present Alps beyond. Sheer white curtains beneath billowed under the soft, sweet air drifting through the open windows. Sunlight fell across wooden floors that gleamed like polished tortoiseshells and she was amazed to look up at the chandelier and see that the floor's design was duplicated in the lofty ceiling. It made her dizzy. She held onto a bedpost until the room straightened again.

She sat down at a writing table adorned with a vase filled with vividly colored saffron yellow and orange zinnias. In this room, she thought, I could get a lot of work accomplished. If only my heart would stop beating so violently. I must rest.

Stephen put her suitcase on a wooden chest. "Thank you Stephen. You should rub something on those bites."

"Yes, ma'am." He slipped out the door.

The low wooden bed covered in quilted green satin welcomed her small, tired body.

LM started unpacking and bustled around the room, disturbing Katherine's rest.

"Please, not now, Jones. Get settled in your room and we'll meet for dinner."

"Are you sure you'll be all right?"

"Here in this room how could I be anything else but all right?"

After LM left, she closed her eyes and fell asleep whispering, "Stay. Rest. You're safe here."

The following morning her heart had quieted and, anxious to start on the new story percolating in her mind, she set Jack's Corona typewriter on the writing table. She had conceived of the idea after watching the caged canaries on the neighboring balcony across from their Paris hotel.

She remembered lying in bed after her séances and listening to their songs. In order to write this story, she thought, I need to get inside that birdcage; their feelings, their dreams, the lives they led before they were caught or the lives their grandparents lived in the South American forests and the coast of the immense perfumed sea...words cannot express the beauty of that high shrill sound.

In a few days of intense work, she wrote *The Canary* and dedicated it to Brett, fulfilling the promise she had made to her, a pact of their friendship. She would send it to her agent who kept asking for more stories to satisfy her growing popularity. What had once been so difficult to do, find publishers for her stories, was now so simple and could have been joyous, if she wasn't ill.

When she was done, she took out a sheet of stationery and wrote to her father who was visiting her sisters in London. *I have just finished a story with a canary for the hero, and almost feel I have lived in a cage and pecked a piece of chickweed myself.*

She couldn't bear to stay indoors when the afternoon outside her window appeared so welcoming and, having just finished a story, a celebration was in order. At first she timidly approached the hotel garden. She was unaccustomed to being outdoors alone and she didn't see LM anywhere but, after resting for a moment, she ventured past the hotel walls.

Deep in her thoughts, she didn't realize how far she had strayed until she looked back at the hotel in the distance but before starting back she stopped to stretch out on a soft bed of grass and looked up at patches of blue framed between tree limbs. This, she thought, is the greatest happiness I shall ever know. I want to feel like this the rest of my life.

She sat up against the tree trunk and wrote in her notebook:

There's nothing to prevent you living like this but it is incompatible with Jack. You are the most stupid woman I have ever met. You never will see that it all rests with you. If you do not take the initiative nothing will be done.

I should be concentrating on the things that count—like the sight of this tree with its purple cones against the blue and wonder how am I to put it that there is gum, on the cones—gemmed? No beaded? No they are like crystals.

There is something I should be learning. What is it? I must find out and start fresh with a new style. Something is missing in my stories? What is it?

A sudden drop in the temperature made her aware of the time. She got up and wrapped her shawl tightly around her shoulders. The hotel was now lit up and glimmering through the evening dusk. How beautiful it is, she thought, I must write a story about it. In the distance she heard LM anxiously calling her.

SHE HAD LOOKED FORWARD to Brett's visit but now that Brett was actually there she made excuses to avoid her. She needed solitude to consider her next step. She told both LM and Brett that if they saw her walking in the garden they should not interrupt her. She told them her writing kept her occupied until mid-afternoon when she joined them for tea. Brett had come to Sierre to paint landscapes and was content to roam by herself with her easel. LM went off on hikes. She and Brett had little to talk about without Katherine's company.

Brett visited Katherine in her room in the evenings but was inclined to carry on too long talking about their mutual friends without noticing that her listener was falling asleep. Katherine told LM to come to her room and scoot her away, saying Katherine needed her rest, which was true. She was tired, more tired than she wanted to admit to herself or anyone else.

She told LM and Brett she needed to be alone to write but it wasn't true. She just needed to be alone. The pen hardly touched paper and the punching of the keys on the Corona ceased. She lied in her letters, too, and told her friends and family she was much better and writing stories. She told her father that her tuberculosis was quiescent. But she didn't tell him that her heart, at any hour, became a loud, terrorizing drum.

Jack came down on the weekends, visited with Brett and often played billiards with Katherine in the hotel lounge. He asked how the writing was coming along and she told him she was working on a short novel, a continuation of two previous stories, *Prelude* and *At the Bay,* with the idea of merging them into a longer novel that would move back and forth between England and New Zealand. It wasn't a complete lie. She was working, but only in her head.

As the days went on, staring at a blank page made her anxious, so she put her pen to paper and wrote whatever came to mind.

One day, Brett came out of her room to find Katherine pacing the hallway looking at door numbers.

"What is it? Have you forgotten your room number?"

"I'm working on a story but I've changed it around so often I'm muddled. I need to find the room where the idea originated. The rooms are exquisitely decorated but most of them are empty. I wander through them. I'm looking for a huge stove. Come along and help me find it."

Brett followed behind down the long dim hall as Katherine slipped in and out of rooms. "Here it is!" she shouted. "Here's what I was looking for." She pointed to an ancient milky white and blue stove in the corner. Exhausted from her efforts she sat down on the bed and took out her notebook. "Brett could you read the figures engraved on it."

Brett walked over to the stove and read out, "Sixteen hundred and twenty three."

"Yes, now I remember," Katherine mumbled to herself, scribbling down more notes. "Too perfectly historical for words, don't you think?"

"What?"

"Never mind," she said. "It's just something Emma says to her sister about the stove. If you want, come back to my room and I'll read it to you. The story takes place in this hotel, which Emma and Emily stay at with their father."

Back in her room, she opened to the pages she'd been working on and stood upright in front of Brett as if she was entertaining a roomful of listeners at a salon gathering, something she had often done in the past:

For a long time now—for how long?—for countless ages—Father and the girls had been on the wing. Nice, Montreux, Biarritz, Naples, Menton, Lake Maggiore, they had seen them all and many, many more. And still they beat on, beat on, flying as if unwearied, never stopping anywhere for long. But the truth was—Oh, better not enquire what the truth was. Better not ask what it was that kept them going. Or why the only word that daunted Father was the word—home . . .

Home! To sit around, doing nothing, listening to the clock, counting up the years, thinking back . . . thinking! To stay fixed in one place as if waiting for something or somebody. NO! No! Better far to be blown over the earth like the husk, like the withered pod that the wind carries and drops and bears off again.

She stopped and looked over at Brett. "Well?"

"Is that all?"

"Yes, for now."

"Why I think it's quite wonderful. I always like it when you read your stories out loud. When you come back to London I must arrange a salon reading."

"My cousin Elizabeth and I are thinking about a reading tour in the States. My books are selling well there and there've been requests."

"That would be smashing! May I come along?"

"Yes . . . why not?" Katherine looked down at her notebook. "But you must leave me now—I have work to do. We'll discuss everything over dinner."

"That's what you said yesterday."

"I'm sorry. I've neglected you, haven't I? I'll come downstairs tonight. I promise."

"I certainly hope so. I'm leaving for London tomorrow."

"No, that's impossible. Have you been here a fortnight already? We spent too little time together. I'll be sorry to see you go."

After Brett left, Katherine sat down to work but she was too tired. She laid down on the bed instead.

That evening, she asked LM to help her get dressed for dinner.

She descended the stairs to the salle à manger, which was the size of a ballroom. It was off-season and bereft of guests and easy to spot Brett in one of its only inhabited chairs. Before going to her, Katherine quickly wrote in her notebook:

All gay, all glittering, the long French windows open onto the green and gold garden, the salle à manger stretched before them. And the fifty little tables with the fifty pots of dahlias looked as if they might begin dancing with . . .

Whom? Katherine asked herself, having no idea where the sketch might go from there or if she would ever complete it—so many unfinished sketches in her notebooks. She smiled over at Brett and approached her.

It was like old times. She performed gaily for Brett all evening, miming their friends and telling funny stories. She gave a brilliant performance and hoped Brett would return to London and tell their friends that Katherine was doing quite well, writing, and happy.

After Brett left, she took to her bed. Without the strength to concentrate on the story she was writing, she turned her pen to poetry:

In the wide bed under the green embroidered quilt
with flowers and leaves always in soft motion
she is like a bird resting on a pool.

She suddenly dropped her pen. "Jones! Jones!"

LM rushed into her room. "What is it Katie!"

"My heart. It's pounding."

When Katherine had palpitations, Dr. Donat had instructed LM to sit with her. Keep her calm. Don't leave her alone. She mustn't panic.

Her banging heart slowed down after a few minutes. LM brought her a glass of water.

"I can't go on like this," said Katherine. "It comes in spasms like my cough used to but it's far more frightening. Each time, I think I'm dying. I must see Dr. Sorapure. He's the only one who will tell me the truth. We must leave for London right away."

"I'll make the travel arrangements," said LM. She too was frightened by Katherine's recurrent attacks.

"Jack is coming down on Sunday. I must speak to him first. He's very content in Randogne; perhaps he'd rather stay and finish his book. You know he's taken up golf. I knew he would someday."

Unable to sleep, she ran over a list several times in her mind of people she wanted to see in London:

Pa (childhood/love)

Orage (soul)

Kot (friendship)

Sorapure (heart)

THE FOLLOWING DAY, her strength returned. She wrote to her father, apologizing for the change in her plans but she would like to meet in London instead of Paris:

To come straight to the horses, my heart has been playing up so badly this last week that I realize it is imperative for me to see Dr. Sorapure before I go on with my Paris treatments.

Jack agreed with her decision. He only asked that she promise to continue her séances with Dr. Manoukhine come September. She was having a minor setback and he was sure that more radiation to her spleen would fix her right back up again.

They played billiards and made their plans between hitting balls in the pockets. He wanted to accompany her to London.

She would occupy the only available small room at Brett's flat so he would have to stay next door with other friends.

It was a relaxing day for them. She let him win at billiards. He told her of his first golf game with Elizabeth. Teasingly she said, "The only women you ever love are the ones who love you. And this time it's my dear cousin Elizabeth."

He stayed the night in her room and the following morning he kissed her tenderly before returning to Elizabeth's to pack.

After he left and LM brought her breakfast tray, she said, "Jones, I want you to witness my will."

"Katie, sometimes I think you say things just to shock me. It's just your heart that has you worried. I'm certain Dr. Sorapure will set you right again. And hasn't Dr. Manoukhine promised that the next séances will cure you?"

"Jones, please don't be like Jack. If I can't prepare for the inevitable with him I would like to know I can with you."

LM looked at her for a long time before she spoke. "I'll help you anyway I can."

"Thank you. Now please bring me my notebook so we can get started." She still felt Jack's tender morning kiss on her lips. "If something should happen to me, I want to leave clear instructions for Jack. Otherwise he won't know what to do with my possessions."

The earlier Will that she had hurriedly written back at the Elephant when she thought she wouldn't survive the winter in Italy wouldn't do. The Will she wanted to write now would be more specific.

Together she and LM went over her possessions. "Nothing of great value," she said. "The larger pearl ring to Jack's brother Richard to have for when he marries; Spanish shawl; fur coat; favorite books to various friends, mother's walking stick to S. Koteliansky, writing cases to my sisters; to my Pa, return the brass pig that has been my loyal traveling companion."

She held up her small gold watch and chain she kept on the mantel. "Jones, would you like to have this?"

"If that's what you want to give me," she said in her tiniest of voices.

"It seems the right gift. It represents our long friendship. Your loyalty has never faltered and you have continued to be my most constant friend. Now what about my Bible? Would you like that?"

"Katie! Please no more of this talk. It's cruel of you to go on like this."

Katherine ignored her outburst and said calmly, "All right. I'll give the Bible to my father."

"Can't we do this some other time?"

"Just a few more things and we're done."

Later, the list completed, Katherine said, "You can leave me now. I want to write a letter to Jack."

LM left the room not bothering to hide her tears.

Katherine picked up her pen:

I have been on the point of writing this letter for days. My heart has been behaving in such a curious fashion that I can't imagine it means nothing. So, as I would hate to leave you unprepared, I'll just try and jot down what comes into my mind. All my manuscripts I leave entirely to you to do what you like with. Go through them one day, dear love, and destroy all you do not use. Please destroy all letters you do not wish to keep and all papers. You know my love of tidiness. Have a clean sweep, Bogey, and leave all fair—will you?

Books are yours, of course . . . monies, of course, are all yours. In fact, my dearest dear, I leave everything to you—to the secret you whose lips I kissed this morning. In spite of everything—how happy we have been! I feel no other lovers have walked the earth more joyfully—in spite of all."

She looked down at the small daisy-shaped pearl ring that Frieda Lawrence had kindly given her off her own finger when Jack forgot to bring a ring on their wedding day. It was iridescent under the gaslight. She would not leave it behind. It would remain with her on the grim journey where she certainly wouldn't wish anyone to follow her, not even Jack.

27

August-September 1922

Return to London

Why hath the rose faded and fallen, yet these eyes have not seen?
Why hath the bird sung shrill in the tree—and this mind deaf and cold?
Why hath the rains of summer veiled her flowers with their sheen?
And this black heart untold?

Awake—William de la Mare

LONDON WELCOMED HER like a loving parent whose adopted child had returned home from far away. She settled into Brett's sitting room in Hampstead and LM went to nearby Chiswick to stay with her sister's family who had returned from Rhodesia. Jack rented the top floor flat in the house next door to Brett's. Too many stairs for Katherine to climb, he'd visit her at Brett's for meals and at teatime.

Without LM to shoo people away, Katherine hung a sign on her door—"Working." It was intended for people who stopped by to say hello without an invitation. She never could understand why people thought writers sat at their desks with nothing to do but entertain people who "thought they would just come by to say hello." Brett was the worse offender. She came to talk at all hours, but Katherine couldn't begrudge her. It was Brett's home and she had hinted that her upstairs tenant planned to leave at the end of the month and that Katherine could rent this flat if she was interested in staying for an extended time in London. She was tempted but wanted to wait until after she saw Dr. Sorapure, before making any decisions about tomorrow.

When she walked into his office he greeted her with, "Why Katherine you do look better than when I saw you last. How long ago was that?"

"I've been gone two years."

"That long? Well then the open-air cure has done you good, or perhaps it's Dr. Manoukhine's radiation treatments? Why come to see me?"

"Quite simply because you're the only doctor I trust to tell me the truth."

"That's a compliment coming from someone who's seen as many doctors as you have. If you want my opinion, just looking at you I'd say whatever you're doing is better than anything I could do for you."

"I'm afraid my appearance is deceiving. I still have debilitating fatigue, my hips are on fire, my cough has returned, and I'm often out of breath. All these symptoms I have learned to tolerate. It's the frightening heart palpitations that brought me to you. My heart thuds in my ears and bangs twice as fast as it should. If my heart is going to stop it's going to stop, but if I'm putting myself at risk because of the radiation I want to know."

"I see. What does Dr. Manoukhine say?"

"He said the palpitations would stop after the treatments stopped. They didn't. They've become much worse."

"Let's have a listen to that pounding heart of yours." The cold metal chest piece pressed against her heart and made her flinch.

"Why aren't you using your anti-chill device?"

"The rubber disc? I'm sorry, I forgot to put it on. Not all my patients are as sensitive as you when I listen to their bodies. Would you like to listen?" he asked.

"No. It makes me squeamish hearing my heart beat and my lungs rasp for air. Besides, I don't need a stethoscope to hear their complaints."

When he was finished with the exam, he told her to sit down and pulled up a chair next to her.

"Here's the good news. You have the heart of a thirty-three year old woman as you should. It's just that it has to pump very hard to keep you alive. The left lung is the problem. Let me try to explain it with a drawing." He took a pencil to paper and drew a simple child's drawing of an inflated balloon and then a deflated one, side by side. He explained, "Here's a normal lung and here's one like yours."

He drew a wide canal around the deflated white balloon and filled it with pencil lead. "The tubercular lesions have leaked air into this dark canal between your lungs and your chest wall. This expanded canal, called an enlarged pleural space, is pressing against your heart. Your heart must pump much harder to circulate oxygen-filled blood. If there was a way to remove the air from the enlarged pleural space, your lung would inflate again and you wouldn't be having these palpitations."

She studied the scribbled pencil drawing and touched the small, white, deflated lung. She looked up and asked, "How do you know this?"

"There are no sounds of breathing over the affected lung because the lung has collapsed. Only your right lung is working."

"And there's no way to release the air?" she asked, pressing her finger on the dark canal. "Can't it some how be released?"

"Unfortunately, no, at least not yet. As I've told you before, it's a long process before medicine and science discover cures for our illnesses. We've yet to discover a way to let the air out of the pleural canal."

"And there's nothing that can be done to stop my heart's violent banging?"

"Exercise the lungs. Not excessively, that could be dangerous, but slow ten minute walks. Deep, slow breathing in fresh air might help expand the deflated lung."

"Then your medical opinion is that I continue with the radiation treatments and take daily walks in the park?"

He smiled. "Ah, Katherine. I always appreciate your sense of humor. Yes I guess you could put it that way but I wouldn't want to be quoted as saying I recommend radiation to the spleen. There is no scientific or medical data to back up Manoukhine's theories. Courageous patients like you that are willing to take medical risks lead us doctors and scientists to these much-needed cures. But, until medically proven, there's only Manoukhine's word and the testimonials of satisfied patients—the ones that are alive, that is.

"I can recommend that you stay in motion, unless your body tells you otherwise. Just don't run up any stairs."

Katherine left his office and following his advice took a slow walk in Hyde Park protected from an early fall breeze by the warm sun above. She sat down on a bench to take in the brilliant day and contemplate what she should do now knowing her heart was not in immediate danger. She felt a sentimental longing to stay in the city that she had once happily called home before she became a wandering consumptive. If I do decide to continue the treatments, she asked herself, why not in London instead of Paris?

Manoukhine had told her about a London radiologist he'd personally trained to irradiate the spleen with his patented X-ray machine. Why stay in a lonely hotel room in Paris when I could undergo the last ten séances here?

And what with Brett soon having an available upstairs flat . . . .

She stood up. There was much to do. Yes, she would stay in London, at least until winter. And if she were fully cured by Christmas, with no chance of another relapse, as Dr. Manoukhine had promised, then maybe she'd stay even longer. With a plan in mind, her spirits high, she hailed a taxi to take her back to Brett's.

Pa (childhood/love)

A few days after seeing Dr. Sorapure she took a train to her sister Chaddie's house outside London to see her father who was visiting from New Zealand and her sister Jeanne who was visiting from Canada with her husband and children. Everyone was delighted Katherine was staying in London and was on the mend. She brought gifts for the young nieces and nephews she'd never met before and made plans to have lunch with her father and sisters the following week in London. They were so welcoming and her father seemed so sincerely moved that she left them feeling she had returned to the fold and was once again Pa's loved child.

Orage (soul)

Third on her list after Dr. Sorapure and Pa was Orage. After reading *Cosmic Anatomy* and other books on mysticism that Orage had sent her, Katherine realized he'd influenced her ideas more than she previously thought. Early on when she was a young writer of twenty-one, he told her she must find her own center where the mind and soul worked together to create art. He had been wary of her promiscuity both personally and intellectually in those early years when she was driven to experience life to its fullest. She'd associated with several men Orage considered irresponsible and a bad influence on her young mind.

"The young artist who is virtuous will live for his art," he told her. But she didn't listen to him or anyone else. Her ambition back then was absolute freedom, whatever the cost. The writing would follow. At the time she'd been angry with him but now she understood that he was right; precious time had been wasted.

Katherine asked Orage to meet her for lunch at a restaurant, as there was really no privacy in Brett's sitting room. She woke up eagerly on that Wednesday morning, two weeks after her arrival in London. As she dressed, her heart beat loudly but she wasn't afraid. It pumped for joy. It had been two years since last they met. As excited as she was, she took time to dress carefully. She checked herself in the hallway mirror, pinched her cheeks, and left to find a taxi.

When she entered the restaurant he had suggested she immediately spied him seated in a far corner. He looked just as charming and handsome as ever though a bit more worn around the eyes, which were shaded under the same unfashionable felt hat that he had worn at their first meeting twelve years ago. He stood immediately when he saw her and looked at her fondly across the room with his charming and cheery smile.

When she was within reach he swept off his hat and crushed her in his arms. Wrapped in his fatherly arms, she didn't want him to ever let her go. A few locks fell down on his forehead and she flipped them back. He slowly released her and smiled.

"Katherine you look—"

"Please don't say it. One feels a great fraud to have a well built outside and such an annoying interior. Yes I can give a very good imitation of a perfectly well and strong person when I'm sitting down but that's all. I can't walk more than a few yards without faltering."

His eyes welled with tears.

"That wasn't a plea for your sympathy. I just get tired of the masquerade, appearing better than I really am. With you I needn't pretend."

"What I was about to say before you interrupted, my dear Katherine, is that the south of France and the mountains of Switzerland have done you well. They've done your writing well, too. I've kept up with your published work and what you have accomplished is most impressive. You will be remembered as one of the finest modern story writers."

"You used to tell me I was 'an empty husk, as promiscuous as a rabbit, as responsible as a bubble and as deceitful as a cat.'" She laughed, put up her small hand and clawed the air, finishing with "Me-ow."

Orage's face brightened. "Oh dear, you haven't forgotten have you?"

"It's not easy to forget such words of wisdom spoken from my editor's beatific lips."

"I didn't mean to hurt you."

"Well you did. But I forgave you a long time ago after I came to understand you were just trying to help me. I just wasn't up to someone being so honest."

They ordered lunch and spoke of small things in the past. In a moment of silence, Orage picked up his wineglass and lifting it recited a poem William de la Mare had written after spending an afternoon with Katherine in London several years before:

To K.M.

We sat and talked. It was June and the summer light
Lay fair upon ceiling and wall as the day took flight.
Tranquil the room—with its colours and shadows wan,
Cherries, and china, and flowers: and the hour slid on.
Dark hair, dark eyes, slim fingers—you made the tea,
Pausing with spoon uplifted, to speak to me.
Lulled by our thoughts and our voices, how happy were we!

By the time the port arrived, accompanied by cheddar cheese and figs, they were sitting back in their chairs sharing confidences. "Orage, there's something I'm most curious about. Why did you ask Jack to review Cosmic Anatomy for your magazine? His intellectual integrity would be held in question if he ever accepted mysticism as a valid philosophy. Did you really believe he might review it?"

Orage laughed. "I meant it for you Katherine. I would have liked Jack to review it but if he didn't, I really hoped you might pick it up and read it yourself. You and I had resumed our correspondence but we spoke more about literary subjects than spiritual matters. I thought it best if you discovered that book on your own. So it actually chose you."

Katherine smiled. "And it set me on an adventure within myself that's far from over. That book understood my dissatisfaction with the idea that Life must be something less than what we are capable of 'imagining' it to be. I feel I've lived a false life but there have been moments, instants, gleams, when I've felt something much more real. I hoped that by coming here, you might introduce me to those people, like yourself, who understand more about developing conscious awareness."

"There is someone I know who may have the wisdom you're looking for. Have you ever heard of G. I. Gurdjieff?"

She shook her head no.

"His lectures earlier this year were so popular that the Home Office became overly concerned. Gurdjieff escaped from Bolshevik persecution in Russia. Our government worried that there might be unpleasant repercussions and they denied his visa. He just left for France a few weeks ago. The French are more receptive to his ideas that without self-knowledge, man cannot be free, he cannot govern himself and he will always remain a slave.

"I'm sorry you won't be able to meet him."

"Where is he in France?"

"He's found a new location for his Institute in Fontainebleau south of Paris. In fact, I happen to know he just signed a lease on a château there today. But there is someone else you could meet. His disciple P.D. Ouspensky will be here in a few weeks lecturing on Gurdjieff's teachings. You can come to his lecture with me."

"Of course, I'll come. I must come. I confess this to you Orage, and you alone: I'm not writing. I pretend that I am and tell everyone to leave me alone so I can write. I even put a sign up on my door that says "Working," but behind that door I sit at my writing table and stare at a blank page. Worse, I've reread many of the stories I've written previously and I don't like any of them. There's something lacking. I'm onto something new but I just don't have a handle on it. Maybe Gurdjieff could help me find what I'm looking for."

Orage covered her hand with his. "My dear, dear Katherine." She felt him tenderly wipe away the tears on her face. "Everything's going to be all right. I'm confident that if anyone can help you find your way it's Gurdjieff."

"Has he helped you?"

"Immeasurably. It sounds terribly banal and Jack would laugh, but Gurdjieff has changed my life. I have been asking myself for a long time: Who am I? Why am I here? What is the purpose of my life, and of human life in particular? And now I've found someone who through many years of searching and practice has found answers and wants to help others find their way."

He hesitated and then said, "Here's a secret for you to keep. I'm resigning from *New Age* to join Gurdjieff's new Institute in Fontainebleau."

"Orage, I don't believe it. You're leaving your magazine?"

"From what I've learned already, I must make changes. Gurdjieff has shown me that through self-observation one realizes the necessity of self-change, it's a means of awakening. If I undertake this task of self-observation, I must put it first in my life. I can't afford to squander my life on trifles."

THE SMALL DINGY MEDICAL OFFICE of the radiologist Dr. Webster, Dr. Manoukhine's protégé in London, was quite different from the sophisticated sterile clinic in Paris. His examination was too brief and he was clumsy with the stethoscope, timidly exploring her chest as if he was afraid of setting off a land mine. Worst of all, after trying several times to listen to her heart with the stethoscope, he impatiently unhooked it from his mousy ears and pressed his ear against her breast.

He then told her she wasn't strong enough to tolerate the radiation. They argued. She told him Dr. Sorapure had found her heart young and strong, just overworked.

"It might be a young heart," he said, "but for now it's old. Rest up for another week and we'll have another listen, shall we?"

Dr. Webster's fee was half Manoukhine's but she felt cheated. He didn't even have a nurse and she would be the first patient that he would treat with Manoukhine's X-ray machine.

THE DAYS TURNED GLOOMY. Even the flat she'd moved into at Brett's with its orange-flowered curtains and her familiar Buddha on the mantelpiece felt like a waiting room. After three weekly examinations under Dr. Webster's stethoscope, he still held off the treatments. Her mind disturbed, she visited her family and close friends for diversion and comfort, including Kot, who was fourth on her list.

LM visited daily to see if she needed anything. Jack had moved to Sussex to stay with friends for the autumn season. She went with him to help him settle in on the first weekend in September and promised to return on weekends but found excuses not to. They had a depressing effect on each other. He blamed it on her new "occult passion."

Orage took her to Ouspensky's lecture as promised. The room was packed and airless. But not a person left. Gurdjieff's Russian disciple mesmerized everyone. He spoke of the loss of the essence that we are born with that creates a lack of harmony. We only develop the other half of our being, the personality, which is a machine that our will has no control over.

He amused his audience by suggesting that on their way home they should try to walk differently than they were accustomed to, even walk backwards to see if by changing their mechanical, automatic behavior they could wake up their conscious mind. "If you practice Gurdjieff's methods," he said, "you can become the master of your life and you might become the master of your death."

Katherine and Orage were sitting in the first row and she felt Ouspensky was speaking directly to her. He spoke of the new Institute for the Harmonious Development of Man at Fontainebleau whose first residents would be Gurdjieff's Eastern European disciples. A few Occidentals would also be invited.

After the meeting Orage introduced her to Ouspensky. She wanted to know if she could visit Gurdjieff at his new Institute. Ouspensky said he might be able to arrange that but first she would have to explain her reasons for wanting to do so. Unfortunately he couldn't see her for another two weeks. His schedule was booked until then.

Several days later Orage invited her to lunch at the home of science fiction writer J.D. Beresford along with John Sullivan, Jack's previous assistant editor at *The Athenaeum.*

Orage spoke of the new Institute in Fontainebleau where one could develop harmony through self-observation. Gurdjieff maintained that, owing to the abnormal conditions of modern life, we no longer function in a harmonious way. In order to become harmonious, we must develop new faculties—or actualize latent potentialities—through 'work on oneself.' The teachings were presented in three forms: writings, music, and movements, which correspond to our intellect, emotions, and physical body.

Katherine sat next to him in Beresford's living room. She felt a sense of frustration in the room, even an undertone of deep regret. She timidly admitted, "I feel that I'm missing something within myself. That I've given up. This is not what I want. If this is all, then Life is not worth living. But I know it's not all." She went on to repeat what she had said to Orage about having instants, gleams, when she felt the possibility of a truer reality.

Outside in the back garden, under the sun's glow, trees waved their glistening leaves. She felt aglow herself. She took comfort in finding other people who were also seeking change, even old acquaintances of hers and Jack's—who didn't laugh at her ideas.

She came home to find Jack's brother Richard there and continued the discussion with him about the possibilities of Life. Sullivan came over for supper. She told Richard and Sullivan that if she could find harmony within her divided self, it might cure her illness, too.

After Richard and Sullivan had gone home she thought of the time W.J. Dunning came to dinner at the Elephant and they'd discussed Eastern religion and thc practice of yoga. Afterward, she and Jack sat up late talking excitedly about approaches to understanding one's consciousness other than the Western intellectual approach. That night she'd felt a change within Jack, a flicker of inner light. What had happened to that flicker? Why wouldn't he look deeper within himself? Why didn't he see the value of self-observation?

She picked up her pen and wrote to him.

I wish you found life as wonderful as it seems to me. Even the least idea—the fringe of the idea—of 'waking up' discovers a new world. And the mystery is that 'all' of us in our unlikeness and individual ways do seem to me to be moving toward the very same goal.

Katherine smiled. Jack would probably think she sounded like the evangelistic Mrs. Jellaby, a Dickens's character who was so zealous in her missionary work that she let her children starve.

ON WEDNESDAY, SEPTEMBER 27, she suffered through her second radiation treatment on Webster's table. When she complained to him of recurring symptoms, he brushed these symptoms off as minor complaints that had no bearing on her treatments. He scheduled another treatment for the following week. She left knowing she would never come back.

That night she wrote Jack in Sussex and told him she'd changed her mind about staying in London. *Dr. Webster doesn't know what he's doing. I will not let him practice on me.* She would be leaving for Paris the next Monday to continue with Dr. Manoukhine. She did not ask him to join her. He did not offer.

She told him she felt their relationship had shifted to brother and sister rather than man and wife. No matter. Everything would change after she was cured.

Jack didn't come to say good-bye.

28

October 1922

34th Birthday

"Do you know what individuality is?" Ouspensky asked.
"I thought I did," Katherine replied. "I'm no longer sure."
"Consciousness of will. Conscious that you have a will and can act. Does this interest you?" he asked.
"Yes, very much so."

KM speaks with Ouspensky

WHEN SHE ENTERED HER FLAT, LM was waiting for her. "Katie you're quite flushed. Where have you been?"

"I've met with Ouspensky." She said quickly, stopping to catch her breath. "I must sit down." She collapsed onto the divan and after taking a sip of the offered glass of water, said, "There's a chance I might meet Gurdjieff at Fontainebleau in a fortnight."

"Gurdjieff? Ouspensky? Who are they? How do you know them?"

"Two weeks ago I attended Ouspensky's lecture on the teachings of Gurdjieff."

"But how can you go to Fontainebleau when you've started radiation treatments here with Dr. Webster?"

"He's inexperienced and not to be trusted. He's a radiologist not a diagnostician like Sorapure, and he doesn't show any concern over the symptoms I'm having. I could burn up on his X-ray table and he wouldn't even notice."

"My dearest, how terrible. Shall I go with you the next time?"

"There isn't going to be a next time. I want to leave for Paris on Monday."

"Monday! That's two days from now!"

"Yes. Manoukhine can give me the third séance on Wednesday so I won't miss any.

"Jones, why are you staring at me like I'm—like I'm crazy. I thought you believed in Manoukhine, too? Don't you want to go to Paris?"

"Yes. Of course I do. It just all seems so sudden. You've moved in your furniture . . . it took weeks to get it the way you wanted and now it all looks so comfy. Even your Buddha has settled in on the mantelpiece. Does Brett know?"

"Not yet. I'm going to ask her to sublet the flat with my furnishings. That way I can hold on to it. I am coming back . . . but please no more questions. Just do as I ask."

"I'll go to the station first thing tomorrow. How many tickets am I buying?"

"Two. Jack's staying in Sussex. There's no reason for him to come to Paris."

"Is he the only one who knows you're going? You haven't told your father?"

"No. How could I? I only decided a few days ago . . . Ida! Stop staring at me like I'm crazy. Come sit down. Let's have our tea. It will be calming for both of us."

Katherine let LM pour and then said, "There is something I want to tell you, but you must first promise me to keep it a secret."

"Of course. You know you can trust me. What is it?"

"I have every intention of continuing Dr. Manoukhine's séances, but if I become terribly sick again as I did before, I'll stop."

"But Katie—"

"I'm fed up with being bedridden and unable to write, while these doctors experiment on me and hold out the false promise that I'll be cured. My God, I'm not an experimental cow. Manoukhine is the last doctor I will give myself over to. If he fails I have an alternative course."

"Where are we going now? The Ivory Coast to see a medicine man?"

"Not exactly but some might think that's what I'm doing. That's why I'm keeping my alternative plan a secret."

"But Dr. Manoukhine has told you the next séances won't be as difficult."

"Yes, that's what he says. As I said, I will try, but I need, shall we say—an escape route. Know that I have thought long about this. This is not one of my impulsive decisions. I have not been hypnotized, even though Jack might think so."

"Well . . . can I know where are you escaping to?"

"The Institute for the Harmonious Development of Man."

"The institute of . . . what?"

"I have learned that it's possible for an individual to transform illness with the consciousness of one's will, to be one's own master in spite of the circumstances. Gurdjieff might be able to teach me the way."

LM put down her teacup, leaned toward Katherine and said, "I don't understand what this is all about or who these people are, but don't worry, I will stand by you regardless."

"Thank you, Jones. I hoped you would say that. Remember this is our secret. I'm only telling you so that you will be prepared for the possibility. I owe you that."

It wasn't until she was sitting in the train's passenger cabin, pencil lines drawn through her London to-do list, that she could relax. She had put off seeing Ottoline, Virginia and other friends, having nothing to say to them and there were some she had seen like that horrible Wyndham Lewis who had attacked Gurdjieff's teachings so unfairly that she wished she hadn't.

Calais was sizzling under a cloudless sky. Old women offered luscious pears from their baskets. LM kept her from being crushed by other travelers as they boarded the connecting train to Paris.

Settled inside, she opened her purse and took out an address Ouspensky had given her. Seeing that she was in such poor health, he insisted that she be examined before meeting with Gurdjieff. Dr. Young, both a surgeon and a psychotherapist, had a practice in Paris and was also G's disciple. Would he be probing my mind, my emotions or my body, or all three? she asked herself. She looked out at the passing French countryside that filled her window frame like an Impressionist painting. Will I pass inspection? She closed her eyes for the rest of the journey.

As they pulled into the station, she lifted the window shades to look out on Paris at dusk. It was warm and shadowy. The gas lamps gave off a kind of glowworm red—not like the harsh yellow lights of London. She felt a glow within and smiled. "We're home."

LM had brought a list of recommended hotels. They started at the Victoria Palace where Katherine had last stayed with Jack. Seated in its elegant red velvet lobby she thought how estranged they had become when only a few months ago they were inseparable.

She was not disappointed when LM told her there were no rooms available. She found its opulence distasteful. It reminded her of her silver-spoon childhood in Wellington that she had run away from as a young girl. She had never been comfortable with the chic and fashionable, and now she had no taste for it.

After several other places turned them away and night fell, they checked into a dim room in a small seedy hotel. Katherine's sleep was disturbed by the ghost-like sounds of water sobbing, gurgling and sighing its way through the rusty pipes.

LM slept soundly as usual and Katherine had to wake her up. They dressed quickly and left. When they went into a nearby café for coffee, Katherine got the feeling they'd been there before. She looked out the window at a small modest hotel across the street. "Why there's our old hotel," she said, reading the familiar marquis out loud: "Select Hotel. I was always amused by that name, as it wasn't a hotel one would naturally select, but at the time we were without options, like now. Do you remember?"

"Certainly I remember. But why would you want to stay there? It will only bring back bad memories. The Germans were bombing Paris when we were here then. That wasn't a pleasant time for either of us."

"No. But I remember its simplicity and the wonderful view from the attic of the roof—tops of the Sorbonne decorated with those distinguished gentlemen carved in marble bath gowns. And those rickety stairs we had to climb. And the short walk to the Luxembourg Gardens. It was also inexpensive and my account is depleted."

"How will you manage those stairs? And since when did you want simplicity? You loved your stay at the Palace."

"I'm no longer that person. She's dying, don't feed her."

Katherine smiled at LM's shocked face. "I'm only speaking figuratively, Jones."

In a few hours they were settled in the same attic rooms on the sixth floor that looked out on precisely what she'd remembered. She called Dr. Manoukhine to make an appointment for the following day, Wednesday, and was delighted when Dr. Manoukhine, Dr. Donat and Sonja, all got on the phone to welcome her back in English, Russian and French. After she hung up, quite touched by their enthusiasm, she put away Dr. Young's phone number. She'd wait a little longer.

Both doctors and Sonja were waiting at the door and she was greeted with many hugs and kisses. She felt she'd returned home to her dearest friends. The dark X-ray room, the clock, the cold metal table were just as she had left them in May. The only noticeable change was Dr. Donat's trimmed beard that tickled her when he listened to her heart.

She gave them Dr. Sorapure's analysis of her heart problem. Dr. Donat translated for Dr. Manoukhine, and after discussion, assured her that when she completed this series of séances, the remaining bacteria would be killed off and her left lung would inflate again and take the pressure off her struggling heart.

The first séance was easy. They lowered the power of the rays and shortened the duration to one hour instead of two. She felt no immediate discomfort. They advised her to rest for the next few days as she would probably have a mild reaction.

They gave her a stack of recently printed pamphlets: *Le traitment de la tuberculose par la leucocytolyse consecutive a la l'radiation de la rate.* Dr. Donat claimed an extremely high success rate for Manoukhine's patented X-ray machine and said it brought about "de veritables resurrections" even with the worst cases. She was asked to distribute the pamphlets in England.

Oui, je suis une resurrection, she thought, reading over the pamphlet back in her room. She enclosed the brochures in a letter to Jack and asked him to pass them on to Dr. Sorapure and anyone else he thought might help promote Dr. Manoukhine's miraculous cure.

SHE EXPECTED TO WRITE STORIES and a table was ordered for her room. On it, she wrote to Jack of her intention to send him a new story but the only work she accomplished was correcting an English translation of some of Dostoevsky's *Letters* for Kot.

A week later, after her second séance, she'd been unable to hold down any food except the soup LM brought her. Too weak to get out of bed, she postponed the third séance telling Jack that she could hardly raise her hand.

After finishing her letter, she sent LM out to post it and took out the folded sheet of paper she'd been keeping in her writing case. She called Dr. Young.

He graciously offered to examine her at the hotel. They set a date for the following week. The appointed day arrived but just before Dr. Young came she received a letter from Jack. A pressed rose fell out and she realized it was her thirty-fourth birthday.

Dr. Young sat with her for a couple of hours discussing how Gurdjieff's teachings were practiced at the Institute. All residents had to spend time working as laborers in the kitchen, in the garden, or in construction of a new building. She told him she was inexperienced in the kitchen but an avid gardener. He listened to her heart and lungs and discussed her heart palpitations and fatigue. He said the diet at the Institute included milk and cheese produced by their own farm animals and she would hopefully regain some weight as she was much too thin. He would speak to Gurdjieff about an invitation to visit the Institute and would call her as soon as he received a medical report from Dr. Manoukhine.

She asked him to tell Orage that she hoped to see him before he left for the Institute. Orage called that night and invited her to dinner. She said it would have to be somewhere locally as she was quite weak.

On their walk to the restaurant they were drenched by a bursting rain cloud. She laughed and said how appropriate since she was walking with *Orage*, French for storm. They hurried into the restaurant to get out of their wet coats. "That was so unexpected and vivid," said Katherine at the table. "Walking in the rain is quite wonderful. It's a sensation that stays with you long after the sun has come out again."

The waiter, dressed in a red vest, white apron and a little grey cloth cap, returned with their orders—big bowls of piping hot beef stew, bread, and a carafe of red wine. She waited until they were having their after-dinner coffee before speaking intimately.

"Jack has a vast choice of sticks in the hall stand when he wants to go walking and even an even vaster choice of umbrellas. I feel I'm unprotected and exposed and I only have a fearful sense of the heavens lowering. He and I are so different. He won't discuss Gurdjieff's teachings.

"I wrote him that Dr. Manoukhine and all the other doctors have failed because they've only treated the physical part of me."

"And what did he say to that?"

"He said the other half is up to me. He said no doctor could help me with my spiritual side. That's true. But then how do I reach the other part of me—the secret self that waits in the dark to be healed? Often now when I sit quietly and go within, I walk down a cellar staircase and find a sick little girl in rags shivering in a dark corner. I want to bring this child up into the sunlight but she shakes her head no and turns away from me. She is my secret self. If I go to the Institute and practice Gurdjieff's teachings, do you think she will come up from the cellar and join me in the sunlight where she can be healed?"

"I believe Gurdjieff can be of great help to you as he has been to me. I've been dissatisfied with my work at the *New Age* for some time but didn't know there was any other way to live that would be more satisfying, more joyous. He gave me the inspiration and courage to transform my life."

"Jack says that giving up Manoukhine for Gurdjieff's 'spiritual quackery' would be criminal. 'Wrong, utterly wrong,' he said."

"Will he try and stop you?"

"No." She smiled. "He was never one to take action with what he feels passionate about. He'll anguish over my decision but he won't try to stop me."

Orage walked her back to the hotel. They lingered in the lobby. She didn't want him to leave but he had a meeting the following morning with Gurdjieff at the Institute. After reassuring her that he was certain she would be joining him there soon he helped her up the stairs to her room and left.

SHE ANXIOUSLY AWAITED Dr. Young's call. She distracted herself with walks along the pebbled path in the park edged with blooming fall flowers but, short of breath, she often simply sat on a bench near the park entrance. LM watched over her from the café across the street.

When she postponed the third séance again, a concerned Dr. Donat rushed to her hotel room. When she suggested that perhaps the séances were causing the symptoms, he told her she must be patient. The unpleasant side effects would stop when the radiation stopped but for now she must continue. She would be absolutely cured by the Noel. He frightened her with notions of what might happen if she suddenly quit and repeated several times that only Dr. Manoukhine could save her.

The following day, with LM's help, she hobbled over to the park and, once seated on what had become her favorite bench, asked her friend to leave.

She couldn't rest. Why hadn't Dr. Young called? She worried that Dr. Manoukhine might not have written the necessary report because he wanted to keep her under his care.

She faintly breathed in the color and vibrancy around her, the children playing on the grass, the sunlit leaves somersaulting one by one from trees shaken by a soft breeze. But she couldn't shut out the chilling darkness that flooded over her. She had no strength left to resist. She gripped the cold wooden bench that became a raft dragging her down into the dark sea.

"Miss . . . Miss . . . Are you all right?"

Her face wet with tears, she looked up into the eyes of a kind old man who was walking by and saw her crying.

"Yes . . . I mean, no." Embarrassed, Katherine tried to laugh and wiped her face with her handkerchief. "I was saddened by some bad news, but I'll recover. One must, you know. Thank you for asking."

She reached for her cane.

"Are you sure I can't help you?" he said, putting out his hand.

"No. I must do this on my own. Thank you. Good-bye."

The phone was ringing when she walked into her room.

"I have good news," said Dr. Young at the other end of the line. "Gurdjieff is inviting you to visit the Institute. Dr. Manoukhine's report said you were too ill to travel and it was in your best interest to stay in Paris under his care, but Gurdjieff wants to meet you regardless. He'll judge for himself."

"Miss Mansfield? Are you there?"

"Yes. Sorry. I needed to sit down. I just walked in and I'm a bit out of breath. This is wonderful news. I'll arrange to come right away."

Her heart pounding from climbing the stairs, she lay down on the bed to rest. Sunlight entered through the window and spread over her, the chill that had clamped onto her in the park melted. A tingling joy passed through her. If I was not so tired, she thought, I would leap off this bed. She fell asleep with a smile on her lips.

That night, LM looked miserable when told. Like Jack, she still believed in Dr. Manoukhine's cure. "We're only going to the Institute for a few days." That was the truth. There was no guarantee that Gurdjieff would let her stay or that she would want to but she had to go there to find out.

"Don't fall apart on me, Jones. Fontainebleau is only a short train ride and I'm told it has a beautiful park. Remember our walks at Queens College and how you used to catch the fall leaves and bring them to me? Maybe we can do that at Fontainebleau. It's the same time of year."

That brought a smile to LM's pale yellow face, which glowed under the gaslight.

The following morning, before leaving, she wrote to Jack:

I'll see Gurdjieff and come back tomorrow.

It sounded like a telegram and certainly didn't express her true feelings, so she added:

It's not sunny today. What a terrible difference its absence makes. It ought not to. One ought to have a little core of inner warmth that keeps burning and is only embellished by the sun. One has, I believe, if one looks for it.

On the train to Fontainebleau she looked across at LM's frightened eyes staring right through her as if into the face of death.

She thinks we're being transported to a slaughterhouse, thought Katherine. She dreads each unfurling of the train's wheel but is helpless to stop it. She's assumed the worst—my death. Poor Jones, if only I had let you go long ago and not asked you back over and over again. How unfair I've been. How false our relationship is. This time I must let you go and never entreat you to return. I've used you all these years because I feared being on my own without your care. And now you're thirty-four years old and have no one to call your own, not even yourself.

29

November 1922

Gurdjieff's Institute

The wise grieve neither for the living nor the dead
Never at any time was I not, nor thou,
Nor these princes of men, nor shall we ever cease to be.
The unreal has no being,
The real never ceases to be.

Bhagavad-Gita

KATHERINE LEANED HER HEAD outside the taxi window and breathed in the long avenue of trees flimsily dressed in last season's still-clinging leaves. The bulk of their shorn garments scattered across the lawn, pooling in soft piles of gold, red and orange. As she drew nearer to the long, low white château, she looked up at the windows gleaming in the late autumn sun and wondered which floor her room was on, which view would be hers? The end of the clear, bright day seemed to stand still, silently welcoming her arrival at Gurdjieff's Institute for the Harmonious Development of Man.

Dr. Young appeared at the front door and guided her into the marble entry hall and up a spiral staircase. He helped LM with the baggage as they walked down the wide hall into a large bedroom. "How wonderful!" said Katherine.

It had been difficult climbing the stairs, but the room was the one she had wished for when she looked up from the taxi. It was way beyond what she had imagined sitting in her Parisian garret—

paneled walls, antique furniture, French engravings, ornate Empire mirrors and wide view over the Versailles-style garden with it's formal beds of red geraniums, dark blue lobelias, lemon drop calceolarias and pink mesembryanthemum. Katherine's first sighting of Mr. Gurdjieff was at an informal lunch that afternoon. He was occupied with his other guests and their introduction was brief. Later that evening, after a second abundant meal, the commune students and guests congregated in front of the salon's roaring fire. G. sat down next to Katherine and they talked with the aid of a Russian interpreter. When he stood up shortly afterward and said it was time for everyone to retire, she noticed that LM must have slipped out.

"JONES, WAKE UP. WAKE UP!" Katherine called out, bending over the mattress on the wooden floor, shaking her. "I have wonderful news. Please wake up."

Groggily, LM sat up, rubbed her eyes and squinted into the illuminated candle Katherine was holding.

"What's wrong? What's happened?"

"I'm fine. Please come sit by the fire and listen to my news." LM sat on the floor in front of Katherine and looked up at her pensively. "Gurdjieff has agreed to keep me under observation for a fortnight to see if I fit in here."

"Do you fit in here? I certainly don't. Who are these strange people? I can't understand a word they're saying and how funny they dress. There must have been thirty of them in the dining hall, all talking and eating. Everyone shouting across the table. I've never seen so much drinking and it went on for hours. You don't want to fit in here, do you?"

"Oh yes I do. I'll have to work like everyone else but he'll make my chores easier until I'm feeling better. Chores I love to do: work in the garden with my hands, or on rainy days help in the kitchen making meals. There's no staff here. Everyone works—even Gurdjieff. And Orage has been digging a trench for water pipes.

"Isn't this wonderful news, Jones?"

"I suppose so, if it makes you happy."

"Then why do you look so tragic?"

LM forced a smile.

"Tomorrow I need you to go to Paris and pack my clothes. Only a few things. I'll give you a list in the morning."

Upon LM's return from Paris, Katherine thanked her for bringing what she had asked for and suggested they go sit by the garden fountain.

Katherine felt the cold cement penetrate her skirt and touch her skin when she sat down. She shivered but before LM could get up she said, "No, I don't want you to fetch my shawl." She saw the sadness in LM's eyes and knew she mustn't avoid what must be said any longer.

"Jones, I think you feel this too but are unwilling to say it—we must separate. You must have your own Life. A Life that I have kept you from by asking you to be my legs. Your devotion has robbed you of your own Life and, to my shame, I've allowed it."

"There is nothing I would rather do than be in your service."

"Yes. You've told me that so many times that even I believed it. But you only think this because I'm all you have and I'm correcting that situation right now. Perhaps you would like to travel? You've often talked about visiting Russia. Jones, what do you want to do?"

"Take care of you."

"That won't work. The Katherine that depended on you has gone away. This Katherine who sits here with you now wants to give you back your Life. Do you understand?"

"My reasoning mind accepts the truth of what you're saying and can even make a list of all the places I want to travel to now that you say I'm free to do so. But my heart cannot imagine Life without you and it's breaking. Who will take care of you if not me?"

"Dr. Young has arranged for one of the students to look after me but only when I need help. You see, part of the practice here is learning to take care of oneself, to be independent. I'll never do that as long as I depend on you."

LM put her hand down in the pool and treaded the icy water with the fallen leaves. She pulled out some drowning flowers one by one and dropped a wet crimson rose in Katherine's lap.

"In time you will find life far more interesting without me," said Katherine softly, trying not to hurt her anymore than she already had. "I'm not saying I'll never see you again. Just not as my nurse. I want you to leave knowing that when we meet again it will be as equals."

LM turned her teary eyes toward Katherine. "I'll leave because you're asking me to, but only to return to Paris where I'll wait until I hear from you. That way, if you change your mind, I won't have to travel a long distance."

"That won't happen when we separate this time but know you will always be nearby in spirit. I want you to think of us as continuing to travel together on the River of Life but we're no longer sharing the same boat. Each of us in our own boat, sailing together but independently."

She looked down at LM's reddened hand still treading the fountain pool. There is nothing more I can say, she thought, and stood up.

"I'm going to leave you now, Jones. You needn't say good-bye. I'll just walk away and you wait here until I'm out of sight. Write to me from time to time, won't you?"

She took her cane and slowly made her way into the château feeling LM's eyes remaining on her even after she was out of sight. She thought she heard a sob but perhaps it was only the wind shaking loose the last of the clinging leaves.

SHE SPENT HER PROBATIONARY FORTNIGHT doing what G. had told her were her chores: walking in the garden, picking flowers for the entry hall vases, eating and resting.

Orage eagerly showed her around, relieved to take a break from digging the trench for pipes that would supply water to the new Turkish bath that was being built. When he showed her where the pipes were being laid, she was surprised to see G. down in the trench digging along with his disciples.

Orage told her that if she stayed on she would also be given more to do and would work with her hands doing carpentry and farm work. He said he looked forward to getting out of the trenches yet it surprised him that he still woke up each morning looking forward to his day of labor—a feeling that he had stopped having in London when he had to get up and go to his office at *New Age*.

She jokingly complained that the hardest chore G. had given her was eating. She'd never seen so much food served at every meal. It was delicious but the courses were never-ending. She might not be cured at the château but, as Dr. Young had warned, she would certainly gain weight on a diet filled with plenty of milk, butter and cream.

After Orage left her to go back to work, she found a sunny bench to rest on. This is all a wonderful dream, she thought. Gulliver must have felt like this when he was shipwrecked and came ashore to find a world that was stranger than anything he had ever known: the food, language, customs, people, music, time. How impoverished my life was before I came here. G. has already brought me back in touch with Life and I've only been here a week.

The perfect weather continued. She'd wake up early each morning, restless to continue her exploration of the château grounds and to meet more of the Russians and other foreigners who were there following G.'s teachings.

One afternoon, seated on what had become her new favorite bench under a massive quince tree like the ones back home in New Zealand, she looked up to admire the deep blue between the branches. In the distance she could also see the Institute's members in the trench. The clarity in the late autumn light made their figures as sharp as cutout silhouettes. As the sun's warmth moved away she shivered but she didn't want to go inside until the vivid autumn colors faded with the falling sun.

She pulled her shawl tighter around her shoulders. Except for her fur coat, she had little in her wardrobe to keep her warm.

At lunch G. had given her the news she had anxiously awaited. She could remain at the château as long as she wanted. Now a member of the commune, and no longer a guest, she would have to take on working in the kitchen and tending the farm animals. She was eager to do so but needed additional clothing.

She wrote a list in her head: a wool jacket for sitting in the salon after dinner to watch the dancers and listen to the music; one or two bed jackets for sitting by the fire in her room with new friends; wool skirt for walks in the garden; galoshes for walking amidst the farm animals. Just then a quince fruit fell on her head, a warning to go inside before she caught a chill.

Back in her room she wrote to LM. She was going to stay at Fontainebleau indefinitely. In case of an accident, she was sending her Will to her father's bank for safekeeping. She asked LM to shop for her list of clothes while she was still in Paris. Then, remembering she had promised to teach several of Gurdjieff's students added:

Would you please send me a book of instruction for beginning celloists.

She knew she was breaking a promise to herself not to ask anything more of her former companion but she was cold and who was better suited to buy her clothes and send them to her than LM? She swore not to ask anything of her again.

LM wrote that she was going to London for a few weeks to visit her sister. She would also see Jack. Katherine suggested that maybe Jack would buy a small farm and LM could be his housekeeper and help him in the garden and tend to the farm animals, like she would soon be doing. LM kept asking questions in her letters about Gurdjieff's teachings so Katherine recommended that she attend Ouspensky's lectures when she was in London and learn for herself about the practice.

In a letter to Jack she suggested he do the same, or perhaps invite Ouspensky to dinner and discuss Gurdjieff's philosophy.

Jack wrote back and asked if she was keeping up her writing and remaining true to her gifts.

She responded:

At the end of my source for now. When I write again—and write I will—I'll write far more steadily, but not until my Life flows, as it has been clogged—distant from the source.

She encouraged Jack to get outside and work with his hands in the ground; to learn something not taught in books. She thought he was only escaping life with his constant reading and chess playing.

Her new supply of clothes arrived just as the evening temperature dropped below fifty degrees. It was also the same day that she was advised that she was to move to another wing of the château: the servants' wing. It wasn't meant as a punishment. G. often moved the residents to different rooms without any explanation. She opened a door on her small sparse room that lacked a view of the park and wondered what she could possibly learn there.

After living several weeks at the château, when all her underclothes disappeared at the laundry, she became depressed for the first time. She didn't have the strength to take a taxi on her own to Fontainebleau to shop. She hesitated but again wrote LM for help, enclosing a detailed list. She would reimburse her for the cost. Soon another packet arrived.

Her new room was not the only change for her at the château. G. had built a small loft overhanging the cow stalls in the stable specifically for her. He wanted her to spend time there breathing in the cows' breath. It was an old peasant cure for tuberculosis and he thought it might help. As Orage brought her out to the stable they passed by many of the animals that she was becoming familiar with: sheep, pigs, rabbits, hares, horses and mules, and as she walked through the pastoral scene, she thought, what a wonderful adventure this is.

In the stable, three cows welcomed her into their home with their soft bovine eyes. She looked up at the loft, amazed that anyone would have built this just for her. The resident painter had painted the ceiling in gay patterns of trees and flowers, animals and birds. He caricatured some of the people of the Institute in the faces of the animals and birds, himself included. The floor and walls of the loft were covered with oriental rugs and cushions. She climbed the narrow staircase and sank into the purple velvet pillows piled on the divan.

That first day she was surprised by the sweet fragrance of the cows' breath and fell asleep on the pillows. She woke up to the sound of teats being massaged and pumped and milk hitting the sides of a tin bucket. She came down the short ladder to find a petite young girl with long thick black pigtails milking the cows.

"Hello, Mrs. Murry," she said and smiled. "I'm Adele Kafian. Mr. Gurdjieff told me to tell you that these are your cows—Mrs. Murry's cows he said. And when you're stronger you will be in charge of them."

Katherine asked her if she could try milking but she had to give up after a few tries.

"Gurdjieff told me to keep an eye out for you in the stable," said Adele. "If there's anything you need just let me know." She then scooped up a glass of goat's milk from another tin bucket and said that he wanted Katherine to drink four glasses a day.

She was surprised by how good the milk tasted. She thanked Adele and asked how she came to live at the Institute.

Adele told her that three years ago, she and some of Gurdjieff's other devotees left their homes in the Caucasus Mountains of Russia to establish schools in the West where his teachings could be spread and practiced. She had also studied painting and helped paint the monkeys hanging from trees on Katherine's ceiling.

Looking up, Katherine thought she might actually prefer sleeping in the stable above the warm bodies and heated breaths of the cows and under the vividly painted roof. She looked forward to spending every afternoon there reading and writing in her notebook or just resting.

When she returned to her small room in the château she sat on her bed and wrote Jack. There was no room for a table, so she put her writing case on her lap. He had complained in his last letter that she didn't write often enough and when she did she told him nothing about what she was doing at the Institute.

Our happiness does not depend on letters, she wrote. *I don't know how to explain yet what it is like for me here. I don't want to falsify my position as I am only on the fringe of what is going on here and can't yet write about it. What I can tell you is that I am very happy and that every moment of the day seems full of Life. I have escaped my illness, which is what I had hoped for by coming here, but I am in a state of transition and it is difficult to talk about it. What I can say is that I can never go back to the old life and can't yet deal with the new one.*

As far as "us" I feel we have no present relationship but I know down deep that there is a possibility of one.

His response came five days later. He told her she had hurt him to the core. What did she mean they had no relationship? He worried that she was being too influenced by Gurdjieff. and it was causing radical changes to her personality.

She quickly wrote an apology.

I have come here for a cure. I could never have regained my health from any other treatment. At last I am understood by someone who wants to treat the whole of me—mentally and physically. My old friends and my doctors only saw a frail half-creature—saw only my illness and not the condition of my withered soul that is now being healed.

Someday when I am fully well you and I will live so happily, so splendidly, just not now. But know we are together. I love you. You are my man. I want to build and live in that reality. I believe it's possible. Your loving, Wig.

30

December 1922

There do exist enquiring minds, which long for the truth of the heart, seek it, strive to solve the problems set by life, try to penetrate to the essence of things and phenomena and to penetrate into themselves. If a man reasons and thinks soundly, no matter which path he follows in solving these problems, he must inevitably arrive back at himself, and begin with the solution of the problem of what he is himself and what his place is in the world around him.

G.I. Gurdjieff

THROUGH NOVEMBER AND INTO DECEMBER, she woke to a brilliant sun that gave her the strength needed to dress and go downstairs for breakfast. She cut the early winter carnations in the gardens and arranged their multi-colored bouquets in the château's crystal vases, and then helped in the kitchen, peeling and chopping vegetables for the midday meal. After lunch she rested in the stable loft, and, if not too tired, wrote letters to friends and family, and scribbled sketches in her notebook for the stories she would write later.

Too weak to participate as a laborer, she was instructed by Gurdjieff as part of her practice to observe every detail of the work being done on the commune. She visited G.'s students planting bulbs and seeds before the first frost, watched them building the Study House brick by brick and remained conscious of the work being done with their hands as if they were her own. At the same time she was memorizing a list of

Russian words, as well as the math calculations taught by G.—it was all a practice of mindfulness.

His students became accustomed to her visits and set up a chaise longue for her after she tired of standing. And if at the end of the day she'd fallen asleep, one of them would gently wake her and slowly walk with her back to the château making sure she was comfortable in her room before leaving her. She'd always tell them she didn't need their help but they treated her like fine china about to break.

On one particularly chilly afternoon, she was in the loft writing a letter. She wished there was a fire to warm her chilled fingers but the letter was long overdue and she felt she had to finish:

Dearest Pa:

After two applications with Dr. M. my heart couldn't take it. I was extremely ill and disappointed. I am now living in Fontainebleau outside Paris under the care of Mr. G.I. Gurdjieff. He has given me gentle exercises and movements. For now I will concentrate on strengthening my heart and then revisit the wings/lungs. I am confident that the lean years in the past will be followed by fat ones.

I wish you could see me now in the stable lying comfortably above the cow stalls breathing in cow's breath. It is part of my treatment – good for the damaged lungs. The château is most beautiful under winter light. The rooms most lovely with central heating and hot and cold running water. It is mostly run by Russians (they seem to haunt me). Though I speak French and German fluently, I am fascinated by languages and I hope to learn Russian and then later Italian when I go south after I finish here with my cure.

I am determined to regain my health though disappointed that it might take longer than I hoped but know I am feeling better already. I will not give up. I will not accept life as an invalid.

I have let LM go as I can now take care of myself. She might work for Jack on a farm he is thinking about buying.

Your devoted daughter,
Katherine

Yes it was true, there was central heating but what she didn't tell him was that Gurdjieff believed it should only be used in freezing conditions. Every decision he made had to do with the practice—the work of healing through constant awareness of the physical, emotional and intellectual self.

She accepted the austerity but the damp chill in her bedroom in the servants' quarters without a fire to warm her was endangering what good health she had regained. She lived in her fur coat and, even though there were ten to twenty pots cooking on the stoves at one time, she still shivered peeling carrots.

After finishing the letter she bundled under the rugs in the loft and considered asking G. if she could move to a warmer room, maybe one with a fireplace. She was anxious that if her cough became noticeable or she became flushed with fever, he would send her away.

As if she'd summoned him, he suddenly appeared right in front of her holding the day's third glass of goat's milk. Though a large robust man, she hadn't heard him climb up the loft stairs. It was as if he'd leaped up like a cat.

She sipped the milk he handed her, and felt his eyes upon her, studying her, absorbing her before he sat down cross-legged in front of her on one of the pillows. "How are you doing, Mrs. Murry?" he asked, handing her his own handkerchief to wipe the milk from her lips.

"I feel better than I have in years." She was amazed to hear herself say it, but it was true. She actually spent entire days without napping. Up at seven in the morning and not back in her room until late at night. If not for the cold . . . .

He asked her what she'd learned living in the servants' quarters, and she impulsively replied, "I've learned I can rough it, stand any amount of noise and put up with untidiness, disorder and queer smells without losing my head."

His wide black eyes twinkled and his belly shook with a laughter that was so contagious she had to laugh along with him though she was rather embarrassed by her candidness. After the laughter the comfortable silence was broken when he said, "Today, Mrs. Murry, you pack your suitcase."

"Pack my suitcase?" she asked, anxiously, putting down the glass. Please no, she cried to herself. This is where I belong. This is where I've found happiness. This is where I'll be cured.

G. must have seen the distress in her face. "Don't you want to move back into your old room? I'm told you were very happy there."

"Oh yes. Thank you very much. I misunderstood you. I was afraid you were asking me to leave."

"Why would I ask you to leave? I'm pleased you are here with us. I only want to make sure you're comfortable." He smiled. "You've learned all that is possible in your present accommodations. Adele will help you pack."

He pulled himself up gracefully and, reminding her again of a black-whiskered cat, silently slipped away. She was so relieved he wasn't sending her away it made her giddy. She looked down at her hand that still held his handkerchief. Should she give it back to him or was it a gift?

SACRED DANCES OR MOVEMENTS, as Gurdjieff referred to them, were rehearsed in the salon every evening after dinner—a mixture of Assyrian, Arabian and Dervish dances, which he had witnessed growing up and later throughout his travels to the East. He considered the Movements an integral part of his teachings and he designed and taught the complicated steps personally with great care and attention.

Katherine would lounge in her favorite chair next to the fireplace and watch the students practice under Gurdjieff's direction, and his choreographer, Jeanne Salzmann. Another devotee, Thomas de Hartmann, accompanied the dancers on piano, playing compositions he and Gurdjieff composed. Other students would join in, playing Eastern instruments, their sounds foreign to Katherine's ear.

The Movements were mechanical, like the interior workings of a clock, but they were exciting in their precision and control. Only through practice, memorization and deep concentration were the dancers able to synchronize each movement, creating a harmonious, flowing piece of work. Katherine was enthralled.

She wrote to Jack after watching her favorite dance, "The Initiation of the Priestess":

I have never really cared for dancing before, but this—seems to be the key to the new world within me. There is one that takes about 7 minutes and it contains the whole life of woman—but everything! Nothing is left out. It taught me, it gave me more of woman's life than any book or poem. There was even room for Flaubert's "Coeur Simple" in it, or Tolstoy's Princess Marya. Mysterious.

One night after a rehearsal, she invited her friend Olgivanna to share a bottle of wine with her at the Ritz, as she affectionately called her large bedroom. Olgivanna, a tall, dark-haired young dancer from Montenegro often came to the Ritz for talks. She also brought Katherine her meals when she was too tired to eat in the dining room. At twenty-three, ten years younger than Katherine, Olgivanna had already traveled with Gurdjieff to many countries. Katherine tried to imagine what these places were like when she watched her dance.

Katherine reclined comfortably on a divan and Olgivanna sat next to her on a footstool from where she could add logs to the fire. Having changed into her warm dressing gown, its fur collar protecting her from the cold, she was amazed that Olgivanna could sit there in her flimsy white dance tunic and not shiver.

"I'd like to speak Russian with you," Katherine said in broken Russian.

"Why Russian? We speak well together in English."

"Yes, but I'm fascinated by other languages. After I master Russian I'll study Italian. Doesn't Gurdjieff tell us how important it is for the mind to practice memorization, to help keep one conscious? What better way than learning a new language?"

"Perhaps easier than the mathematical problems he gives us to memorize," Olgivanna said.

"They are dreadful, aren't they? I prefer memorizing words I've looked up in my Russian dictionary."

Olgivanna read through the list of words Katherine had written in her notebook and covered her mouth to stop laughing.

"What's so funny? Are they all wrong?"

"No, not at all. But this reads like a poem of your experience here at the château." Olgivanna read in English: *"I am cold—bring paper to light a fire—cinders—wood—matches—strong—because no more fire—white paper—what is the time—it is late—it is still early—is there a glass of wine?* A very cold experience one might think."

Katherine smiled and lifted her wineglass and clinked Olgivanna's. "That couldn't be further from the truth. I've never been happier than I am now. This place is like a dream—or a miracle. You must help me add Russian words that express that happiness. Someday strangers might read my notebooks."

"You want strangers to read them?"

"I don't mind, if my notebooks might encourage people to overcome difficulties. That's how they'll find the happiness they are seeking."

"That's what you did, isn't it? I hope to have your will power and determination someday."

"You already have or you wouldn't have followed Gurdjieff this far from home. You are very fortunate to have had such a powerful and positive teacher in your youth. I left my home to follow the ways of my teachers too, but I didn't have anyone like Gurdjieff to help me when I got lost and made mistakes."

Olgivanna poured wine into Katherine's empty glass and filled her own. "Who were your teachers when you were my age?"

"Mostly writers. When I was a young girl living in New Zealand, I read Marie Bashkirtseff's *Journal of a Young Artist.* She started her journal at age twelve and she believed, like Gurdjieff, that you have to be true to yourself. She wrote down her uncensored thoughts and shared them with her readers, thoughts that encouraged me to follow my own individual path regardless of what others thought I should do.

"Marie knew she was dying from tuberculosis and was afraid her parents would find her uncensored journal and destroy it." Katherine recited, *"Then nothing would be left of me, nothing, nothing, nothing. To live, to have so much ambition, to suffer, to weep, to struggle, and in the end to be forgotten; as if I had never existed.*

"After she died in 1884 at the age of twenty-four, her mother did publish her journal but only after a thorough editing, which removed her humanity. The original manuscript was later found and published as Marie would have wanted—uncensored."

Olgivanna put another log on the fire. "I think Gurdjieff would have considered Marie a positive influence. What were the 'mistakes' you mentioned?"

Katherine sipped her wine before answering. "Oscar Wilde."

"Oscar Wilde?"

"Yes. An English writer. I don't know if there's a Russian translation of his work. He said, 'A man who is master of himself can end a sorrow as easily as he can invent a pleasure. I don't want to be at the mercy of my emotions. I want to use them, to enjoy them, and to dominate them.' "

Katherine smiled. "Unfortunately he lived before Gurdjieff. Wilde failed, and his uncontrolled emotions corrupted his marriage, his career and his life."

Katherine felt familiar ghosts enter the room and gather around her. A log fell, sparks landed in her lap. She jumped. The ghosts dispersed.

She held up her glass of wine and as she stared through it at the fire, the flames broke into a thousand golden teardrops.

"I have acted out my sins, too," she said in a soft voice, "and then excused them, or put them away with 'it doesn't do to think about these things,' or, more often, 'it was all experience.' But it hasn't all been experience. There's been waste—destruction, too."

Olgivanna moved onto the divan so that she could hear more and Katherine began: "Shortly after my boyfriend left me, my mother took me to Bavaria. She left and took the ship back to Wellington without knowing . . . . Unhappy in the hotel, I moved into a pension. I was writing . . . taking long barefoot walks in the woods . . . part of the water cure for hysterical women . . . but I was content . . . my hand on my belly . . . the new life growing within.

"One day stretching up to shove a chest onto the top of the wardrobe closet I curled over with cramps. I was alone. I screamed in pain. My landlady found me curled up on the bed, a bloodstained sheet under me. There was nothing the doctor could do . . . but remove the stained sheets and . . . ."

Her eyes clouded over and closed.

She felt a strong warm grip on her icy hand as she was yanked out of the darkness. She opened her eyes and saw Olgivanna's frightened face.

"That was quite a scare you gave me," she said, still gripping Katherine's hand. "You were telling me what happened in Bavaria and then you fainted."

"I'm fine now," said Katherine, "you needn't worry."

"I'm so sorry about what happened to you there. You're a remarkable woman. I don't think I could ever be as strong as you are. And to keep it a secret all this time."

"I'm glad I'm finally able to talk about it." She smiled.

As she looked into the fire a wave of relief rolled over her and then a feeling of lightness as if she was floating on a calm turquoise sea warmed by the bright sun above. A feeling she hadn't felt for what seemed years.

She turned away from the fire to Olgivanna. "I'm sorry. Where did I leave off. Should I tell you about Floryan? Yes. I suppose I must."

She picked up the wineglass and took a sip.

"I met him in Bavaria after my . . . my miscarriage. He translated English and Russian literature into Polish. He read to me and sang songs—a beautiful soothing voice when I woke from my nightmares. He was very gentle and when he wanted to make love, I didn't resist. I had nowhere else to go. He offered me safety and I curled up in his kindness. Later, I found out I'd made a terrible mistake. The short time I spent with Floryan has cursed me all these years and prevented me from ever having a child."

"I don't understand."

"He gave me an infection that's transmitted sexually. And when I tried to have the infection removed surgically, I only made it worse. That's why I'm an invalid today. And then there's the tuberculosis . . ."

"How terrible for you. But you certainly can't blame yourself."

"No, I don't. At least, not anymore."

She suddenly felt very tired and laid down on the rug to get closer to the fire. Olgivanna put a blanket over her, placed a pillow under her head, and laid down next to her with her head propped up on her elbow.

"It wasn't all bad," said Katherine, watching the flames rekindle. "Floryan introduced me to the work of Anton Chekhov. After I read his short stories about the Russian people, I began writing about the Bavarian people I'd been living with. Orage published those stories and that was the beginning of my writing career."

"You mean that grumpy old man who digs all day in the trench and never stops moaning about how sore his body is?"

They both laughed. "Yes the very same. I was a bit younger than you when we met and I guess you could say he discovered me. He published my first short stories."

"I love your enthusiasm and mimicry when you entertain the children living here. It would be quite wonderful to hear you read your own stories."

"I like to give readings. My cousin Elizabeth is also a writer. We're going to do a reading tour in America . . . when I'm well again."

"Have you ever written a novel?"

Katherine's heart constricted when she thought of the notebooks filled with starts and stops. "No, only short stories. Some day I will write a novel; that's ahead of me."

As Olgivanna turned away Katherine saw fear or was it grief reflected in her eyes. Am I the only one, she thought, who believes in my cure?

* * *

One afternoon, excited about her ideas, but unable to put anything down on paper, she put on her fur coat and went out on the grounds to find Orage. He had helped her in the beginning of her career and she was confident he would help her now.

She laughed when she came upon him in his mud-splattered overalls. They returned to the château together. He helped her take off her fur coat and they sat by the fire in the salon.

"Look at you," she said. "No one would recognize you on Fleet Street without your old hat and bow tie."

"Well for that matter Katherine I wouldn't recognize you either though I find that simple dress quite charming on you."

Katherine stood up and turned around to model the plain dark blue dress.

"And what are you doing with your hair? I've never seen you without bangs. I like it. It brings out those dark expressive eyes of yours.

"Come sit down and rest with me. I've been digging holes since dawn. We have to finish the new Study Room by mid-January. Many guests are coming to see a performance of the Sacred Dances.

"I look forward to that. Will it be finished in time?"

"Gurdjieff won't leave us alone until it is. He works right alongside us and seems to have more strength than anyone. You know how unaccustomed I am to physical labor. My work was always inside my head."

"You're not regretting your decision to come here are you?"

"Certainly not! I belong here. I complain about it, but I like spending time outdoors working with my hands. I've spent too much of my life in dank offices. Just look at these blisters." He held up his hands proudly.

"And what about you?" he asked taking her hands in his. "Do you sometimes wish I'd never introduced you to Gurdjieff?"

"No. I admit I had a hard time at first following his instructions to just sit and watch, but now I'm quite enjoying myself."

She closed her eyes. "I never thought I could feel so complete and I don't need anything more than what I have right here—sitting next to my dear friend."

She felt Orage's eyes on her and opened hers.

"I remember so vividly the first day you came to me with your manuscripts," he said. "Now here we are, can it be twelve years later, comrades again." She smiled up at him.

"It's good to see you happy, Katherine. I've been very worried about you but now there's color in your cheeks. Your face actually shines."

"Stop it Orage or you'll have me blushing like a young school girl."

"But it's true. You're radiant."

"I only wish Jack and LM would believe me when I tell them how happy I am. Jack worries that I've been hypnotized by Gurdjieff and LM grieves for me as if I'm already dead. She thinks I'm being consumed by illness and wasting away and sends me clothes that are too small. If she could only see how I've filled out on goat's milk." They both laughed.

"How do I explain the joy I've found here to Jack and my family and friends?" She raised her hands in the air taking in the salon in all its splendor, a microcosm of the world she now dwelled in.

"You're the writer. Find a way."

She smiled. "That's actually what I wanted to talk to you about. I seem to have lost my technique.

"I now see that I've been a camera in my writing—a selective camera. My attitude has determined the selection of the pictures, and the result is that my slices of life have been partial and misleading, and a little malicious. I don't want to write like that any more. I don't have all my ideas worked out yet but each day I know I'm a little closer. Soon this hand," she held her hand up against the sun streaming through the window, ". . . soon this hand will write about heroes and heroines measured by the quantity and quality of the effort they put forth and not by their successes." She sighed as her hand dropped in her lap. "I've only written one sketch that exemplifies what I'm trying to do."

"Tell me about it."

"It's about a couple who consider loving each other as an art. Both struggle to have meaningful lives, to forget the past and not worry about the future, to live in the present. They live each day with full consciousness of its fleeting joy, bravely accepting their circumstances, be it poverty or illness, and turning them into an opportunity to deeply feel their love for each other. They are true heroes.

"The reader's sympathy is maintained by the continuity and variety of the effort of one or both of the characters. They sulk after their first failure but we admire their endurance or sympathize with their suffering or laugh at their ineptitude.

"When I'm ready, and I'm not ready yet, I must make the commonplace virtues as attractive as the vices in today's novels. I want to present the good as the witty, the adventurous, the romantic, the gay, the alluring; and the evil as the platitudinous, the greedy, the solemn, and the conventional.

"Oh, listen to me. It 's that old habit of mine to speak without having solidly formed my thoughts. I'm so excited about this new attitude I have toward life that I'm really bursting. Forgive me. I wanted to ask for your advice and here I am running away with my own thoughts. Does this all sound ridiculous?"

"Not at all," said Orage, pulling her up from the sofa. "I like the new Katherine very much." He drew her hand to his lips and said, "I look forward to reading the many stories that this small, delicate, powerful hand will write."

31

January 1923

I want to be all that I am capable of becoming
so that I may be . . . a child of the sun.
Notebooks—KM

THE CHRISTMAS CELEBRATION ended with nine wide-eyed children gathered around Katherine in the salon as she told stories. She entertained them with different voices and dialects to hold their attention as few could understand English.

Maybe it was my facial mimes they enjoyed the most, she thought, slowly climbing the stairs afterward to her room. She stopped to catch her breath and looked down at the green holiday laurels adorning the staircase.

She couldn't believe that Jack's Christmas at the Denning's could have been as wonderful as hers. Even though mostly Easterners lived at the château, Gurdjieff had organized a traditional Christmas feast for the British and other foreign guests. Sixty sat at the table eating soup, spiced meats, fish, vegetables of all kinds, delectable salads, dishes of oriental tidbits, exotic fruit, fragrant herbs and puddings and pies.

Through the frosted windows she could see the barren trees outside. It seemed like it was years ago not just a few months, when she had arrived and the leaves still clung to the trees. Soon spring would arrive, her favorite season. She looked forward to seeing the flowers bloom below her window.

"Oh my!" she gasped, surprised and delighted to find a small Christmas tree in her room illuminated by three flickering candles.

"Do you like it?" asked Adele, stepping out from behind the door.

"Ah oui!" exclaimed Katherine, collapsing onto the couch. "Why are there three?"

"One for you, Mrs. Murry. Another for myself." She hesitated.

"And the other?"

"It is for the one you wish to come here." She blushed.

"You mean Mr. Murry? How odd you should mention him. Just tonight, Gurdjieff told me I could invite him to the opening night of Sacred Dances at the new Study House. I had planned to not see him until the spring. Do you think I should see him sooner, before I'm cured?"

Adele nodded her head up and down enthusiastically.

Katherine turned her attention to the little tree. "What a lovely gift. Did you carry it all the way from the forest? The pines smell so fresh."

Adele joined her on the divan and rested her head on Katherine's lap. Katherine gently plaited the thick strands of Adele's hair with her fingers. "You know," said Adele, "my mother used to sit with me by the fire like this and discuss the day's events, just like I'm doing now with you."

Katherine watched the candles burn and breathed in the sweet smell of the pinecones hanging from the tree. She thought longingly of her Christmases at home with her family when they were all together and her mother and brother were still alive. She felt them near her now.

After a while, Adele sat up and asked, "Do you find life here very difficult?"

"No, but I don't work as hard as you do. I do really wish I could participate in the Movements. When I hear the music and watch you and the others dance, I have such a strong desire to join you."

"Have you asked Mr. Gurdjieff if you could?"

"He says not yet. It's too strenuous. For now I watch and memorize the steps so I'll be ready to join in when I'm stronger."

Adele put her head back in Katherine's lap just as one candle sputtered and went out. "Oh dear, that's me, isn't it?" gasped Katherine.

"No! No!" said Adele, jumping up and snuffing out the other two with her fingers. "See, they all went out and who's to say which was yours? I'm certain you will dance with us very soon. Perhaps when your husband comes to visit."

"Yes, of course I will. But now I must get some sleep and so should you."

After Adele left, Katherine took up her pen:

Darling Bogey, Would you care to come here on January 8 or 9 to stay until 14-15? Mr. Gurdjieff approves of my plan and says you will come as his guest. On the 13th our new theatre is to be opened. It will be a wonderful experience.

She went on to explain which train to take to Paris and where to get the cab to Fontainebleau and then told him specifically what she wanted him to wear. She wanted to show him off to all her new friends.

I hope you will decide to come my dearest . . . We can sit and drink kiftir in the cowshed. Your ever loving, Wig

TWO WEEKS LATER, the morning of Jack's arrival, she dressed quickly as she wanted to have her chores done before he arrived. She looked around and, pleased with how lovely the Ritz looked, she imagined them sitting in the Victorian needlepoint chairs in front of the fire, sipping tea. How perfect it will be. Maybe she should invite Adele or Olgivanna to join them. No, she thought, I don't want to share him with anyone. Certainly not on his first day. She giggled at her schoolgirl behavior and with one last smile at her mirrored reflection left the room, forgetting her cane in her excitement.

Downstairs in the kitchen it was quite hectic. She'd written to Jack describing the kitchen three months ago:

It's a large kitchen with six helpers. Madame Ostrovsky, the head, Gurdjieff's wife, walks about like a queen exactly. She is extremely beauti-

ful. She wears an old raincoat. Nina, a big girl in a black apron—lovely, too—pounds things in mortars. The second cook chops at the table, bangs the saucepans, sings; another runs in and out with plates and pots, a man in the scullery cleans pots . . . and it's so full of life and humor and ease that one wouldn't want to be anywhere else.

Jack would see it for himself today. Just then Gurdjieff strode in and took up a handful of shredded cabbage and ate it.

She walked across the kitchen floor to her corner worktable. A stack of carrots awaited her. She shoved up the sleeves of her fur coat and went to work, looking up occasionally to say hello to someone rushing by. The festivities for the gala planned for that evening had already started in the kitchen. She felt the gaiety bouncing off the walls. After the carrots were done she cut bread, making a mountain of breadcrumbs.

She wondered why she had ever hesitated in asking Jack to visit. What better time then right now?

She finished her kitchen chores and went outside to cut the Christmas roses to put in the vases that she had lined up on the banquet table between bottles of wine and candleholders. This took her the rest of the morning. Tired, she climbed the stairs to her room, stopping along the way to take slow deep breaths to calm her racing heart.

She fell asleep planning what she would wear when she greeted Jack later that day.

Yes, that's it, the purple dress, she thought, rising an hour later. She studied her face in the mirror and took out her brush and retrained her bangs to fall over her forehead. She'd wait until Jack had been with her a few days before showing him her new look. First he would need time to get used to the changes within her.

She just finished putting on the matching purple jacket when she heard his honking cab and hurried downstairs to open the gate.

"Oh, Katherine is this really you? Why you look radiant," he exclaimed upon seeing her. He enfolded his arms around her and held her tight under the quince tree she had described in her letters.

"Come, I want to show you the stable," she said, reaching for his hand.

He laughed. "Wait a minute. Won't you show me your room first so I can leave my valise there?"

"Of course, how silly of me." She changed directions and guided him to the entry hall.

"Jack, why not leave your things here in the downstairs closet? I don't want to go upstairs quite yet. I'm saving that for teatime."

"All right. Then take me to your wonderful stable so we can drink . . . what did you call it in your letter . . . oh yes, kif-tir." He hung his hat and coat in the closet and put his valise on the floor underneath.

Outside they met up with Adele, who shyly shook Jack's hand and walked with them to the stable and then left. They climbed up the ladder to the loft. They didn't drink kiftir but Jack enjoyed himself immensely lying down and looking up at the trees and flowers painted on the ceiling as she pointed out "who was who" in the monkey faces.

After the stable, she showed him the farm animals and the vegetable greenhouse. "We eat the food grown here," she said. They walked over to the Study House where the construction was going on with great intensity. Several people were using translucent paint to color the windows like stained glass. After introductions, Jack was handed a paintbrush and he added a few strokes to the vivid green, red, blue and yellow patterns, which glimmered in the late afternoon sun.

By the time they got up to leave, thunderclouds had darkened the sky and it started to rain. Jack said, "Shouldn't we wait till it clears?"

Olgivanna offered her umbrella but Katherine said, "No thank you. I love the rain. I want the feeling of it on my face."

In the château, they dried off in front of the fire in the salon. Katherine wanted to take her time before taking Jack upstairs. She pointed out things along the way, the Christmas roses she'd arranged in the banquet room for the dinner, the Christmas tree Gurdjieff had cut down in the forest and the decorations everyone had made that now hung from its branches. They peeked into the kitchen and she pointed to the table where she worked.

At last she brought him up to her bedroom. The moment she walked in she knew Adele had been there. The fire was lit and there was a tea tray on her writing table.

"What a gorgeous room," said Jack, quite taken aback. "No wonder you're so happy here. You live like a queen."

"Not exactly," she said, "but the king does live next door."

"The king?"

"Mr. Gurdjieff lives next door with his wife Madame Ostrovsky, though I hardly ever see him and she's always working in the kitchen. He gets up before everyone and is always the last to bed, and he often makes trips to Paris.

"Come sit down Jack. Let's drink the tea while it's still hot."

Jack watched her pour, without spilling a drop. "And you live here on your own without anyone taking care of you. I keep expecting LM to walk in the door any minute."

"Oh, everyone helps a bit. Adele brought the tea and slipped out before we came in. She'd do more for me if I let her. She's adopted me as her mother and I love her as the daughter I never had."

He smiled sheepishly. "I thought from your letters that you'd been hypnotized by Gurdjieff and that this château was filled with devout theologists who would grab me when I arrived and force me to join their cult."

Katherine laughed. "Don't let Gurdjieff hear you say that. He'd throw you out. He hates being accused of being a theologist."

"What does he like to be called?"

"A teacher of dance."

"Really?"

"You'll see tonight. There'll be a dress rehearsal of the Sacred Dances for next week's performance in the Study Hall."

"You mean that giant hangar where I helped paint the glass windows? That will be finished by next week?"

"Yes. If Gurdjieff says so, it will happen. Even if he does it all himself."

They sat together for a while enjoying the silence, comfortable with each other's breathing.

"Now off with you," said Katherine, suddenly getting up. "Why don't you take a walk around the grounds while I dress for dinner?"

"Am I all right like this?"

"Yes you look very handsome. Even more handsome than that drawing you sent me that I've shown everyone. I'll be proud to show you off tonight. Meet me downstairs at six in the salon. Everyone gathers there before dinner in the banquet hall."

She took particular care dressing. She wore the black chiffon gown and draped the black shawl embroidered in vivid colors over her shoulders. She knew it had been worth the trouble when she saw the way Jack looked at her as she came down the stairs and pressed her into his waiting arms.

At dinner she watched as Jack talked to Orage, their past differences put aside. Jack seemed quite comfortable talking to the students. Perhaps he will stay awhile, she thought, now that he sees what loving people my new friends are; even though they may seem a little strange to him as they're so open and not ashamed to be themselves.

After dinner they retired to the salon and watched the rehearsal of the Sacred Dances. Katherine was a bit irritated at first that she wasn't one of the dancers Jack was admiring, but she settled for the pleasure of sitting near him.

At ten, Gurdjieff and the dancers left for the Study House to rehearse on the newly built stage.

Katherine took Jack's hand and pulled him toward the spiral staircase. "Come, Jack. Maybe I'm not well enough to dance yet but there is something I can do."

At the foot of the stairs she smiled at him and said, "Watch me!"

She let go of his hand and leapt up the stairs. Halfway, she stopped, overcome by a coughing spasm. She pressed her hand against her mouth trying to stop the blood oozing between her fingers and collapsed on the landing.

Epilogue

On the evening of January 9th, 1923, Katherine Mansfield, at age thirty-four, collapsed from a lung hemorrhage. She died thirty minutes later. She was buried on January 12th in a nearby cemetery in Avon attended by her husband, John Middleton Murry, Richard Murry, Ida Baker, her sisters Chaddie and Jeanne, Hon. Dorothy Brett, G.I. Gurdjieff, A.R. Orage, Dr. James Young and many residents from The Institute for the Harmonious Development of Man. The epitaph on her grave from Shakespeare's *Henry IV* reads:

But I tell you, my lord fool,
out of this nettle, danger,
we pluck this flower, safety.

Acknowledgments

This novel wouldn't exist without the encouragement and unwavering faith in my writing of my husband, Jim Payne, whose own story compelled me to recreate Katherine's. He had endless patience in following me in my pursuit up into the hills of Menton to find Katherine's villa Isola Bella and then to Fontainebleau to visit G.I. Gurdjieff's former Institute and then on to the Avon graveyard where Gurdjieff and Katherine are buried.

And thank you to my children, Amie and Sam, who never fail to inspire me with their willingness to climb mountains in pursuit of their own dreams and who helped me to achieve my own. Amie accompanied me on my pursuit to Bandol, France to find Katherine's past and, between tears, read Katherine and Jack's love letters on the drive home. And Sam, who often tells me to "keep going," allowed me permission to use his painting on the book cover.

To my dear friends in and around Teyssières, Brisou, Henri, Eddie, Philippe, Carole, and Pascale, who left me alone to work but always knew when I needed a break from Katherine and invited me for wine tasting or a meal; to Ina who gave me the keys to her Floridian retreat so that I might write in silence; and to sister Kate who knew to be silent when I was writing in her desert home.

To my editors, Steve Lewis and Jim Payne; I would never have finished this book without your support and advice. To the Duckdog writers' group that sat through the late hours hearing my fledgling attempts at reshaping Katherine's story. Go Avatar!

And to Katherine Mansfield who taught me so much about what it takes to be a writer.

A Note on Sources

While Katherine Mansfield, John Middleton Murry, Ida Baker and other people who actually lived appear in this book as fictional characters, I have tried to render as accurately as possible the outward particulars of their lives.

I am deeply indebted to Margaret Scott and Vincent O'Sullivan for collecting and editing Mansfield's notebooks and letters into the five volumes of *The Collected Letters of Katherine Mansfield.* And to C.A. Hankin for *The Letters of John Middleton Murry to Katherine Mansfield.*

I depended for information on a number of other sources, most prominently the insightful biographies of *The Life of Katherine Mansfield* by the late Anthony Alpers, *Katherine Mansfield: A Secret Life* by Claire Tomlin, and *The Life of Katherine Mansfield* by Ruth Elvish Mantz and J. M. Murry. Ida Baker would never have been so fully rendered without the honesty and courage with which she wrote her own book, *Katherine Mansfield: The Memories of L.M.* John Middleton Murry's autobiography *Between Two Worlds* and F.A. Lea's biography, *John Middleton Murry*, allowed me to enter into the life of "Jack." I also learned about Katherine's volatile friendship with Virginia by reading Hermione Lee's chapter, "Katherine," in her marvelously definitive Virginia Woolf biography.

About the author

Joanna FitzPatrick lives and writes in New York City and Teyssières, southern France.

Her first foray into writing came about when she wrote Hollywood screenplays and learned to see through the eye of a camera. The result was the movie *White Lilacs and Pink Champagne.* She then turned to the music field and had a successful and vibrant career giving Bette Midler her first driving lesson and managing The Manhattan Transfer. Later she left Hollywood for Manhattan to become the managing director of Gramavision Records, promoting jazz, blues, and eclectic classical music.

She left the music industry several years later and returned to her first passion, literature.

Majoring in English, she returned to college, graduated *cum laude* from SUNY Purchase and went on to receive a Master's degree in writing at Sarah Lawrence College.

This is her first novel. Visit her website joannafitzpatrick.com for information on her memoir, *Princess of the Lanes: A Hollywood Girl.*

Made in the USA
Lexington, KY
29 September 2013